ONE HONEST SOUL

A SAM HALLORAN THRILLER

TOM GOLDEN

First Edition: June 2021
E-book edition ISBN: 978-0-9994363-3-2
Paperback edition ISBN: 978-0-9994363-4-9
Hardback edition ISBN: 978-0-9994363-5-6

Cover by *Damonza.com*

For Marcia, thank you for saying Yes 50 years ago

"He who passively accepts evil is as much involved in it as he who helps to perpetrate it. He who accepts evil without protesting against it is really cooperating with it."

—Martin Luther King, Jr.

"Courage is contagious.
When a brave man takes a stand,
the spines of others are often stiffened."

—Billy Graham

ONE HONEST SOUL

A SAM HALLORAN THRILLER

INSPIRED BY A TRUE STORY

Before…

"Javier, thank God you're here. Momma has been calling for you."

"How is she, Saida?"

"Resting now. You should go in to see her."

"I want to talk to the doctor first."

Javier Mendoza approached the nurses' station, laid his hands on the counter, and asked to see the doctor attending to his mother.

"Inmediatamente," said the nurse as she hastened to a glass-paneled office, closed the door, snatched up the phone, and rapidly spoke into it, her face taut.

Javier leaned on the counter surveying everyone moving about with no one making eye contact with him. Three minutes later, a young, slightly built, dark-haired man wearing black horned-rimmed glasses with a stethoscope around his neck and a clipboard in his hand came around the corner. "How can I help you?"

"I want to know what you are doing to attend to my mother."

"And you are?"

"You know who I am," Javier said slowly, defiantly.

The man extended his hand, "Doctor Ricardo Morales. I am pleased to meet you, *Señor* Mendoza. I do know who you are, but I need you to properly identify yourself before I can discuss a patient's health with you. This is the law. I mean no offense."

Javier considered the doctor's request for a moment. "I am Javier Mendoza. Nilsa Mendoza is my godly mother. I want to know her condition and prognosis." He looked directly into the doctor's face, vein throbbing in his forehead.

Dr. Morales removed his glasses and took a half-step back. "Please follow me, *Señor* Mendoza."

The doctor stepped into a small windowless office, his hand on the inside doorknob, waiting for Javier Mendoza to follow.

"Please sit, *Señor* Mendoza," he said as he closed the door and took his seat behind a metal desk strewn with clipboards, assorted pens, and a rim-stained coffee cup still full, now cold. The doctor glanced briefly at a picture of his young family frolicking at the beach on a sunny day last summer and then to the small desk clock his wife had presented him when he graduated from medical school three years ago. It was approaching nine o'clock in the evening.

Mendoza sat straight in the metal chair positioned directly in front of the desk. He watched the doctor's every move... should he make a wrong move.

"Your mother has lung cancer which has metastasized to other parts of her body, *Señor* Mendoza. We have performed some tests and are awaiting the results, but she is terminal, and it is just a matter of time."

"I know that, you idiot!" he exploded, pounding his fist on the metal desk. The picture of the doctor's family bounced up and then fell forward. "I asked what you are doing to care for my mother."

The doctor sat rigid, his eyes wide, and glanced at the fallen picture of his family before reaching over to right it. It gave him a moment to consider his response.

"I have reached out to her oncologist, Dr. Mendico. He is currently on holiday in New York City."

Again, Mendoza pounded the desk. "I don't care where the fucking guy is. Get ahold of him and get the damn test results. Report to me by tomorrow morning."

The doctor did not make eye contact with Mendoza. He nodded his head and said, "I understand. I will call him again, and I will have a report for you in the morning. I am sorry we cannot meet your needs—"

"Take care of my mother, or you'll wish you were a fucking plumber."

"I understand, *Señor* Mendoza."

Javier Mendoza took one deep breath, stood, smiled amicably, and extended his hand to the good doctor, taking it gently when the doctor also stood. "Please forgive my outburst. But this is my mother.

I care for her deeply. I am certain you will do all you can to make her comfortable and in need of nothing while in your care."

When Dr. Morales met Mendoza's eyes he saw the gentle glow of a son caring for his dying mother and had a moment of sympathy. He then remembered that Javier Mendoza was not a man to be taken lightly. The doctor would not challenge him on this day or any other. He would talk to the oncologist even if he had to travel to New York City personally. At least then he would feel safer.

Javier stood outside his mother's room watching his sister walk toward him.

"Javier, what did the doctor say?"

He took Saida's hand and warmly said, "He is doing all he can, making her as comfortable as possible. I am afraid her time is near. All we can do is be by her side to let her know how much we love her."

"And pray for her! Javier, please promise me you will pray for her!"

"I promise, Saida. I will pray for her as I always do." He looked toward his mother, now asleep in her bed, a dim night light illuminating the floor. So peaceful. He would return to her soon.

Saida hugged her older brother and sobbed. Javier said, "It's OK, Saida. Let it out. Let it out. I'm here to comfort you." He patted his sister's back. "Just like I have been and always will. Let it out, my dear."

Saida's husband moved close, and Javier released his whimpering sister to his care, nodding his head and backing away. "Take her inside my mother's room. I have things I must do," he said dispassionately.

Javier turned and walked away, catching the eye of one of his bodyguards who leaped to attention with his boss approaching. "Get my car. I am returning to the office."

"Right away, *Jefe*," he said as he quick-stepped his way down the hall and out the hospital doors.

Javier liked order, but keeping order was stressful. He was about to relieve his stress.

His men almost toppled the dominos game they were enjoying on the front porch when Javier's BMW 7 Series pulled up to the administration building of the Abello plant in Palencia, Guatemala, about thirty-five miles outside of Guatemala City. Javier quickly exited.

"Everything ready?"

"Yes, *Jefe*."

Javier walked up the narrow, dark stairway to his office on the second floor of the plant.

The door was open. The ceiling lamp dimly lit the room and a fan turned slowly and rhythmically as he stood under it. Not a typical day, but soon all of that would be forgotten.

Javier surveyed the room. All appeared to be ready for him.

She was seated on the sofa, facing him, naked. Her hands were bound in front and tethered to a similar binding at her ankles. He had ordered a young one for tonight but the creases in her face belied her supposed youth. But then, maybe those were ripples of fear.

He wanted to be sure. It was important. He grabbed her bound wrists already beginning to bleed from her bindings. He looked at the tattoo on her inside forearm. It read *Lily1981*.

Javier knelt in front of her and stared into her face. "There is nothing to fear, Lily. Javier will take good care of you."

"That is not my name," she said defiantly but trembling.

"No matter. Tonight, you are Lily," he said placing his hands on her thighs, slowly moving them upward. Immediately, she pushed herself into the back of the sofa and began rocking, violently. Then, he put his hand behind her neck firmly and pulled her slowly toward his face. As she began to plead, he mashed his mouth onto hers and then pulled away quickly and slapped her across the face. She rolled onto her side sobbing, pleading, bleeding from her mouth. Javier stood and turned away from her.

"Tie her down."

"Which way, *Jefe?*"

"Legs over the end of the sofa. Ass up."

"*Sí, Jefe*. Where are you going?"

"Bitch bit my lip. Be right back. Make sure her hands and ankles are tied tight."

"*Sí, Jefe.*"

When Javier Mendoza returned, he was pleased his bodyguard had complied with his instructions. It wasn't as though they hadn't been through this routine many times before, although this one was a bit feistier. He would shape her up, like breaking in one of his horses. First couple of rides were a little rough. Not such a bad thing. Compliant sex was getting boring. After too many times with the same worker, they acquiesced too quickly. A fresh one like this was a rewarding challenge.

Javier viewed her from behind, not yet ready to mount her. He touched her lightly in the small of her back. Her skin was prickly with sweat. She moaned and strained against her lashings. Javier's man had used a knot which would tighten with her every movement; her pain would increase with any struggle, thanks to the rough-hewn hemp rope Javier favored—the same kind he used to rope his cattle at the ranch.

Her petrified moaning communicated she knew what was coming. Still, she squirmed, trying to break free. She cried as her bindings cut into her skin. It was best to stop fighting and accept what had become an almost daily ritual. At least, that was what she had heard… even though she hadn't believed the rumors. Now, it seemed she should have… and stayed away from him.

It excited Javier to watch her writhe and moan. He touched her again, and again she cried out but louder this time.

"Shut up, bitch."

"I am begging you, *Jefe*,"

Jefe, or "Boss," was how all the workers had been taught to address Javier Mendoza. *El Jefe* when referring to him: "The boss." Only his closest associates could call him by his Christian name.

Lily, or whatever her real name was, had been working in the plant for the past week. Juan Romero, his foreman, had skimmed her from their latest shipment of women from Columbia. The ID tattoo on her forearm put her at sixteen. Perfect. Javier assumed she was a virgin. He would determine that for himself in a few minutes. As she squirmed, he began to unbuckle his pants. This one was indeed a treat, although he knew he could no longer partake like this every day. Too strenuous for a guy his age—too many burritos and beer over the years.

At fifty-one, Javier had to take it easy. Last summer, a session like this landed him in the hospital with what his doctor called a mini stroke. It left him weak on his right side. His doctor said that unless he took it easy, exercised, and watched what he ate, another attack might be more damaging, maybe fatal. That wasn't going to happen to him. Life was too much fun.

But his doctor was right. Javier took his advice, bought a treadmill, and dropped twenty pounds. He limited himself to maybe one session like this a month. It hadn't been quite a month since his last one, but all in all he felt like he was taking better care of himself.

As he began, she resisted and moaned, and then cried out. She twisted and contorted as he maneuvered her hips with his hands. He could almost feel her pain from the lashings digging deeper into her skin. Her moaning reminded him of one of his cows giving birth.

Still, she resisted as the lashings cut deeper into her wrists, which were now dripping blood.

As she let out a sustained, guttural scream, he wasn't worried he might be discovered. He didn't care.

It was going on eleven o'clock in the evening. His office was situated on the second floor of the administration building attached to the plant. The night shift was operating with nearly two hundred of his workers at his distillery. Even if someone heard her screams, they knew better than to do anything about it. With all the bribes he paid police, politicians, judges, and union leaders Javier Mendoza was the most powerful man in the region and probably all of Guatemala. All the more reason he deserved all he had. It was his right.

They were no longer laughing at Javier Mendoza.

ACT I

PREPARING TO CONFRONT EVIL

CHAPTER 1

SOME WOULD SAY fifteen years is a long time. At least long enough. But not for Sam Halloran. He would never live long enough to remove the stain of that day.

I just wanted to expose them. I didn't mean for her to die.

"Sam, pick up on one," Maggie called out to him.

He could use the distraction.

"Sam Halloran speaking. How can I help you?"

"Mr. Halloran, this is Dennis DiNardo calling from the Middlesex County Prosecutor's office in New Jersey."

Hearing that name, Middlesex County, reset every sensor in Sam's body to high alert. "I know where Middlesex County is. Why are you calling?" Sam said harshly.

"I'm sorry, but we must have gotten our signals crossed here. This is not how matters like this should be handled."

"Look, I'm pretty busy. Could you please get to the point?"

"Yes, sorry. It's just a courtesy call to inform you Thomas William Halloran was released from Rahway State Prison on November 30th. The document I am looking at says you are to be notified upon his release."

This time, it wasn't fifteen years that fell away exposing a raw wound still pulsing with pain. It was more like thirty.

"Mr. Halloran, are you still there?"

"You mind telling me what took you over a month to make this *courtesy call*?"

"Sorry, Mr. Halloran, but they had a difficult time tracking you down. I don't know the details beyond what I am reading in the file. I'm interning with the prosecutor's office. I don't see much here, except... I see another reference to an Olivia Halloran, but... wait a minute—"

"Yeah, that's my mother. She's dead."

"Very sorry, Mr. Halloran. I am sorry to upset you. I should have looked over the file closer before I called."

"Are we done here?"

"Ah... yes, sir. Really sorry for the late notice and... well—"

Sam laid the phone down gently in its cradle.

Maggie came into Sam's office, her arms wrapped around herself like she always did when she felt she had not handled something in her usually efficient manner. "Sorry, Sam. Sounds like I should have screened that call better. When he said he was a prosecutor I thought it was a potential client. It's my fault. I understand if you're upset with me."

"Maggie, you didn't do anything wrong. Just not a good day. What's up?" he said as if trying to flip the switch on his mood.

"While you were on the phone, Dan Berg called to confirm the timing of your presentation to the new audit associates this afternoon. I confirmed you still planned to be there a little before two o'clock."

Maggie Walsh had worked as Sam's secretary ever since he transferred up from Indianapolis to Chicago five years ago. She was conservatively dressed with short hair and minimal makeup, and she was tall and slight—all packed in an efficient frame, the product of her deep-south upbringing. It took Sam months to break her from calling everyone *sir* and *ma'am* when she started.

Sam studied her pained look. "Maggie, there's nothing you could do to upset me. How many times have I told you you're the best secretary I've ever had?"

"More than once, but you seem so uptight today."

"And you think it's something you've done?"

"Well, you're usually in such a positive mood, and—"

"Remember we had a similar conversation last year about this time? And probably the year before? Trust me. It's not you. Bad memories each year when I have to recount the GEL investigation in front of the new kids."

"But then, why do you keep doing this speech each year if you know it will upset you?"

Sam hesitated. *Maybe as penance*, he thought, but said matter-of-factly, "Because they need to hear it."

"Can't someone else do it?"

"No."

CHAPTER 2

SAM HALLORAN WAS a partner at Hamilton Pierce, one of the Big Five—the five largest accounting and auditing firms in the world. He was also the partner-in-charge of HP's Chicago forensic accounting investigation practice; a practice he started in Indianapolis in 1983 and had transferred at the firm's request to build a larger practice in Chicago. Not only was he successful, Sam's practice had grown to become the largest forensic accounting investigation practice in Hamilton Pierce's US firm.

There were two reasons for his success. He had been remarkable at building his client base, not only in Chicago but across the nation. He was so good at turning opportunities into new clients that the firm enlisted him to teach his marketing and selling techniques to newer partners and promising directors.

When Sam received a call to discuss a new engagement opportunity, an investigation, they never asked Sam to bid on the job against his competitors. No, they never asked how much it would cost. The only thing they asked was how quickly he could get a team to some remote part of the world and fix their problem.

Sam was also a master at recruitment. He had a knack for hiring not only the best and the brightest from the best schools but those who would do whatever it took to succeed. He'd find those rare few during the office interview process. He told them they would work long hours, needed to travel anywhere in the world at a moment's notice, might miss holidays and their kids' soccer games, and—most important of all—they had to be exceptionally confident individuals, not afraid of taking risks and occasionally failing. Sam especially stressed they would learn and grow through failure. He said to expect it because he would constantly challenge them and push them to their limits, sometimes beyond. For those sacrifices, he committed to making them the best they could be. No extra salary. No special perks. Just the opportunity to work in one of the most dynamic practices at Hamilton Pierce. They'd apply their accounting and auditing skills investigating financial fraud—accounting fraud— perpetrated by those who stole millions using calculators rather than guns. Others in the firm called Sam's team the Navy SEALs of the accounting industry; *auditing with an attitude*, some would say.

Veronica Martinez was one such recruit. Sam had found her eight years before at Mizzou—University of Missouri, one of the best accounting schools in the country. Today, she was Sam's most promising director. Her next step was partner, although that was still about five years into the future.

She'd do any project anywhere in the world. She loved to be pushed and tested beyond what most others could handle. There was no project she would not tackle when Sam called. She was also unflappable… and drop-dead gorgeous.

"So, did you and Laura have a good dinner after your speech?" Veronica asked, tilting her head and displaying her famous smirk. Sam could read her like a book.

"Bullshit, you were in on it."

In a horrible Scarlet O'Hara impersonation, she said, "Why, Sam Halloran, how could you accuse your best forensics investigator of something so underhanded?" She knew exactly why Laura

Wittford made the trip from San Francisco, and it wasn't just to see Sam's presentation to a bunch of new audit associates. Hell, Laura knew all about the GEL investigation fifteen years ago. In a way, she was part of it.

Sam didn't respond, favoring instead to continue working on something in front of him as he sat at his desk.

"Silent treatment?" Veronica said demurely.

"Get out of my office," Sam said with one of his manufactured attitudes.

"So, are you going to approve her transfer?"

Sam ignored her.

"Dammit, Sam. You know she'll do well here. You have to approve it."

"I'm the practice leader, the partner-in-charge. I don't have to do anything I don't want to do." Like flipping a light switch, his attitude toward her changed. "By the way, you did a nice job handling that question and the following melee on stage in front of those audit newbies last Saturday," Sam said, attempting to change the subject.

"My, my… is that a compliment coming from the big, bad practice leader?" she joked with her poor Southern accent.

"I'm hungry. Let's grab a bite," Sam said as he stood abruptly from his desk. He grabbed his overcoat and walked out of his office knowing Veronica would be close behind.

"Can I at least grab my coat? It's freezing outside."

"Hurry, I'll meet you at the elevators. I have something serious I need to discuss with you."

"Not this place again!" Veronica shouted as they approached the restaurant. Sam was now five steps ahead of her racing through the revolving door. "I didn't think an old man like you could move so fast."

"The older I get the thinner my blood gets!"

The hostess said, "Mr. Halloran, Maggie called ahead. Your usual booth is ready for you."

"Thanks, Emma," Sam said, following her to his booth.

"How come you always gripe about this place? Where else could you get this kind of service?" Sam jokingly admonished as they slid into the booth.

"Please, Sam. Every person in our practice hates this place. Do you know what we call it?"

Pointing to the top of the menu Sam said, "Emil's."

"Wrong, again. We call it *Slime*. I'm certain even the owner knew his cooking sucked and spelled backwards what he really felt about it."

"Do you know what you want?" Sam said looking at the menu.

"Yeah, same thing I get every time. Vegetable soup. At least I know they boil it. Gives me confidence all the germs are killed."

Sam gave Veronica a sideways glance hoping to change the subject. "So, like I said, you did a nice job handling that associate at my presentation."

"Thanks, not much of a challenge, though. He was a kid, for God's sake... please," she said rolling her eyes. "Give me a challenge."

Sam crumbled saltine crackers into the steaming chili the waitress placed in front of him. He had the feeling Veronica would want him to talk about what happened fifteen years ago in Indianapolis. The big reveal he had disclosed on stage in front of, well, the whole firm by now, but Sam had no intention of going there today... maybe never.

"So, like I said, I need to update you on a potential new engagement. I've got a conference call with the client tomorrow to discuss it. Do you remember Walter Hopkins? He ran Chicago's consulting practice but moved to the Philadelphia office a couple years ago to turn them around like he did Chicago."

"Didn't he have something to do with getting you to transfer up here? Then, you dragged me along."

"I don't see you complaining. Chicago is a twenty-something's dream city."

"OK, serious time," Veronica said as she pushed her half-eaten bowl aside. "What's going on?"

"He's arranged for me to talk with a Hampton Enterprises divisional CFO tomorrow."

"Awesome! They're in the news every day about boring stuff. About time they did something stupid."

"What makes you say that?"

"Come on, Sam. Big, global, public company like that. You know they've got to have at least some shithead managers. Now we get to nail them!"

"Not very impartial today, are we?" Sam said, knowing exactly where she was coming from. Greed was present in all industries and companies. It was just a matter of degree.

"I don't have anything to take notes on. Can we do this at the office?"

"Not to worry. You'll have plenty of time to take notes later."

"Are you telling me I'm your *man* to run this one?"

"I can't believe you just said that. How about *woman*?"

"Don't tell me you've lost your sense of humor and get all *PC* on me now, Sam."

"You're amazing," he said smiling and shaking his head. "So, here's all I know at this point. Hampton's Abello division operates a liquor distillery in Guatemala, mostly for the manufacture of rum. It's their largest and most profitable distillery plant in the world."

"Ha, so the truth comes out. You want me for my language skills. You racist!" Sam shot her a derisive glance.

"OK, so you're serious. I'll shut up," she said, folding her hands and giving Sam her full attention.

"In my earlier call with Walter, he faxed me a copy of an anonymous letter apparently from an employee at the Guatemalan plant alleging three claims against the general manager: he's cheating on his expenses, forces employees to work on his ranch, and… " Sam paused, "this seems to be the worst of it… he takes advantage of the female employees."

Veronica's expression didn't waver but knowing her the way Sam did, he was certain that would strike a chord with her. Hearing Latinas were being taken advantage of would roil her. Sam knew a little about her Mexican heritage. Her father was an immigrant. He wasn't sure about her mom but knew Veronica had two older sisters.

"Anyway, it appears this GM, Javier Mendoza, supervised the plant's construction eighteen years ago and has apparently done quite well running it for them," Sam said smirking sardonically.

"I know why you're smiling. I still think you're a racist."

"And why do you think that?"

"Because I am about to hear speech #104 that all Latin Americans in powerful positions are corrupt."

"Well, how about we change roles this time and you tell me what *you* think. I'm sure you will not give opinions and stick to your own experience." Veronica thought for a minute. She'd want to say something snarky, but then Sam saw her jaw tighten, her lips purse as she looked over his shoulder.

"So, you want me to say my hypothesis of Mr. Mendoza is he's probably garnered his power by regular payments to just about every official in the country for everything from permitting to solving labor issues to who knows what else."

Sam was looking into Veronica's face to measure her. "Are you scared yet?"

"I think you know the answer to that," she responded with steely-eyed determination.

Veronica tensed. He suspected she was visualizing what the women working for Mendoza had to endure.

"Sam, I'm sure you considered this but aren't we getting far afield from what we do? Not that I'm suggesting we walk away from this one, but where's the accounting fraud in all this? Where's the sufficient predication you've taught us to look for before beginning an investigation?"

"Good point, but surely you've worked for me long enough to know if you find a bad actor with access to cash and the books—"

"You need to look at everything they've touched," Veronica said glibly.

"As for predication, I think the anonymous letter is sufficient predication to begin an investigation. No telling what could surface once we begin to poke the beast."

Walking back to the office in the freezing wind and dodging clumps of ice along Wacker Drive, they didn't talk anymore. It was too early to tell her, but Sam was grooming her to succeed him as the practice leader. No doubt, Veronica still had some rough edges, most notably her penchant for flirting, drinking, and partying.

Sam didn't want to pry into her personal life, but if the rumors were true, she needed to tone it down a few notches. Still, he felt in time he'd level her out. After all, she had just turned twenty-nine years old, and Sam, at only forty-seven, hoped to have at least another decade growing the Chicago practice before he was ready to retire.

"You don't need to answer my earlier question about Laura's transfer request. She called me right after you said she *could* transfer to our practice!" she said laughing like she had pulled one over on Sam.

"Of course, she did… right after I gave her permission to tell you." Veronica's smile turned quickly into a frown. He'd trumped her yet again.

Still, Veronica and Laura were close and would remain so. He would need Veronica close by to calm Laura down after he delivered some unwelcomed and unexpected news when she arrived in Chicago.

CHAPTER 3

Friday, December 5, 1997 (One month prior)—Palencia, Guatemala

THE INTERNAL AUDITORS from corporate stayed only a
week, and Javier was the perfect host. The Abello Distillery was
one of nine facilities across the globe distilling spirits, mostly
rum, owned by Hampton Enterprises. But Javier's plant was special,
the largest and most profitable of them all. Such success in the corporate world garnered men like Javier certain privileges—like being
left alone by corporate.

Usually.

Someone had betrayed him. Someone broke the veil of silence.

They didn't tell him it was a woman, but he knew it had to be.
If one got away with something like that, soon he could lose control
of the entire plant. Then where would he be? No, he would find the
bitch and beat her in front of the whole plant.

Then… maybe not. Too much attention. What if someone else
wrote a letter? This could get out of hand. He would calm himself.
Things would quiet down and get back to normal. He just had to
deal with those pesky corporate internal auditors. He had done it
before. Child's play.

Herbert Richmond was the lead guy. He was an Accounting
major who graduated from the University of California, Berkeley,

seven years ago and was now the Director of Internal Audit for a division of Hampton Enterprises. Herbert sometimes forgot to mention the *division* part in his interviews. He had been looking around for a new job, having finally passed the CPA exam after six attempts. At least, that's what the private investigator Javier hired had reported to him.

Javier was a thorough man. When he received that call from corporate HR two weeks prior informing him of the required internal audit visit, he had to act quickly. He needed information. HR also informed him why they were investigating him and his operation. All because some *slut* made accusations against him. So, he prepared himself. That included learning as much about Herbert Richmond as he could.

The dossier was a comprehensive piece of work. Javier was surprised his investigator could learn as much as he did so quickly, but he didn't come cheap. Still, Javier appreciated competence. He also did not suffer fools well. Herbert Richmond seemed a complete fool. Just another gringo with no clue about how things were done south of the border.

All things considered, Herbert had it rather good. He lived in an upscale area of Chicago called Wrigleyville with his wife, Susie, and their Maltepoo, Misty. No kids. Their favorite pastime was gathering with their other Gen Xers at the local tavern most nights to talk about how they would change the world, one beer, reefer, and ecstasy at a time.

Javier suspected the kid was proud of his position in the company, so he played along. He invited him to his favorite restaurant in Palencia after meeting in his office on Monday, the first day of the audit.

"*Señor* Mendoza, I am truly sorry for the unexpected notice of this audit," Herbert told Javier at lunch, and he meant it. He appeared apologetic and nervous. He had been warned by corporate to do his job but "to be respectful of Mr. Mendoza." Javier had many different attitudes he could have displayed, but the kid looked like such a lightweight, Javier went easy on him.

"Not at all, and please call me Javier. After all, we both work for the same great company and are here to address this disturbing issue. I am only sorry you are troubled to make the long journey to my plant. I and my entire staff are here to make your stay as efficient as possible so you can be on your way back home to your family. Whatever you need, please ask. We are your servants. These charges I have heard of are very upsetting to me."

"No, *Señor* Mendoza, it is I—"

"Javier. Please. Call me by my Christian name."

"Yes, sorry." Herbert seemed to stumble searching for the right words. "So, I meant to say, Javier, I'm sorry to have to disturb a successful executive as yourself on such a matter, but I am sure you know these allegations must be investigated."

"But then, you have me at a disadvantage since you have seen this letter. I have not seen the letter," Javier said, barely making eye contact with stooped shoulders, almost appearing subservient. All for show, of course. Javier Mendoza was subservient to no one.

"Yes, I am sorry, sir—I mean, Javier. It's standard procedure, you see. Please do not take offense."

"But I do not know how else to take it. I was embarrassed to hear of it two weeks ago. I have not had a good night's sleep since; I am filled with dread and worry my reputation may be tarnished by whatever is in that letter." Javier flailed his hands like a distraught schoolteacher whose students were most disobedient.

"I totally understand where you are coming from—"

"But how could you? You are so young and coming from America, you have little understanding of what someone like me goes through here. Taking illiterate peasants off the streets and training them so they become successful and can provide for their families. I work so hard, and this is how I am repaid," Javier said, finally slamming his hand on his desk in apparent frustration before covering his face with both hands and leaning on his elbows… waiting.

"Would it… help… maybe this is all right… if I show you the letter, and we could go through it together?"

Javier almost leaped out of his chair, a wry smile on his face, with both hands extended. Waiting.…

Herbert looked uncomfortable but sympathetic. He was aware Javier was well regarded at corporate. When a corporate HR manager first discussed the assignment with Herbert, she appeared apologetic he would have to travel with his team to, of all places, Guatemala, like it would be the gravest of hardships. While Herbert was not usually opposed to travel, he was hopeful he'd be back by the following Sunday. He had tickets for the Bears versus Bills game. He could only hope this was just a one-week project.

Javier was quick to rise from his desk, motioning Herbert over to his small round conference table. As they sat next to each other, Herbert pulled the letter from a folder and handed it to Javier. In a moment, they were interrupted.

"*Señor*, the production line belt is down again, section 35. You are wanted immediately," said Gabriela Castillo, Javier's secretary, appearing anxious.

Javier leapt from his chair, still holding the anonymous letter in his hands. Herbert stood as well. Javier looked at Herbert and then at his secretary. He handed her the letter and said to Herbert, "I am so sorry, but things like this will take some time to resolve. How about you and I meet first thing in the morning to go through this?" Javier turned and walked out of his office.

"But.…" Herbert tried to object to this change in protocol, but it was too late. Gabriela had already placed the letter in her copier and pushed the copy button. Herbert thought it wouldn't be right for the accused to take a copy of the letter, but what could he do?

Gabriela returned the original and rescheduled him for the next day. Moments later he walked out of her office looking somewhat bewildered.

The next morning Javier was effusive with his apologies as he welcomed Herbert back into his office. They sat at his conference table and Javier warned that he had only thirty minutes, as he had received a last-minute call from Palencia's mayor asking to meet with him. He seemed sincere in his desire to assist Herbert… for at least the next thirty minutes. "I am totally at your service. How can I help?"

Herbert appeared flustered, not expecting he'd only have thirty minutes to go through the letter, and now all element of surprise was gone since Javier had the entire evening to read the letter and prepare responses to all of Herbert's anticipated questions. Again, child's play.

Thirty minutes later, Gabriela Castillo walked into Javier's office to remind him of his meeting with the mayor, and in a flash Javier left like the wind.

The audit went on as expected—well, Herbert followed his audit plan. He interviewed several supervisors and workers in a room Javier had arranged, the one with a hidden listening device and camera that everyone except Herbert knew about.

Herbert made a list of some test selections of the expense reports his associate would audit. Of course, those reports were not immediately available. That wasn't what he was told, but each passing day brought more apologies from Gabriela as the one coordinating the entire project.

Although he made several attempts, Herbert did not see Javier until Friday, forty-five minutes before he had to leave to catch his flight back to Chicago. The exit interview went a little rough. Herbert complained he still didn't have the expense reports he had requested, but, with apologies, Javier promised his team would work all weekend and FedEx them to Herbert's office at Hampton's headquarters in Chicago no later than Monday. They arrived the following Friday. Javier was confident no one would object. He was Javier Mendoza, and he ran the most profitable distillery in the world for Hampton Enterprises.

Herbert arrived home in time to see the game. The Chicago Bears destroyed the Buffalo Bills by a score of 30 to 3. Child's play.

Javier called together his foreman and supervisors for a celebration back at his office. The occasion called for drinks and smoking Castro's own Cohiba Especiales cigars. Tomorrow was another day in paradise.

"It is celebration time. Drink up, men. I told you this would be no trouble."

"*Jefe*, you are right, always. To *El Jefe*!" Mendoza's foreman, Juan toasted to their boss.

"To *Jefe*!" cheered the seven managers and supervisors gathered around Mendoza. They clinked their glasses of rum, celebrating the end of the audit. It was not just any rum. This bottle of Havana Club Maximo was from Javier Mendoza's private stock. His associates could avail themselves of Abello Rum, produced on the plant floor below them, day after day, but such was not good enough for Javier Mendoza. No, he would have the best of everything: rum, wine, motorcycles, guns, and of course, women. Any woman. Any woman of his choosing any time of day. They owed him their very existence, as he would remind them on a regular basis. Especially the young ones Juan would select from those being trafficked north to the brothels in Mexico and America. *Save them*, Javier would declare when he would survey the latest crop.

Then, there were those from the girls' orphanage on the outskirts of Palencia, the one Javier funded. Most would say this was because he was a kind and generous man, but those most loyal to him knew differently. Javier's intent and purpose for sheltering these homeless young girls was not made known to those who cared for the girls—the sisters from Saint Joseph of Anchieta Parish, which was also funded by Javier's *generosity*.

Ten minutes later, the laughter and gaiety quieted.

"Leave me."

As they cleared the room, Javier said to Juan, "And bring... them." Juan stopped and turned to face him, "Put them in there," Javier said pointing to his side room. His office apartment. "Lock the door. Be sure you collect them in the morning. Clean them up this time."

Juan nodded as he walked out of Javier's office. He knew the routine but tried not to think of it. He had daughters. They were both at university, courtesy of Javier Mendoza. Juan didn't think it was right, but he would comply with *El Jefe*'s wishes. He believed some people were simply less fortunate than others. This was just the way of things.

Javier sat alone in his office, listening to music, thinking, drinking, snorting. When he heard the girls being shuffled outside his closed office door, he began to prepare himself. Just one rail of snow tonight. He wanted to enjoy himself and stay out of trouble remembering his heart issues. After all, he worked hard and deserved all he had. God was good.

CHAPTER 4

SAM HAD NOT been in the office much since his presentation on Saturday. This year's version revealed something he hadn't intended. Again, he told the story about his discovery on the GEL audit fifteen years ago when he uncovered the fraud that previous auditors had missed. All of that went as planned. The Q&A, though, went a little different than in prior years. He hadn't planned to reveal his *mistake* from fifteen years ago—all prompted from that kid's very perceptive question, one that no one had asked in his previous presentations.

It was uncomfortable being in the office so soon after his unplanned on-stage confession. He wondered how his staff was reacting to it. *They must all be talking about it*, he thought. He'd have to address it sooner or later. True to form, Maggie didn't even bring it up. She always gave Sam the space he needed.

"Is there anything I can do for you?" Maggie asked Sam on the phone.

"Just tell the staff I'm busy this week, and I'll be available only for emergencies. Client calls I'll take."

Twenty minutes before Sam had to join the call, he remembered the first time he had met Walter Hopkins.

When the firm approached Sam to transfer to the Chicago office in 1993, they dangled the carrot of giving him the opportunity of building a much larger forensic accounting investigation practice in the country's third largest city. It was a tempting opportunity, for sure, but Sam expected a compensation package to accompany the opportunity. It wasn't offered. Sam kept trying to enlighten the Chicago managing partner, Bob Ebert, of the stark cost-of-living differences between Indianapolis and Chicago, yet Ebert kept referring to the *opportunity* and wouldn't budge on a better compensation package. So, Sam kept saying *no* to the transfer.

Finally, one day Sam got a call from one of Ebert's lackies, saying if the sun set that day and Sam had not yet agreed to transfer to Chicago, then Hamilton Pierce would process his removal from the partnership. At the time, Sam had been a partner for only three months, and now they threatened to force him to withdraw. They obviously didn't realize whom they were dealing with.

Sam faxed his voluntary partnership withdrawal letter the next day. He had enough emotional scars delivered by his father's frequent alcoholic binges. It was impossible for any human being to intimidate Sam into doing anything he did not want to do.

Sam withdrew his letter a few days later when Walter Hopkins, the leader of Chicago's struggling consulting practice, stepped in and made it right. Walter viewed Sam's forensic accounting investigation practice as a promising new service offering in his consulting practice. He was intimately familiar with the success Sam had enjoyed in the Indianapolis marketplace, and he wanted him to be happy when he transferred to Chicago. Even after Walter's transfer to the Philadelphia office, he and Sam had remained close. They would soon be working together again on Walter's largest client.

Sam picked up on the first ring.

"Sam, it's Walter Hopkins. I appreciate you taking the time for this call. I'm holding Steve Lemly on the other line. If you're ready, I'll connect us."

"Let's do this."

"Steve, I've got Sam Halloran on the line, as promised. Tell him what you told me, and I'm sure he'll have better advice for you than I do."

"Sam, I really appreciate your time today. I need to jump on this before it gets out of hand. This fraud stuff is not in my wheelhouse, so I'm glad Walter found you."

"Happy to help."

"As you probably know, I am the CFO of Abello Distillers, a division of Hampton Enterprises," Steve Lemly began. "Have you had a chance to read the anonymous letter?"

"I read the translation and have one of my staff currently checking it against the original."

"Good, then as you are aware the author claims to work on the production line at our Palencia, Guatemala, location. My internal audit folks tell me they believe the author is a woman. They spent a week in-country doing whatever they do but could not prove-out the allegations contained in the letter. Lead guy's name is Herbert Richmond. He's the Director of Internal Audit for Abello. I've heard he's competent, but I don't have any experience working with him. Anyway, his team has completed a report my assistant is faxing to both of you right now. He addresses fraud risk, but it seems pretty generic. I was hoping you'd have some words of wisdom for me."

"I have some initial thoughts, but you know the parties involved and the operation better than either Walter or me, so I'd like to hear your thoughts before I speak."

"Well, I don't have much at this point," Steve said. "Let me get to the allegations. The writer talks about the plant and the living conditions, which I doubt you would have any interest in."

"Steve, everything in that letter is of interest to me. It all goes to the credibility of the writer. It's possible what you may have is simply a disgruntled employee seeking revenge against the GM, and the veracity of the claims can be measured in what is said in the letter and how it's said. But, if you'd like to begin with the allegations, I'm fine with that."

"All right, as you likely noted, the letter contains three allegations. Our corporate HR director has reviewed the letter, and his initial reaction is none of the charges are the sort of issue requiring the attention of our outside auditors."

Walter was quick to chime in. "Steve, your HR director may be right in his belief, but I certainly appreciate you informing me of this letter so we could discuss it internally and make up our own minds as to its materiality to the audit."

"Well, to be honest, I agree the HR director may be correct," Steve said, "but I have had some unpleasant experiences in my past life at Kraft. We once received a letter from an employee alleging harassment by her male supervisor. A quick review of her file revealed she was not what one would call a model employee, and she was making accusations against one of our best people. We dismissed the claims. A few months later, she quit. Most felt relieved she had decided to move on. Six months later, another employee quit, and on the way out the door she made similar accusations against this same supervisor. This time we took a closer look. Turned out the allegations of harassment and abusive behavior were true. Had we investigated him earlier, we might have discovered he was also taking kickbacks from local suppliers. The guy was a real scumbag, stealing from us and harassing our employees in the process, which ended up costing us a bunch in a civil suit filed by several female employees. So, where do we go from here, Sam?"

"Steve, I applaud your tenacity," Sam responded. "You're doing the right thing. If it's any consolation, I should be able to recommend some minimally invasive and cost-effective procedures to take this to the next step, but I need to spend a little more time reading the letter and thinking about options. For now, let's keep talking."

"Actually, guys, my assistant just slipped me a note. Garrett Barclay needs me to call him. He's not the kind that likes to be kept waiting, so how about I do that now, and we reconvene in an hour. Will that work for both of you?"

Walter and Sam agreed.

Sam read the translation again. She talked about her children, the lack of opportunities for the plant workers, and the squalor living conditions the workers had in makeshift houses behind the plant. Her pay may have been market wages for the area, but Sam wondered how $5 a day could sustain an individual, let alone a family. He pitied them working ten-hour shifts in a distillery and then attending to their children in the evening.

Then, the writer stopped ranting about the conditions and described Javier Mendoza. "He makes us honor him like he is president. We must call him *El Jefe*. One woman, she is a mother, and he forces her to lay down with him. Sometimes, he takes her in his office. One time, I needed to get work order, so I go to second floor. I hear grunting and look to his office. There he was humping her on his desk with his door open for all to see. What man would do such things and with no fear he gets caught? It's like he is proud of what he do. This woman, she work and she go to her home with no husband but a sweet little girl. Another that he fancies, she is just a child…. He forces her to lay down with him…. She so sad all the time. He is a pig…."

Sam laid the letter down momentarily and thought it distressing, but from what he understood about most developing countries, this kind of tyrannical behavior was commonplace.

Sam sat back in his chair and began to analyze the letter in more depth. First off, it looked like Mendoza was at least having an affair with one of his female workers, and likely other females at the plant. *Affair* was too antiseptic; more like he enjoyed raping his female workers. From the demographics Steve had included with the letter it looked like the GM had a lot of victims to choose from. Of the plant's 983 employees, ninety percent were female.

Another allegation appeared to indicate he was using a few male employees to do landscaping and other maintenance at his cattle ranch. Again, not uncommon, and not surprising given he clearly views himself as lord of the manor. Lastly, it appeared he was cheating on his expense reports. The writer said she knew his secretary must make fake receipts every month to cover up his "thievery from the company."

The hour had passed quickly, and it was time to rejoin the conference. Sam had a few more questions, but he had already determined what the first steps in this investigation should be, and he felt certain he could sell it to Steve.

Steve called Walter and connected the three of them again.

"Sorry for that interruption, guys. When Garrett Barclay calls, we jump, but I'm guessing you know that, Walter," Steve said with nervous laughter.

"I get it, Steve. I jump too when Garrett calls," Walter said.

"Okay," Sam cut in, "who is this guy?"

Steve was the first to respond. "Sorry, Sam. Garrett Barclay is the CFO of Hampton Enterprises. My boss. I'm sure that title speaks to why we jump, but you would have to know the man to understand why we jump so quickly. He selects each of his words with diligent care. When he speaks, everyone in the room is pensive. I venture all who know him, including every board member, would describe him to you in the same manner as I did. Garrett Barclay is a god around here."

"Thanks, Steve. I get the picture," Sam responded. "Steve, what was your first reaction to these allegations? I'm assuming you know the man, Javier Mendoza?"

"Well, setting aside it's hard to really know someone all that well after just a few encounters, these allegations don't rise to the level of massive corporate fraud, but they are still something we need to look into. That was my thought when sending down internal audit. But now it seems their efforts failed to resolve the allegations."

"Did that surprise you?"

"Not really, I suppose. I initially used internal resources believing it the responsible thing to do from a cost standpoint, but I'm now ready to pull the trigger on bringing in the big guns. That's why you and I are talking."

"Good, now tell me what you know about your GM."

"Sure. Javier Mendoza has been with us from the start, and I mean from the inception of the entire plant project. As Hampton Enterprises considered locating a new distillery, mostly for rum production, we wanted to locate it in an area already producing rum by our competitors. In that way, we believed we'd have a certain source of materials, a cooperative government, and a workforce accustomed to producing our product. Workers might move around the various local employers and wouldn't need to be retrained. Local politicians would understand the economics of what we produced and would be reasonable in assessing taxes and granting permits. They would also understand the waste products resulting from rum production and would be more tolerant and reasonable in the administration of environmental regulations, which could get way out of hand since rum production smells and throws off a great deal of waste. Not surprisingly, it's a lot cheaper to dump that waste in a nearby creek or river rather than build expensive containment facilities. With other rum producers already in the area, the government gets it. This alone would save us millions."

Sam was taking copious notes and said to Steve, "Okay, I get it. Now, tell me about Javier Mendoza, the man."

"A US citizen but a native of the region, he was educated in the US, receiving a civil engineering degree from NYU. He told us he wanted to return to his home to help bring prosperity and modern conveniences to his people. We were impressed by his sense of loyalty and compassion, as well as his credentials, so he was immediately fast-tracked for the GM position. Besides this, he was bright, resourceful, and from what our recruiter was able to discern, the kind of manager who would not let obstacles stand in his way. Somehow, he would get the job done. That attribute proved quite handy. Let me give you one example.

"During the initial permitting process, we ran into some issues we hadn't anticipated. Something about the water aquifers that were unique to the seventy-five acres we had purchased for the plant site. I suppose his engineering degree came in handy as he worked with city officials, explaining why our plans would comply with local laws and regulations given construction techniques and the plant layout. In the end, they agreed with him and permitted the plant's construction. I could give you other examples, but the bottom line is the Palencia facility has been in operation for eighteen years, and its growth and profitability speak for themselves."

"So, he gets high grades on making you a lot of money, but what kind of a person is he?"

"Not sure what you mean, Sam."

"I'm looking for a description of his character, Steve. For instance, tell me how he treats others, particularly his employees."

"Not sure I can answer that. Not even sure how that's relevant. Keep in mind this is a foreign plant that is not burdened by all the fluffy, make-nice-to-your-employee requirements imposed on US facilities. I'll be perfectly honest with you, Sam. Everything is very labor-intensive in a plant like we have in Palencia because labor is so cheap. While we still bottle in the US, we no longer produce here due to cost considerations. We shut down our last US distillery six years ago. That facility was about the same size in terms of production as the Palencia facility. We had it manned with only 90 production people. In comparison, the Palencia plant requires a ten-fold increase in the number of employees depending on the shift and time of year.

"Now, for the most part, management believes having fewer employees is always better. Machines don't get sick, die, or work at random outputs, nor do they complain and strike. But when one compares developing nation production costs to that of the US, cost per unit on a cash flow basis is fifty percent lower south of the border, all due to the extremely low labor costs. It's easy to see we make a lot more producing our products in Palencia. There's a reason we no longer have distilleries in the US. On a comparative basis, it's simply too expensive."

Walter knew that response to Sam's question about Javier's character would not satisfy him. In fact, he knew Sam would want to respond in a manner that might move things in the wrong direction. He quickly interjected, "So, Sam. What do you recommend?"

Sam bit his tongue. "I'm operating under the assumption you both want to get to the bottom of this as quickly as possible. So, I recommend we conduct some information gathering about Mr. Mendoza so I can have a fruitful conversation with him."

"What do you mean by *fruitful*?" Steve asked.

"I will need to ask some questions of Mr. Mendoza... to test his propensity to lie or tell the truth."

"And if he lies?"

"If he lies, we've got a big problem."

"How will you know if he's lying?" Steve asked.

"Because for a few well-timed questions I will ask of him, I'll know the answers."

"And you'll get those answers how?"

"Beforehand, I need to employ CRI to perform some in-country fact-gathering for me. CRI, Corporate Risk International, is a global firm comprised of ex-law enforcement and ex-military types who do things I need done but in areas we are not trained in, such as surveillance, dumpster-diving, etc."

"You sure this is necessary?" Steve asked, sounding a bit downtrodden.

"CRI will find facts I will use to test Mendoza's integrity. If Javier Mendoza lies to me, that will be instructive as to how to proceed."

"OK, you hire CRI, they get you some information about the GM, and then what? You call him?"

"No. I need to do this in person. I need to see how he reacts sitting across from me. I fly in for a day or two specifically to meet with him. When you call to let him know I'm coming, label me as *assisting the audit team* in preparation for the current year's audit. Don't mention the anonymous letter. If he brings it up, merely comment that while I might bring it up, as far as you were concerned that issue has been resolved with internal audit's visit and subsequent report. Nothing further to discuss. I want Javier Mendoza's defenses low. Under no circumstances should my visit be characterized as an investigation. I want to be clear about that."

"Sam, could I chime in?"

"Sure, Walter, it's your audit."

"Thanks for reminding me of my liability," Walter joked.

"Sorry, I didn't mean to imply—"

"No need to apologize. I get it. Believe me, I do. I am well aware of the risks. HP has had a few partners who signed off on bad audits. We don't shoot them, but we do put them out to pasture, and I'm not ready to start making cheese quite yet."

Amid their laughter, Walter checked his watch and said, "Guys, I'm going to have to drop off here. We have tickets for the opera. Sam, could you give me a synopsis of the rest of this discussion sometime tomorrow?"

"Enjoy the opera, Walter. We'll talk again tomorrow."

"Right. It usually turns out to be an awfully expensive place to take a nap, but my wife enjoys it, and that's what matters!"

With Walter off the phone, Steve continued. "So, Sam, what do you need from me?"

"Your verbal approval so I can begin making the arrangements and to alert CRI. I won't engage them until I get a signed engagement letter from Hampton."

"Which means I need to be meeting with Garrett Barclay soon," Steve said.

"Well, I'd strongly suggest we be retained by outside counsel to protect the privilege. That's usually coordinated by your Office of General Counsel."

"Sam, you don't know yet how things work at corporate. This falls clearly to Mr. Barclay's decision. And besides, we have a new general counsel. He'll take his instruction from Garrett Barclay or his tenure at Hampton Enterprises will be a short one. No, I need to sit down with my boss and the sooner the better. Besides, I want to jump on this now. If we run this by outside counsel, there's too much opportunity for a bunch of lawyers foisting their *concerns* on us at $600 per hour. Politics will slow this down."

"I like the way you roll, Steve."

"Sam, if I can get Garrett to approve your engagement letter by tomorrow how soon could you get down there?"

"I could most likely fly to Guatemala on Sunday and meet with Mendoza on Monday."

"Perfect. Could you then plan on flying back Tuesday and meeting with the management committee on Wednesday, say at three o'clock in the afternoon, to give them a preliminary report of what you learned?"

"I'll make that work."

"I know I'm moving the board pieces fast, Sam, but it sounds like that's your preference as well."

"Absolutely."

After Sam hung up, he needed to call Derek Dorn from CRI. They had worked together on numerous occasions in the past, and if Sam played his cards right, if he could sell this investigation, they'd be working together again very soon.

"Sam Halloran! As I live and breathe. Tell me you have a new job for me. Please say it!"

"Actually, I may. Haven't officially sold it yet, but you know me."

"Hot damn!" I'm on stakeout in DC waiting for a certain senator to get his rocks off with a beauteous Russian hooker. Got some good photos I'm thinking I could retire on if only I had the balls to call the tabloids."

"You've got too much integrity to do something like that. But I'm kinda jealous you're having so much fun without me."

"So, what's cooking?"

"Got a possible job in Guatemala. CRI got people down there?"

"For you, we'll send people anywhere you need us. What can you tell me?"

"Derek, I feel quite certain I'm going to be able to sell this job, but I need some information on an individual, and I need it as soon as possible. Like... I need someone to begin immediately, before I have a signed engagement letter. That possible?"

"Just tell me what you need, Sam. I'll do it myself if I can't get it approved on my end."

Sam gave Derek all the information he had about his target, Javier Mendoza, even though he was not yet authorized to do so. "Sometimes, you just gotta bend the rules to seize the advantage," Sam had said more than once.

CHAPTER 5

GARRETT BARCLAY WAS raised in England on one of London's most expensive streets, Kensington Palace Gardens, in the lap of luxury. His father was a British aristocrat from old money. His mother, an American, was the daughter of a steel worker from Pittsburgh.

Like most Oxford graduates, Garrett had a liberal arts education but didn't follow most of his classmates into medicine, law, or accountancy. Garrett always enjoyed working with his hands. So, upon the death of his father during Garrett's final year at Exeter, his mother decided to head back home to Pittsburgh. Garrett tagged along. He recognized liberal arts majors had to grow up and learn something they could use in the real world, so he entered MIT and obtained a degree in mechanical engineering.

Garrett started in one of Hampton's bearing factories in Camden, New Jersey. Three years later, he had secured five patents. Although Camden Bearings was a small company, Garrett quickly caught the eye of Rutherford B. Hampton III, then CEO and Chairman of Hampton Enterprises. Throughout the years, the company name never changed. Tradition ran deep in the Hampton family.

Hampton III introduced Garrett to a whole new world of

opportunities… literally, the world. Garrett traveled for the next two decades, expanding the company's interests globally. In the late 1970s, it was Kate Hampton, the granddaughter, who summoned Garrett back home to help her manage her growing company. Kate owned the company lock, stock, and barrel courtesy of her grandfather upon his death. It was Garrett who convinced Kate to take the company public a few years later. Titles never mattered between them. They ran the company together. Kate attended to the politics and relationship building. Garrett handled everything else—particularly, if there was trouble on the horizon as there seemed to be now, with a stirring in Guatemala.

After Steve Lemly and Garrett discussed the Guatemala issue, he made a call to his new, untested general counsel, the officer whose job was to keep the company out of trouble as may have been the case in Guatemala. Garrett left him a voicemail asking that he arrange to meet with Garrett to discuss the matter first thing in the morning.

Aaron Schmidt did not have Garrett Barclay's aristocratic background, but he was no slouch either. He was valedictorian of his high school class at the competitive Lake Forest Academy in Chicago's suburbs and then attended the University of Illinois, majoring in accounting, but soon tired of debits and credits and compliance work. He was accepted to and graduated from Harvard Law in 1985 and then began his career with the prestigious Chicago law firm of Bruce & Bishop, making partner in only nine years. Known for his work in securities law, he was a transactional lawyer, not a litigator.

During the interview process, he didn't seem to have the street smarts Garrett was seeking, but upon the advice of others Aaron Schmidt had the credentials Hampton Enterprises needed.

While Garrett kept his opinions about lawyers close to the vest, he didn't care for them much, but he was savvy enough to know what he didn't know… and he didn't know much about the law, especially securities law. After this first meeting with Aaron Schmidt, he hoped he would get a good start on the law which might rear its ugly head high enough to threaten Hampton Enterprises with respect to something going on at their Abello plant in Palencia, Guatemala.

Garrett Barclay stood to greet his new general counsel—a little stoop-shouldered and shorter than his formerly muscular, six-foot frame when he played rugby all through university. Grey, thinning hair revealing age spots, wire-rimmed glasses and a forest of hair growing out of his ears gave him that Max von Sydow look from the movie *The Exorcist*. Still sharp as a tack at seventy-eight, he remained one of those old salts who would one day die quietly at his desk.

"Let's sit by the fire," Garrett said as they moved toward the massive fireplace which was the centerpiece of Garrett Barclay's office. It was an exact replica of the one back in London in the house he grew up in.

Looking up at his new general counsel, Garrett stared into his face, measuring the man. At six and a half feet, Aaron Schmidt towered over his boss. Closely cropped blond hair and blue eyes atop an athletic frame gave authenticity to his German heritage. Packaged in what had to be an expensive, expertly tailored suit one would expect to see on Wall Street, Aaron Schmidt screamed of a privileged upbringing. His long piano fingers, smooth skin, and perfectly manicured fingernails telegraphed the man had never touched a shovel in his life.

This was the first meeting between the two men since Aaron Schmidt had begun work for the company.

Aaron was seated to Garrett's right in a massive Queen Anne chair that consumed even him. Garrett was seated in a rocking chair that looked even older than he did.

"So, Aaron, I know you've been here only a week but what are your impressions so far?"

"Well, sir,—"

"Please, you're an officer now. It's Garrett."

"Of course, Garrett, thank you. Yes, it's only been a week, but I knew enough about the company to recognize early on in the process that if offered this opportunity I would take it in a heartbeat," Aaron Schmidt said with the enthusiasm of a high school senior on a first date trying to impress the father of the most popular girl in school. Not a good start, but Garrett was willing to give him a chance.

"Really?" Garrett said lifting his chin to gaze upon Aaron, who suddenly appeared nervous and fidgety. Garrett could smell someone sweat a block away.

What had begun as a conversation involving two corporate officers by a fireplace in the CFO's office quickly devolved into what seemed to be a job interview all over again. Garrett did not intend to put his new general counsel on the spot. He asked a simple question about the Guatemala matter. Garrett liked direct, honest discussions about matters such as this. Maybe it was Garrett's tone and mannerisms. He rarely questioned his thoughts, actions, or comments. He simply followed his instincts.

Later, Aaron Schmidt would be kicking himself for how he answered his CFO, but it was too late. First impressions were lasting impressions. Without pausing, he launched into his experiences, first with a Foreign Corrupt Practices Act (FCPA) investigation in South Africa and how he had advised his client who, at first, hadn't taken his advice but later did when it was too late. "That was the first *client* I had ever fired," he said with a smirk as if he was actually proud of it. He went on to explain the details but then quieted himself when Garrett waived a dismissive hand.

Bottom line... he didn't answer his CFO's question: *What do I need to know about the legal issues surrounding the Guatemala matter?*

After forty minutes of listening to shameful boasting, Garrett abruptly stood in the middle of Aaron Schmidt's oration. He didn't say anything immediately, favoring instead to stare at him. It caused Aaron to stop talking and stand as well. Garrett did not want to ridicule his newest corporate officer as he had done hundreds of times with lower-level managers. Instead, he looked directly at him and said, "Thank you for coming. Have a nice rest of your day." He then turned away from him, took a few steps and hit the button opening the massive ornate, hand-carved door separating Garrett Barclay's office from the rest of the human race, and walked out.

Ashley, having seen this routine many times in the past, surreptitiously watched Aaron Schmidt slouch toward the door. She purposely did not look up when he passed her desk.

Garrett walked by Hampton Enterprises' CEO and Board Chairwoman's secretary like she wasn't even there. All she did was press a button under her desk to open Kate Hampton's office door in time for him to walk through exclaiming, "That new general counsel you hired is an ass."

"*I* hired?" Kate Hampton laughingly said as she walked over to a cozy chair that looked more at home in someone's suburban living room. Still talking, or rather complaining, Garrett took a seat in a similar chair across from Kate, who sat patiently waiting for her CFO to get comfortable and stop talking, or jabbering, as she would often accuse him. Over the years, she had become accustomed to this routine.

Kate Hampton and Garrett Barclay were more like husband and wife, although neither was married. Garrett had been married, four times. Never had any children, or if the lore was true he had fathered several by accident, but he drowned them at birth in Lake Michigan. Kate had never been married. Those who knew her well said she really was married but to an inanimate entity—one she loved as much as someone could love another person.

Garrett and Kate would get together often like they were doing now to commiserate, mostly. They understood each other's peculiarities and motivations, and most importantly, they gave support to each other in ways that helped them do their respective jobs. At this moment, Kate knew Garrett needed her to just listen. She'd nod when appropriate or say "I understand" or offer a gentle comment trying to help Garrett find his way, or simply listen in silence. After a time, she might say something more substantial or might not.

The company sort of ran itself, except on those occasions when there seemed to be trouble brewing—like now, several thousand miles south of them.

"Total, egotistical ass, he is."

"Now, Garrett, you know how you can get sometimes. Maybe you were too hard on him. He's only been here a week. Give him some time," Kate said as she stared fondly into his face. He wasn't looking at his CEO and Chairwoman. He rarely looked into someone's face unless he was trying to make a point the other person seemed not to get. That was rarely the case with these meetings with Kate. She was one of the few people who understood what made Garrett Barclay tick. They were truly soulmates. Many wondered why they never married each other.

Garrett stopped railing on his poor decision making. He had made a bad hiring decision. He knew it just as sure as rain. He would have to deal with that later. He seemed to pause for a time. Kate said nothing, simply watching Garrett at work with interest. She realized he was working through the problem and soon would get to where he needed to be.

"For almost forty minutes, he told me what he thought I wanted to hear. I need people around me who will tell me what I *need* to hear."

"I agree. You'll find that person, Garrett. You always have in the past and you will again."

"Already have. He calls himself a forensic accountant, and he's about to fix our problem in Guatemala."

CHAPTER 6

JAVIER MENDOZA HAD to prepare. He'd been having second thoughts about how Hampton would react to the internal audit visit. Those thoughts informed him that Hampton would not be satisfied with the work Herbert Richmond did. Javier didn't have proof of that; no one had called since Richmond's plant visit last month; he just knew Hampton would do something more. He trusted his instincts—which had never failed him.

Javier was the adoptive son of Luis and Nilsa Mendoza. Luis was a successful New York businessman, who traveled often to Mexico and Central America. On one of those visits to Guatemala, he met a woman, a secretary for one of his clients, and married her. She was pregnant. Luis was the father. He did the right thing.

Complications during pregnancy prevented Nilsa from having any more children after the birth of their daughter, Saida. Then, they happened upon Javier. Well, Nilsa did, anyway.

At the age of six, he was tied to the church door, abandoned. A kindly priest took him in. *Kindly* was how he was known to the community. That wasn't how Javier remembered him though. At the tender age of six, most children begin to accumulate memories that last throughout their lives, memories of times with family and those special celebrations: birthdays, holidays, and the grandest holiday of all—the birth of Jesus Christ. Who didn't enjoy the celebration of all celebrations called Christmas?

Not until Javier became an adult and began making his own memories had he ever known a Christmas he would want to remember. His childhood Christmases held bad memories but none so bad as his first with Father Benedict when the *kindly* Father showed Javier just how much he really loved his new charge. When Javier would return that love in exactly the manner the Father had instructed him, he'd be loved and cared for. When he resisted, the Father would beat him with a lead sap on the soles of his feet where they would not leave a mark.

Over the years that followed, the visits to Javier's bedroom continued until Father Benedict met with a tragic accident. Falling down the altar steps he had traversed a thousand times, he cracked his head open when it made contact with the marble. Well, at least that was how the police reported it... just a tragic accident. But Javier knew differently. One time too many.

As fate would have it, one of the congregants, Nilsa Mendoza, had desperately wanted another child. Javier had a new family, or at least a new mother. Everything happened so fast that she didn't have time to run the adoption of Javier by her husband due to his infrequent visits to Guatemala.

When Luis finally did return to Palencia for a visit with his Guatemalan family, it had grown to include a new addition, Javier. He didn't take kindly to his wife's choice because Javier wasn't quite right, an issue Javier was not fully aware of until transferring to a new school after the church school closed upon the death of Father Benedict.

At the church school, Javier was bigger than his classmates and older. It was a small school. Everyone fit into one room. At his new school, he was assigned to a class of students his own age. It was then that Javier realized he was much larger than his classmates. It turns out he had a pituitary gland disorder in his earlier years that somehow had corrected itself, but it left its mark.

At the age of sixteen, Javier was just over six feet tall and weighed 240 pounds. The disorder affected only his upper body, leaving him with enormous hands that seemed like marshmallows attached to forearms like tree trunks. His head was the size of a pumpkin and seemed directly attached to a chest, a chest that resembled the casks used to age rum at the local rum plant.

On his first day at his new school he found he had a new nickname: No Neck. He found it difficult to take issue with it, as he really had no neck. Others had a neck. Not Javier. His mother had told him it was God's gift to him, that he was a little different than the other children. She told him that God had special plans for Javier, and he should thank God in his prayers for making him a little different.

Well, that story seemed to fall short on his new classmates, the girls, especially. The boys pretty much left Javier alone. They got the message after one made fun of Javier in the classroom. It had been going on about a week and Javier had had enough. His size had advantages. The kid had called him *No Neck* just once too often.

Javier walked up to him as they were leaving class, grabbed him by *his* neck and held him down as he sat on him and pummeled his face like a butcher tenderizing a chicken breast. The kid left in an ambulance and never returned. Nope, Javier never had trouble with another boy, but the girls, they were relentless in their ridicule of him.

This being Central America, there were few girls in his school. Many were abandoned shortly after birth. Those who were able to remain in a home were not in school. After all, they were girls. Fathers saw their value lower than oxen. As soon as they were old enough they were put to work. When they would reach the age of sixteen, they were introduced to a new profession—the sex trade. They would either be rented out locally by their fathers or many would strike out on their own—a *prostitutas*! After they proved themselves, they got picked up by a handler—a *chulo*. Days were filled with getting high and nights being raped for money. Most didn't live past their thirties.

The girls who were privileged to be admitted to secondary school were special. They usually came from wealthy factory and land-owner families. They took many liberties with their special status and enjoyed mocking No Neck every chance they got. Javier learned early on he could not touch them, except for the first and last one.

The girl's father was well known in town. He owned the local concrete and block company. He was a big guy in stature and size. He cornered Javier after school one day and beat him with a baseball bat, broke his arm. Javier would remember his name.

Years later when Javier began construction for the new Abello plant, that man still owned the same company now under contract to provide block and concrete. He never indicated if he remembered Javier. He was simply happy to have won the contract.

One evening, Javier invited him for a drink. When he went to leave, Javier beat him unconscious with a baseball bat, then he ran his body through the woodchipper, which ran all day clearing the forest for the plant and administrative building site. Javier saved the gruel his body now represented and dumped it into the cement truck mixer the next day. He became the concrete threshold Javier would step on as he walked into his building each day as the GM of the Abello plant.

Javier looked as big as a baby elephant, and he also had a memory like one.

Throughout secondary school, those girls mocked him, making his life miserable. Even after his body caught up to its premature size and the abnormalities were not as pronounced, he still had no neck and enormous hands. The girls mocked on. He could not shake the *no neck* moniker… that was until he went away to college in America and returned an engineer to build a rum production facility for Hampton Enterprises.

They were no longer laughing at Javier Mendoza.

CHAPTER 7

THE WALK HOME east on Wacker Drive and then north on Michigan Avenue was usually a pleasant one during most of the year, but not during January. The day was cold but the usual wind was absent, making the walk home at least bearable.

Sam often walked home. It gave him time to think, to contemplate the day's events. Tonight, he was thinking about his conference call with Steve Lemly and Walter and trying to reconcile what they discussed with past events—investigations that didn't go exactly as planned—all still spinning in his head. Like fifteen years ago in Indianapolis.

Instinct informed Sam that Guatemala could be like walking into the barrel of a loaded gun, and not just for him but his staff. Not enough bad facts yet to draw such a conclusion… just a feeling. He could decline, but then knew he could not. If not him, who?

Monday, he'd be facing off with Javier Mendoza on his home turf. Sam would sit in front of him and make his own assessment.

Every past Latin American investigation he had done revealed some manager or politician who took advantage of those who worked for him. They'd use them and, in many cases, abuse them…

especially the women. Every piece of scum he had encountered south of the border.

Sure, he was profiling. The political correctness police would be up in arms, but they didn't know how investigators like Sam, the cops, military combat soldiers, or anyone facing dangerous situations worked. Profiling in the absence of suspected criminal activity is wrong; using accumulated experiences gained from working in certain countries and with people of certain professions and cultures resulted in certain profiles. Those profiles led to following specific procedures enabling good to triumph over evil and keep the investigator safe and alive. So, we profile, and the *PC* police be damned.

Nearing Chestnut Street where he'd turn left just fifty yards from his building, Sam briefly thought of Sue. She wouldn't have enjoyed Chicago condo living. Better off they divorced long before he moved to Chicago. So much time had passed. *Why couldn't I let her go?*

As he entered his building, he gave a quick wave to one of the doormen, Harry, who was assisting someone with their luggage. Al and Harry were Sam's favorite doormen. Al was the lead doorman but tonight Harry's ear-to-ear smile was a welcome distraction.

Once inside his condo, the quiet was palpable. The absence of sound was strangely soothing, especially considering all the traffic below. Sam poured himself a scotch and sat in the Barcalounger next to one of his condo's floor-to-ceiling windows. From his fifty-second-floor perch, Michigan Avenue looked surreal. A few minutes before, he had been walking on that famed street. He was now viewing cars, trucks, buses, and other obstacles he had to negotiate, but from this vantage point they all seemed like small pieces on a massive playing board.

Looking east over Lake Michigan, he could see the distant light standing watch over the entrance to Monroe Harbor warning summertime boaters of the breakwaters. The foghorn sounding a warning to all to avoid the rocky shoals upon entering could not be heard through the glass, but Sam could hear it in his memory. He had been through that narrow opening many times on his own boat.

Sam's thought drifted to his childhood. He tried hard to avoid remembering, but at that moment he failed. His alcoholic father had tormented him, derided him. He told him day after day that he'd never achieve anything. He hated his father more than anyone could hate another human being, and now the monster was out there, uncaged.

How could that be possible? True, he had served thirty years, but he murdered someone, Mr. Miller, the next-door neighbor who only wanted to break up one of the nightly fights Sam's parents would engage in. That night wasn't much different than any other except for the gun. The gun was introduced into the mix by Sam himself. Sam failed to use it to bring down his father once and for all. His father had wrested it from Sam and used it to shoot Mr. Miller, who was just trying to stop the monster armed only with a baseball bat.

Sam wondered how he would react if he ever saw his father again. He prayed he would not have a weapon in his hands should that day ever come.

Sam's thoughts shifted to Javier Mendoza and how he might view Sam's visit. Did he view all his surroundings like pieces on a massive playing board, Sam just another obstacle to be dealt with? Would Sam's investigative team become additional pieces consumed by Mendoza's network of crime? Would Sam, again, miss the signs like he did fifteen years ago?

It was wrong for Sam to think that way. They were just allegations. Except for the letter, they were baseless allegations. Still, it was enough to require an investigation. Innocent until proven guilty. Sure. All attempts to move his thoughts to think impartially, to think like the expert investigator he had trained himself to be, were absent.

Someone once told Sam that we were all just a summation of

our past experiences, the good and the bad. Sam was laboring to remember the good ones. Surely, he had had some of those, too.

Sam's favorite scotch, now consumed, was failing him at the moment. He drank it too fast and needed another. He stood abruptly, losing his balance, but he grabbed onto one of the pillars outlining the windows with one hand, the other lay flat against the window. The glass felt cool. He pressed his face against it and then the rest of his body until he was solidly in contact with only the glass, leaning against it, feet on the floor. He turned his head so he was looking south along Michigan Avenue, still leaning against the window. Only two panels of quarter-inch glass separated him from the comfort of his luxury condo and certain death—yet Sam wasn't afraid. He was confident the glass would hold fast. All the same, it was exhilarating to tempt death like that.

As Sam mentally prepared to battle with Javier Mendoza, he wondered what would keep him and his team safe. They would rely on Sam to keep them safe. Others had relied on him before. His track record was spotty, at best.

He was getting ahead of himself. Steve had notified him earlier in the day that the quick trip to interview Mendoza was approved and he immediately informed Veronica—but selling the larger investigation was quite another challenge. Of course, the Hampton management committee would discuss the matter with their lawyers; they would advise that if the company pursued an investigation, bad facts might surface. *Bad facts*: a euphemism for illegal activities possibly coming under the auspices of government regulators and all the havoc that might cause. Hampton's lawyers would at least discuss the option of doing nothing, walking away, at worst simply firing Javier Mendoza. You can't get in trouble for not reporting what you don't know. That's what a good lawyer would say. Sam was certain Hampton Enterprises would hire good lawyers to advise them of their available legal strategies: send a team of investigators down to Guatemala, learn bad facts, and have to deal with those bad facts. That's what the Hampton executives would be hearing from their lawyers.

Yes, walking away, turning one's head, was always a legitimate option any responsible management committee should consider. At least those beholden to shareholders worried about how bad facts would most certainly have adverse effects on market value. Hampton's lawyers would say that too. Sam wished he could be in the room when that discussion took place. He'd been involved in such discussions many times. Why this one seemed to possess him he couldn't say. His skin grew taut, his eyes winced, and his fists clenched around the cocktail glass holding his third scotch when Sam recalled parts of that letter.

She is just a child.... He forces her to lay down with him. Sometimes he takes her in his office.... She so sad all the time. He is a pig....

Sam walked into the kitchen, still clutching his drink. Opening the refrigerator, he realized he should eat something, but there was nothing there but condiments. But then, he knew that before he opened it. Even before they split, Sue and he rarely cooked except after he got fired from Benson Distributing. Bean soup was a favorite. Then, launching into that crazy scheme to get an MBA and pass the CPA exam, all to get hired by an international accounting firm. *How in the hell did Sue calmly agree to such a risky venture?* He thought. *Because she believed in me... more than I believed in myself.*

At the time, they had been married nine years. That was when the journey really got interesting. The crazy plan actually worked, but not for long. Sam had worked hard for two years re-educating himself to become a financial statement auditor while Sue slaved away teaching, tutoring, coaching, and working summers to support his crazy plan. She would say it was *our* plan, but she really did it for him. She always did things for him, for Will and Ben too, never putting herself before her family. *Then I screwed it all up. Why?* Sam still didn't have an answer. *I'll probably never be able to rationalize it.*

As far as career accomplishments, the path for Sam was clear after being the hero on the GEL audit. That was the start of his career taking off, and at the same time, it was the primary reason for the failure of his marriage, a marriage he believed from the moment he met Sue would last forever. They would have a couple of kids and grow old together, watching them succeed in their chosen fields and raise their own families one day. Then Sam had to get involved with someone else.

He wanted another scotch, but he was hungry. Fortunately, Sam lived across the street from Mike Ditka's restaurant, which made lonely nights like these all the more bearable.

Two more scotches later, he slid off the bar stool at Ditka's and found himself in a booth savoring a perfectly cooked bone-in, dry-aged fillet, twice-baked potatoes, and steamed green beans, all paired with a Turley Zinfandel. Life was good.

"Hey, old man!"

"Veronica, what are you doing in my neighborhood?" Sam said with gleeful surprise.

"Eating alone, again? Didn't we tell you don't ever eat alone?"

"Join me," Sam said as he motioned for her to sit across from him.

She laid her purse down on the table. "Give me a minute. I've got to dump some baggage." In a flash, she disappeared around the corner. Who knew what she was up to, but Sam suspected it would be something to do with a guy, someone tempting her to make poor choices.

She came back looking a bit frazzled but sighing with relief. "OK, that's done. Now, I can visit with you without that boat anchor," she said as she slid into the booth across from him. Sam motioned his server to get her a drink.

"Boat anchor? What are you talking about?"

"Oh, just a date."

"Where did he go? I want to meet him."

"Trust me, Sam, you don't," she said rolling her eyes with a coy smile.

"So, how was your day?" she said with a bit of a slur informing him she had a few past her limit; the glint in her eyes revealing she wanted to pry about something. He decided to ignore the question and address the larger issue concerning him about her: breaking his privacy rule.

"Veronica," Sam said as he shook his head and looked at her. "You have so much going for you. Why—"

"Don't go there, Sam. Besides, exactly when were you going to give us the rest of the story?" she said deftly, changing the subject away from her inebriated state that gave her confidence to push the envelope.

"About what?"

"Please… you know *what*. That bombshell you dropped on stage last week when addressing all the newbie auditors… right before I stumbled around trying to defend you from that little shit auditor trying to take you down during the Q&A."

"Oh, that," Sam said tipping back another glass of Turley.

"Yeah, *that*," she said with her head leaning on her right hand and staring directly into his face like she expected an explanation.

He hadn't planned it. "So, what is everyone saying?" Sam said.

"Sam, you know how we feel about you. It was obvious you were in a world of hurt. Something you've been dragging around for a long time. Something for which you can't forgive yourself. We were angry when that first kid started the ball rolling and then furious when the second guy wouldn't let it go."

"Robert Freeland."

"He's the kid who ridiculed you?"

"No. He's the one who asked the question that got it all rolling. That I failed to do what I should have. And had I done that, Carol Wittford would still be alive today."

"Sam, shit happens. You've told us time and time again, we all make mistakes. That was yours. It was fifteen years ago. I realize I am not qualified to be giving you advice, but you need to let it go."

Had Sam done the right thing... but Sam didn't... all because he feared he might be wrong. He was a new auditor. He'd be fired, he thought at the time.

"To this day, I don't know if that bullet was meant for me," Sam said, blankly staring into the candle on the table.

Veronica stared at Sam. She seemed to be able to piece together all that had happened without need of asking any more questions of him.

"Either way, it was my fault, as if I had pulled the trigger. And that piece of shit just disappeared, causing Carol's young children to grow up without their mother."

Veronica placed her hand on Sam's forearm. "Call it what you want, Sam, but don't forget those two young kids got to experience the love of someone who took care of them and is still watching over them. Speaking of which, I hope you realize how happy you made Laura. I talked to her again last night. She was packing. Moving van coming Friday. I want to be assigned as her mentor and expect you to make that happen."

Sam had already considered it. "That makes sense," Sam said, waking from his trance and focusing again. "You would be a good influence on her, *professionally*," Sam said, attempting to engage her on an issue she continually dodged. She was not willing to go there now and ignored his comment.

"You're the best!" she said as she hopped up, grabbing her purse and giving Sam a hug. "It's 11:30, and I have to get my beauty sleep." Lingering next to Sam's ear she said, "Don't come in at your usual time. I'll talk to the staff. What happened last week on that stage will never come up again. Go home, get a good night's sleep, and we'll see you sometime tomorrow."

She began to walk away and then stopped and turned back toward Sam. "Oh, almost forgot. You're all set for your meeting

Monday in Guatemala. I got you one of Mexico City's most capable women from their audit practice. Sorry, no forensics practice in Mexico."

"So, you're making me work with another Latina?"

"Hey, you got any complaints working with this one?"

"No, but you've been Americanized."

"You'll have a good time. And besides, she's hot! Ha! Looked her up in the firm directory. Could be my twin sister. Be careful, Sammy boy. You know how we Latinas can get with a little alcohol in us." She gave him a devilish smile. Sam shook his head.

With that, Veronica was gone.

Sam motioned for the check. When he did, he noticed a woman sitting at the bar boldly looking at him. When he met her stare, she didn't look away. She grabbed her drink and stepped away from the bar.

The waiter finally walked by, and Sam handed him his credit card. As he stepped away, she stepped up.

"Mind if I sit?"

"Depends. Who are you and what do you want?"

"I want to test your memory."

She slid into the booth across from Sam.

Sam didn't look at her. He'd be leaving momentarily.

The waiter returned with Sam's folio and laid it in front of him. Sam opened it, grabbed the pen, and scrawled his signature. He still wasn't looking at her, but she was looking at him.

"Test my memory, huh? Look, any other night I'd be offering you a drink and begin to question you about that provocative intro. Not tonight, dear. I'm headed home, alone."

"I'm sorry, can we start over?" she said stiffly.

Sam closed the folio and slid it toward the table's edge, looking at her now. Searching his memory. Nothing.

"Catherine Jennings, but my friends call me Cat," she said extending her hand.

"Look… Catherine Jennings, I don't want to be rude, but I'm beat. I don't know you, and I'm afraid if I sit here with you, I will pay for it tomorrow," Sam said as he gripped the table's edge, pulling himself sideways.

She lightly touched Sam's forearm before he stood. "Look, I know this is awkward, but I was in your forensic accounting class at DePaul about four years ago.

Sam looked at her face trying to remember. It was useless. He taught only one class of eighteen students but would never remember any of them.

"Again, I'm sorry. You're right, it's late," she said apologetically. "You mentioned during our first class you enjoyed mentoring young professionals. Sitting at the bar and watching how you and the lady were relating to each other, I knew she had to be on your staff… at Hamilton Pierce, right?"

Sam didn't respond but did recall mentioning mentoring in that class. That was before he became disenchanted with his first and last teaching position as an adjunct professor. Grad students, it seemed, were more interested in getting their A and moving through the MBA program than engaging in any real learning. It was a waste of his time, and he turned it over to his staff to teach the class going forward. Sam looked at her again but still couldn't remember her, although with that bright red hair he was surprised he could not.

As if she suspected he was searching his mind, she said, "I wasn't a redhead back then. Long story, but I was a brunette. Lost my mind for a couple of years but now back to my natural hair color."

"Good choice. I'd keep it natural if I were you," Sam said, now standing and getting his bearings after consuming at least five scotch neats and a bottle of Turley Zinfandel. She stood too, standing in front of him.

"Look, Mr. Halloran, I do understand. It is late, but if it's not too inconvenient I would really like to have a coffee with you. I need some career advice. I got fired today, hence why I found myself drinking at the bar by myself. Then, I saw you and your staff person...."

Upon hearing of her difficult day, Sam softened a little. "Veronica, and yes, she is one of my directors."

"Pretty name, but anyway, I need some advice. I probably should have availed myself of your mentoring offer four years ago, and maybe I wouldn't be in the predicament I find myself now," Cat said quickly, as though she thought Sam would cut her off any second.

Sam looked at her and then away at the back bar, then down at her feet not saying anything... thinking.

"Again, I'm sorry to have disturbed your evening," Cat said. As she turned to take her leave, Sam reached out and touched her elbow. She turned immediately.

"I do remember the mentoring offer to your class," Sam said. He looked at his watch, noting the time was a little after midnight. "There's a Starbucks across the street. How about we meet there at 4:00 this Saturday? Looks like today's events opened up your calendar a little."

"That would be so kind of you, Mr. Halloran."

"Please, call me Sam. You're no longer my student, and I feel old enough already these days."

"Thank you, Sam." They stared at each other without uttering another word, a moment longer than new acquaintances would normally do.

They walked through the revolving door at Ditka's, exiting on Chestnut Street.

"I'm going just a few blocks north to my home. Want to share a cab?" Cat said as she walked into the street.

Pointing to the building directly across the street, Sam said, "I live there."

"Oh," Cat said, now looking at the entrance admiringly. "Very nice."

"In fact," Sam said, motioning toward a familiar face and getting his attention, "Al here will be happy to hail you a cab."

"Yes, sir, Mr. Halloran. Right this way, miss." Al motioned where Cat should stand while he went out into the middle of Chestnut to hail a cab.

While Sam waited, he now had a chance to take Cat in. He was pleased with what he saw. Maybe he should not have been so hasty to dismiss her.

CHAPTER 8

SAM SHOWED UP at Starbucks only a few minutes late. It didn't take long to spot Cat waving her hand and beaming like a college kid at a concert flagging over her friends. He felt bad he was late, but she wore a big smile and extended her hand as she leapt from her seat.

"Sam, I can't tell you how much I appreciate you agreeing to meet with me. I hope this isn't a bother for you."

"Not at all. I'm happy to meet with you, Catherine."

"Could you please call me Cat, now. After all, this is our second meeting." They both laughed. Not a nervous laughter. A warm one, as between friends.

Cat spoke first. This being Chicago, she began with the weather. Sam allowed her to direct the flow of conversation, knowing at some point she would lead them into a discussion about her career... her need of a job. When she finished, Sam stared at her, anxious for her to get to the point. Saturday was like any other day of the week.

"So, I'm not really sure where to begin," Cat began haltingly.

"Well, all I know is you were a student in my forensic accounting class at DePaul four years ago, and you got fired from your job two days ago. So, how about you fill in the time in-between," Sam said smiling.

Cat smiled too and held her gaze for longer than Sam expected. He was happy to accept it, even though it did feel a little awkward. Sam was forty-seven and Cat was… well, younger… nearly a generation apart.

"Yes, I did get fired, and here we are today, both of us laughing about it."

"Now I feel bad for the humor. I apologize—"

"No, don't think twice about it. Trust fund baby and all. I'll be fine."

"Trust fund baby? OK, am I sitting in the company of royalty?"

"I'll never tell," Cat said playfully. "Even so, I want a career, and I want to be successful. Bad enough I was not the son every father hopes for and there ain't no more… but let's not go there either," Cat said flailing her hands as if she didn't want to discuss any more of it.

"So, I worked in the internal audit department of the Crown Group."

That started a two-hour discussion, both laughing as they discussed their individual experiences like they were old friends who hadn't seen each other in years until finally Cat touched Sam's forearm gently. "Sam, look at me going on and on. I'm so inconsiderate of your time."

"No, Cat, I'm enjoying this. It's been some time since I've had a pleasant conversation with a woman outside of work. You are quite the conversationalist," Sam said with sincerity.

"You are kind, Sam, but truth be told sometimes I don't quite know when to shut up."

Sam paused, waiting for Cat to make eye contact, and looking directly into her face he said, "No, seriously, I am enjoying myself. Yes, this is Sam enjoying himself. It doesn't happen often enough, so, again, thank *you*." He continued staring at Cat as she began playing with her long, bright red hair like a schoolgirl might on a first date.

"So, how about we talk about fixing me?"

"Suppose we begin with the central question: Why were you fired?"

"If you had asked me that the other night, I would have said I had no clue, but... I do know," Cat said as she looked down into the center of the table as if she was embarrassed. "I trust you won't judge me."

She played with her napkin. "I was having an affair with my boss." She quickly looked up at Sam, but he sat stone-faced, nonjudgmental.

"Why him?" Sam asked.

"Because I wanted to. I liked him. Make that, did like him. He made me feel secure. But then, it came down to him or me. I learned after I left that he told the company I came on to him, seduced him. He was sorry. Married with two children, he swore he would never allow that to happen again. They took his side," Cat said dismissively as if believing him correct in his assessment. "Maybe it was my fault."

Sam allowed that to float on the surface for a moment. Cat was twisting her napkin. "Didn't you anticipate what problems could result from sleeping with your boss?"

"See, that's just it. I didn't. I mean, I know I should have, but I block things out. Things I don't want to think about. Daddy calls me a lover, not a fighter. Then, he would add that's why I would never be successful in business."

"Maybe he's right."

"He encouraged me to go into teaching or social work. I hated him for it," she said gritting her teeth.

"Why?"

"I thought you'd have some answers for me. I don't know *why*. You tell me why."

"I suppose the *why* doesn't matter at this point, and besides, I can't do that. I don't know you well enough to have an opinion."

Cat looked up at him. She seemed not to understand.

"Let me ask you this, Cat," Sam said, doing what he typically did—move from the problem and on to the solution. "Did you enjoy what you did? Auditing, that is."

She lit up like a Christmas tree. "Sure. I liked the company environment, the people, our interactions, especially how we used to meet outside of work."

"I'll be more specific. Did you enjoy the *work* you did? The world of internal audit? Do you get a shiver down your spine when beginning a new project?" Sam asked it lacking the excitement he was sure matched how she really felt about her job.

"What do you think?"

"I think you don't seem like an internal auditor."

"What's that supposed to mean?" She started to cry.

"Cat, why are you crying?"

"I don't know," she said with disgust.

"I think you do."

A few moments passed as he let her think about it. He was prepared to sit there all day waiting for an answer. He would let the silence work on her.

"He's always right, and I hate that about him," she said, now fiddling with a tissue she pulled from her purse.

"You're talking about your father?"

"How did you know?"

"Well, it's obvious you love him, and you want to make him proud of you." Cat stared into Sam's face, frowning, as if wondering how he could be so right about her after just meeting her. "There seems to be something preventing you from expressing your true feelings. You're holding back."

"I do want to make him proud of me."

"For him and for yourself."

"Easy for you to say, Sam. You probably knew what you wanted to do forever. How could you relate to my circumstances?" More muffled sobs.

"Cat, what are you passionate about? What makes you come alive?"

She thought for a moment. "People! I love people! Not all people. Not the mean ones. Mostly the defenseless ones. The ones that continue to suffer from life's injustices and are powerless to change their circumstances." Cat smiled as if recalling a happy memory.

"Why are you smiling?"

"Just remembering. I went on a mission trip when I was seventeen. It was my last year in high school. We went to Cuba. I had no idea... no idea people could live like that. I mean, they had nothing. Well, they lived in a communist country. No wealth, no property, nothing material beyond basic shelter, food, and services. I wouldn't even call them poor because that's a relative term. Poor compared to what? Who? No one in Cuba had anything.

"But they had something the government could neither give them nor take away. They had God and family. The more time I spent with them, families, to my amazement, that was all they needed to live fulsome lives. God and family.

"After spending about a month with the Cuban people I became ashamed of the way I lived. They had so little, yet were so happy; I had so much, yet little appreciation. In the end, the more I had, the more I wanted even though I knew it would not make me happier or satisfied. Sadder still, I saw no way out of my predicament." She laughed at the seeming irony of it all.

Cat continued talking about her mission trip to Cuba with an enthusiasm Sam didn't expect given their previous dialog. Before she began talking about that mission trip, even her short bursts of happiness seemed contrived. But then, she started talking about Cuba and came alive.

Sam was pleased Cat had found a happy topic to talk about. It gave him a reason to stare into her face. Her creamy smooth, silky white, and flawless face, her glossy, bright red lipstick, her high cheekbones, slim features, delicate chin, perfectly straight and pearly white teeth. Periodically, a lock of her red hair would fall into her face. She'd let it dangle there for a time, continuing to talk, and then gently pulled it back, looping it over her ear without interrupting her dialog. Sam would nod like he was listening and absorbing every word she said, although he was only half listening, instead making an assessment of all he had seen over the last two-plus hours.

The moment he walked into the Starbucks, he immediately focused on Cat. Maybe it was because he had just recently met her, but maybe because she was quite pleasing to look at. Even the schoolgirl manner in which she presented herself caused Sam to smile, but only briefly, causing Cat to pause in mid-sentence, look up at Sam, smile, chuckle, and say, "Sam, why are you smiling?"

Her question caused Sam to break his concentration and mumble something that would not reveal his inattention to what Cat was saying... in favor of how she was saying it. "I'm simply marveling over your enthusiasm. You could be the poster child for mission work."

"I'm hardly a child. I'm thirty-four years old," she said in a more serious tone but still smiling, causing Sam to go on the defensive, fearing he might be found out for his slowly developing feelings. He was out of practice. After Sue, he knew he'd never marry again. He'd never be able to fall in love again. He still felt that way, but it was about time he found a woman he could enjoy just being with.

"Sorry, I didn't mean that the way it sounded. It was meant as a compliment. You are clearly a strong advocate for bringing attention to the underserved," he said diplomatically.

Cat continued to smile, seeming to evaluate Sam's intentions, maybe making her own assessment of Sam beyond the mentoring meeting they were supposed to be having.

She paused. Sam waited, hoping he hadn't disclosed an awakening feeling he now worked hard at quelling. Cat appeared reflective for a moment and then continued.

"I learned something from that mission trip to Cuba, living and working alongside the Cuban people. For the short time I was there, I was changed. Convicted. Unfortunately, I came home, and quickly reengaged in the same desperate plight most Americans suffer… to find the secret formula to happiness. A decade-plus later, it seems as elusive as it's always been. I feel destined never to achieve such a state."

"You're wrong, Cat. I think you are closer to achieving your goal than you know."

"You really think so?" she said wistfully.

"Listening to you today, I think you know exactly what to do with the rest of your life. You are resistant only because of one factor."

They stared at each other showing no emotion. Sam was waiting for Cat to come to that realization by herself. She was so close. No one could tell her. She had to figure it out for herself.

"All because *he* would be right again," she said with an admiring tilt of her head.

"Is that so bad?"

Cat appeared contemplative.

They both sat for a few moments, neither saying a thing.

"Make a dinner date with your dad."

"What for?"

"Tell him you want to run something by him. That you need his advice."

Cat smiled. She understood. She would be fine.

She continued to stare into Sam's face, regarding him in a way she hadn't before. Even though the place was brimming with people talking and laughing all around them, Cat was totally focused on Sam.

"I'm hungry," she said with a smile.

"I'm also hungry," Sam said, happy to extend the evening.

They hopped in a cab. Before Sam could tell the cabbie the restaurant he had in mind, Cat gave him another address. Ten minutes later, the cab pulled to the curb in front of a luxurious four-story, red brick and limestone townhouse on North Lake Shore drive. Cat took Sam's hand. She was completely focused on him when she asked, "Would you like to come in?"

At 1:45 a.m., Sam began gathering his clothing that was strewn from Cat's bed to the door. He tried to be quiet and not wake her. He was unsuccessful.

"You don't need to leave, Sam. Please stay."

"I'd love to, Cat, but I can't. I have a flight in six hours."

"Where are you off to now?"

"Guatemala."

CHAPTER 9

Sunday, January 11

ON THE FLIGHT to Miami, Sam tried hard to focus on the CRI report he was reading, but his thoughts continually moved to Cat. While he was inexperienced with the dating scene he struggled to understand where this new relationship might be headed. There were no doubts about what he most enjoyed about her, but was there another attraction? He scoffed at the thought there might be a future as he compared her to Sue, the only true love he had ever known.

There was no comparison. Sue and Sam were the same age. Cat was thirteen years younger. Sue was a wife and mother from the start. Cat was free-spirited and lived mostly for the present moment. Even last night, the first night they were together, he was sure she decided to invite him into her townhouse on a whim. There was no planning to it. One moment they were in a cab, the next they were having sex.

As the flight attendant announced they were beginning their descent into Miami International Airport, he concluded that Cat was fun, like a Cancun vacation, but soon he'd have to return to the real world. He could never be serious about her. Still, Sam enjoyed being with Cat more than any other woman since Sue.

The flight was quick and painless. When Sam reached his connecting gate to Guatemala City, he thought about meeting Alicia Lopez and became somewhat anxious.

Sam nestled into his seat at the gate area. He had checked on Alicia's incoming flight from Mexico City. It would be arriving in an hour. They made plans to meet at the gate for their flight to Guatemala City. He began people watching. It was especially interesting in Miami Airport because of the Latinas. Sam had run investigations in Mexico and several South American countries and was exposed, more than a few times, to the Latina flair for life.

One such investigation in Caracas, Venezuela, several years ago proved particularly instructive. His target, Carlos, educated Sam one night on the town. Sam was doing what he always did with his targets—befriending them... like a black widow spider.

"Caracas is the world capital for cosmetic surgeries," Carlos said. "Look around while you are here, and you will enjoy." He was right. The simple act of walking was an art to Latinas. They strutted in seductive, provocative movements with complete disregard for the hot-blooded, leering men splitting a path for them to parade down the sidewalk or through office corridors. Their passion for sex, for living, for attention, brought new meaning to the nine-to-five workday.

"Our Latinas' raw beauty is impossible not to notice," Carlos bragged. "Ladylike is a complement to them. They enjoy being sexy and hold a great deal of pride in being feminine. They revel in it and love to show off their assets." Everywhere Sam looked confirmed what Carlos had said. One Latina told Sam her first pair of shoes were high-heels. He didn't believe it but got the point.

Before dinner, Sam and Carlos went to a bar. In seconds, they were surrounded by beautiful Latinas, but they quickly tired of Sam, as Carlos later told him why. Apparently, Sam was too nice, offering to buy drinks and asking them about themselves. That was a big mistake if he had planned to impress them.

Carlos, on the other hand, was acutely aware of how to play the game. As he explained to Sam, "Latinas are impressed by strong men, repelled by weak ones… " like Sam appeared to be. "And they want to be dominated." Crazy, Sam thought. But, at least for one evening, the fantasy was real and alive, although, as a single man, Sam had wished, at least that one evening, he could have impressed the ladies. He didn't. Two of the ladies they met at the bar did join them for dinner, one on each side of Carlos. They wouldn't pay Sam the slightest bit of attention, and they both went home with Carlos. Sam walked into his hotel room alone.

Sam was jealous of Carlos. The next day, in an admission-seeking interview with him, Sam did get revenge when he led Carlos to confess to stealing $300,000 from the company. Ironically, some of it was to pay for his secretary's breast, buttock, and tummy-tuck surgeries. She made out big-time! He was probably still in prison— no Latinas for a very long time.

The Latin culture hyper-sexualized their women and made no apologies, but the old expression *you can't have one without the other* was definitely a big downside for Latinas. Sultry, sexy and beautiful was also interpreted by many as dumb and careerless.

Veronica suddenly came to mind. She was smart, beautiful, and sexy. She knew it, was proud of it, and never apologized for it. Still, Sam wanted to tame the beast within her. It was just a matter of time before it would get her in trouble. Latina, for sure, but she was working in an America that didn't tolerate such freedom of expression.

Just then, one came walking around the corner of the Hudson News stand commanding his attention, her bouncing long dark hair meshing well with her curves, all cloaked in a red dress that looked like it had been spray painted on her, topped-off with dark sunglasses revealing a mysterious nature to her and wearing a smirk she knew demanded attention. Everything went into stop frame motion. Her essence and captivating features caused her to stand out in any crowd. At that moment, she appeared to Sam as the only woman in the terminal.

Suddenly, Sam realized she was walking, no, strutting toward him in animated slow-motion. Directly toward him. Looking right at him, now smiling. Then he remembered Veronica's description of Alicia Lopez: *She's hot! Be careful!*

"You must be *Señor* Halloran," she said as she dropped her purse, which looked the size of an overnight bag, at Sam's feet and then extended her hand toward him as he stood to greet her. "It is very nice to meet you, *Señor* Sam Halloran. I'm Alicia Lopez."

"Yes, you are. I mean, yes, I am Sam Halloran, and you are Alicia." He sounded like a third grader meeting his over-the-top, hotter than hell teacher for the first time.

"How did you recognize me, Alicia?"

"Why, you are most handsome and smart looking," she said as she took the seat next to Sam, sitting on the edge and toward him, never confessing how she picked him out from the crowd. All part of the mystique she was creating. It was working.

Sam took his seat again next to Alicia but ignored the comment. "So, how was your flight to Miami?" As if he really cared. He just needed to get some distance away from whatever intended course she might have in mind. Or maybe that was an innocent comment made by a young foreigner wanting to impress, or rather suck up, to a US partner.

"I have heard so many amazing things about you and it is so glorious to meet you today and thank you for the pleasure of working with you."

"Well, it may be premature to thank me," Sam said, feeling a little off-centered by Alicia Lopez.

"I cannot tell you how excited I am to be working this fraud case with you. I hope you find my skills useful," she said, smiling seductively.

Sam couldn't believe she just blurted that comment out with twenty people around them. As he took a quick look, it was clear that some heard her say "fraud case," glowering at them like they were government secret agents. Hell, some of the folks on this plane could work for their target. After all, this was a direct flight to Guatemala City. *Dammit, she may be great eye candy, but with that slip it's pretty clear she doesn't know a damn thing about how to conduct a clandestine investigation*, he thought.

"Alicia," he said, as he took her by the elbow and directed her to stand and walk away with him, "you can't be talking like that in public."

She seemed initially stupefied, but when she removed her sunglasses the expression on her face informed Sam she was crushed. She spun immediately in front of him gripping both his forearms. "*Señor* Sam, I am so sorry. Whatever was I thinking?"

"Look, Alicia, it's not that big a deal. It's just best if we don't talk in public about what we do. We're probably fine, but better to act like we're tourists."

They sat again. She placed her glasses back on, pulled her chin into her chest, crossed her arms, pursed her lips, and began to sulk. *Is it possible she could be this sensitive?* Sam felt like he was working with a child.

After a few minutes, Sam said, "Look, Alicia, relax. You just need to be more careful, all right?"

She said nothing but nodded her head in a manner mimicking an adolescent. Then, she slouched back into her chair, looking down into her lap, arms now tightening across her chest.

Sam's mind was racing, desperate to get into a business discussion, anything but this crap.

"Alicia, now that we have some privacy over here, how about we talk about this project?"

She lifted her head and with little feeling said, "I would like that very much."

"Good. Let's go over a few preliminary things."

"You have my undivided attention, *Señor* Sam," she said with a Julia Roberts smile revealing astonishingly white and perfect teeth.

Sam was trying desperately to act like a professional. In this environment, he was her boss. The last time he forgot his role on an engagement, it didn't turn out so well.

"OK, Alicia, first off, please keep in mind we are here to check out the situation based on very preliminary evidence. We don't know if a crime has been committed. Hopefully after tomorrow, we'll have a better idea of what the story is."

"Yes, *Señor* Sam. I understand."

"Alicia, please call me, Sam? Just Sam will be fine." She nodded her head.

"What is our plan of attack?" she said with a pleasant demeanor like she might be able to move past the first ten minutes.

"Did you get useful information from CRP?"

"CRI," Sam corrected.

"Yes, CRI. That's what I said."

"OK," was all Sam could muster.

"When do we bring in a team to find out what was stolen? How big this fraud is do you think?"

"Whoa, Alicia. Like I said, we don't yet know if any crimes have been committed. As far as we know, our target could be a very competent manager with self-indulgent leanings. If that's the case, it won't be the first time a successful manager fell into the entitlement pit and rationalized a few pleasure-seeking activities. And if that's the worst of it, then we can turn this over to HR and be done with the matter."

Alicia was looking at Sam with an intensity demanding he instruct her. It was becoming clear Alicia Lopez had no investigative experience.

"OK, Alicia, here's a quick synopsis of what experience tells me at this point." Sam talked about his experiences, especially on Latin American investigations where pompous, dictatorial executives took liberties with everything falling under their purview. Alicia appeared to listen and take interest, but Sam wished Veronica were by his side on this one, but she had an important matter to tie up.

Sam finished telling Alicia all he knew about the case at this point.

"You make it sound so sensual," Alicia said breathlessly. He was clueless where that came from and ignored it.

He checked his watch. They wouldn't be sitting together on the plane, and he wanted to say something positive before they boarded hoping they had crossed a difficult hurdle. "At any rate, Alicia, I am happy to have you assisting me. Sometimes I feel like I'm getting too old for this."

"You don't look so old, Sam. You look wise and handsome, and I am so pleased to be with you today." She wrapped it all up in a big red bow with that smile of hers.

Damn. This is going to be harder than I thought.

Over the loudspeaker Sam heard, "American flight 667 to Guatemala City will be boarding in fifteen minutes."

The announcement thankfully broke the tension.

As Sam stood preparing to move over to the business class line, Alicia stood with him, still close as if they were tethered together.

"So, what is happening when we land?"

"We don't land until late; I think close to midnight. I'm guessing we'll cab it over to the hotel, hit the sack, and meet for breakfast at seven to go over the plan. The GM is sending a car for us at ten o'clock. That should give us plenty of time to review our meeting agenda."

"I am so *excited* to be experiencing this," she said, arms raised like she was a celebrating cheerleader at the big game.

"Good. I hope you feel the same way after spending a day with the Buddha."

"The *Buddha*?"

"Oh, sorry. Forget I said that. Most successful organizations have a Buddha, or two. Entitled… privileged," Sam said still working hard to keep the discussion focused on the task at hand.

"Do you feel such entitlement sometimes? You are so successful yourself?"

After the briefest of pauses Sam said, "No, never, and if my thoughts did wander that way, the firm has controls that would expose me in a heartbeat. There is no way my mind could wander."

"That's a shame," she said as she looked away.

Just then, some guy bumped into Sam and he apologized immediately. Timely distraction.

That's a shame. What the hell is on her mind?

CHAPTER 10

THEY LANDED IN Guatemala City a little after midnight. A moonlit night revealed the same surroundings one would expect at an airport: hangers, maintenance and emergency vehicles, trucks, and passenger cars. Disembarking was a flashback to a bygone era. Passengers descended the air stairs much like Clark Gable might have back in the day. The air seemed unexpectedly cool. Eerily quiet, also.

The lateness of the hour had its usual effect on the disembarking passengers. No one was talking. Not even the flight crew. Everyone seemed exhausted.

Sam waited at the bottom of the stairs for Alicia. International business-class travel was a luxury afforded only to partners of the firm. Alicia was flying economy coach, but she was young and easily adaptable to narrow seats with no leg room and intermittent service.

Sam stood on the tarmac, waiting. He wondered why no Alicia. *Could she be asleep?* Hopefully, she had forgotten whatever was on her mind just before they parted. Maybe it was simply a language thing he had completely misinterpreted. Serious work was the only thing on the agenda for tomorrow, rather, later in the day, and Sam needed a professional by his side, not a concubine.

At last, she sauntered out of the plane and elegantly descended the stairs as if being greeted by reporters and admirers on a different kind of runway, hips swaying, purse clutched in the crook of her arm. She stepped on the tarmac with a sensuous, subtle smile, her eyes slightly closed and said, "Did you have a nice sleep, Mr. Sam?"

Ignoring the salutation with an intentional yawn, Sam slurred out, "I feel as though I'm still nestled in my seat and this is just a dream. I can't wait to lay my head on a real pillow."

Alicia followed along by Sam's side without comment.

"So, here's the drill. We hopefully get through customs quickly, hit the hay, and meet for breakfast at seven. I realize that's only a few hours from now, but there are some important things we need to discuss before we meet with our guy."

They walked at a brisk pace to try and catch up to the others now entering the customs area. "How do you expect *Señor* Mendoza to deal with us?"

"Alicia, now that we are in-country, no names. Refer to him with your favorite pronoun of choice, but no names from here on out."

"Sorry, but of course that makes sense."

"We'll have ample time to talk in a few hours at breakfast, so let's walk, heads down, get through customs, and cab it over to the hotel, which I'm guessing at this hour would be a ten-minute ride."

They finally reached the others and found themselves at the end of an exceedingly long, single-file line queuing up to a lone customs table with one guy stamping passports and two others looking over these new entrants to their country. Never a fan of lines, Sam found his impatience bubbling to the surface like a launch at Cape Canaveral.

"Damn, this is a two-hour line! There's got to be a quicker way to get through here," Sam said as he looked around for some alternative.

"This is my fault. I should have hurried," Alicia said.

She was right, but no sense in making her feel bad about it. "Not a big deal. We'll be fine."

Five minutes passed. "Alicia, how about you run up and have a look to see if we can get through this line a little quicker. Maybe you can work your Latin charm on them."

She immediately perked up with this new mission and hustled to the customs desk. Sam felt a little bad for his impatience.

She was talking to someone now. It was an object lesson to watch her work those customs officials, swaying her hips toward the seated guy doing the stamping while flirting with one of the standing guys. *Good work, Alicia.* Now, she was playing with a long curl of her hair. He was smiling and the guy stamping passports was gawking.

Suddenly, Alicia stood erect, one hand on her hip, the other flailing above her head like a metronome, a last-ditch effort to right the sinking ship. Soon she spun around and walked back toward Sam, head down, no sexy swaying of the hips with her arms crossed, quickly pacing. Translation: no luck.

"I take it they were not moved by your appeal."

"Pigs. That was my best act, and they enjoyed with no payment."

"Well, nice try. I suppose we'll have to wait our turn like the rest of the folks. Nothing we can do about it now."

Over her shoulder Sam noticed three large and serious looking men making a headlong pace toward them, appearing to have a purpose in mind with their eyes fixed on their position.

"Don't look now, Alicia, but behind you are three rather surly looking guys walking toward us for reasons I do not know. Don't make eye contact and continue talking to me like they don't exist."

The trio stopped and fanned out around them. "*Señor* Halloran?" said the big guy in the center.

"Yes, I am Sam Halloran. What can I do for you gentlemen?"

"*Señor* Mendoza instructed us to take you to the hotel. Please follow us."

Before Sam could say anything, two of them grabbed their overnight bags and walked toward the customs desk at a good clip. Sam began to question the whole scene, instinctively knowing they should not be following these guys. But that was thinking rationally, and all Sam could think of was getting into a nice warm bed a lot quicker.

"Gentlemen, what's the plan here?"

"Please follow us, *Señor* Halloran. All has been arranged."

Arranged. That sounds like mob talk for shut up and follow me or I'll whack you.

"So, is there some kind of VIP line you are taking us through?" Sam said.

"Please follow," said the big guy.

Another of them said something, the others laughed. Alicia threw Sam a sideways frown. He got the hint and shut up.

As Mendoza's men moved Sam and Alicia alongside the customs table, the officials didn't say anything or even give them so much as a passing look. Soon they were a safe distance past customs and walking straight for the terminal exit doors. Sam's first thought was *That was cool. No VIP line for them. We're too important even for VIP treatment.* But then, as he and Alicia were helped into a black SUV by their hosts, reality hit Sam squarely between the eyes: Government officials don't look the other way for free. Strike one.

While Sam was checking into the hotel, his BlackBerry buzzed. It was a text from Derek Dorn, the CRI investigator.

It's important we meet before your meeting with Mendoza.

CHAPTER 11

MORNING REVEALED WHAT Sam had expected. Sipping his coffee, he walked through the sliding doors and onto his balcony overlooking a sprawling and vibrant business community filled with Guatemalan commuters on their way to work. From Sam's twentieth-floor perch he could hear and smell Guatemala City preparing itself for another day. He texted Derek, changing their meeting to Sam's room at 6:30.

The air had an acidic smell to it. Sam doubted anyone cared. It was still dark, but according to the forecast it would be sunny with a high of 75 degrees and no rain was predicted… until June. Sam's only concern was to get through the day without an earthquake. He'd been inside many foreign countries but never one whose capital had changed as many times as Guatemala's, mostly due to earthquakes. Earthquake destroys the capital and the natives just leave that city and go find another.

He was beginning a new investigation. There was nothing better in his world.

Right on time, Sam opened the door and the two men embraced.

"Man, it is so good to see you again," Derek said.

"Agreed! When was the last time? Nigeria?"

"Sam, you are getting old. Dubai… last Spring. Nigeria was the year before."

"You're right! How could I forget? Experiencing Ramadan in a Muslim country and getting chastised by a guy for eating peanuts during the day. You've got a better memory than I do. Maybe I am getting too old for this."

"Well, I hope you brought all your faculties for this one. You've picked a formidable opponent," Derek said getting right into it.

"Sounds like you've got more intelligence to add to your excellent report you faxed to me yesterday. Great facts that I'll use in my interview today. There's the coffee pot. Meet you on the balcony," Sam said, then walked through the sliding doors and sat waiting for his friend to join him.

"It really is good to see you again, Sam. I've got a bit of personal news to share with you, but first let's discuss what I learned about your target that wasn't in our report."

"Sounds good."

"Not sure where to start. I know you like to address the financial issues, but, Sam, this guy Mendoza is as bad as they get."

"Start anywhere you'd like."

"Now, keep in mind I've just been digging several days and none of this has been corroborated, but I believe I have a good source. At least I got him from a trusted source."

"Who are we talking about?"

"Guy used to work for Mendoza. On his personal security detail. Former Guatemalan military. Said he couldn't stand it anymore."

"Couldn't stand what?"

"Mendoza's extracurricular activities."

"I'm listening," Sam said, putting down his coffee and focusing on Derek.

Derek hesitated. "Women and drugs. Trafficking. From Columbia, through Guatemala, then to the Mexican drug lords, then to the US. He owns the market, or at least acts like it. Nothing gets through or around Guatemala unless Mendoza gets a cut."

"So, who anointed him king? Why Mendoza? He's just a distillery plant general manager."

"He's a lot more than that. Happens to have a very connected cousin in Columbia." Derek looked at his notes. "José Santacruz Londoño, also known as Chepe Santacruz or *El Gordo*, The Fat Man. Along with the Rodriquez brothers, they started what is known today as the *Cali Cartel*."

"I've heard of *Cali*. But don't they play second fiddle to the *Medellín Cartel*?"

"You've got old Intel there, Sam. The *Medellín Cartel* disappeared shortly after Pablo Escobar got clocked a few years ago. He was taken down by the Columbian government, but most suspect *Cali* had a hand in it. Without Escobar around, *Cali* is getting bigger all the time. At least, they control Guatemala through their resident boy, Javier Mendoza, or as my source called him, *El Jefe*."

"And *El Jefe* means what?"

"A name Mendoza adopted. Now, again, this is all uncorroborated, but apparently Mendoza's idol is Fidel Castro, who used the title *El Jefe*, the boss, when he was militarizing his people in preparation for the overthrow of Batista... and the rest is history."

Sam sat up and frowned at his friend.

"Hey, I'm doing the best I can here," Derek shot back.

"I know. And I appreciate it. I know this is all preliminary."

Derek was staring into his notepad.

Sam glanced at his watch. It was approaching 7:00 when he would be meeting Alicia for breakfast. He polished off the last swig of coffee in his cup as he stood. "OK, well that's something, at least."

Derek stood too. "Sam, my source really seemed disturbed about the women trafficking. How he chooses them. What he does to them."

"How's that?" Sam said, seemingly losing interest. Like he

was only concerned about the typical crimes he investigates. Money crimes.

"Part of his job was to check out every shipment of women. He was instructed to find the prettiest ones but then to make sure they were sixteen. Then, he'd turn them over to the plant foreman."

"So, he interviews them to find out how old they are?" Sam said sarcastically.

"Apparently, they are tattooed in Columbia. On their inside forearm. Name and birthdate," Derek said quizzically. "Don't know why. That's just what he told me," Derek said as he closed his notebook.

Sam contemplated for a moment... *Bring him the prettiest sixteen-year-olds....* Then, seemingly dismissing it he followed with, "I've got a breakfast meeting at seven. What was the personal news you had?"

Derek extended his left hand and smiled.

"You're married! When did that happen?"

Derek pulled out his wallet and proudly showed Sam a picture of his new bride.

"And a white woman! And here I thought you were a racist!"

"Oh, don't get me started with the racist barbs again," Derek said laughing. "Too many memories!" The big deal isn't that she's a white woman. She's a Brit and MI6 agent. Met her in Dubai after you headed home. Three months later we were married by her preacher father."

"Well, says a lot that they welcomed a black man into the family."

"The Brits aren't racist like you Americans!" At that, Sam fondly remembered when they first met a couple of years ago. Investigation in Lagos, Nigeria, Derek's birthplace.

"Don't get me going again. We'll have to defer this for another time. I'm late."

"Damn, almost forgot," Derek said opening his notebook again. "My source called me just before I texted you last night. He learned from a friend still working for Mendoza that one of the plant workers committed suicide in front of everyone on second shift yesterday. Jumped headfirst into the sugarcane chopper."

"Oh, my God!" Sam said looking at his friend. "What a horrible way to die." Sam sat contemplative, neither speaking for a moment. "You get a name?"

"Sort of," Derek said again, referring to his notes. "She had a tattoo on her arm—*Lily1981*."

"That's it?"

"I've asked him to keep digging. I figured you'd want more information. I'll call you if I get it."

They embraced one last time. "Thanks for the excellent work and in such a short timeframe," Sam said somberly to his old friend. "Not sure how I might use this additional information, but keep it coming."

"Will do, Sam. And seriously, Mendoza seems like one really sick dude. You be careful down here."

"Job one," Sam said as he led Derek to the door.

Sam finished getting dressed and headed for his meeting with Alicia. It was a little after seven o'clock. He was running late—not a good start for the day.

He walked fast to the elevator bank on his floor. He pushed the down button and heard the hum of the elevator motor click into service. Telltale signs caused Sam to realize he was far from home. The floor showed worn carpet at the metal molding edge of the elevator shaft, grime around the buttons on the wall. Off to the right, a table lamp sat with one of the three bulbs burned out and behind it was peeling wallpaper—all confirming he was no longer in America.

This was Latin America, where even the five-star hotels didn't have the spit and polish Sam was accustomed to seeing back home or in most developed nations. Most Americans had no idea how good they had it. It was no wonder people risked their lives, often placing their own children in danger and traveling thousands of miles for a chance at having the Great American Dream. Who could blame them? He thought about Derek's comments, his concentration broken by the *ding* of the elevator arriving.

The doors opened to a family apparently going out to enjoy the pool even though it seemed a little early for that. The mom, dad, and the little ones were dressed in swimwear. Dad looked like a fireplug standing at about five-foot nothing with sunglasses and an unlit cigar in his mouth. He was holding the hand of a shorter version of himself who looked about ten years old. Standing next to him was the mom, also short, overweight, and dumpy. She was holding the hand of the little brother, who was trying to retrieve a booger out of his nose.

Seeing Alicia standing and waiting for him at the entrance to the restaurant snapped Sam back to their purpose for being in this place at this time. They were about to engage in a little planning, informed guesswork, and determining how they would test Sam's hypothesis about Javier Mendoza. Crook or innocent man? At least for now, in this place and in Sam's own mind, Javier Mendoza was a bad actor.

"Alicia, good morning. I hope you were able to catch a little sleep."

"Good morning, Sam. I am feeling happy and alert and ready to do our battle for good to destroy the evil," Alicia said, all wrapped in that killer smile.

"Ah… yes," Sam wondered when she would stop with the clichés, jumbled that they were. "Well, let's grab a bite to eat and discuss our upcoming battle for good against the evil, shall we?" he said, trying to play along. "I reserved a conference room where we can eat and talk in private."

In the conference room, they helped themselves to some food and coffee. Sam allowed Alicia to sit, and then he sat a safe distance away.

"So, what is the plan? When do we meet with *Señor* Mendoza?"

"I got a voicemail that Roberto, Mendoza's driver, will be picking us up at ten o'clock, so it looks like all is going as planned. I want to go over the CRI report with you. There are a couple of findings I intend to use to test Javier's integrity," he said as he opened a folder containing the report. Alicia scooted her chair closer to Sam.

Sam laid out the purpose of the meeting in the same manner he had explained to Steve on their conference call… to test Javier Mendoza's integrity. He gave her specific instructions as to her role. Alicia had some questions, but he didn't get the feeling she got it.

An hour passed. "Alicia, it's important you follow these instructions to the letter. Are we clear?"

"Clear as a drum," she said in a serious tone.

Sam let it pass without comment. He wanted to review his questions in solitude, so he gave Alicia a rather long article he had previously published about how to conduct a financial crime investigation. Surprisingly, she sat and read it with a highlighter and without interruption. He considered if any of the information Derek had provided that morning might be used but then discounted it all as personal. Anecdotal.

"Our ride will be here in fifteen minutes. Do you have any other questions for me?"

"No," she said with a smile. "I have it, and I understand the plan and my role in it. What you had to say about your interview techniques in the article are helpful. I obviously can learn much from you and eager to begin my experience," she said with less enthusiasm, more seriously, like she might just be catching on. It was promising. Maybe, just maybe, he could pull this off with her by his side.

CHAPTER 12

IN THE HOTEL lobby, Roberto Cuesta approached them, his arm extended, and his mustached-draped mouth stretched from ear to ear with a smile exposing a perfect set of white choppers. Too perfect.

"*Señor* Halloran, I am so pleased to meet you on this day and your associate, I take it?" he said as his eyes fixated on Alicia's cleavage. Sam couldn't believe she wore a dress like that but said nothing.

"Roberto, thank you, and it is a pleasure to meet you as well. Yes, this is Alicia Lopez. She is an audit manager from our Mexico City office."

He looked back and forth between Sam and her. "And she also is pleasing to the eyes, no?" Roberto said exposing those huge pearly whites again.

Alicia offered a demure smile. Sam ignored his comment.

Roberto pointed to a freshly washed Jeep Cherokee outside the lobby doors. He rushed ahead and grabbed the door handle on the front passenger side. Alicia was a step ahead of Sam and enjoying Roberto's attention. It seemed her maturity was short-lived.

He was wearing combat fatigues, an untucked and unbuttoned blue linen shirt atop a tucked white tee-shirt, and black polished combat boots with his pants neatly tucked inside. As he opened the door a wind gust caught the front of his shirt, wiping it aside to reveal his compact sidearm, probably a 9mm, Sam suspected. The way he wore it informed Sam he knew how to use it. Roberto, still eyeing Alicia, swung the front door open. "*Señorita*," he said as he helped her inside the jeep.

Alicia smiled and took her seat without a passing look at Sam. Climbing in, she and Roberto exchanged glances and comments, in Spanish, of course, like they were going on a first date.

Roberto dashed around the front of the jeep, so Sam opened his own door to the back seat and felt like the husband of a movie starlet but made no comment. Alicia appeared accustomed to this kind of treatment and enjoyed every minute of it.

Sitting behind Alicia trying to get comfortable on a bench seat with little leg room, Sam glanced at Roberto, who was now seated comfortably behind the wheel—maybe too comfortably, as Sam noticed him leering at the passenger next to him.

Sam slid behind Roberto to capture his view. As if Alicia's mini skirt wasn't short enough, she had pulled it higher to reveal too much thigh sitting askew with her right leg across her left facing Roberto. Alicia was doing everything she could to exaggerate her breasts and cleavage, even dappling it with a white linen cloth. "Is it always this hot so early in the morning?" It hadn't even reached 70 degrees yet.

"Shall we go?" Sam said, hoping to break Roberto's trance-like stare.

The ride to the plant was mostly on back country roads. A big stretch of the drive was on a dirt road filled with potholes and no guardrail keeping them from a fall should Roberto's continual activity of visually undressing Alicia get the better of him. She looked like a stripper about to do a pole dance and Roberto was like a dog in heat. Sam buckled his seatbelt.

Thirty minutes into the drive, Sam became impatient. "Roberto, how much farther?"

"The turnoff to the plant is just ahead. Then, we will be on some bumpy and narrow dirt roads for another few kilometers. We should be there in twenty minutes."

"Roberto, how long have you been in *Señor* Mendoza's employ?" Sam asked.

"I don't work for *Señor* Mendoza, directly. I work for *Protección* who has the contract to provide security for the plant."

That was news to Sam. "How many men like yourself provide security for *Señor* Mendoza?"

"Hard to say. I know we provide 24-hour security, and I work an 8-hour shift during the day, so I can't say how many others the company provides to *Señor* Mendoza."

"We are soon there," Roberto said as he took a sharp right onto an even bumpier road. On the left was a tall cinderblock wall about twelve feet high and covered in vines as if the wall would fall without its support. The terrain close to the road was very old-world, looking like something you'd see in a Tuscan village in Italy.

"Roberto, is this wall surrounding the entire plant?"

"Yes, *Señor*," he said with a casual glance to Alicia's legs again, although these diversions were not as frequent giving consideration to the steep embankment to a creek which looked like something out of a Louisiana bayou. Also adding to the spectacle was Spanish moss and vines cascading from beefy branches protruding parallel to the water from massive trunks along the banks.

As they approached the front gate Sam took note of the large number of security personnel. "Roberto, is it like this everywhere?" Sam asked.

"*Sí, Señor*. They say if you want to do business in Guatemala, you'd better bring your own security, or you will end with the fishes." Sam was already stressed out from the ride and didn't need to hear anything about fish.

Roberto motioned to the guards to open the gate. Eight to ten of them were milling about on both sides of an imposing gate constructed of partitioned metal exposing rusting bolts and seams like the side of a cargo ship. At its top and the adjoining cinderblock walls was a double spiral band of concertina wire. Sam could not recall when that wire appeared along their journey and now wondered why it was necessary. *It's a distillery. Why all the security and protection?*

The guards were walking about dressed in cargo pants and tee-shirts of different varieties. Each carried varying pieces of armament: short-barrel shotguns, AR-15s or AK-47s. Sam never thought his interest in guns and shooting would have a business purpose but was pleased that interest was benefiting him now.

The air had a thick syrupy odor, leaving no doubt this was a distillery, but the wall, the gate, and the guards all resembled a military base rather than a production facility.

Roberto morphed into his tour guide role as he began to describe what they were passing. "We are headed for the main administrative building just ahead. It is two stories with the windows wrapping around the corner, do you see it?"

"I do, Roberto. Is that where *Señor* Mendoza's office is?"

"*Sí,* on the second floor," he said and then pointed out an attached building resembling a large airplane hangar with high walls cresting to a steep peak. Along the ridge was a long line of windows seen in images of WWII vintage manufacturing plants providing for light to enter the plant floor. Sam guessed the buildings were constructed during that time period. He thought about the letter when looking up at Mendoza's office.

As they parked and exited the car, everyone was staring at them. It was the first time Sam regarded the Guatemalan people up close. They seemed starkly different from those on the plane and in the hotel. They were darker with deep-set eyes and pursed lips set in wrinkled skin canvased on plump, round faces. Their hair was slicked back and greasy, many sporting a ponytail. One woman displayed the body frame and stature of an 80-year-old woman, but Sam somehow knew she was not that old. She was carrying a box and approached the door. Roberto said something to her in a harsh tone that caused her to halt, step aside, and look down as they passed. Sam glanced at Alicia, but she offered no reaction.

"Right this way, *Señor* Halloran," Roberto said as he held the door open, motioning them inside and toward a narrow stairway. Sam reached for the wood banister, smooth to the touch like it had guided many others navigating the stairs over the years. The walls were painted a lime green but were grimy just above the banister, cracked and chipping in places revealing white plaster walls. Even though the stairs were poured concrete, the many years of foot traffic had hollowed out an indentation on each stair tread. Ascending the stairs, Sam thought this was not the place one would want to visit after dark. Creepy.

A guard sat at the top of the stairs, a short-barreled 12-gauge, pump-action shotgun balanced across his thighs and shouldered a bandoleer filled with shotshells. Another guard sitting next to him was munching on some fruit, oozing juice cascading down his unshaven chin. He looked at Sam with piercing eyes and a vapid expression, pausing his chewing momentarily while they passed. When Sam made eye contact with him, he did not look away. He stopped eating, throwing what was left of his snack in the trash, and then he stood, hooking his thumb under the sling of his AK-47 rifle to reposition it over his shoulder. At all times, he kept his eyes focused directly on Sam. It was the first time someone regarding them did not immediately switch their gaze to Alicia. They were likely ex-military or law enforcement seeing Sam as the more probable threat.

The three of them walked into an open room with several people seated at a round table playing cards. They immediately noticed Alicia, paying no attention to Sam. They smiled, revealing the most grotesque sets of tobacco-stained teeth. Alicia was looking down. Sam could only imagine what was going through her mind.

Roberto led them into a large open room overlooking the entire yard and gate they had traveled through. In the room were four other guards, all dressed in the same cargo pants, shirts, and caps. No long guns. Side-arms. All were positioned somewhere along the windows taking up half the wall space, coming together at the corner of the room. Roberto made no comment as they walked past them, their gaze on Alicia.

Their procession abruptly stopped. A moment later, a huge, strapping, mustached man came out from a doorway to the left and greeted them. Roberto stepped aside dutifully. It was Javier Mendoza in the flesh. Massive, thick. No neck.

"At last, our guests have arrived," he boomed.

CHAPTER 13

JAVIER MENDOZA EXTENDED his hand and covered Sam's palm with his puffy, fat fingers and gave a slight twist causing Sam's hand to turn to the right, thereby ensuring Mendoza's hand was on top. This was his home turf nestled in a fortress-like compound. Sam had never felt so vulnerable at meeting a target in any previous investigation. Whatever Mendoza's intentions, he arranged this introduction to instill fear in Sam, and it was working. He quickly turned his attention toward Alicia. His handshake lingered as his other hand lightly touched her forearm, as if touching a delicate butterfly. She looked like a child standing next to him— Beauty and the Beast.

Mendoza continued gently shaking Alicia's hand and speaking in Spanish. Alicia handled it well, smiling graciously and almost curtsying, showing him deference in every way. He appeared to be undressing her in his mind. She had to feel uncomfortable. This whole show seemed staged for Mendoza's plan of intimidation for them.

Whatever his talents at running this plant and whatever games he had going on the side, he was certainly good at both. Javier Mendoza appeared to be a master manipulator.

Suddenly, it was show time and Mendoza turned on the charm.

"*Señor* Halloran, may I offer you something to drink or eat? Anything? Anything at all?"

"*Señor* Mendoza, possibly some black coffee for me and I can guess Alicia would love some green tea."

Alicia nervously responded, "Yes, green tea with a little *leche* and sugar would be lovely. Thank you."

"It is my pleasure," Mendoza said with a smile. "You are most welcomed in my plant, and I am hoping you have received only the best treatment thus far in your journey to us," he said glancing between Sam and Alicia. "Please come into my office and have a seat," Mendoza said, motioning for them to enter ahead of him through his outer office.

There, they were greeted by his secretary, who stood from behind her desk, extending her hand and announcing in surprisingly good English, "Welcome, I am Gabriela Castillo, *Señor* Mendoza's secretary. Please let me know if I can attend to you in any way."

Cutting her off, Javier said, "Yes, Gabriela will take good care of you." He then said something to her in Spanish and she hurried off.

With that brief introduction, Sam and Alicia were motioned into his office. Sam considered it austere and spartan for a plant manager by US standards. At the center of the room was a grey metal desk, 1950s motif. Behind it was a padded chair, some foam stuffing peeking out of the torn back.

As Mendoza poured his massive frame into his chair, it completely disappeared, creaking as he shifted his weight to get comfortable. He motioned for them to sit in straight-backed metal chairs in front of his desk, the back and seat covered in forest green cracked vinyl. Mendoza continued to stare at Alicia as Sam took the opportunity to take in the rest of his office.

Behind Mendoza's desk was a large window, no curtains, flanked on each wall with metal shelving sparsely filled with a few books, three-ring binders, and bottles of the company's distilled products. Sam got comfortable in his chair, now watching Gabriela enter the office with their beverages. He attempted to survey her for any noticeable tells, but she was forcing her gaze downward. Only once did she look into Sam's face and then immediately downward again, her face revealing nothing.

Most auditors and even some investigators tended to ignore the administrative staff. Not Sam. She appeared a sympathetic character. Sad. He made note of her name.

Mendoza had been virtually silent since they entered his office, almost as if he wanted to give Sam time to look around. His office was completely unimpressive, which did not follow the expected pattern of an overzealous manager enjoying his entitlement with lavish spending for his own purposes.

Alicia bent down to place her purse and briefcase on the floor next to her chair. Javier's silence and fixed gaze upon her informed Sam what likely was capturing his attention. *He is a pig.…*

In front of Sam, in the center of his desk, was a placard about a foot wide and six inches tall—a point-of-sale ad for Mossberg shotguns. It was no doubt a subliminal warning to those who found themselves in the presence of *Señor* Javier Mendoza, plant manager and local boss.

Gabriela had placed their beverages on a small table between Sam and Alicia. She offered to pour Alicia's tea all the while moving deliberately as if Mendoza had her on puppet strings.

"Gabriela, that will be all," Mendoza said gruffly. She offered a sideways glance toward her boss, dropping a spoon on the tray as if to honor his wishes immediately. Without a moment's hesitation, she was out of his office, closing the door behind her.

Sam was careful to allow Javier center stage and the feeling he was in command, which of course he was. All settled in, Javier started. "So, I am here at your disposal. How can I help you?"

Mendoza looked directly at Sam, in no apparent hurry to speak.

"*Señor* Mendoza—"

"Please, call me Javier."

"Thank you, and please call me Sam."

Javier deferentially nodded his head.

"Javier, before we begin, I must pass along what I believe is an exemplary compliment from your superiors at corporate. They told me, in no uncertain terms, you run the company's most profitable distillery plant. They further said I would be doing the company a great service if I could figure out what makes you so successful, bottle it, and bring it back so they might enlighten your peers into running such a profitable and successful plant."

"But, Sam, I am just a humble servant of the company and very pleased and happy I can be successful to help them reach their goals," Javier said beaming. "They are a good company, and I owe my success to their great leadership."

Sam smiled but said nothing in response, hoping Javier would continue to talk. His patience was rewarded.

"Sam, I must begin by telling you I was disheartened when I learned someone had made baseless charges against me in a letter sent to corporate. I would never do these things I am accused of doing. I hope you can understand my agitation hearing such accusations. I only want to help you in any way I can to bring your investigation to a quick end so I can get back to making money for this great company."

Sam looked at Javier appearing puzzled. "Javier, I am aware of the letter you speak of, but you may be giving this visit too much importance."

"But I was under the belief you are here to investigate me for these charges."

"We are here to perform some preliminary audit procedures ahead of the year-end audit, but I don't want you to get the impression you are being *investigated*. That would be a mischaracterization." Alicia crossed her legs and folded her arms across her chest, wearing a frown.

"But I am very confused. What will you be doing here?"

"I have a small team coming down next week to conduct some

data interrogation and interviews. All very routine audit procedures these days. It is certainly nothing to be concerned about."

"So, you are not investigating these charges?"

"We won't be bringing it up in our interviews."

"Then this is good news, no?" Javier said with a smile.

"Well, I'm not one to say that being on the receiving end of any audit procedures is desirable, but it sure beats an investigation," Sam said with a friendly chuckle. He could see a heavy burden lifted from Javier instantly—just the effect Sam wanted to deliver. He liked to sneak up on cockroaches.

"Then I have this worry for no reason."

"Javier, you are a savvy enough manager to know auditors don't find things of importance; they're more or less check-the-box, procedural financial types. Obviously, we will be doing what auditors do: getting in the way, but Hampton Enterprises is a public company with rules and regulations to follow. Of course, you know this." Sam could see all concern visibly disappear from Javier's face.

"Then I should take you both to lunch, and we should have a good time!"

Javier's phone rang. "Excuse me, this is my private line, and I must take this call." Sam nodded, and Javier began to speak into his phone. Sam was hoping Alicia was taking note of what Javier was saying, but after a few words he covered the mouthpiece and looked up at them. "I apologize but I must take this call in private. Would you both please wait for me in the hallway? After this call I take you both to my favorite restaurant. I think you will find it pleasing," he said with a smile that would tempt the devil to follow him.

Sam held up his hand, signifying he understood. They stood and walked through the outer office and into the hallway. Sam looked in both directions. The four guards were still seated and playing cards but down at the other end there was no one. Sam touched Alicia's elbow and nodded toward the far end of the hallway where they would be alone.

Alicia followed Sam, both stopping at a window. She leaned on the opposite side of the hall against the window frame, her arms folded across her chest, still frowning.

Before she could speak, Sam said, "Alicia, we can't discuss it now, but I think you have the wrong impression."

"But, Sam," she said in a whisper, "Why did you say those things? I thought we were here to investigate the letter. And can you not tell from meeting with him for this short time he is *¡Bestia animal serás fusilado como un perro!*"

One of the guards was peering at them from about sixty feet away. Sam gave him a casual wave. He nodded, maintained his position, and took a long drag on his cigarette.

Sam refocused on Alicia. He held up his finger and with a tilt of his head indicated to Alicia, *I know what I'm doing.* "Later. Not now. I get it." It seemed to placate her for now, but she was a completely unknown commodity. Soon, they would be at lunch, which had to be managed like a high-stakes poker game, and Alicia didn't know the rules. This could be a disaster.

CHAPTER 14

WITH PERFECT TIMING, Javier exited the outer office into the hallway. "Ah, there you two are. Many apologies for the interruption. It seems we have an engine problem with one of our trucks which will cause a change in our production schedule. It is nothing for you to be concerned with, but I wanted you to know what has taken me away from our scheduled time together."

Sam walked toward him. "Not a problem, Javier. I took that as another example of why you are so successful." Eating up Sam's compliments like a plate of sweet dates, Javier demurely smiled and motioned for them to follow him. "Come, let us enjoy a bite to eat, shall we?"

"Yes, indeed," Sam said as he turned toward Alicia. "Alicia, let's do it."

"Yes, we shall!" Alicia said and then smiled, signaling to Sam all was good. The stage was set.

Descending the narrow stairway on their way to exit the building, the guards moved in and out opening and closing doors like they had rehearsed this routine a thousand times. Javier continued to walk as others attended to his every need. He was also preoccupied walking alongside Alicia and talking to her in Spanish, doting over her like a school kid wanting to impress his teacher.

Twenty minutes later, they arrived at an uncommon one-story stucco structure with a garden courtyard entrance surrounded by a low wall covered with climbing vines. They walked past a line of patrons, some smoking, talking. All stopped talking, most stood straight and looked away in deference to Javier Mendoza, Sam presumed.

When they entered the restaurant, the *maître d'* snapped to attention as if a puppeteer pulled the right strings to place him into action, "*Señor* Mendoza, *¿Cómo está usted hoy? Su mesa esta lista.*" With a tilted nod of his head and pleasant smile, Javier responded, "*Hoy tengo invitados muy importantes para disfrutar de su cocina.*"

Alicia looked toward Sam, but as their eyes met she gave no indication of trouble, her demure smile indicating a comfort that Sam was close by. They followed the *maître d'* down a narrow hallway and away from the general seating area.

The small private room they were ferried into was dimly lit with three four-top tables covered in white linen with a single rose centered on each table, which seemed more fitting for an evening meal rather than a casual business lunch. When they arrived at their table, Sam held back so Javier could choose his seat, which he did without hesitation and then displayed brash confidence again, snapping a few orders to the *maître d'*. As Sam suspected, Javier chose the seat where he could enjoy a full view of the room, wall to his back. Very primal. Sam sat to Javier's right and Alicia sat to Sam's right. Sam gave Alicia a casual and approving nod. So far, so good.

They situated their napkins as the *maître d'* exited the room. A young boy dressed in white entered with a water carafe and an expression on his face appearing more fearful than inviting. Without comment, he poured the water for each of them as if he were handling nitro and any wrong move would blow them all to hell. Mendoza paid him no attention, still very occupied with the Latina beauty now sitting directly across from him. He and Alicia were exchanging comments in Spanish, which Sam gathered from Alicia's warm and friendly responses were not important.

A short, stocky man entered with menus in hand. More Spanish was exchanged by Mendoza to him, and again Alicia signaled all were routine pleasantries.

Javier told Sam of the trout, Javier's favorite meal, he exclaimed. He highly recommended it followed by a description as if he were a gourmet cook. Sam asked where it was listed on the menu, at which Javier laughed heartily. "The menu is for tourists. Whatever you would like, they will cook. If they don't have, the chef will go kill it and serve it to you," Javier said laughing. Sam only half-believed him but then who knew? Sam ordered the trout. Javier did as well. Alicia ordered a salad.

Sam spoke to break Javier's leering at Alicia. "Javier, it looks like you are a frequent guest of this place."

"Yes, I do come here occasionally when accompanied by important guests and I have the time, but usually my day is filled with work. Rarely do I take time to leave the plant for lunch."

With their orders placed, the waiter collected the menus and swiftly left the room. They were alone.

"Javier, before your call you were discussing some of the reasons for your success, and I'd like to continue along those lines."

"Well, I am not sure where to begin."

Sam hoped he wouldn't start with grade school and then offered him direction. "Tell me a little about your management philosophy."

"Yes, Sam, I suppose that is a good place to begin because I truly believe the manner in which I manage my people is at the core of my success."

And there it began. Through lunch, dessert, and coffee, he labored on and on and on. Sam thought it worse than an Italian opera. Of course, it was all bullshit, but Sam had to humor him and play this game, which required interjecting compliments and an innocent question here and there. At least it kept him awake. Two hours passed.

Throughout his droning on, Sam and Alicia exchanged glances

and head nods feigning interest. Sam felt confident Javier was totally convinced they were his pawns. At least he appeared completely comfortable in their company. Sam was looking for the right time to test him using the CRI information gleaned from their report, but he was cautious and patient, knowing that the critical time was approaching. Patience was not one of Sam's strong points but too soon or too awkward and the whole cover could be blown. He had only one chance, and if he forced it, the entire trip would be a waste of time.

"Sam, would you enjoy a little Grappa?"

"An excellent idea, Javier, let's all have some." *Finally,* he thought, *we are close.*

Mendoza shouted to their server who was dutifully standing near the door but very attentive to them.

"Waiter, a bottle of your finest Grappa for me and my friends!" shouted Javier with an enthusiasm Sam would expect at a sporting event.

"Javier, you are the perfect host!"

"Indeed, I am, Sam!" he said laughing as he grabbed the bottle from the waiter and unabashedly poured the moonshine-like liquor sloppily into three glasses. His excitement climaxed with a toast. "To our new friendship and exciting times ahead!" He chugged down his drink and looked directly at Sam, expecting him to do the same, which Sam did, though taking a bit longer to avoid choking it back up. Sam thought it tasted like molasses mixed with diesel fuel.

Sam finished and noticed Javier pouring another round. Before he could object, Javier tossed it back, consuming all its contents. Sam reluctantly did the same.

"I love Grappa. You too, Sam?"

"Yes, Javier. A big *yes* for my new friend!" Sam yelled slamming the shot glass on the table. He glanced at Alicia, who appeared to be struggling with that second shot.

Javier appeared jovial, relaxed, and completely removed from any thought of conducting himself in a guarded, business-like decorum. At their table and in that moment, they were three friends enjoying each other's company and completely at ease. At last, the time was right.

"So, Javier, tell us, what you do when you're not working so hard? What are you passionate about?"

With what seemed like total careless abandon, Javier responded, "Oh, Sam, I wish I could muse on about some outside interests I have, but I must honestly tell you my job as plant general manager *is* my life. I sadly have no outside interests. I know that makes me look like a boring person. Yes, it is sad but true," Javier said with a booming "HA!"

By that response alone, Javier made it all the way along the guilt scale right into the bucket labeled *Thief, Crook, Scumbag.* Sam thought it would take more time to *prove* he was a bad actor, but his response did him no favors and moved Sam closer along the path to obtaining the evidence expected to surface in a full-scale investigation.

Javier mentioned nothing about his collection of twenty-one Harley-Davidson motorcycles, nothing about his motorcycle club and the palatial surroundings where he and his foreman, supervisors, and managers met regularly, a building Sam felt certain was entirely and unknowingly funded by Hampton Enterprises. *Bless CRI,* he thought. *They are good.*

Such expenditures confirmed beyond any reasonable doubt Javier's passion for motorcycles reached the highest levels one could imagine. Why he would not talk about such a passion, especially considering he was so relaxed and comfortable with them, was compellingly instructive. Passions are to be expressed. If we are not enjoying them, we are talking about them. It had always proved true, and Sam felt certain Javier had made a huge mistake.

Sam looked at Alicia. "See, I told you this man was the real deal." She nodded in agreement. "The company is incredibly lucky to have you, Javier. The man has passion only for his work and ser-vice to this great company," Sam said as he lifted his glass to Javier. Alicia followed. What Javier didn't notice was Sam taking a mouth-ful of Grappa and depositing it into the half-empty glass of water he feigned as a chaser. He looked toward Alicia noticing her shot glass was now empty. It was her third, and she wasn't looking so good. He needed to bring this party to a quick close before she passed out or worse: let something slip. Fortunately, Javier was cooperating famously, and the interview would shortly be over. Sam had one more important fact from the CRI report to test.

"Javier, tell me about your wife. You said earlier you met her in the States, I think you said New York City, while you were both studying there." His glassy look toward Sam informed him the Grappa had won over him.

"Sam, I didn't do a whole lot of studying as my lovely Sabina would attest to if she were here." Javier let off another bellicose laugh, totally drunk.

At first, Javier seemed to ignore Sam's question. That might be cause for concern to someone with less experience than Sam, not investigative experience but rather the experience gained growing up with an alcoholic father. That experience was coming in handy now. Javier had that same look. It was not the look of deception or withholding information. It was the same look Sam's dad had after drinking too much and momentarily forgetting where he was and what he was going to say. That blank, vapid look when you were trying to reconcile your senses to the reality of being totally and completely smashed. Sam knew exactly what to do.

Repeat the question knowing he'd already forgotten it. But before he could, Alicia chimed in.

"Is she pretty?" Alicia asked, which was like hitting Javier with electronic shock panels to the chest. Her timing was perfect, and Sam was certain she had no idea what she was doing. No strategy. Simply conversation between two drunks.

"Huh?" Javier said, seeming initially startled by the question. "Did you ask me if my wife is pretty?" he slurred out. From the glow on his face it was the perfect segue for Javier to launch into more bluster.

"Sabina is the most beautiful woman in all of Guatemala. I am so lucky to have her by my side," Javier said through a couple of burps, pauses, and lots of slurred speech. He didn't seem to care how he sounded.

"Sabina is not only beautiful, but she is a very, very smart person, at least for a woman."

Sam felt it was time to take the reins. "So, Javier, what does Sabina do all day while you are slaving away at the distillery?"

Taking another gulp of the Grappa, eyes darting between Alicia and Sam, Javier said, "Sabina is such a dedicated wife taking care to assist me in my work. This is what she most wants to do. I am so fortunate."

Thanks to the CRI report, Sam knew differently. Javier was lying again. "Helps you with your work? I didn't know she was an employee of Abello."

"No, she does not do so for pay. She voluntarily helps me, mostly with personnel issues where her insight is invaluable. You may have noticed, Sam, there are quite a few women at the plant."

Sam said nothing. He didn't want to get in the way of Javier self-immolating. But then Mendoza began drifting off again.

"So, she voluntarily helps you with personnel issues? She sounds like such a dedicated wife. But what else does she do when not assisting you?"

"I'm telling you, Sam; she only helps *me*. Oh, maybe her real passion is reading. She likes to read a lot. She is a caring person. Not the hard-driven businessman I am. She is an excellent complement to me, and I am lucky to have her by my side."

"You are truly a lucky man in so many ways, Javier. A stable and successful career as a plant manager admired by the company you work for and all the while having a beautiful and dutiful wife by your side. I envy you." In a ridiculous sort of way, Sam did, at least some aspects of Javier's life. The part about having a beautiful and loyal wife by his side. He wasn't so much admiring Javier as he was lamenting his own bad decision-making many years ago. When he was young, immature, naïve, and stupid. But he couldn't get bogged down in that thought process now. He had an interview to wrap-up and possibly a colleague who might need medical attention. He began to worry about getting Alicia into the car and back to the hotel.

Mission accomplished. Time to go.

Sam stood from the table and helped Alicia up from her seat. Her condition was obvious to Javier. "It seems the little lady can't hold her liquor," he said inches from Sam's ear. "Maybe you are lucky very soon, eh?" he said while smiling at Sam.

"Javier, you are indeed perceptive, and I'm thinking this gal's day is through, and maybe mine is as well."

"Yes, I would imagine you will soon be enjoying each other in ways that make me jealous."

"Oh, Javier, if only I worked for you in this wonderful land you enjoy, but I must remember where I work and what perils could befall one who takes such advantages."

Javier patted Sam on his back. "I understand my friend, but at least you can still enjoy the privacy of your fantasies."

CHAPTER 15

JAVIER SAID HIS goodbyes. It took both Sam and Roberto to pour Alicia into the back seat. She was still conscious, but the Grappa had sent her to a different place. Sam sat in the front seat and buckled his seatbelt and silently hoped Alicia would fall asleep on the journey home. Fifteen minutes into the trip she was snoring. Sam looked back to check on her and smiled to himself.

Pulling up to the front of the hotel lobby's doors, Roberto hopped out and opened Alicia's door first. Sam slammed his door, awakening Alicia as he stepped down from the Jeep. Roberto reached in to grab Alicia's hand, careful to steady her descent. He quickly handed her off to Sam who clumsily placed her arm over his shoulder to steady her in what he felt would be an appropriate manner. He thanked Roberto and bid him a good rest of the day.

Walking through the lobby and past the registration desk on their way to the elevators, Alicia slurred, "Have I made a fool of myself?"

Sam pushed the elevator call button. "Alicia, you did great. I'm proud of you. You are a woman inexperienced in knowing what Grappa could do to you. That's not such a bad thing. You have nothing to feel guilty about." The ping of the elevator interrupted his thoughts.

"So, you think I am a woman, Sam."

She was leaning on him. Sam looked into her face, inches away. He felt her silky curls against his face. Combined with her scent and his own slight buzz it was all working like a powerful aphrodisiac on his hormones. He refused to break his stare. Their rooms were across the hall from each other.

Alicia's eyes informed Sam she would welcome his lips onto hers. Her every action indicated she wanted Sam in other ways as well. This was how the game was played in her country... and she was good at this game. Sam was bad at this game.

Another guest entered the elevator giving a judgmental stare at the two of them. Sam loosened his grip on Alicia, but she tightened her grip on his shoulder. She wasn't going anywhere and continued staring into his face.

As the elevator continued its rise, the other guest didn't say a word, but the casual glances back to them signaled disapproval.

It felt like the longest elevator ascent of his life, but they finally reached the guest's floor. As the doors opened the man took a final glance leaving with a parting comment, *"¡Disfruta de nuestras prostitutas!"* Alicia's reaction was immediate pulling away from Sam and leaning on the elevator wall. Sam didn't need any translation. The doors closed.

When they reached their floor, she walked out first. Her gait was slow, wavy, and uneven. Sam hung back several feet. Upon reaching her room, Sam noticed her fumbling with her room key. He wasn't about to go near her and hung back until she finally succeeded in opening her door. He wasted no time and promptly entered his room.

Alone, Sam breathed a sigh of relief. After setting his room key on the table he moved quickly to close the drapes blocking out the bright sunlight. Loosening his tie, he began reflecting on the day's events.

He brushed aside thoughts about Alicia's issues, concluding the meeting with Mendoza went well, and Alicia was a big part of that success. She had done well. He saw potential in her and wished he'd have an opportunity to work with her more. She'd be a huge plus to their Latin American investigations. But then, reality hit him: *she's an HR nightmare.* If Hampton's management committee would approve an investigation going forward, he would not be requesting Alicia to return. That wasn't fair, but life wasn't fair, and he had to consider the risk.

Sam opened the minibar and selected a seltzer and then settled comfortably in a soft side chair. *Lunch was truly a home run!* he thought before he dozed off.

Four hours passed. The knock at the door was slight and hesitant. Sam awoke but ignored it, not because he always ignored knocks but rather because he had work to do to prepare for his meeting with the Hampton management committee. He slid in front of his laptop and turned it on.

The knocking continued. Ignoring it didn't seem to be working. This time it was a louder, *knock, knock, knock, knock* followed with "Sam, we have to talk. Please let open the door, so we may talk."

"That's not a good idea right now," Sam yelled at her through the door as he began typing away on his laptop.

"But, Sam, I have already napped, and my headache is almost gone, and I want very much to talk with you about my conduct today."

Sam ignored her. *She'll go away soon.*

"Sam, I know why you are upset with me, and I want to explain to you."

Still she persisted, "If you are not going to open the door, I will make my explanations right here in the hallway, and I don't care who hears me. So, please open your door."

The phone rang. The red light was flashing. *What the hell is that about?* He wondered. *Answer the door? Answer the phone?*

The phone won. "Hello," Sam said abruptly.

"*Señor* Halloran, I am deeply sorry to disturb you, but the person knocking at your door I am now understanding from other guests has been doing so for some time. She is disrupting and I will have to send security to remove her unless you tell me you can bring this to a happy conclusion."

Sam told the caller what he wanted to hear, walked to his door, flung it open, and walked back to his chair to continue his typing. He didn't even glance at Alicia, who was now sitting on his couch. She sat with her elbows on her thighs, fiddling with a tissue in her hands.

"Sam, I know right now you do not want to be here with me. You do not see me as the professional I want you to see me as. Even if you felt I could make contributions to the solutions you are seeking you are afraid of where having any relationship with me might lead. You're thinking as soon as you get out of this country you will never, ever call me again, much less have me work on what I feel will be a most excellent investigation."

Sam stopped typing and looked over at her. She was rigid and stoic. "This is all true, is it not? Have I left anything out?"

"Alicia, that is not true, and I feel you have been a great help and hope you will help in the future if Hampton decides to move forward in this—"

"Stop with the bull… shit. Please, stop," Alicia shouted and abruptly stood, facing Sam with fists clinched.

Sam could see in her eyes she had no empathy for his circumstances.

She resumed in a calmer manner and moved closer to Sam. "Look, Sam, I'd like to make a bargain with you. Let's go to dinner now, and in the next, say, two hours, if I cannot convince you I will be immensely critical to the success of this investigation, then I will get on a plane, return to my home, and you will never hear from me again. I will also promise you will not experience the fear of HR I see written all over your face. Please give me a little time to convince you. Dinner…. That's all. It will be your decision, and

I will honor it no matter what." About thirty seconds passed with neither of them saying a word.

Sam stood with no idea where this was going. While she posed a fair suggestion, Sam was still prepared to part ways with her. A bit of empathy was leaking into his tired and weathered thought process, however. He still was fearful of what he didn't know. Alicia broke the silence. "Will you strike this bargain with me, Sam?"

He was impressed. It was like she was reading his mind. "I think that's fair. And after the day we both had I am famished, and I know you must be, too."

"May I take a few moments to freshen up?"

"Certainly. Not a problem. Take all the time you need. I'll meet you at the lobby bar."

"Good. I shall meet you in the lobby bar in a little while."

Opening the door to leave, she turned to look at Sam, pausing momentarily, and with a solemn and downward glance ending with direct eye contact, she said sincerely, "Thank you, Sam."

At the lobby bar, Sam kept a watchful eye on the entrance. He set his eyes upon a tall, attractive, and professionally dressed young woman standing at the entrance, hesitant, obviously looking for someone. Their eyes met and she advanced toward him. This was not the Alicia he had expected to show up.

He moved toward her and greeted her by taking her elbow and escorting her to the bar before guiding her up onto the bar stool. He signaled the bartender, who ran to them like a puppy eager to hear his next command. Sam looked toward her. "Alicia, what will it be?"

"Just a seltzer, thank you." The bartender looked at Sam. "No thanks. I'm good right now."

Alicia wasted no time getting to the point. "Thank you, again, Sam, for this meeting." Sam nodded his head. This was her show, and he deferred in saying anything. He'd follow her lead.

Sam signaled the *maître d'* for their table. They sat across from each other.

Alicia was struggling with her thoughts. She knew what *she* wanted but she'd have to think in his terms—to recognize his concerns. After a minute of silence, Alicia began. "I know how you must feel about me. How you view me. I do not blame you. I know I've been carrying on like some cheap hooker. I know this because that is how I am. This is how I have achieved what little success to my position as a manager. This is how most women make it in my country, especially the pretty ones. It is the burden we carry, and I am sick of it and want to change."

Sam said nothing, but he was listening.

"It is a curse for a businesswoman to have beauty in my country. Men run everything. They run the government, they run every business, and the only way a woman makes it to success is to either marry one of them or be mistress to one of them. I chose the latter. Yes, you could say I've slept my way to the top, but then I am not at the top yet.

"There are yet many beds I must do before I am to be a success. It is disgusting, and I do not know any woman in my country who does not feel as I do, but we are all feeling trapped by this system. It is so unfair. We are smart, capable, and want opportunities, but they escape us. We sleep with them, and they throw us bones. This is why I am… this is why you have seen me the way you have. Without thinking when I met you in Miami, I fell into that role. I see you and know you are a partner. A successful US partner and all I see is how I can get into your bed so I would pleasure you into helping me continue to advance. That is why I have been with you the way I have. This is how I have been, and I am so ashamed." She lowered her head.

Sam wanted to think differently of Alicia. He felt sorry for her circumstances, but he quickly realized he was not in Chicago, and Alicia was not on his staff. Sam was a caring person but practical as well. That sad tale of woe she shared with him may all be true, but he didn't feel it was his problem.

"Please, Sam, say something. I am hanging out here on a tree."

Sam chuckled to himself. He was softening... slowly but still conflicted by memories. There were too many scars in Sam's past from trusting the wrong person.

The waiter showed up and gave them both a moment to take a breath. He handed them menus to peruse. Moments later he returned, and they ordered.

Sam looked at Alicia sitting across from him. "After watching you over these past two days and listening to you this evening, I'd like to ask you something I hope is not too personal."

"But of course. Ask me anything."

"What would make you feel satisfied? Is that even possible in your current position?"

No response. She stared blankly into the candle in front of them.

Then a tear appeared out of her left eye, so subtle, so slight as to almost pass unnoticed, but then it was nudged along by several others, and soon Alicia wiped them away with her napkin. Sam decided to take a break as all the emotion she obviously felt now had hijacked the moment. Alicia's tears were flowing. Sam handed her his handkerchief.

"I'm sorry, Alicia."

"No, you did nothing wrong except hit a very exposed nerve. Please... a moment longer."

While she never answered Sam's question, all was revealed in her reaction. It was time to change the mood.

The rest of the evening was pleasant. They told stories of their childhood, friendships, schools, and careers until nearly three a.m., and it ended on a positive note. Sam was surprised the restaurant didn't throw them out. If this were Chicago, they most certainly would have been asked to leave hours ago.

Sam left a hefty tip for their waiter and gave him a nod in appreciation as they exited the restaurant.

In the elevator, both were silent as it ascended to their floor. Sam was conflicted. Still, he had to make a decision knowing they would meet only one more time for breakfast before they flew back to their respective offices.

The elevator doors opened. Alicia stepped ahead of Sam, and he followed her down the hall toward their rooms. Having reached their destination, Alicia was facing her door and Sam watched her. She turned to face him, and with an innocent smile and a confident and warm countenance, she extended her hand and took Sam's. "Sam, I cannot begin to thank you for all you did for me today and especially for the caring time you spent with me this evening. I believe you are changing my life and all for the better. I very much want to continue working with you, not just because I know I will learn how to investigate financial crimes. I believe working with you I am certain to become a stronger business leader and, most importantly, a better person."

Sam paused for a moment to consider her comment. "Alicia, I'm glad we talked, and I appreciate your honesty. Get a good night's sleep, and I'll see you at breakfast tomorrow."

"You mean in a few hours," Alicia said, yawning. They both chuckled.

CHAPTER 16

SHORTLY AFTER SAM and Alicia had left him at the restaurant, Javier sat by himself in the courtyard drinking Black Label scotch and smoking a Cuban cigar. He was recounting the last several hours, trying to determine how he had performed for his corporate guests. While he felt he had been the perfect host, he thought he could have done better, but then, he usually did feel that way. He credited his mother's persistent nagging on him while growing up. She made him the perfectionist he prided himself to be. "You can always do better," she would say to him.

He knew they would return. While the *auditor*, as he began to refer to Sam, would return, Javier had already formulated a plan that would stymie them. Something they would not expect. They would never see it coming.

One thing was for sure: he would determine how to separate Alicia from the protection of Sam Halloran and show her how a real Latino would bed her. He'd have to be gentle since she was from a respectable firm and might take wrong impressions back with her. He'd leave no marks. Still, he would enjoy her and she him.

"*Jefe*, can I have a word?" asked his foreman, Juan Romero, who came to stand next to his boss, albeit not too close.

Javier gave him a sideways glance, hardly noticing him. Like a trained dog, he would patiently wait until Javier decided to give him his attention. Javier sipped his scotch and then took a long draw on his cigar, slowly exhaling a stream of smoke. Only then did he notice his foreman. "What is it?" he said gruffly.

"I have the background check on *Señor* Halloran you ordered."

"Read it to me."

"It is quite long so I have highlighted some parts you might have a close interest in reading when you have a moment."

"Set it over there," he said with a tone causing Juan to take a step away, wishing he had simply given the report to his secretary. Still, he felt the need to alert his *Jefe* and reap some benefit for his diligence.

"*Jefe*, there are things in this report I should like you to pay close attention to. This *Señor* Halloran may be different than others you have encountered from the States."

"He's a fucking auditor, you babosa. The day will never come when I fear an auditor. Now lay the goddamn report down like I told you and be gone."

Juan moved quickly to honor *El Jefe*'s wishes.

Mendoza looked over his shoulder and saw no sign of him, thereby questioning his own sanity and then blamed it on the touch of the *nieve* he had sampled shortly before lighting up. A little taste test of the latest cocaine shipment.

Mendoza returned to the plant after their lunch. He was drunk and high, a bad combination for any man but it was explosive for Javier Mendoza.

There were those extremely rare times when Javier failed to manipulate his surroundings. Then there were even rarer times when someone under his direct control would dishonor him. So rare that Javier struggled to recall the last time it had happened.

Castro had not been in Mendoza's employ for long. A year or so. Javier didn't know his full name. Just went by Castro. He had taken a delivery to a customer in Guatemala City last week, and not of the rum variety… their off-books product line.

Castro did not return when expected. That's what the caller said earlier in the day, interrupting Mendoza's meeting with Sam and Alicia.

After making his delivery Castro noticed a church while sitting at a red light. The same one he attended with his family. He didn't think he was doing anything wrong when he stopped to give his confession to the priest. It had been a long time. The last time he did, he had a different name, the one he now gave to the priest, who knew him and was glad to see him again.

Some years ago, Castro left his home in Guatemala City after an argument with someone he now desired to see again, to reconcile with. He didn't go far… just to the Pacific Coast. His three years there gave him time to think. He realized it wasn't right to blame this person for what happened. It's just that when tragedy occurs, someone is to blame.

The priest was helpful and gave him no penance, only to seek reconciliation. God had already forgiven him for breaking one of His Ten Commandments, the priest told him.

Ninety minutes later, Castro was on the road again headed back to the plant. He'd have to think about the timing, but he would honor his promise to the priest and to God. It was time, and God's forgiveness had given him hope for the future.

But Castro was never able to honor that commitment. That reconciliation would need to wait for some other day… in heaven. Javier's men had determined who the snitch was. Javier would deal with him later in the day. He ordered his men to prepare.

Last Friday morning, before the first shift had started, DEA agents made a surprise raid on the Abello plant. They were accompanied by PNC, Guatemala's national police force. Men on Javier's payroll. But he understood they had to put on a good show. After all, while

Javier paid well, US aid paid better. Best to make it look like the American War on Drugs effort was top of mind with the Guatemalan government. Still, this was no problem.

Javier acted surprised when DEA showed up. They demanded he pull back his security to allow them to search within the walls of his plant. If that wasn't inconvenient enough, they took bolt cutters to the padlocks on the storage room doors even though Javier told them he had the keys and was happy to open them. The agents entered and tore through several buildings, searching for what, only Javier knew thanks to a tip from the PNC. He made sure the DEA would not find what they were looking for.

After they had searched several buildings and gathered to leave, their leader glanced at Javier long enough to catch his wide Cheshire grin, but Javier would not be grinning when he dealt with the informant.

Javier regretted the fate that awaited Castro because he, too, was a great admirer of Fidel Castro and hated to bring such pain to one bearing his name. Not that he would want to live under Fidel Castro's rule. He only wished he could live *like* him. Maybe someday.

Juan brought Castro to him. He had no real proof that Castro had ratted to the DEA. Only that he was late returning from that delivery to Guatemala City last week. It had to be him… maybe, but Juan knew what his *Jefe* expected, and he would deliver according to those expectations… or he might end up suffering what Castro was about to suffer.

The smoke indicated his men had fired up the furnace, just the way Javier had ordered them to do. When he arrived, Castro had been gagged and lashed to a flat board.

Javier approached Castro on the ground, writhing and attempting to speak. He had pissed his pants. His eyes were wide open.

Javier ordered a few of the plant workers to witness what happened to workers who did not respect him. Only a few would be

112

all that was necessary to spread the word about what they had seen that day.

Trying without success to break free of the cutting hemp, Castro's wrists and ankles were bloodied from his rapid movements. When Javier stood directly over him, he smiled. "Castro, we are honoring you today as a great teacher. The one who will teach others it is a terrible mistake to talk about what goes on at my plant."

Castro tried in vain to scream through his gag. He pulled on the ropes, his body almost convulsing.

"It seems you have some last words to share with us," he said, motioning to one of his men to remove the gag.

"I beg you, *Señor Jefe*. I do not know why you are doing this to me for I have done nothing to dishonor you." Castro sounded honest, probably because he was speaking honestly. He really hadn't ratted out his *Jefe*. It was just an unfortunate coincidence his delivery to Guatemala City was just a block from the US Consulate where DEA had an office. If only he hadn't returned so late. Of course, he was the one… or so it seemed.

No, what was about to play out for Castro was unfortunate and the product of Javier Mendoza's terror campaign to treat his workers less favorably than he would the chickens that would supply his morning breakfast and evening meal. It mattered not that Castro was innocent. Javier had to punish someone and do so quickly. Castro was as good as anyone. A big plus was Castro had no family that could be determined, so no others needed to be silenced. No loose ends. Swift and hedonistic justice.

Hilmer, another of Javier's supervisors, signaled all was ready.

Javier made the sign of the cross with his hands. "*In nomine patris et filii et spiritus sancti, Amen.*" Everyone about to die deserved a proper Christian blessing, even those who couldn't hold their tongue. He couldn't rely on God to punish Castro for his mistake—his sin.

Javier took a step back and nodded to his chief metal worker, who was now holding a red-hot ladle at the end of a six-foot long iron rod. The worker moved forward, positioning the ladle directly above Castro's open and screaming mouth.

Some of the workers—witnesses—looked away.

"Enough of this. Do it!" Mendoza ordered. A worker looped a metal hook over Castro's lower jaw and then pulled, stretching open his mouth. That silenced him. Castro closed his eyes as if that could stop the fate awaiting him. The red-hot ladle was tipped slowly, allowing the molten lead to pour like firewater into Castro's mouth. His flesh evaporated like water poured on a hot grill.

Even though Castro's eyes were still open, he had mercifully passed.

Through it all, Mendoza smiled until there were no more sounds emanating from his latest victim. Not his gurgling. Not the sizzling sounds of his burning flesh. It was done. What remained was something unrecognizable. Javier thought of the unconscionable pain that young man must have experienced. It pleased him.

Javier sighed as if his fun was over for the day. He pulled a handkerchief from his back pocket to wipe his forehead and then looked at his watch. "Juan, tell Roberto to bring the car… then clean this up. Dinner awaits. I mustn't keep them waiting.

"Right away, *Jefe*."

That morning, about an hour before meeting with Sam and Alicia, Javier learned that his mother had passed. He called his sister to gather the family. He'd make dinner arrangements at his favorite steakhouse, Del Griego in Guatemala City. He would also invite his lieutenants and political friends. Surely they would want to be with him as he grieved for his sainted mother.

As they all gathered at the restaurant, Javier said solemn words to honor his mother. She deserved that even though he felt little emotion with her passing. It's not that he didn't appreciate her; he even loved her. It's just that Javier never liked to get too close to someone.

He hated to be disappointed, and in his world, anyone—his men, even his family—could disappoint him, and he would be required to send another message.

When he finished his eulogy, his attitude changed in an instant. Soon, the banquet room he had arranged turned into a party atmosphere complete with a calypso band. His sister looked at her brother in disgust, but she knew she had no sway over him. She and her husband were the first to leave, followed immediately by the rest of the family. Javier made no notice of them filing out. He was too busy flirting with the singer about to perform for him and his men. It was party time.

Soon the band was in full swing like they were playing for a wedding celebration on a Caribbean beach. Lambchops were his choice for the evening. As Javier ate and drank, he laughed unabashedly at his own jokes. Others did too, of course. They would be foolish not to.

Javier looked at everyone at his table. Times like these he was happy to eat and drink with them almost like they were his equals. Almost. He was aware he must keep one step ahead of them, all of them, all those who worked for him: the police, judges, politicians, plant workers, even those closest to him, even his security team now surrounding him. All of them kept a close eye on their *Jefe*, their benefactor. They were his loyal and humble servants… maybe.

There was always the possibility that one would be waiting for Javier to relax his guard. All for an opportunity to have a go at him. Even though Javier believed that impossible, he sometimes wished it might be true. It would give him another opportunity to revel in another's pain. Javier believed there was at least one such person out there, one who would be bold enough to accept such a challenge. After all, if he would ever work for such a man as he, he would take that chance. Surely others might think that way. Some might try to challenge him. He would find them, and in the process of searching for him, he would do what he was so good at: enjoying life.

CHAPTER 17

SAM AWOKE AROUND 9:30 a.m. and was functioning on about five hours of sleep. He'd nap on the plane back to Chicago.

His meeting with the Hampton management committee was scheduled for three o'clock tomorrow. They likely were anxious to hear Sam's thoughts on how Guatemala might impact their bottom line. In Sam's mind, he'd already taken it to the next level, beyond financial. He couldn't quite pin it down, but his instincts were in hair-trigger mode.

As he left his room, it pleased him to see a *USA Today* newspaper at the foot of his door. He couldn't wait to get back to the States.

Sam's BlackBerry vibrated.

"Steve, hey. Good to hear your voice."

"What's your status?" Steve Lemly asked, his voice cracking once. Sam ignored it.

"Alicia and I are getting ready to meet our ride to the airport. Are you calling to confirm our meeting for tomorrow afternoon?"

"I am, but I also wanted to tell you to be prepared for a number of executives at the meeting. I'm not sure who all will be there, but I was told the site was switched from my division's conference meeting room to the board room, which can only mean the big guys are planning on hearing your presentation. Probably our CFO Garrett Barclay, for sure. So, I wanted to prepare you."

"I appreciate the warning, Steve, but it really doesn't matter to me who is in attendance. It won't change what I intend to present."

"I have no doubt you will be prepared. Can you give me a preview of tomorrow?"

"I'll be recommending an investigation. Beyond that, I can't say what it might look like. Right now, there are a lot of thoughts spinning around in my head. Tomorrow I plan to disclose the basis for my recommendation. Details to be worked out later."

"So, you think this guy has done the things suggested in the letter?"

"Well, yes, that and more. Much more. You will know everything I know tomorrow, and you can make up your own minds as to what to do."

"I hear you. Well, I know you have a flight to catch, so I will let you go and see you tomorrow afternoon. Safe travels."

"Sounds good, Steve, and thanks."

As usual, Sam was running late. He didn't take time to pass through his room ensuring he had everything. Whatever he may have left behind was a trifle issue compared to what awaited him in the lobby.

Exiting the elevators and passing the front desk, he saw Alicia talking to two men dressed in the familiar uniforms he had seen yesterday. The conversation they were engaged in seemed somewhat terse.

"Can I help you gentlemen?" Sam asked, now standing next to Alicia.

"These men work for *Señor* Mendoza and are instructing us we are not to leave yet," Alicia told Sam. "It seems *Señor* Mendoza needs a meeting with us immediately."

"I'm sorry, gentlemen, but we have a flight to catch, and I was not aware of any scheduled meeting with *Señor* Mendoza. You will have to relay our regrets to him. He is free to call me later today." As Sam tried to walk past them, the bigger of the two stepped in front without saying a word. Alicia was upset and broke away.

"*Señor* Mendoza will be disappointed with such news, and we are not in the habit of disappointing *El Jefe*, so you will please come with us."

Without responding, Sam moved to step around him when the other guy grabbed his bag.

"Get your hands off of my bag!" Sam shouted with the expectation of drawing attention.

Fortunately, a couple of hotel security guards stepped up with one of them saying something to the guy now holding Sam's bag. Still, Sam was blocked. Alicia was leading several more hotel security guards over to Sam. They separated the two Mendoza security men from restraining Sam. He and Alicia now headed for the front doors. Behind him Sam could hear heated conversation. He did not wait to see where the discussion was headed and exited the hotel.

"Sam, I think that's our driver over there waving his arm." Alicia pointed.

A couple of hotel security guards caught up to Sam and one held open the door to their awaiting limo. Sam asked the guards to follow them to the airport.

He and Alicia hopped in the back seat, and the security guards jumped into a car just behind them. Sam smiled to himself upon their escape and then realized it was all a harbinger of trouble to come. Mendoza didn't seem the type of man to take rejection well, and Sam would be returning… he hoped.

They merged onto the highway as Sam watched their hotel fade into the distance.

"Sam, I am thinking Mendoza may have figured out your stated purpose is not the true reason for our visit."

Sam was still trying to take it all in. He held up the back of his hand to Alicia. "Alicia, please give me a minute. Driver, keep that hotel car in your rearview. They will be following us to the airport. Don't lose them." Alicia translated.

Thoughts about what had just transpired were racing through Sam's head. Alicia was keeping a watchful eye on the hotel car hanging on their bumper.

There was an obvious tension in the air their driver seemed curiously unaffected by. He appeared as calm as one could be. "There is no need for translation. I speak English," he said to Alicia through the mirror.

"Can you tell me what you witnessed back there at the hotel?" Sam asked him.

"It seems you have made an enemy of a powerful man. A man you should want to avoid."

"You know of this man, Javier Mendoza?"

"Mendoza is the most powerful man in this city and maybe even all of Guatemala. He has his hands in all things illegal: women trafficking, booze, drugs."

Hearing the magic word, Sam stopped him, "Did you say drugs?"

"Yes, mostly cocaine. His cousin is *El Gordo*."

"*El Gordo*? The Columbian drug lord?"

"The same," the driver said casually.

Sam stared ahead, blankly. It was all confirming what Derek Dorn had told him.

Now taking the exit following the Departures sign, their driver appeared as relaxed as one would be drinking a beer on his back patio. He continued talking about Mendoza, seeming quite knowledgeable. Sam was further impressed by his willingness to disclose it all to them. He suddenly became as interested in him as the information he was giving them.

"Driver, can I ask your name?"

They had arrived at the airport. The driver pulled the car alongside the curb directly in front of the Departures Terminal, reached into his breast pocket, and handed his business card to Sam. "Here is my information. I am happy to drive for you if you decide to return to Guatemala City. Maybe I can also help you in other ways."

Sam looked at the card. "What other ways, *Señor* Escapa?"

"Pablo. I have specific military training. If you are dealing with the likes of *Señor* Mendoza, my services and knowledge of this country and its people could assist in whatever you are doing. You have my card. You should keep me in your mind."

Pablo hopped out of the car and opened Alicia's door behind his. He took her hand to steady her exit. Sam exited on his side and watched him. Pablo was the only man on this entire trip who treated her respectfully. Everything he did impressed Sam.

"Pablo, thank you very much for your help. If we decide to return to your city, I will give you a call. It sounds like you would be good with that?"

"This would be good. You will be safe in my care."

"Good to hear," Sam said as he shook Pablo's hand. He paid him in US Dollars, which included a $50 tip.

When Sam and Alicia reached the doors to the terminal, he looked back, pleased to see Pablo still standing by his car and watching, first behind him and then a last look toward them. Sam gave Pablo a final wave which he returned.

As they walked into the terminal, Alicia said, "It looks like you have made us a new friend." She smiled.

"A guy like that could help us a great deal," Sam said.

Sam gave a sideways glance toward Alicia as they walked up to the American Airlines counter. "So, you were not scared away with what we just experienced back there?" he said.

"Not at all. It only makes me more excited to be working on this investigation. I will learn much. And… I know you will do what is right to protect us from any harm. I trust you will make good decisions."

That's what it's really all about, Sam thought. *Hampton's executives will be expecting me to tell them what to do. Good decisions. That's what everyone will expect from me.*

After checking into their respective destinations, Sam and Alicia walked away from the ticket counter discussing the events of the last hour. They paused at the junction where they would part, faced each other… Sam, feeling he should say something along the lines of their dinner conversation opened his mouth to speak, but Alicia quickly held up her hand inches from his lips. "I am hoping I will see you soon. Godspeed, Sam Halloran."

Before Sam could react, Alicia kissed him first on his left cheek then on his right and hurriedly turned and walked away. Sam watched her walk down the empty concourse and around a corner. She never once looked back.

Moments later, Sam buried himself in his business-class seat on a Boeing 747. With all the emotion of the last two days swirling around in his head, he began to steady himself for his immediate challenge—providing good advice and making good decisions. Whatever personal goals confronted him, Sam knew none of them were even a footnote in the equation. The only relevant questions to ask were: What is in the best interests of the shareholders of Hampton Enterprises, and does Sam Halloran have the resources to help his client achieve those goals? Period. This will consume him for the rest of the day.

Hearing the engines revving up, Sam looked out his window toward the terminal. He stared at the sign wondering why he hadn't focused on it earlier. Gate F8… *Fate.*

CHAPTER 18

S AM WAS USHERED into the board room at Hampton Enterprises headquarters a little before 3:00 p.m. Steve led Sam around the massive board table, introducing him to the players he would soon be addressing. The first was Hampton's CFO, Garrett Barclay. Sam had heard enough about him to have a good sense he would want to do the right thing… if that made sense financially. He stood slowly to greet Sam, taking time to first button his suit jacket and then extended his hand. "Sam, it is a pleasure to finally meet you in person." He seemed gracious enough, but his next comment disclosed what side of the fence he sat on. "I know you realize how important that operation is to our company and our bottom line."

"Mr. Barclay, I can assure you your financial goals are of paramount concern to me."

"I knew you were a perspicacious businessman of the first-order when Steve first described you to me. Good to know we think alike." With that not so gentle cautionary salvo, he regained his seat and mumbled something to the Global HR director, Bernard Fuchs, who stood to meet Sam.

After acknowledging Barclay's comment, Fuchs greeted Sam

with a rather limp handshake and a nod and shifted his attention back to Barclay as they settled in for the show to come.

Next was Dorothy Mumfry, heir to her late husband's supermarket empire, and according to Steve's summary notes she devoted most of her time these days to philanthropic causes. As one of Hampton's longest serving directors her presence at this meeting was representing the board, or rather the shareholders. As she stood to greet Sam, he could see in her eyes a lady who was serious about anything that mattered… and if you weren't sure if it mattered, she would focus you in an instant. Her handshake was firm and assuring as she held her stare and grip throughout their brief but purposeful introduction. "Mr. Halloran, I want to tell you how pleased I am with your service to our company. I'd like to talk with you about your impressions of our efforts to help the indigenous people of Guatemala. Not today, but at some point in the near future."

"Mrs. Mumfry, I would be pleased to spend as much time as you would like to discuss a topic I expect is very dear to your heart." She had to be in her late seventies as the many fine lines on her face revealed, but everything about her dress and bearing foretold this was a woman not to dismiss. With just this brief encounter, combined with what Sam had heard about the woman, she would be a compelling force.

Steve then moved Sam on to meet the remaining two participants. From their looks and bearing they needed no introduction. Aaron Schmidt, the first to stand and greet him, was Hampton's general counsel, distinguished in the way that old money would groom someone for power. As he shook Sam's hand, his stare was both commanding and controlling. He then turned slightly. "To my left is Rodney Phillips. Rodney is my, rather, *was* my partner at Bruce & Bishop before I accepted my position here as general counsel. He's here to assist us with the important decisions we expect to be presented with today." Schmidt touched Phillips's shoulder as if to break his concentration away from the documents he was reviewing.

As the Bruce & Bishop partner stood, his phone rang, immediately diverting his full attention to it and away from Sam. Talking into his phone, he greeted and then dismissed Sam with his raised hand like a crossing guard at a busy intersection.

Everyone being present, the meeting was called to order by Steve, at this time the only advocate Sam had in the room, or so he thought.

Steve wrapped up his introduction of the issue at hand. "And now I'd like to turn the meeting over to Sam Halloran, who leads the Chicago Forensic Accounting Investigation practice for Hamilton Pierce. We are fortunate to have Sam's insight fresh from his initial visit to our Guatemalan operation. Sam, the floor is yours."

After briefly complimenting the company and its management, Sam got into the meat of it. "The purpose for my trip was an attempt to provide a quick assessment to assist you in deciding the path forward regarding the issues you now face at your Guatemalan facility."

Sam paused and quickly scanned their faces. He had the attention of Steve, which was no surprise, and Mrs. Mumfry, a pleasant surprise. The CFO, GC, and HR director were giving him blank stares. The Bruce & Bishop partner was hammering away on his BlackBerry with an occasional glance at Sam.

Sam took them through his initial conference call with Walter Hopkins and Steve to go over the anonymous letter and immediately began receiving pushback. First, the GC said, "Sam, let me see if I have this correct. The anonymous letter you refer to, which source we cannot verify as one of our employees, outlines three specific allegations against a general manager who I understand is a long-term, and I might add very successful, executive of Hampton Enterprises. If I heard Steve correctly, one of those allegations was related to his use of company property for personal use, a second was cheating on his expenses, and the last was having an affair with an employee. Did I state them all correctly?"

"You did, Mr. Schmidt, with a slight modification to the

characterization of the *affair*. It would seem the author's implication was he sexually abused a number of—"

"Whatever. I don't think it is proper to introduce one's personal moral judgement on top of the ramblings of an assumed employee. And even if it's proven she is an employee of the company, we have no idea of her motivations to accuse someone as proven and valuable as our general manager."

"But—"

"All I am asking, sir, is you limit your comments, for now, to just the facts. We'll get into interpretations later."

"Fair comment. I'll continue."

Aaron Schmidt was treating this like a courtroom and the more he could do to disrupt Sam's direct testimony the better.

"And while on the subject of this assumed employee's complaint," Schmidt continued, "I think I speak for all of us in our desire to see some solid evidence of a crime presented to us today. Well, I don't want to speak for this group, but I, for one, would consider the letter evidence to be, at best, weak. Maybe HR might want to look into it, but I'll leave that to Bernard's consideration."

Bernard Fuchs, the HR Director, was quick to chime in with a dismissive laugh. "These kinds of things happen here and there. We would deal with this being sure to place it in its rightful context, which would be an HR issue of somewhat minor proportions."

This was definitely getting off track. Sam had to get control quickly, or it would be a short meeting not ending well.

"Gentlemen, your comments reflect my exact thoughts when I first read the letter," Sam said, attempting to right the ship. "Without having the benefit of traveling to Guatemala, you could certainly resolve yourself to that action and no one would fault you. But please hear me out, and your impressions may change.

"My objective in making this trip was to get a firsthand assessment of the plant's environment and to measure the character of

Mr. Mendoza, our target. As you will hear from me later, I feel both objectives were accomplished."

Dorothy Mumfry raised her hand and began speaking before being recognized. "Mr. Halloran, maybe you have incriminating evidence to show us later in your presentation, but I am surprised to hear you label our plant manager as a crook already. I don't think that's appropriate."

"I'm sorry, ma'am. I don't believe I have characterized Mr. Mendoza as a crook. Why do you think that?"

"Well, first off, please refer to me as Mrs. Mumfry."

"Please forgive me, Mrs. Mumfry."

"You just told us he's your *target*, implying you are after him. Right? That's what a target is."

Before Sam could respond, Rodney Phillips interrupted. "Mrs. Mumfry, as the only outside lawyer present here, please allow me to compliment your understanding of the legal terms it would seem Mr. Halloran is misusing." He gave Sam a glint of a smile, and Sam knew immediately he had screwed up.

"A target of an investigation is labeled as such when sufficient and probable evidence has accumulated to indicate they have likely committed a crime which can be proven by such evidence. Mr. Mendoza is a *subject* of unsupported allegations. Hopefully, Mr. Halloran will provide us evidence of a crime which at this point is nonexistent, but I do not want to presume until I have all the facts." He glared at Sam. Sam was kicking himself for taking liberties with the legal terms.

"My apologies, Mrs. Mumfry," Sam said, "and thank you for catching that. I agree entirely with Mr. Phillips. It was wrong of me to take liberties with such characterization. I will refer to Mr. Mendoza by his name only." With a nod to Rodney Phillips, Sam said, "Thank you, Mr. Phillips, for clarifying." It killed Sam to concede to a smug Phillips, but it was the right thing to do. Acknowledge the snafu and move on.

"So, back to Mr. Mendoza and our principle focus to determine if he might have the capacity for doing bad things that could jeopardize the company's standing not only in-country but with regard to US laws and regulations. Now, I caution you to note that we only spent one day in Guatemala, but I will say the time we spent with Mr. Mendoza was significant in terms of the attention given him."

"Mr. Halloran, I don't want to appear rude," Phillips interrupted again, "but can't you just get to the evidence of wrongdoing you found, if any, so we can evaluate it and decide what to do? I mean, we are all busy people here, and I'm trying to step things up in respect of everyone's time."

Fortunately, Sam paused before answering, long enough for Garrett Barclay to seize control of the meeting from Phillips, who obviously wanted Sam out so he could run things his way.

Barclay held up his hand toward Phillips. "Rodney, let's give Mr. Halloran a little respect here and allow him to say what he has to say in his own way, shall we?"

Sheepishly deferring to the obvious power in the room, Phillips appeared reluctant in his retreat, "Of course, you're right, Garrett." He then gave Sam an impatient, irreverent look. "I apologize, Mr. Halloran. Please proceed at your own pace."

"Thank you." At least it was now obvious who the pack leader was. The rest of the room were influencers, important players, but not decision makers. It was time to clarify a few things.

"What I will present to you are a few facts and then my impressions. Please keep in mind my primary purpose was to determine the measure of Mr. Mendoza's integrity. All I can do is relay the observed facts as accurately as possible. I recognize I am a factfinder, and my impressions are subservient to yours which will be translated with the benefit of your legal counsel's learned opinions of the best course of action dictated by the circumstances."

Pausing to permit further questioning on the same point and hearing none, Sam continued. He told them about getting through customs without having to show their documents. He looked toward Phillips for his assessment and possible law violation. Phillips didn't say anything but did take notes. That was a good sign. When Sam communicated the plant working conditions, particularly those of the women workers and the conditions under which they had to endure, it struck a chord of disgust with Mumfry, who shook her head, seeming to memorialize those observations in her leather-bound Moleskine. She was likely the only one at the table who cared about the workers. When Sam mentioned the number of armed guards, Steve pulled out a copy of the plant's security contract.

Steve reported that while the number of security personnel and duties were not specifically addressed in the contract, the annual fee for such services was in a range of $20,000 to $50,000. Further, it seemed unlikely the observed level of security could be provided for a cost in the contracted range. He also noted those levels of protection seemed excessive given the job of protecting the plant's assets, which included its personnel during plant operations. Lastly, he noted the security company, *Protección*, which Roberto Cuesta had communicated to Sam, was different than the contract he had on file. When questioned about his knowledge of the actual cost, Steve said that would be determined if further investigation was ordered by this committee. He also indicated there were ways the plant manager could disguise higher security expenditures.

Sam then disclosed the CRI report and how he used it. He received some strange looks from everyone at the table except Steve. When Sam characterized Mendoza as a liar, it was clear some thought that a bit of a stretch, simply based on his failure to talk about his motorcycles or his wife's activities which Mumfry was quick to point out were none of their business. She didn't get it, but Sam was not about to correct her thinking, at least not yet.

Rodney Phillips was the first to push back. "So, let me get this straight. You're telling us just because our very hard-working and successful plant general manager, who supervises a thousand employees who occupy the bottom of the food chain... this man who makes this company millions of dollars each year... just because he didn't tell you he enjoyed motorcycles, you labeled him as a liar and a crook. I fail to see the inference."

Sam thought Phillips so adept at mischaracterization he almost admired him... for a lawyer. But he deferred responding, hoping someone in the room would take him on. He wasn't disappointed.

"Mister Phillips," Dorothy Mumfry began tersely, "might I remind you that our sainted Mr. Mendoza couldn't make a dime of profit were it not for those *bottom of the food chain* employees you so disparagingly referred to in your insensitive comment." Before Phillips could respond, she cut him off. "One does not have to imagine where you place your priorities if you so callously and blithely dismiss the hard and dedicated work of our employees in favor of profits. Maybe you have other clients who do not care about the welfare of their employees, but let me remind you that you are now in the presence of one company who is disgusted with your comments, and I'll thank you to keep such opinions to yourself in the future."

Phillips back-tracked his comments, apologizing profusely to Mumfry.

Glibly, Sam continued, "OK, I guess that puts it all in the right perspective. Mr. Phillips, I will explain my negative inference from Mr. Mendoza's comments this way. First off, he doesn't just have an interest in motorcycles; he owns twenty-one Harley-Davidsons and built a rather elaborate structure where he and his associates can enjoy their mutual passion on a regular basis. Given Mr. Mendoza makes approximately $80,000 annually, one must wonder how he was able to afford those kinds of proclivities.

"Secondly, I introduced the topic at our lunch with Mr. Mendoza only after we had both engaged in personal stories that indicated a trust was forming, allowing two strangers, now sharing alcohol and war stories, to venture into a casual discussion. Thirdly, Mr. Mendoza's personality is obviously one whereby he very much enjoys boasting with the purpose of elevating his stature in the minds of his audience, me in this case, and he chose to pass on mentioning his motorcycle passion. Droning on and on about such a passion would have been expected unless one would rather keep such information secret.

"Lastly, he lied again when he told me his wife spends all her time helping him with personnel issues at the plant. She is not an employee of Abello. The CRI investigators learned she is the sole owner of a three-story office complex of businesses for which the services provided are murky. Most of those businesses had long records of lawsuits and police calls, the resolutions of which could not yet be determined. Whatever his wife is involved in, I seriously doubt it is confined to helping her husband sort out personnel issues at the plant. I find that extremely odd and instructive as to his willingness to lie."

"Well, Sam, let's not distort the record," Aaron Schmidt shot back. "He didn't actually *lie* about the motorcycles. He just failed to mention them."

Schmidt didn't realize it yet, but he had just slipped up.

"Mr. Schmidt, I don't know a nice way of saying this, but you are flat out wrong with that comment."

"I didn't know you had a law degree, Mr. Halloran."

"I don't need a law degree to know what a lie is. I raised two boys."

Several chuckled. Not the lawyers.

"Further, I believe if you reference *Black's Law Dictionary* you will find there are two types of lies," Sam continued, addressing the entire group. "First, there are the lies we are most familiar with when someone tells us an untruth—lies of commission. They *commit* a lie by telling a falsity. There are also situations where people hold back information, or truths. They are smart enough to realize, rather evil enough to realize, that should they disclose the information you are seeking, it would not be in their self-interest, so they hold back certain truths. *Black's Law* calls these lies of omission.

"I would contend with complete confidence Mr. Mendoza knew full well if he disclosed his passion for motorcycles I might soon find he owned a lot of them, as well as where he housed them. Mr. Mendoza is a sharp man, and he'd quickly discern I might decide to investigate how he came to acquire all those pleasurable assets. That might lead to discovering other thefts and bad deeds he had perpetrated, possibly exposing crimes he may have committed. I can comfortably stand before you today and confidently assert Javier Mendoza is a liar. As for Mr. Mendoza's failure to be forthcoming about his wife's activities—"

"Sam, I think we get it," said Garrett Barclay. "Point made. Please continue with the rest of your findings."

"Mr. Halloran," Mumfry injected, "I believe what you are implying is that if Mr. Mendoza can rationalize lying to you, a Hamilton Pierce partner representing the interests of our shareholders, then he could lie about anything to anyone. Do I have that correctly?"

"You are exactly correct, Mrs. Mumfry."

"That being the case," Mumfry continued, "I could not agree with you more fervently. Thank you for your commentary on Mr. Mendoza. You have certainly influenced me. While we do not yet know if the allegations in the letter are true, I am beginning to see where you are coming from. If there are no further questions around the table on your observations on this particular point, I encourage you to continue with your reporting."

"Thank you for your patience. I realize in the absence of solid evidence it is difficult to come to any hard-and-fast conclusions, but maybe this last observation might persuade you into making the appropriate decision."

Sam laid on them the confrontation they had with Mendoza's thugs in the hotel lobby prior to their return flight demanding to meet with him and the comments of their driver, Pablo Escapa. When Sam finished recounting those events, the silence in the room was unambiguous. He was finished with his presentation and made a last-minute decision to defer any specific recommendations. He did not want to boldly state them, feeling it would be self-serving. He had delivered his presentation such that the path forward should be clear. He was done. It was now up to them.

Garrett Barclay stood and cleared his throat. "Sam, I want to thank you for your work and service to this company. It is obvious you are very skilled at what you do, and we are fortunate to have you working for us and in our best interests. To this group, I would ask if there are any further questions for Mr. Halloran?"

Barclay looked at each person individually. "Hearing no further questions, it is time for us to deliberate and decide on a course of action." He looked at Sam. "As such, we have no further need of your services at this time, and I would ask you to leave us to our deliberations. I will instruct Steve to call you as soon as we have come to a decision. Again, thank you for your help."

Acknowledging Garrett Barclay's comments and instructions, Sam packed up his materials and left the conference room.

Sam's thoughts shifted to executing what he was certain would be the committee's decision. He began to consider the possible dangers of an investigation and weighed those against making the right decisions… good decisions. Mendoza would be a challenging adversary, but Sam was used to those. His father had prepared him well.

CHAPTER 19

Wednesday evening

IT HAD BEEN a little more than fifteen years. The first time she met Sam Halloran was at Staff B school—orientation for all new recruits to the Hamilton Pierce firm. The firm had conducted richly rewarding training at various points over Ann Williams's career; they were just not highly creative in how they titled their courses. On the first day of training, Ann realized she was the only woman in a class of fifteen, and she felt uncomfortable.

On the third day, Ann went to the happy hour after a long afternoon of instruction. She didn't necessarily want to but felt it would look bad if she didn't. She had been there only fifteen minutes and it began. It wasn't like it was the first time she had felt uncomfortable in a group of men, but she didn't expect it at a Hamilton Pierce event.

Three of them surrounded her. The conversation began innocently enough. *Where did you go to school? Why did you choose Hamilton Pierce? Why did you choose to major in accounting?* Maybe it was the way she answered that last question.

Ann's mom was a bookkeeper at a small, regional accounting firm. It was just the two of them. Her dad died in a car crash when she was only six, and her mom never remarried. For some reason,

Ann was fascinated with books and records. The way everything had to balance out fascinated Ann. In high school her mom let her help occasionally. She took her into the office on some weekends when she knew no one else would be there. No doubt it was that experience and her mom's lament for never graduating from college and pursuing the CPA certification that influenced Ann to pursue a career in public accounting. That's what she told them—the men surrounding her.

Then, their questions became more pointed. *Didn't you realize you were entering a man's profession?* It was like the flip of a light switch. Ann shot back curtly that maybe it was time they modernized their thinking. Soon, it was three against one. She wanted to leave but felt boxed in. She was getting anxious. And then he appeared.

"Hey, Jeffrey, maybe you should be asking Ann how she was able to best you in tackling that tax accrual in class today. Maybe you might learn something." It went downhill fast… for Jeffrey and his cohorts. Sam possessed a confidence and maturity they envied. It was obvious every time he spoke.

When they slithered away, Sam extended his hand and introduced himself. It was the first time they had a chance to talk, and talk they did until one a.m. in the lobby bar at the hotel. They got to know each other well. They had some things in common. Both were raised by strong moms. Both were on the outs in their class—her because of her gender and Sam because of his age; he was a decade older than the average Hamilton Pierce recruit. They remained friends throughout the years, even making partners together. That orientation meeting went a little smoother than their first one.

As the years passed, both Ann and Sam were successful based on their individual achievements: Sam for his marketplace success and Ann for being the youngest woman ever invited to join Firm Council, the twelve most powerful partners at Hamilton Pierce. They ran the US Firm.

Reading the report in front of her, she knew there had to be more. This was not the Sam Halloran she had grown to admire and respect over the years.

Vince Mattingly, US Senior Partner and Chairman of Firm Council, got right to business after entering Ann's office. They moved to the conference table. "Ann, I appreciate you making time to talk with me so quickly about this," he said, laying down on the table his copy of the same report she had just finished reading.

"I'm glad you called me, Vince. How can I help?" Ann and Vince didn't always see eye-to-eye but were generally able to work things out in the best interests of the firm. They were about to tackle another thorny issue together.

"I understand that you know Sam Halloran pretty well. At least, better than any of us on the Council. I've spoken to several of the other members. We're all concerned."

"I'm happy to help. I think I can shed some light on the matter. As to the facts, I know only what is in the report. But I do know the man and I can tell you that these facts, if they are facts, do not depict the man I know."

"When was the last time you talked?"

"Just a week ago. Sam was getting ready to begin a new investigation. In Guatemala, I believe. Beyond the friendly relationship we've maintained over the years, we have always been honest with each other, even when we disagreed."

"So, you trust him?"

"Yes, I trust Sam. I understand your concern with the information contained in this anonymous report, but it does not sound like the Sam Halloran I know. I'm sure there's an explanation."

"But, Ann, did you see the pictures of them together? Did you see the way she was dressed? She was hanging on him in that elevator. Their rooms were across from each other. And then there's that incident on the GEL investigation back in '83. He slept with a manager at our client, for God's sake. Looks like a pattern with this guy."

"Hold on, Vince. I think *pattern* is a stretch. GEL was fifteen years ago, and we've had no other reports of the kind of behavior contained in this report. Look at the success of his Chicago practice. And I don't mean just his market success. He's a model for what we want all our practices to look like—over fifty percent women and minorities. I do know about GEL. We've talked about it. I doubt he could explain his actions even today, but again, Vince, that was fifteen years ago, and there's never been another incident."

"Until now."

"That's not fair. We have an anonymous report. It needs to be investigated, I agree, but let's not jump to conclusions."

"But he's been engaged in an investigation at Hampton Enterprises, one of the firm's largest clients. There's a lot of risk here."

"I'm aware of that, but keep in mind he was engaged at the insistence of Walter Hopkins, the client partner and the one who brought Sam to Chicago. I think we should trust that Walter knows Sam well and knows what he's doing. Speaking of Walter, have you reached out to him on this?"

"Got a call into him, but he's on vacation hiking with his son in Washington. Secretary said she'd try to reach him but didn't know about timing," Vince said with his head down looking at the report in front of him, seeming to ponder his next move.

"Look," Ann said, "I'm no investigator, but consider the circumstances surrounding our receipt of this report. The type-written letter and photos were faxed directly to Martha Crunchner. Not through our hotline. Doesn't that seem odd to you?"

"Not really. Martha is the Global HR leader. Makes sense it was sent to her."

"Sure, on its surface, but that alone takes some sophistication. It would require some research to know who the HR leader of Hamilton Pierce is and then obtaining her private fax number. Plus, consider the timing. Sam is just in the beginning stages of his investigation. The last time we talked he mentioned it to me. That he thought this would be a big one and the accusations were being made against a powerful and politically connected man in Guatemala. It's not too far-fetched to believe this guy could be trying to pressure the firm to get Sam to back down."

"I'm listening. Keep going," Vince said.

"Sam also told me what the guy is being accused of. Sounds like a real piece of work. And if he's as powerful as Sam suspects, he's surely checked out Sam and may be concerned. Concerned enough to try and use this firm to remove Sam from the investigation."

"Maybe, but we have no evidence of that."

"Look at the last paragraph." *If you do not remove Sam Halloran from this investigation, the contents of this package will be delivered to The Wall Street Journal.* Now who does that? Suggest a remedy like that? What anonymous letter have you ever seen with such a threat? Allegations like this are done for personal gain—like threatening a lawsuit, not threatening publicity. Think about it, Vince."

"I hear you, but it's still possible it's legit and you can't ignore the risk to the firm's image."

"Granted," Ann said. They both sat for a moment, neither saying a word.

"How about this? I call Sam. Tell him of the report. See what he has to say about it."

"But don't give him the details," Vince said sternly.

"Come on, Vince. Sam is arguably the best forensic accounting investigator in the firm, possibly the nation. You really want to play it like that?"

Vince frowned and shook his head back and forth in frustration. "I suppose not." He paused momentarily. "Look, Ann, I trust your judgment and you know Sam better than any of us. You make that call, and you handle it as you deem best. Just please do it soon and keep me apprised."

"I'll call him today and I'll let you know what I learn."

As the phone rang, Ann felt a little guilty in the role she was assuming, but when Sam answered she felt reassured that all would be well.

"So, I'm guessing one of your partners pulled his head out of his ass long enough to make you call me and tell me to drop this investigation. Well, you can tell them to stay the hell out of my practice affairs and go back to counting beans!"

"Well, *hello* to you, too. What's got you all bent out of shape?" Ann said, smiling. This was the Sam that she was so fond of hearing. He never pulled punches with her.

"I'm sorry, Ann. I've just been expecting this call and disappointed they forced you into making it."

"So, tell me why you think I'm calling you, if you seem to know so much."

"Look, I know there's a lot of risk to the firm by me doing these types of investigations, but it's not like I make this stuff up. I happen to be helping one of our largest clients with a major problem. Besides, it's too late. I met with the Hampton management committee today. I don't have a signed engagement letter yet, but I feel certain they will want to engage us to proceed with an investigation."

"Look, Sam, you have trained the firm leadership well over the years. No one is going to challenge you when it comes to something like this. Sure, they're concerned with the type of work you do, but we all get it. And frankly, every one of us in leadership knows you are the best partner to be leading such an investigation. Trust me, no one is questioning your judgment in accepting this engagement."

"OK, so far so good. So, why are you calling? We just talked a week ago."

She filled in Sam on the anonymous report she and Vince Mattingly had been discussing. When she finished, the other end of the line was silent.

"Sam, you still on?"

"Yep."

"Why the silence?"

"Just trying to piece it all together. Give me a minute," Sam said calmly.

"Take your time."

A moment later, Sam spoke. "I'm back in Chicago now, but on my last day in-country there was a bit of an incident with a certain Hamilton Pierce manager, a female manager, from our Mexico City office. I'm guessing you got a call from an anonymous person indicating something inappropriate between her and me. How am I doing?"

"Not disappointing. Your intuition is uncanny. But not a call. A fax received this morning including photos."

"OK, probably of Alicia Lopez hanging on me in the lobby of the hotel, drunk as a skunk as I shuffled her to her room. And that's exactly what happened! I deposited her in *her* room and then went to *my* room. Nothing happened!"

"Well, I could play snarky and ask why your manager, quite attractive manager I might add, and scantily clad from the photos I saw, was drunk in the middle of the afternoon, but I'll allow you some leeway to explain."

Sam was not upset in the least. He knew he had done nothing wrong. He knew he was talking with a friend, and he trusted Ann Williams completely. "OK, Ann. Short story is it's all bullshit."

"I'm sure it is, Sam, but I'm going to need a little more to flesh this out for Firm Council."

Sam relayed his experiences with Alicia Lopez since he met her at the Miami airport and their meeting with Javier Mendoza and how she got drunk. He even told her about their dinner meeting and how they left it at the airport as they parted. Through it all, Ann did what she always did: listened without comment. She was one of the best listeners Sam had ever encountered.

"Look, Ann. I've decided I am not going forward with Alicia Lopez on this investigation. With what I know so far, this Javier Mendoza is a scumbag, and I feel certain that the evidence we will uncover will bear all that out. I don't need any advice from your partners, and if there is nothing else, I need to prepare for this investigation."

"Not so fast, Sam, and besides, they're *your* partners too."

"Seriously, you're pushing back at me?"

"No, Sam. You know me better than that. I think I have enough to allay any concerns of Firm Council, but I'm curious about Alicia Lopez. Particularly, why you are so quick to dump her from this engagement."

"You can't be serious. She acted like a fricking hooker! She knows nothing about how to conduct an investigation, and I'm through with her. Hell, you saw how they are using her to end this investigation. She's an HR nightmare, and she can't add a damn thing to what we are trying to accomplish here."

A moment passed. "That rant make you feel better?" Ann said rhetorically. She wasn't angry. Sam needed to vent, and she gave him that time, certain he would extend her the same courtesy.

"OK... my turn. Sam, without going into detail, we have had reports of situations like you described with Alicia that disturb us greatly. Not just from Mexico City but other offices in Latin America and other developing countries. As you know, the US firm has limited authority over foreign offices, as they're sovereign in their own right. Sure, we license the Hamilton Pierce brand to them, but pulling that would be a last resort. I prefer to tackle these problems one issue at a time. I'm asking you to reconsider cutting Alicia loose?"

"Do I need to repeat myself? She's a moron and I don't need the risk."

Silence. "Sam, if you really believe that Hamilton Pierce would hire such people and that there is absolutely no hope of helping the situation then, fine, walk away. It's your investigation. If you find she has no redeeming qualities, then do as you please. I'm simply asking you to reconsider.

"Sam, I've watched you over the years with admiration—what

you have done in building your Chicago practice... especially what you have done to advance women in this firm. From the moment I met you, I knew you were a cut above the rest. You care, and that shows in the leaders you produce. Take Veronica Martinez. The way you talked about her on our last conversation. You told me of her personal issues, yet you haven't cut loose of her."

"Veronica is different. I hired her. I've trained her. She's—"

"Sounds like she's still a work in progress. Like I said, Sam, it's your practice and your investigation down there in Guatemala. I'm just asking that you think about what I've said and reconsider my request to keep working with Alicia. I don't know her particular situation, but I do know that if anyone can help her, that person is you."

Sam thought for a moment. "We did have a good talk our last night there. I feel for her situation, but... I will do as you ask. I'll think about it."

"Can I ask you to keep me apprised of the situation?"

"Why so formal? Of course I will. We're friends."

"We are, and for that I am extremely thankful. Be safe down there, Sam."

"Count on it."

ACT II

BE CAREFUL WHAT YOU WISH FOR

CHAPTER 20

Thursday, January 15

SAM GOT THE call shortly after his conversation with Ann Williams. Steve said that while there was little dissension among the committee members on the need for an investigation, there was a great deal of discussion over who would do it. Of course, the lawyers were all over it. They would be the ones to run the investigation. And they had come prepared. It took them nearly an hour to lay out their approach. Barclay did what he usually did; he listened. Then, without offering an opinion, he looked to Steve for his thoughts. When Steve said that, Sam knew he had won the engagement.

Now, he had to develop a detailed plan. Hampton imposed no constraints as to money or timing; just to be engaged through Bruce & Bishop.

Sam spent the better part of the morning reviewing the status of his other cases, ensuring they were moving along as expected. Others were assigned to ensure his practice would continue functioning as he headed to Central America. The planning meeting with Dave Rogers and Veronica was set for ten a.m.

Dave was Sam's first hire after transferring to Chicago. He was a career FBI, but they force you to retire at age fifty-seven, which was perfect timing for Sam. They met for lunch, and three hours later Sam extended Dave an offer to join him. He accepted immediately. Dave was not only an outstanding investigator; he brought to the practice what Sam lacked… Chicago contacts. Dave knew every big-ticket former federal prosecutor in Chicago from working cases together when he was an FBI Special Agent.

"Good morning, Sam," Maggie said as she brought in his mail and a cookie.

"No cookies. Get out of here. I'm busy," Sam said in his usual sardonic manner.

"Oh, stop! I made these just for you. Well, maybe not *just* for you but for all the staff. You have to eat one," she said as she smiled, never backing down.

"OK, since you made them, I'll have one for dessert after lunch."

As she was trying to organize his desk, he was grabbing things from the same stacks in preparation for his meeting. They were at cross purposes. "Dammit, get out of my way."

"Hush up."

"Fine, you do what you want. I'm out of here," Sam said as he grabbed his gathered documents and Franklin Planner and headed out the door.

As Sam walked through their section of the floor, the cubicles were filling up with his staff greeting him. Coffee in one hand and papers in the other, he nodded to all and smiled, but the quickness of his pace communicated it was not the right time to hit him with anything. They knew his mannerisms well and steered clear this morning.

Once he reached the meeting room, Veronica was at the white board outlining what Sam imagined would be her presentation regarding the preparations she had arranged for their upcoming investigation in Guatemala. Sam thought it time to tell them the good news.

"Steve called… we're on for the full investigation!"

Neither of them broke stride, not even to look at him. Veronica said, "Of course we are. Why do you think we're having this meeting? Did you ever doubt it?" She continued writing. Dave was unmoved as well.

Sam was a little disappointed they weren't excited at the news, but then Dave confessed that Steve had called early that morning with some logistics questions. All three had a good laugh.

"Dave, I appreciate you helping out on this."

"Not a problem. I only wish I were going with you."

"I know, but—"

"I get it. Someone needs to stay behind and keep the place afloat."

"Glad you understand."

Sam liked to let the staff run meetings like this. He believed they took the time to research and plan it, and they should have the leeway to control the agenda. He felt it was a great learning opportunity as well. After all, one day they would be running their own investigations, mentoring their own staff. But today, Sam was really disquieted about getting on to the substantive parts.

"I hate to break your stride, Veronica, but I'm eager to get into it. Can we cut to the meat of it? What do we want immediately, and how do we get it?"

Dave jumped up as Veronica handed him the marker and relinquished control of the meeting to him. "That's where I come in. CRI has continued to provide us with some valuable information. We plan to keep them involved. I've talked with Derek on several occasions." Dave was firing on all cylinders.

"What about what Pablo Escapa told us about Mendoza's cousin being *El Gordo*?"

"Derek is on it, and I have a call scheduled with him later today."

"Good, so how do we nail this scumbag, Dave?"

"That's not going to be easy. Javier Mendoza is a man who has run things his way for quite a long time. For all practical purposes, Mendoza *is* Hampton Enterprises in Guatemala."

"What's the likelihood we can compromise someone?" Sam said.

"Not a lot of choices. Most of Palencia's inhabitants are living in sub-poverty conditions, at least by our standards. Due to the lack of laborers in and around Palencia, the company constructed housing for their workers. That housing wasn't the best to begin with, but the years of earthquakes and flooding have taken their toll. They are totally dependent on Mendoza for their livelihood. Not likely they would bite the hand that feeds them."

"Sounds like they're all pretty destitute," Sam said.

"Half the country is illiterate, and I'm guessing nearly all the production workers would fall into that category."

"I agree they would not be likely targets for compromise. That leaves office workers, vendors, and Mendoza's inner circle."

"CRI has been looking into that. He pays that group of loyalists top dollar. CRI still has more work to do but said not to get our hopes up. They also cautioned against the possibility of them playing us."

"Meaning?"

"Meaning that Mendoza is a savvy guy. It's entirely possible that we could believe we've compromised someone when in fact Mendoza saw it coming and set that person up."

"So, it looks to us like this compromised source is cooperating but in reality he's still working for Mendoza and feeding us erroneous information while providing him information about us. I hadn't considered that," Sam said, nodding his head.

"With limited chance of compromising the line workers or his inner circle, how about vendors and office workers?" Veronica asked.

"My favorites are the secretaries," Dave said.

"I'm with you on that, Dave. While their crooked bosses may destroy documents and emails, their secretaries never do. They save everything just to cover their own ass."

"Any possibilities?"

"Sure. One comes to mind," Sam said flipping through his notes. "Mendoza's secretary, Gabriela Castillo. I met her. Presented herself quite well, attractive too, but guarded. She seemed scared to death of him. Do we know anything about her?"

Dave was flipping pages. "I do. This comes from one of the guys on Derek's team, Hector De Salvo. Gabriela Castillo has been Mendoza's secretary the entire eighteen years the plant has been operating."

"Bingo!" Sam said. "Tell me she's not a wealth of information."

"She may know a lot, but how do we get it out of her? Let me read on. She has a daughter, no husband. No record of any marriage. Lives in a better-than-average house. Her mother and sister live together in a separate, fairly decent house a couple miles away. Neither of them has any source of income, so the secretary must be supporting them."

"All of that suggests that Mendoza is likely subsidizing her either for personal privilege or because she may be the keeper of all the things we would like to know about him. Either way, she's definitely on my short list of people to talk with, maybe compromise."

"Sam, aren't we forgetting the most important person in this mix… the whistleblower herself?" Veronica said.

"What if Castillo is the letter writer, our whistleblower?" Sam said.

"But the letter said they worked on the production line."

"Which means they *don't* work on the production line," Dave said. "Included that just to disguise themselves."

"I agree," Sam added.

"How do we run that down?"

"Veronica will run it down. Mission objective *numero uno*, kid. See if you can get close to Castillo," Sam said to Veronica.

"On it, boss," Veronica said while making a note.

"OK, let's talk about data. When do we get it?" Sam asked.

"Ah, yes, data," Dave said. "We'd be nothing without data, so let's talk about that. We need to get it and get it now before Mendoza can manipulate it."

"You mean any more than he's already done!" Veronica chided.

"Exactly," Sam said. "We can't move forward accomplishing any of our goals until we seize all relevant data and begin to interrogate it."

"Emails, too," Veronica followed. "Email is God's gift to the investigator!"

"That's a problem," Dave said. "They use MS Office feeding Outlook. The license with Microsoft is with officials at the plant and not with Hampton personnel in Chicago; therefore, Microsoft won't even discuss handing over those files. I called when I got off the phone with Steve. They actually hung up on me when I persisted. I'm working with Steve to see if there's a way around that snag."

"Financial data on Abello from corporate?"

"That's a problem too. The only thing corporate has are Hyperion schedules sent to them from Abello. All transactional data resides in Guatemala."

"Are you kidding me!" Sam said.

"Well, at least that's something," Veronica said.

"It's worthless, kid. Hyperion is just a big spreadsheet. Mendoza can put anything he wants on it. Could be, and probably is, total fiction. Get what you can, but don't place too much reliance on it. You're going to have to go down, meet with their head of IT, and extract the financial data, probably emails too, directly from their network. Better make those arrangements now," Sam said looking at Veronica.

"Lastly," Sam said, "can we talk about staffing?"

"Sure. You mean for just the initial discovery?"

"Yep. I'd imagine this will expand, but I don't want to take a dozen staff next week and get surprised. I'm thinking me, Veronica, and maybe a couple staff."

"Maybe a manager... from Mexico City?" Veronica said.

"Sure. I called Alicia last night, and she's ecstatic we are going forward."

"I'm eager to meet her," Veronica said with a wily grin.

"What are you implying?"

"Nothing, boss. She sounded pretty sexy over the phone, and that picture in the firm directory confirms it."

"Yeah, about that. I guess I never followed up with you on your initial impressions. Turns out you were correct. Alicia fits the Latina stereotype to your predictions. But we talked."

"About what?"

"Alicia wants to learn a different way to be successful. She's actually talked about working more closely with our group going forward."

"You mean you!"

"Dammit, Veronica," Sam said with more curtness.

"Sorry. What can I do to help?"

"A lot, actually, if you can focus on your professional skills and keep your issues well-hidden, I think you can help Alicia quite a lot."

"Issues?"

"You know what I mean. You really want me to go there now?"

Dave had been watching the two welterweights in the ring without comment. Each now went to their respective corners for a needed rest.

"OK, Sam. I do get it, and I would like to work with Alicia," Veronica said, relenting and wearing a dispassionate look. "Seriously, I do. We Latinas need to stick together!"

Sam seemed pleased yet cautious with her response. "We'll talk more about that later. Anyway, she's landing tomorrow evening and will come in the next morning."

"That's Saturday."

"And your point is?"

Veronica smiled again. This time sincerely. "Guess it makes sense to break her in early to the way we work."

Sam looked at his watch. "Guys, we've been at this pretty intensely for a while. Let's take an hour break and then reassemble here at 12:30 and keep hashing it out. Lunch will be catered in when we resume."

They all scattered off to check messages. Sam stopped by Dave's office and sat at his conference table. Dave joined him. Neither of them said a word for a few moments. Sam was hoping Dave would start but then realized his former military training would compel him to respect the chain of command.

"Dave, I'm really worried I'm pushing my staff into this investigation. I fear my own excitement is yielding a bias toward moving forward on this one."

"Sam, you're giving yourself too much credit. Stuff like this keeps me young, and as for Veronica, I think you know the answer to that. She's an adrenaline junkie. All your managers are, as well as the staff that follows them. These guys like and respect you, but you have raised them to be pretty independent. I don't know one of them that would hesitate to push back if they disagreed. I've been watching them closely, and quite frankly I'd be amazed if any of them wanted to bow out. Behind the scenes, they are chomping at the bit to be assigned to this gig, and nothing short of termination or death will stop them."

"Dave, between you and me... I'm scared."

"I know you are, and that's a good thing. Stay scared. It'll help you make the right decisions at critical times." As if he didn't have a care in the world, Dave said, "Now get out of my office so I can check my messages."

Sam chuckled to himself. Typical Dave. He stood and looked at Dave but didn't speak.

"Sam, you're doing the right thing, and you are going about this in the right way. Don't be so hard on yourself."

Sam returned to his office. Maggie buzzed him. "Sam, Steve Lemly is holding. Should I take a message?"

"No, transfer him in here."

"Steve, what's up?"

"Not sure how you want to play this, but I just got off the phone with Mendoza. He called *me*. Says he feels like you may have misinterpreted him and apologized for the hotel lobby incident, saying it was entirely his fault by not supervising his men properly. Said his mother died the night before, and he took out his sadness on you. Wants to make amends. Asked what he could do. I honestly don't know what to make of his change in attitude."

"Interesting, Steve. Did he call you before or after he learned I'd be returning?"

"Likely after our VP Operations, Chuck Holland, read him a statement I had prepared simply saying you would be returning with a team of auditors to assist the upcoming audit. Short and simple. I'll fax it to you."

"Thanks. Right now, I'm having a difficult time believing he doesn't think this is an investigation. He's too sharp for that. He knows what's coming, and he'll prepare for the worst."

"I hear you, and I'm not telling you how to react. I'm just passing along this information. I wish I could be of more help."

"I get it. But I'm thinking I should call him and have a chat."

"That sounds like the right thing to do. But it's your decision. Aside from that, how are your preparations going?"

"Going well. We'll conclude our planning meeting shortly. Dave gave me the nuts on what you and he talked about with regard to data collection and logistics this morning."

"I wish I had better answers for you."

"Veronica is probably on the phone right now arranging to fly down there on Monday. We'll know a lot more by Tuesday or Wednesday.

"Sounds good. I'll be in the office both days. Tell Veronica to call me if she runs into any trouble."

"Will do, and I'll reach out to Mendoza and call you if anything remarkable happens, but I expect he'll be a prince on the phone… and I'll kiss his ring. He and I are both good at this game."

"I hope you're a little better."

"Me too."

CHAPTER 21

THE THREE OF them reconvened after the break and sat again in the conference room, each grabbing a sandwich Maggie had arranged.

The caller ID on Sam's mobile phone read "Private." He knew who was on the other end. "Hello, this is Sam Halloran."

"*Señor* Halloran, this is Javier Mendoza calling. Am I catching you at an inconvenient time?"

"Not at all, Javier. How can I help you?"

"This morning, I have talked with *Señor* Lemly and have learned to my distress there was an incident occurring on your way to the airport when last you were in my country. From the way *Señor* Lemly has described the incident, he and you understand a very wrong impression of your visit and of our relationship. I am calling to see if I can help correct any misunderstanding."

"Javier, thank you for calling. I must say that meeting your two associates in the hotel lobby gave me the impression they meant us harm."

"*Señor* Halloran, I was not there and will accept without question your explanation of the incident, and therefore, I must apologize most sincerely for the behavior of my men. I think what happened is my fault. You see, my mother passed away the night before, and my instructions to my men were given when I was in grief for her. My men are very loyal and work hard to please me, and it is now clear they were overly assertive when I asked them to bring you to my office. I cannot express to you in stronger terms that I regret they have upset you. I have already spoken to them upon learning of the incident, and I hope it has not influenced you on this important matter."

"Javier, my condolences on the passing of your mother. Under such circumstances, there is no need to apologize, and we'll forget the entire incident and pick up where we left off at lunch. But thank you for your call."

"You are most welcome, *Señor*."

"I continue to be impressed with the manner in which you present yourself, Javier. How should we proceed?" Sam said, hoping for him to suggest the path forward.

"Sam, you are the expert in such matters, so I defer to you."

He knows what's coming, Sam thought.

"We need data in order to proceed with our examination. Access to your records, both digital and otherwise."

"This is no problem. This is what I told *Señor* Lemly. He asked we give your staff access to our records, and while I could not give him direct guidance at that time, I have since looked into the possibilities. Forgive me, but I am not a financial man and had to inquire myself of such records. I am happy to say we do have the records you need and will make them available to you at your convenience."

"Good to hear, Javier. One of my directors, Veronica Martinez, has already made arrangements with your IT director and will be arriving in Guatemala City on Monday."

"Yes, Miguel and I have talked. I have given instruction with him to cooperate fully and please have your director contact me at once if she encounters any difficulties. Is there anything else that I can do for you?"

"Javier, you are being more than gracious in your offer of

assistance, and I will pass along such news to Steve. At this point, that is all I need. We will be in touch. Thank you again for your help."

"The pleasure is all mine. Please call at any time."

On balance, Sam was surprised Mendoza did not push to hear more details about how much data interrogation they would actually perform. But that was smart on his part. It would betray his cover requesting such information. His back was definitely against the wall, and he was smart to give in to the pressure… for now.

Sam's phone rang. He looked at the ID. He could use a break.

"You're back and you didn't call. How am I supposed to take that?" Cat said innocently. Playfully.

"And how did you know I was back?"

"You're not the only investigator."

"Is that right?"

"Al, your doorman, is helping me keep tabs on you."

"So, you're stalking me now?"

"Maybe. Does that excite you?"

The invitation to have a quiet dinner at her place on Sunday didn't make it past the living room. Inside the door, all she did was touch Sam. They were kissing instantly. The rest moved so fast Sam felt a little embarrassed at how aggressively he made love to her.

"Wow, I guess I don't need that run I was planning for tomorrow?" Cat said smiling, out of breath. By the look on her face, she was both surprised and pleased, relieving Sam's angst.

"I really missed you," Sam said as he slid his arm around her neck, pulling her closer to him on the sofa, the Afghan up to their necks. Their nakedness felt warm, comforting. He closed his eyes and took in a deep breath and let it out slowly.

"Well, I'm glad I could relax you. How was your trip?"

Sam didn't answer. He closed his eyes and breathed slowly. He didn't want to talk. He didn't want to move.

"Sam. This is the part where you talk to me. Otherwise, I feel like a hooker." That got Sam to open his eyes and look at her as she smiled and nuzzled in a little closer. "It's OK, Sam. You don't need to talk. Not now, anyway. Maybe at dinner."

"I thought this was dinner."

"No, just the appetizer."

Cat chose the place tonight. A bar around the corner. They sat inside next to a faux waterfall. The sound of water gently cascading over the stones was comforting. It was also soothing having Cat sitting next to him, her leg wrapped around his and holding his hand.

"Thoughts?"

"Sorry, thinking about Guatemala."

"You probably can't talk about it, big investigator that you are, but know that I am curious. I am happy to talk about it anytime." She kissed Sam's hand.

That was unexpected. Cat wasn't like other women, especially thirty-something women. He began to allow the last feelings of stress to melt away. He tightened his grip on her hand, raised it, and kissed hers.

"I'm starving!" Cat said as she released his hand and picked up the menu.

Sam did the same.

It was dark on the walk back to Cat's place. A stillness contributed to Sam's calm. He needed to do more of this, be in the company of calming people and enjoy the peace. No pressure. No commitment. Still, it all reminded him of the way it used to be… with Sue… when they first began seeing each other. It made him want to be with her. Remembering made him regret.

"Hey, Sam. This is my place. Where are you?"

"Sorry, lost in thought."

She turned toward him, pressed closer, and kissed him gently on the lips. She separated and stared at him.

"What?"

"Dessert?"

Not waiting for Sam to answer, Cat climbed the steps to her townhouse pulling his hand, but he was not resisting in the least. He wanted her.

After they made love again, he lay on her bed staring at the moonlight leaking through the curtains and parting the ceiling. He blocked out everything else, allowing peace to enter him as he drifted off to sleep.

CHAPTER 22

SAM WAS AT his desk by six-thirty.

"Sam, Laura's here. She wants to talk with you," Maggie said, cautiously.

Damn. Just like her to show up unexpectedly, he thought. He had taught her well.

"Send her in. Hold my calls."

"How was Guatemala?"

"Not so fast. Give me a hug," Sam said, deferring for a moment the conversation he had been dreading. "How was the training?"

"A week didn't seem long enough. I learned a lot about investigations, but it exposed so much more I need to learn. I did like being in New York City for a week," she dropped that exactly like Veronica had suggested... as a prelude to what would come next.

"Don't get any ideas! I'm never letting you leave Chicago." They both laughed.

"So, my turn. Tell me about Guatemala," Laura said. "I want to hear all about it. Every detail," Laura said as she sat and scooted her chair up close to Sam's desk.

Sam gave her summary details. Not enough to satisfy Laura.

"Sam, if I'm going to work on this project I need to know more."

Sam didn't speak immediately. "What's up?" she said, now sitting upright in her chair. "You look like you are about to say something. Something that will disappoint me."

"Laura, not this one. It's not the right one. Not for your first."

"What do you mean? I've got two years of audit experience. I know I have a lot to learn about forensic accounting investigation, but it seems a good place to start. You'll be there. Veronica told me she's running the project. You *have* to assign me to Project Vista." She crossed her arms, sat erect, and gave him a cold stare. All classic reactions Sam had seen Laura engage in when she found herself in doubt. Not that she wasn't a confident young woman. Anyone who saw her performance on stage defending him could never doubt her confidence. No, she had that look when she knew she was about to lose an argument and not sure how to get her way. Sam had had that effect on her. He loved her as if she were his own child, and that was the problem.

"You're not assigning me because you feel the need to protect me. This is bullshit!"

"Watch your mouth." She had done that purposefully knowing how Sam hated it when his loved ones acted in an unloving or unprofessional way.

"It's bullshit because you're not treating me fairly. I know who's been assigned, and I have more experience than any of the first-year associates, and you know it. You can't coddle me, Sam. I'm no longer that little girl you met in Houston." She stood, hands on her hips, regarding Sam with a countenance daring him to disagree with her. Still, he would not give on this one. He knew why but could not say it. Laura also knew why but did say it.

"It was fifteen years ago, Sam.... It's not your fault my mother was murdered! This isn't fair! Why the hell did you let me transfer out here if you intended to treat me like a child?" She stared at him; her tone and demeanor demanding an answer, one she could accept. But Sam didn't have that kind of answer.

"Laura, I have every intention of training you to be a valued and successful member of my Chicago team—"

"I don't believe you! Biggest mistake of my life transferring out here!" With that, she gave Sam one last exacting and critical stare, and then she turned and stormed out of Sam's office.

Sam got the message. *Use me or lose me.*

He remained in his chair, elbows on his desk, his chin on his hands staring at the doorway Laura had exited. She had made excellent points, but still he would not relent. He would not assign her to Project Vista. She would have to be patient. Her time would come.

CHAPTER 23

LAURA HAD BEEN gone from Sam's office no more than ten minutes when Maggie burst in. "You're not going to like this, but your favorite HR director is coming up to see you?"

"Not my problem. Yours."

"Not this time, Sammy boy. He's all yours."

Without lifting his head from his work, Sam said, "Why do you think I pay you so well? Close my door and deal with him. Tell him I'm not in."

"He knows you're here. Maybe he saw you come in. I don't know, but he's already told me he knows you're here and said it's important he speak with you immediately. Hung up before I could say a word."

"Maggie, I don't have time to argue with you. Leave, and deal with him."

"Surely you are not talking about me?" Louis Bittle said as he stood in Sam's doorway.

Maggie backed away from Sam's desk and walked toward the door as Louis entered Sam's office.

Sam did not look up, still attending to whatever was in front of him.

"Mister Halloran. Might I have a word with you?" he said closing Sam's door. He walked over in front of his desk.

"Not today, Mister Bittle. Too much important stuff to deal with. Schedule a time with Maggie."

"Then I'll have to chat with New York HR without your input and what happens, happens."

That was the secret password, and that ass knew exactly how to get his attention. Sam peered into Louis Bittle's face.

"So, Louis, what brings you to my neck of the woods? Someone overheard me saying something politically incorrect putting the good name of this firm at risk?" Sam said mockingly.

"May I sit?" Louis said rhetorically and sat down.

Sam gritted his teeth. He said nothing, but his look and demeanor telegraphed his lack of enthusiasm and respect for this man who fed off anything that violated his precious policies, which Sam thought were developed by trolls who have never managed a real practice of top-notch professionals.

"Sam, I know you and I don't see eye-to-eye on things our firm believes extremely important, but—"

"Louis, can we for once skip the histrionics and simply get to what's on your mind?"

Louis had not adjusted his look and seemed especially glib and confident this time. Sam paused in deference to his presumed authority. "OK, the floor is yours, Louis," Sam said, looking deferentially but stoic at Bittle.

"Veronica had an affair with Brian Metcalf this past summer."

Sam was not sure what his face foretold, but it gave Louis pause in the middle of his reporting. Sam didn't immediately respond but was certain his reaction revealed his complete shock upon hearing his star director slept with an intern in his practice. And not just any intern. Brian was assigned as one of her mentees. Complicating matters even worse, Brian was the son of one of the leading litigators in Chicago, who happened to be a name partner at the largest law firm in the city—a firm that contributed about twenty percent of their revenue last year.

"That is the most ridiculous thing I have ever heard. What's the source of this bogus allegation?" Sam said.

"It came from Brian himself, and before you dismiss that as biased, I have independent confirmation from two other interns."

Sam shot back, "Who are they? Where are they? I want to interview them myself. And besides, Brian was our only intern last summer."

"I cannot reveal their names to you, but I can say they were interviewed separately by someone from our Tampa office on the last day of the Disney World Intern Retreat."

Sam stood and placed his knuckles on his desk while inching his face closer to Louis. "They're lying. I don't believe a word of what you are telling me. Veronica is a tough gal, and I'm sure she did something or said something likely pissing them off. Now the spoiled, privileged little piss-ants are trying to make life tough for her. You may be forgetting, Louis, that Veronica was honored by the firm's leadership committee as top-ten female staff just last month, and she's about to be featured in a commercial produced to promote the firm on campuses all across the country. Do you have any idea how ridiculous your accusation is? You need to reexamine your evidence and take another look at this and this time do it in an unbiased fashion."

Sam was rambling and feeling he was losing the argument. He pointed to his door. "You need to leave, Louis. Now!"

To Sam's surprise, Louis remained in his seat and turned the next page of his open file to reveal a frame from the hotel security video which he placed in front of Sam without saying a word. Sam looked in horror at it and slowly lowered himself into his seat, placing his elbows on his desk, hands on his temples.

He was staring at a picture of Veronica with her lips glued to the face of a kid who surely resembled Brian, locked in an embrace that appeared a little more passionate than the typical Latina greeting he had seen Veronica use on more than a few occasions. Next to Veronica's head he could see a room number on a door. Sam stared at the picture, not saying a word. Louis revealed another picture which appeared to be the next scene in this horror film of that same door open, clearly showing an excited and happy Veronica pulling young Brian into the room. Most likely her room.

Louis had Sam. He was speechless. But when he looked up at Louis the smirk was gone, replaced with a compassionate look Sam didn't believe him capable of having.

"Look, Sam. You and I have had our differences in the past, and it's been quite clear from our interactions you don't agree with me on many issues. Even so, I have to say in an off-the-record observation that I think what you have done with this practice is nothing short of amazing. In a firm with eighteen percent annual turnover, your practice has not seen any voluntary terminations or transfers in the five years you've been here. You built this practice from nothing to over forty professional staff, and from my interactions they all appear happy, motivated, and extremely loyal to you and this firm. I am not saying I condone all you do and say, but one would have to be blind, dumb, and stupid to ignore the results you have achieved. In ways I cannot explain, I do admire you."

Sam didn't respond. Likely, he was trying to deal with the burden of what Louis Bittle had communicated to him about his star director. He continued blankly staring at the pictures in front of him, desperately searching for a remedy to this distressing revelation— news that could derail Veronica's career in a heartbeat. He wanted to believe, even in the face of this evidence, that Veronica did not sleep with an intern, her mentee.

Sam finally lifted his head and looked at Louis in a new light. No longer did he see him as an annoyance to be ignored and avoided. Rather, he saw him now as an ally.

"Louis, how do we fix this?" Sam asked humbly.

"Sam, I don't want to build up your hopes that we *can* fix this. I know you know this, but I'm going to say it anyway. We, who know Veronica personally, wish it had never happened and want desperately to make it disappear, but the firm has a history of fixing problems like this by severing the problem from the firm quickly and dispassionately. I have a call with the firm's US HR leader tomorrow morning to discuss what to do, but I know how the firm has responded in the past. Sam, I may leave that call with a directive to terminate Veronica Martinez immediately. If that's the case, there will be no recourse for either of us.

"Everyone who is addressing this issue will be working for a resolution which is in keeping with protecting the firm's brand. It's always about the brand, and right now Veronica has put our brand at risk. It appears the only acceptable action is to terminate her. I wanted to give you fair warning. You have less than twenty-four hours to suggest and support an alternative decision. I'm really sorry to have to be so blunt, but that's the reality we face, and we'll have to accept it and move on."

Looking at Louis directly with the focus of a pit bull on its prey, Sam said, "Louis, you are wrong to lay this at my feet, telling me this is *my* problem. It's *our* problem. You and I are no longer at cross-purposes. We are united in a common goal. And let me say this, Louis, if you help me get out of this with Veronica keeping her job and giving her a way to regain her good reputation, I will owe you big-time."

"Lord, I never thought I would ever hear the great Sam Halloran say that."

Sam smiled in agreement. "I need you, Louis. Like I have never needed you before." Louis got it. He clearly seemed to recognize the dilemma.

They stood and shook hands. "Please help me help Veronica on this. We are all depending on your wisdom and political savvy."

"Sam, please know that I will do whatever is in my power and call in every chit I have with firm leadership to make this happen. I agree Veronica is an excellent leader, and I desperately want to fix this as much as you do."

With that, they parted. Sam was aware the clock was ticking with little time to find a solution that would be acceptable to firm leadership. He was secretly afraid they may have already moved on to their next big problem, believing a decision to terminate Veronica was the only one that made sense. Well, maybe for them but not for Sam. He was determined to find a better solution. He thought about reaching out to Ann Williams but decided to defer that, hoping Louis could find a solution. That was better than putting Ann in an awkward position, but he'd make the call if it came to that.

The rest of the day, Sam sat in his office with instructions to Maggie not to allow anyone or anything short of a catastrophe to enter his sealed domain. Undisturbed, he was able to keep himself occupied, but mostly he thought about Veronica.

While he was angry at her for her indiscretion, he began to examine his own actions. *Could I have influenced this to play out the way it did, my blatant disregard for the rules often implying, even sometimes saying outright, how the only reason we should know the rules is so we can break them one at a time? Was all this my doing?* These kids were Sam's second family. He was supposedly much older and wiser. *They follow my lead.* Sam thought of Carol Wittford. How he himself had broken the rules. Suddenly, it seemed time to leave.

He packed up his briefcase to call it a day. He was spent.

While home was just a ten-minute cab ride, there were some evenings when Sam preferred to walk. Tonight was one of those times. Alone, it gave him time to sort things out without distractions. The city sounds enabled him to relax... to concentrate.

He hadn't paid attention to the time, but before he knew it, he was already at the corner of Chestnut Street and Michigan Avenue. It was too soon. He needed more time for thought, more time to find a solution to the Veronica problem. Or maybe he needed to set it aside, if only for a little while.

He continued walking north on Michigan, past Division. Soon he was standing in front of a familiar place. He dialed her number.

"Are you hungry?"

"Sam, it's eight-thirty. I've already eaten. Where are you?"

"Standing outside your townhouse."

A moment later, Cat opened the door and pulled Sam inside. They kissed. It was exactly what he needed.

Cat led him up the stairs holding his hand until he stopped mid-flight. "Cat, I'm sorry I came here unannounced."

"I'm happy to see you," she said looking into his face. "Now, let's go," she said tugging him along. He followed for a few more steps and then stopped again. "No, this isn't right," he said dejectedly.

She pulled him up her stairs, placed her arms around his neck, and kissed him again. "You look like you could use a friend. And I am suddenly extremely interested in some dessert." She smiled. He followed her up another flight and into her bedroom.

CHAPTER 24

CAT MADE BREAKFAST for Sam. Scrambled eggs and veggies, no meat.

"How can you eat like this? I don't know where you get your energy without protein."

"I get plenty of protein, just not from eating dead animals. Besides, I don't hear you complaining about my performance."

Sam got up from the table and walked toward Cat as she was placing the dishes in the dishwasher. He drew her close, hugged her, and kissed her sweetly on the lips.

"Any chance you can spend the day with me? Kick back and enjoy each other? We can—"

"I can't. I mean, I would love nothing more than to spend the day with you, Cat, but really, I can't."

She hugged him again, ending with a long kiss. "Are you really sure about that?"

"Cat, you bring me peace and comfort. Really, you do. But I've got problems to solve."

Sam let her go and put on his coat and then grabbed his briefcase.

"I do understand. Really, I do. I just miss you. How's Guatemala?"

"We're just getting started. I should get a report back from Veronica today."

"She's the one you were with the night we met at Ditka's, right?"

"She is. She's my best director. A future partner with the firm. And right now, she's in a dangerous place, and I need to protect her. To do that right, I need to be with her."

"So, more than being with me?" Cat said smiling.

"Of course not. Not even close."

"I'm just kidding. Come on, I'll walk you out," she said as she put her arm around his waist and walked him to the front door.

They kissed one more time at the door. "I will miss you, Cat."

"Call me when you get back. I'll miss you too, Sam."

Sam walked down the front porch steps and turned one last time before hopping in a cab. Back to the real world.

In the cab, Sam suddenly felt he was back at the console of managing his business life with the precision of a machinist working in close tolerances. He had a lot to do, and people were depending on him, which always focused him. He'd stop by the gym for a workout and shower, and then he'd check on Veronica.

His phone rang. It was Veronica. Could she know about his talk with Bittle yesterday?

He wasn't ready to talk with her about it yet and almost didn't pick up, but then he thought of her in Guatemala. That's all it took.

With adrenaline coursing through his veins, he blurted into his phone in anxious tones, "Veronica, are you all right?"

"Sam, chill out. I'm fine, but you sound strung out. Are *you* all right?"

"Sorry, I've got a few things on my plate and a little more stressed than usual. What's up?"

"I've got some really bad news to report."

"Go for it."

"So, Miguel, the IT guy I was scheduled to meet this morning, picks me up at my hotel and tells me there has been a break-in at their facility overnight."

"The plant?"

"Yeah."

"Someone broke into the plant last night?" Sam asked.

"No, the Walmart down here. Of course, the plant. Focus, Sammy."

"So why do we care that someone broke into the plant?"

"We care because apparently they broke into their data center, and Miguel tells me the electronic records we requested are no longer available."

Sam tensed up and punched the headrest of the passenger seat in front of him, thinking Mendoza found a way to keep them from getting the data. *That son of a bitch!*

"You have got to be kidding me. This is complete bullshit! Where are you now?" Sam yelled, ignoring the cabbie's stares through the mirror.

"I just walked into the computer room, standing off to the side so as not to be heard."

"OK, Veronica, tell me what you see. Walk me around the room. Give me every detail. Start at the beginning. Miss nothing. Go." Sam was anxious and it certainly showed.

"I always laugh when you say start at the beginning. Like where else am I going to start? OK, to my left there is a hole in the wall where an air conditioner used to sit. It's now on the floor. The opening is not large, but any of these starving Guatemalans could easily have made it through. As I look around the room I see overturned desks, a couple of metal file cabinets looking battered and beaten like someone took a baseball bat to them, some are on their side on the floor, others still standing but with many of their drawers opened, mostly empty. I see files scattered across the floor, and worst of all I see every computer tower pulled from their storage rack and laying in the center of the room. Looks to be about eight of them."

"Do they look intact? The towers. Do they look like they've been damaged?"

"You're not asking the right questions, Sam. They look fine, but Miguel tells me... are you sitting down?"

"I'm in a cab on the way to the office but about to get out. What did Miguel tell you?"

"The hard drives are missing from each and every one of them."

"From what?"

"From the computers. From the towers. The hard drives are gone!"

"Hard drives are screwed into the towers. Even if someone took a baseball bat to them the hard drives would still be screwed in place."

"They're gone, Sam. How else can I say it? The hard drives are missing. I saw it with my own eyes!"

"Is Miguel expecting us to believe some peasants broke into their computer center armed with small Phillips screwdrivers and calmly and precisely took the time to unscrew the hard drives from each of the towers? Then, they knocked over a few filing cabinets and scurried off into the woods to bring the stolen hard drives home to their starving and destitute families as their bounty for an evening's work? Tell me there's another story here. Something that's actually believable."

Sam's rage in the back of the cab was agitating the driver as he motioned they had arrived, yelling at Sam in some foreign language. Sam was still digesting the news. The more he ignored the cabbie the madder he seemed to get.

"Hey, cab number 4995," Sam said as a warning that if he didn't shut up, he's making the call and this cabbie is off the streets for a few days. The cabbie got the message. Sam tossed him a $20 bill and got out, still on the phone with Veronica.

"Sam, you need to calm down and breathe. I'm guessing you have not yet entered our office building, which means you are standing on Wacker Drive and beginning to attract a crowd. Women and children are taking great pains to walk in the opposite direction. So, please get a hold on yourself. I need you down here and not in a Chicago jail cell."

"OK, I think I get the picture. What do you want to do?" Sam asked in a calmer tone.

"Well, I thought you'd want to hear the news as quickly as possible, so I need to spend some time with Miguel to assess the damage and implications. Maybe they have backups, and we can still move forward with our data extraction plan, but I'm doubting that will be an alternative. I'm thinking this was all staged to keep us from getting the data we need. You got any thoughts?"

"I think your assessment is spot on. I also think it's best to play along. Don't let Miguel or anyone see any negative reaction from you that would indicate you don't believe him. Act concerned and ask if there's anything we can do to help them. Then, of course, work your way into asking Miguel what implications this all has on our data requests. Don't help him by suggesting anything. Let him talk at his own pace. Make sure we have a contemporaneous record of everything you see and hear.

"Stupid hocus-pocus all-time worst lie I've heard in my entire career!" Sam said balling his free hand into a fist.

"Noted. I'm going to walk over to Miguel to have a chat and then call you back. You're going to go to your office and tell Maggie to book you on the next available flight for Guatemala City whereupon you and I will meet, with alcohol in front of us, and figure out our next move. How does that sound?"

"About to hop on the elevator. I'll have Maggie book my flight and let you know when I'll arrive. Stay safe. I'm worried about you."

"Count on it, Sam. Safe travels."

CHAPTER 25

"**M**AGGIE, BOOK ME to Guatemala City and let Veronica know the arrangements. Don't book a return."

"Well, I'd make a pithy comment, but I think your day is about to be ruined."

"Why?"

"Louis Bittle said he needs to see you when you get in, and he had a sour demeanor."

"That's his natural state." Sam feared the worst. "Send him in."

Sam sat at his desk… waiting.

"Morning, Sam. I'm afraid I have some bad news, so I'll get right to it." Louis walked up to Sam's desk not taking a seat. "Martha Crunchner called this morning telling me it was leadership's decision to terminate Veronica Martinez immediately. She didn't care who informed her, but I'm guessing you'd prefer to carry that news."

"Louis, this is bullshit, and you know it!

Louis had no response.

Sam stood, hands on his hips, looking down at his desk seemingly searching for a way out. "I want a name."

"I told you, Martha Crunchner is who—"

"Not a damn admin person. I want to talk with those in leadership who made this decision."

"Sam, Martha's a partner serving on Firm Council in her capacity as the Global HR Director. I'm guessing leadership voted, and she was elected to be the one to serve up their decision. It's done, Sam. We simply need to carry out their orders."

Sam thought some more. "It's *not* done. I want to be heard."

"Sam, it is done. It's now our—"

"You're not hearing me, Louis," Sam said leaning into him, his knuckles on top of his desk. "I want an audience with whoever made this decision. I don't care who I need to meet with, just make it happen. I am the leader of this practice and one of the top revenue-producing partners in this firm. I'm pissed, and I want to be heard."

"Sam, I don't think you understand—"

"No, Louis, *you* are the one who doesn't seem to understand! So, let me make this easy on you. I sit on the Chicago leadership committee, and in a few months, we will be discussing the performance of a lot of folks in this office, and you are on that list. If you want me as a supporter, then you need to make this happen."

"That sounds like a threat," Louis said, his body rigid, standing a bit taller, fists clinched at his side and frowning at Sam.

"It is!" Sam said staring at Louis Bittle as if he could will him to do what he demanded. Louis's demeanor softened immediately as he got the point.

"I'll see what I can do, Sam… but I can't make any promises."

Sam brushed by him on his way out the door. "Get this done, Louis, or I will remember your failure, and it won't go well for you in this year's evaluation." Sam left his office without a glance at Louis Bittle. He knew what a weakling he was and preferred not to see him stand there trembling and mouthing excuses. Louis would also know Sam was a man of his word, and he had no desire to update his resume. Sam was confident the show he just put on was enough to get him in front of someone who would see it his way. He now had to figure out what to say.

Maggie informed Sam there was a flight leaving O'Hare in four hours and landing Guatemala City at 11:30 tonight. He went home to pack.

He was stressed to the limit and poured himself a scotch and then fell asleep in his Barcalounger. Sam's BlackBerry vibrated awakening him. "Veronica, are you—?"

"Sam, we've got a situation here I haven't encountered before. I'm scared. I don't know what to do!"

"Veronica, where are you now? Are you safe? Tell me what's going on."

"The note reads: *We will slit your throat. We will send you home in a body bag.* I'm scared, Sam. I don't know what to do. What should I do? I'm so scared," she said menacingly, her voice trembling.

Sam was on his feet now. "Veronica, calm down. Please calm down and tell me where you are."

"OK, sorry, I'm in my hotel room."

"Are you alone?"

"Yes, I'm alone. Oh, it's so good to hear your voice. I'm feeling better already. I'm sitting down. Keep talking. It's so good to hear your voice."

"Is your door locked?"

"Yes, the door is locked, and the chain is on too."

"Take a deep breath, Veronica. Relax. It doesn't sound like you are in immediate danger. I'm not going anywhere. I will stay on this phone for as long as you need me."

The usually calm and confident Veronica was returning rapidly, her tone now communicating an embarrassed young lady who wanted desperately to replay the last sixty seconds.

"Oh, I'm so embarrassed. I wish I could blame it all on being under the influence. I'm so sorry for sounding like a child."

Sam could hear her fighting back tears and trying desperately to mask it. "Please, Veronica, you are the toughest person in this practice, and you are on an incredibly stressful and difficult investigation. You have nothing to apologize for. Now, as soon as you're ready, I'm not rushing you, take your time, but tell me everything that happened since we last talked."

The long pause would have concerned Sam, but he heard her heavy breathing and felt she needed a little more time to compose herself. This was his star athlete, and he was happy to grant her all the time she needed. For a rare moment in his life, Sam found himself actually being patient.

"So, I finished up with Miguel at the plant, you know, the break-in at the computer room we talked about earlier."

"Was Miguel helpful? Any new findings?"

"Nothing new, and yes, Miguel was helpful."

"He wasn't threatening?"

"No, Miguel's great. I didn't get upset until I returned to my room and found this note shoved under my door."

Sam could sense her about to get upset again, but she quickly regained her composure and continued, "It was the note that upset me."

"Veronica, do you feel comfortable reading me the entire note?"

"Yes, I'll read it. It's in Spanish, so I'll translate, *You are swine and like swine we will slit your throat and your blood will drain and slowly and painfully you will die. We will send you home in a body bag if you do not leave now.* That's it. That's all it says. No signature, no letterhead, no indication of where it came from. I can't call the police. I'm sure Mendoza has them on his payroll."

"Unfortunately, I agree with you. Give me a minute."

Sam had a dozen questions about the letter itself but did not want to belabor it as he was no expert in these matters anyway. The important thing was Veronica was terribly upset, and he needed to assure her nothing could harm her. That was the best thing he could do for her right now.

"Veronica, here's what's going to happen: I'm calling Derek Dorn with CRI as soon as I hang up with you. I think he's still in-country. We'll need their guys to begin work before we send down a full team as originally planned. Derek will identify a security team to remain with you twenty-four/seven, and I will call you with the name of your contact person."

"Sam, that won't be necessary. I'm OK now."

"I'm not doing this for you. I'm doing this for me. I would kill myself if anything happened to you. So, we are doing this, and I'm not asking for your permission. Now, be quiet and listen to me, please."

As she acquiesced and they continued to talk, Sam could tell his concern for her safety was restoring her well-being, and she appeared pleased with his reaction to this latest event. Sam knew it would not be long before the old Veronica was back and fully functional, but first things first, he needed to be assured she was safe. Then, he needed to figure out the meaning of this turn of events and how it might alter their plans.

"So, Veronica, are we clear? You are not going anywhere until I call you back with the security guard's name and ID number. You are to stay put. No room service either. Clear? Agreed?"

"OK, Sam. We're clear. But make sure they send over the best-looking hunk they have on staff. If I'm getting a new friend, he'd better be gorgeous."

"You know I couldn't care less about what he looks like, but I will assure you he will lay down his life to protect you. Sit tight, I will be calling you right back. Pour yourself a drink and watch Telemundo."

"Ha! I'd call you a racist, but I get what you're doing. I'll stay put and wait for your call. You still coming down?"

"Actually, I'll be landing at eleven-thirty tonight. I'll see you very soon. Stay safe."

Sam called Derek. He was no longer in-country but still had a team there. Sam then called Veronica back with the credentials of her new security guard who would be knocking on her door in an hour. He had one more call he had to make before he could call it a day.

He wanted to update Dave Rogers, especially about the threatening note.

"Hey, Sam. You miss me already?"

"Dave, you know I can't get through a day without your constant supervision."

"Ha! I think I know a lie when I hear one. What's up?"

"I wanted to update you on something that happened in Guatemala today. Veronica is OK, but she received a threatening note… slipped under her hotel room door."

Sam proceeded to update Dave on the data center break-in at the plant—well, at least what was reported to Veronica. Dave laughed at the news. He too recognized the lunacy of it all but had to admit it was a sure-fire way to keep them from the data. Just say it was stolen. Dave said thus far in the investigation, he'd score it ten points for Team Mendoza and zero points for Team Halloran. Sam cussed him out… just a little.

"I do have a bit of good news," Dave said.

"Please give it to me. I need it badly."

"Got a call from Henry Metcalf at Lawrence & Metcalf. He wants to engage us in the Chicago Public Schools scandal you've probably been reading about in the *Trib*."

"Sorry, Dave. I haven't read a paper in weeks. I have no idea what you are talking about."

"Began a couple of weeks ago. Apparently, there've been anonymous reports to a reporter at the *Trib* about all kinds of fraud at CPS. Links to the State House, Mayor's Office, Aldermen, local businesses. Looks like a big mess. Even roped in some of the local mafia families in alleged construction bid-rigging allegations."

"Dave, sounds like a great case. Congratulations!"

"Thanks. Henry feels confident he can get authorization to sign an engagement letter with us by end of the week. His client is the Illinois Inspector General. Wants us to begin as soon as possible."

Sam thought for a moment about his issue with Laura. "Dave, anyway you can assign Laura Wittford to that investigation?"

"Of course. She'd be great with her audit experience. Consider it done. You can call and tell her."

"Actually, I'd appreciate it if you could let her know. I don't think she'd want to talk to me any time soon."

Dave laughed. "So, you told her you weren't going to assign her to Project Vista and now I've got to bail you out."

"You're used to bailing me out. That's why I keep your old sorry ass around."

"Seriously, Sam. I totally understand why you made that call, and no one would fault you for it. Hell, with just today and that mess you told me about with Veronica proves you've got good instincts. Don't worry about Laura. She's going to be a great addition to the practice."

"At least I'll feel more comfortable that under your tutelage she won't go running off to New York. She can learn a lot from you."

"Not a problem, Sam. Glad to have her."

"Well, I've got to get to the airport for my flight to Guatemala City. Better signoff now. Thanks again, Dave."

Sam didn't let Dave know about his problem with Veronica, what the final verdict was on her future. He may enlist his support later, but Dave just gave him an idea. He'd have to think about it a little more, but it just might work.

CHAPTER 26

"MIGUEL HERRERA, IT is your *Jefe*, Javier Mendoza. Is this a convenient time to talk?"

"Yes, of course, *Señor* Mendoza. What can I do for you?" Miguel said.

"Are you in your office?"

"*Sí, Señor.*"

"Are you alone?"

"*Sí, Señor.* What can I do for you?"

"Is your office door closed?"

Miguel now stood from his chair. Javier Mendoza was acting unlike any time before. Miguel steadied his nerve. "*Sí, Sí, Señor, Jefe.*"

"I need you to do something for me. Something especially important. Something that must be done with precision. Something that if not done properly can make things extremely uncomfortable for me… and for you."

"*Señor Jefe*, have I done something to displease you? Please tell me what this is, and I will fix it."

"Relax, Miguel, you have done nothing which displeases me.

Not yet anyway. But I know you are a religious man and what I am about to ask of you may cause you to become… uncomfortable."

"Nothing could be so. I am here to do anything you wish. Just ask it of me, and I will do it," Miguel said as he felt himself begin to sweat.

"This is good to hear," Javier said smiling, then laughing, as if talking to a friend and sharing good times. "You are telling me comforting words. Maybe I am concerned for no reason. But tell me something."

"Yes, *Jefe*, anything," Miguel said, sweat broken out across his forehead, his hands shaking.

"Whose decision was it to paint your daughter's bedroom pink? It is such a lovely color for a little girl. Especially one so pretty as her. Was it her idea or someone else perhaps?"

Miguel Herrera fell back into his chair and could not speak. He began sweating profusely, shaking, knowing Javier Mendoza was talking to him from his sixteen-year-old daughter's bedroom. He immediately imagined the worst. "*Jefe*, please. This is not necessary. What have I done to displease you?" He began to cry. "Please, *Jefe*. What have you done to my family?" He was sobbing when he fell to his knees.

"Miguel, get a hold of yourself, for God's sake," Javier mocked him. "What kind of man do you think I am?" Miguel knew exactly what kind of man Javier Mendoza was and, more importantly, what he was capable of. "I was in your neighborhood and simply stopped by to visit with your lovely family. Valeria. Am I correct? Valeria is the name of your little girl?"

Miguel was trying to think clearly of where his family was at that moment. His wife Mariana would be working at the market and his precious Valeria would be in school.

"Miguel, you must gather yourself. Your family is fine, but I need you to listen carefully."

"*Sí, Jefe*. Anything. I will do anything you ask of me," Miguel said with laser focus. He was sitting now at his desk so he could write down *El Jefe*'s orders word for word.

"Juan will be there in a few minutes. Simply do as he instructs."

"Juan, yes, *Jefe*. Juan is coming, and I will do as he says. Always, *Jefe*. I will stay here. It will be done."

"Very well, Miguel. You have always proven to be a trusted and loyal servant. I know you will carry out Juan's instructions to the letter. Now, I must go. I am leaving you an envelope on your pretty daughter's bed. It contains a thank you and a reminder that I am a man of my word. Rest easy, Miguel, and do exactly as Juan says."

Miguel hung up, sat in his desk chair, and focused his stare at his office door. He would not move until Juan Romero walked through that door. He began to pray.

Fifteen minutes later, Juan walked into Miguel's office as Javier Mendoza had promised. Miguel was still seated behind his desk, still petrified. Juan pulled up a chair, sat, and told Miguel what he must do. When they finished talking, Miguel would head home. Tonight, he would return to his office. He and Juan would… prepare things. Tomorrow morning, he would pick up Veronica Martinez at eight o'clock at her hotel and bring her to the operations data center located just outside Miguel's office.

Juan handed Miguel detailed instructions including the script of what he would tell Veronica tomorrow. Juan waited until Miguel read it and received confirmation he understood his mission.

"Any questions, Miguel?"

"I understand what I must do. Please tell *El Jefe* I have no issue with this. It will be done exactly as it is written here. No problem. It will be done." Miguel wiped his brow.

"*El Jefe* will be pleased to hear this. Any problems, call me."

"It will be done," Miguel said while trembling, staring blankly at Juan. He repeated it until Juan left his office.

Miguel headed home. He wanted to see for himself that all was in order. He also wanted to retrieve the envelope and its contents before his family got home.

He walked first into his daughter's bedroom and picked up the bulky envelope lying atop his daughter's pillow. The only thing out of place was her favorite doll. It was lying face down on the floor, all clothes stripped from its body. He shuttered at the symbolism. He fell to his knees, broke down, and sobbed.

Moments later, he was in his backyard, alone. He had resealed the contents inside the envelope and set it on fire. He could have used the two extra months' pay but could never forget what it was rolled into—a torn pair of Valeria's underpants.

CHAPTER 27

SAM ARRIVED IN Guatemala City close to midnight. It was not as chilly as Chicago, but it was not like visiting a Caribbean island either. No matter. He didn't expect he'd have a lot of time at the pool.

It would be reassuring to have their own security team. "I'm Manuel Diego from CRI. Your flight was good, no, *Señor* Halloran?" Manuel asked as he met Sam at the gate, holding out his ID badge. It matched what Derek had told him.

"Is Jorge at the hotel with Veronica?" Sam asked, opting to pass on a more courteous greeting.

"You mean Fernando?" Sam nodded. "He is, *Señor*." Manuel didn't think it odd at all that Sam used the wrong name for his partner. He knew what Sam was doing. "Fernando has already informed her of your arrival. *Señorita* Martinez has instructed us to take you to the hotel and get you checked in. She is a nice lady."

"Yes, she is in more ways than you could know."

After wading through customs for over an hour, Sam climbed into Manuel's black SUV. "Do they make any other color of SUV?" Sam asked.

Manuel seemed confused as he pulled out on to the highway for their short ride to the Hotel Barcelo. "I'm sorry, *Señor*?"

"Never mind." Manuel still wore a puzzled look.

"The last time I was in your country my security team skipped the line and took us right past customs, which was very convenient."

"*Sí, Señor*, but they were working for a man who either pays you off or makes you pay. Either way, he controls you, and he owns you. Now you are with Manuel," he said with a smile. "I may take more time to get you where you are going, but I work for you and no one else. 'I have your back,' your American actor Tom Cruise would say, no?"

"Yes, Manuel, you have that right," Sam said with a chuckle. He and Manuel would get along fine. "I like this arrangement much better. So, is Veronica behaving herself?" Sam said while looking into Manuel's face to gauge his reaction.

Manuel paused for what seemed a long time as if searching for the right words. "She is energetic. A happy sort, no?"

"I would have chosen other adjectives, but I think we agree. She will be difficult to keep in line." They came to a stoplight. Sam held his index finger up as if to emphasize what he was about to say. "But understand this, Manuel. Veronica means a lot to me. You need to understand that. If anything should happen to her—"

"*Señor*, she is our primary concern," Manuel said. "I know where you are coming from. I have instructed Fernando. He is my brother. He will listen to me. Also, Derek filled me in of your conversation. She will be safe."

"If she will not listen to you or Fernando, you are to inform me immediately. Is that clear?" The light turned green.

"Perfectly. I, too, have a daughter. She is just fourteen, but I do understand a father's love for his daughter. How I must ensure her protection."

"Well, Veronica is not my daughter, but I worry for her as you worry for your daughter. I think we understand each other."

"*Sí*." Manuel nodded his head.

"Manuel, I noticed several custom officials appeared to be searching the crowd for someone."

"*Sí, Señor*, they are again looking for someone. This is not unusual. This is Central America. We are right on the line of drug trafficking: Produced in Columbia, then transported to your country by the Mexican gangs. We know they travel through our country all day and every day. We want no trouble, and most days that is how we have it."

On the drive to the hotel, Sam began to reflect on the task that lay ahead. Not the investigation... Veronica. At least he was able to buy some time. Leadership would have to meet with him. They might have their heads up their asses on most days, but they would grant Sam this accommodation. Not that he expected them to set this whole mess aside, at least not with the stakes currently on the table. If they didn't, Sam would increase those stakes. He would do whatever it took to retain Veronica.

Still, Sam would have to faceoff with Veronica on the substance of the issue. He knew she played it loose with her personal choices. He could not have his management team sleeping with their staff. What was she thinking? He knew what she'd say. That she wasn't thinking. How would he answer that one? He didn't want to. He'd rather face trying to extract a confession out of a serial killer than confront Veronica about this, but there really was no alternative. He'd have to sit down with her... soon.

As Manuel pulled up to the hotel lobby's entrance, Sam was thankful they had arrived. It would be their base of operation, their safe space.

"What time is it?"

Manuel glanced at his watch. "It is zero-one-forty-five, *Señor.*"

"Well, that answers one of my questions. You are former military, yes?"

"*Sí, Señor.* Most everyone I know in this line of work is former military. It is good training for what we do. It is a good job what we do. Fernando and I, we make good money and someday we will have things, beautiful things." Manual opened the hotel lobby's door and carried in Sam's bags. The hotel valet attempted to take the bags, but Manuel grunted him away.

After Sam checked in they entered the elevator, and Manuel pushed the button for the twenty-fifth floor. "I want to check on Veronica right away," Sam said.

"Her room is the first on the left. We will find Fernando sitting in the hallway outside her door. Yours is at the end of the hall—the penthouse." Sam was so focused on her he missed the *penthouse* part.

Walking down the hallway, Sam became nervous seeing an empty chair... no Fernando. He moved quickly and pounded on the door to Veronica's room. Momentarily, Fernando opened the door. Manuel was the first to walk in the room, followed by Sam.

Veronica jumped up from her chaise lounge on the balcony wearing a tight top that revealed her ample breasts, lots of skin, and... about the total amount of cloth to make one of Sam's handkerchiefs.

"About time you got here!" She walked over and hugged him.

He looked at Fernando, who was standing close by, hands on his hips. He shrugged as if to say, *She's a wild one. What do you want me to say?* Manuel looked confused. Sam's face showed his displeasure. Veronica sluffed off the whole scene.

"Oh, relax, Sammy. Fernando and I were just lounging outside in the cool night air having a nightcap and waiting for you. I wouldn't try anything knowing you were coming. Now, what can I get you to drink?"

"Not for me. It's late, or early, rather. I'm hitting the sack. Let's talk at breakfast," Sam said in businesslike fashion.

Sam turned away from Veronica and looked at Manuel who could read his mind. "Yes, *Señor*. Fernando and I are sharing a room directly across the hall." Sam wondered if that was too convenient.

"We will have a night security guard positioned in the hallway where he will remain until zero-seven-hundred. If you require nothing further for tonight, we, too, will retire."

"Sounds good, Manuel. Let's all get a good night sleep. The battle begins bright and early tomorrow. Veronica, I will see you at seven-thirty for breakfast. We have an appointment with our Guatemalan lawyer at ten o'clock. We both need to be on our toes for that meeting."

"Wow, you waste no time. When did you arrange that?"

"Returned Rodney Phillips's call when I landed. He arranged it. Loved getting him out of bed. At his rates, he won't complain."

Sam gave her one last stern look. "So, seven-thirty. Be on time."

"Yes, sir, on time. Yes, sir!" Veronica saluted in mock military fashion coming to attention. Sam ignored her.

The three of them walked toward the door to leave. "Goodnight, Fernando," Veronica said, playfully. Sam purposely did not look at either of them fearing what that comment might portend. He silently wished Fernando were not the Latino hunk he was certain Veronica was thrilled to have by her side. It was all bad timing.

Sam entered his room and flipped on the light. He marveled at the sheer size of the... suite of rooms he'd be living in for who-knew-how-long. He wanted to tour it, but his exhaustion won out. Moments after walking into his bedroom, he was asleep almost immediately.

He awoke just a few hours later. This would be a big day and he wanted to go over his notes before meeting with Veronica. He needed her alert and sharp for this meeting. Sitting on the edge of his bed, he began to take in his room and thought he might be in the wrong place.

The bedroom alone was half the size of his Chicago condo and looked more like a player's suite in Vegas—satin furniture, gold leaf wallpaper, and elaborately flowing drapes that extended from a ceiling at least ten feet high, vaulted, mirrored, and lighted. It all seemed way overdone. No doubt, this had been the scene for parties of the rich and famous and now wasted on Sam.

Meandering out his bedroom in search of the coffee pot, he flipped on a couple more lights and walked into a full-sized kitchen that doubled as an elaborate bar. Continuing through his *new home*, he stepped down into a lavish dining room that opened into a massive living room with another vaulted ceiling more modestly stated but just as prodigious. Before him was a coffee table as big as a bed surrounded by an L-shaped sofa grouping. As he stood there taking it all in, he was reminded of his mission to find the coffee pot about to be deferred upon noticing a wall of somewhat transparent drapes. Through the drapes, Sam was looking at an enormous patio that beckoned him to enter.

He pulled the drapes aside, slid the patio doors open, and stepped onto a tiled floor surrounded by ivy covered walls, bordered with shrubbery and flowers. His was the top floor. Nothing above but a slowly dawning sky. He was immediately transported into the gardens of the Tuscany region of Italy where he'd visited many years ago. The place seemed more like an elegant vacation home. Fortunately, the doorbell ringing brought him back to reality, and for a moment, the challenge was to find the entry door, allowing Manuel to enter.

"Good morning, *Señor* Halloran, I trust you had a pleasant night's rest."

"Manuel, please come in and experience this place. I am blown away by it."

"Not to bother you, *Señor*. I only wanted you to be aware my brother and I are here and at your service. I will sit here just outside your door and await your instructions.

"No, please come in. There is no sense for you to sit outside. Is Veronica up?"

Manuel looked sheepish. "She is. She and Fernando are having coffee on her balcony." His look foretold Sam would not be pleased hearing how well the two of them were getting on.

"Manuel, I realize Veronica is a handful, but you need to instruct your brother—"

"Do not worry, *Señor*. Fernando is a professional. He knows his duty and his limits. We talked last night."

"Good, so come on in."

Holding up his hands and refusing to cross the threshold was a polite way to communicate he was the consummate professional and knew he could better fulfill his appointed duty of securing their safety from the hallway, especially considering his brother was otherwise occupied. Sam honored his wishes and acknowledged his better judgment saying, "You're right. You should know what is best when it comes to security, and I appreciate your insistence. I need to shower and change and should be ready to go down to breakfast in thirty minutes. Please inform Veronica."

"*Sí, Señor*, I am at your disposal. Just call if you need anything."

Dressed and now ready for the day ahead, Sam exited his room. Manuel immediately leaped from his hallway chair.

"Please check on *that*?" Sam said pointing to Veronica's door. "I'll meet you in the restaurant."

"*Señor*, Veronica and Fernando are in the restaurant about ten minutes ago."

As if she was watching him, Sam's phone vibrated.

"Morning, boss. Just checking in, mainly to mollify your concerns about my whereabouts, which happen to be in a booth in the lobby restaurant, eager and famished to have breakfast. Where the hell are you?"

"I'm coming now. See you soon."

Sam looked at Manuel. He shrugged his shoulders as Sam shook his head.

As they walked toward the elevator Manuel asked, "May I ask what is the schedule today?"

"Certainly. After breakfast, Veronica and I will have some things to discuss. We are due at the attorney's office at ten o'clock followed by a meeting with the IT director from Abello. I'm not sure where that meeting is taking place. Veronica arranged it. Then, I suppose we play it by ear."

"Very well, *Señor*. May I have the address of the law firm so I can plan our route?" Sam gave it to him.

The elevator doors opened to a lobby sparsely populated with hotel guests beginning their day. It was still somewhat dark outside, a reminder that regardless of the milder temperature it was still winter. Manuel led the way to the hotel restaurant, and Sam felt ready to tackle the day knowing Manuel and Fernando had their backs. Still, he was not looking forward to meeting with another lawyer.

CHAPTER 28

Wednesday, January 21

SAM WAS PLEASED to see Veronica across the restaurant sitting in a booth, alone. Fernando sat at the bar. His brother positioned by the kitchen door.

"Good morning, *Señorita* Veronica," Sam said.

"Don't start with me. My head feels like it's about to explode."

"What happened to that vibrant person I just talked with on the phone?"

"She's still here, just buried deep within."

"That's what happens when you overindulge in the spirits and deprive your body of needed sleep. Well, at least that's what I'm told, anyway."

"Can we please dispense with the father-daughter diatribe and get down to business? I need more coffee," she said, scanning the restaurant in search of their waiter.

At first, Sam thought she was kidding, but now it was obvious she was not in the best of moods. Regardless, he let her have some space. This was an important day, and even at seventy-five percent Veronica was the best in her class.

"Did you arrange for our own private section over here?"

"I figured you'd want some privacy. Manager told me he expected a light crowd. Not exactly tourist season. He was happy to close off this section. But maybe he should have told his waiter to take better care of us!"

With an anxious wave from Veronica, their waiter finally came, and judging from her tone, Veronica made him pay for his tardiness. That course correction at least produced our breakfast in record time. Seated across from her, Sam leaned in a little, and she did the same. "So, main topic with the lawyer today is to find some legal cause of action to remove Mendoza. If that's possible, it will save us a great deal of time, worry, and our client's money. If not, we're in for a real battle, more likely a war, especially considering the size of Mendoza's security."

"I don't think you told me about that."

"Sorry, so here's the deal, CRI estimates his security team numbers upwards of 160 guards, which greatly exceeds the contract Steve had on file. Recently, CRI determined he's been using a different company, *Protección*, owned and operated by his brother-in-law. They further estimated he paid them $2,000,000 over the past twelve months. Steve couldn't confirm anything close to that number. God only knows how Mendoza is hiding that from the company and our audit brethren."

"Not difficult to hide even that amount of cash in an operation this big."

"Point taken. Anyway, let me go down the list of issues you found as you searched the computer room to ensure I have them all when we meet with the lawyer," Sam said as he glanced at his watch. "According to Manuel, we should be leaving here around nine o'clock to arrive by ten o'clock. Apparently he wants to take the long way."

Sam went through all the items on her list regarding the break-in at the computer room, and they agreed on the approach to take with the lawyer. They also did a little role-playing with Veronica playing the lawyer. Trying to anticipate....

Veronica finished her toast and jelly and what was now her third cup of coffee. She seemed perfectly fine, alert and engaged.

"So, boss, are you going to send staff out to the plant if you can't do anything about disbursing Mendoza's army?"

"Not a chance. Too dangerous. I think he's capable of anything, and I am not putting any of you in that kind of danger.

"Here comes Fernando," Sam said as he stood.

Moments later, Fernando helped Veronica into Manuel's SUV, Sam jumped in next to her as Fernando slid into the passenger seat.

"I am noticing a lot of security personnel walking around with automatic rifles or machine pistols. What's the deal, Manuel?" Sam asked as they drove through the business district of Guatemala City.

"We are no longer in the tourist section. A lot of business, legal and illegal, is transacted every day here. If you are a businessman and you do not have your own personal security, you are asking for trouble."

When they arrived at the office building housing the law firm, Manuel pulled close to the main entrance and stopped. Fernando was quick to jump out and hold the door for Veronica. Sam exited on the other side and moved around to join them while Fernando did a 360-degree visual sweep. He said something that prompted Veronica to translate. "He's telling us to hurry." Sam obliged without question. In a moment, they were standing in the lobby of the law firm with Fernando at their side. "He said he would not be permitted to accompany us to the law offices, but we would be safe in the building," Veronica informed Sam.

Fernando pointed to an area where he'd be waiting for them after the meeting and under no circumstances were they to step outside the building without him. Sam looked to where he was pointing and saw a smoke-filled area with a dozen or so guards. He assured Fernando they would do as he instructed and thanked him. Manuel would remain with the SUV, pointed in the right direction for takeoff, his motor running.

Sam and Veronica walked through an area in the lobby much like the entrance of the federal building on Dearborn Street in Chicago. They passed some athletic looking guards—not at all troubling to Sam. Actually, it made him feel safer.

Enrico Blanco extended his hand first to Veronica and then to Sam, but he lingered his eyes on her longer than Sam felt appropriate. Veronica didn't seem to mind; she appeared to enjoy the attention. She could handle anyone who tried to overstep her bounds—at least, that's what Sam hoped.

Blanco was a short, rather plump man dressed in a suit that made Sam's look like he'd bought it from JC Penney. The offices were well-appointed, which surprised Sam from the poor condition of the outside of the building. After seating them in a small conference room and attending to their beverage needs, they got down to business.

Sam deferred his typical casual get-to-know-you demeanor. His experience working similar engagements was that no successful lawyer could operate in a country like this unless he was corrupt. It wasn't fair but that's the basket he'd already thrown Enrico Blanco into. He doubted seriously if he would hear anything close to what they wanted to hear—some legal way they could remove Mendoza. He was here only at the insistence of Rodney Bishop, his *client*. Well, at least in form. "*Señor* Blanco, I understand you have had at least an initial discussion with Steve Lemly?"

"Yes, *Señor* Lemly and I spoke on two occasions now. He instructed me to treat you as my client and you would be conducting an investigation into allegations discovered in a letter sent to him anonymously."

"Yes, that's correct."

"And how is your investigation proceeding?"

"We are in the beginning stages. I first met with *Señor* Mendoza on January 12th at his office. During that meeting, it was clear Mendoza was, let's say, less than authentic."

"Could you please expand?"

"Mendoza lied to me on two occasions, and it was clear he did not want me to proceed with an investigation into the allegations identified in the letter."

"Yes, the letter. *Señor* Lemly was kind to forward me a copy." Blanco lowered his head, wiped his mouth with a white linen napkin, and cleared his throat. "You do understand, *Señor* Halloran, the status of the employees at *Señor* Mendoza's plant, do you not?"

"What do you mean by *status*?"

"But you see, these are mere peasants. It is most likely one of whom doesn't like *Señor* Mendoza and desires to damage his reputation. Matters such as this surface from time to time in my country. We deal with them in a manner that is instructive to the kind of respect someone like *Señor* Mendoza deserves," he said with a glib smirk. Sam held his polite but uncompromising manner. Sam's concerns about working with local counsel seemed to be confirmed.

"Yes, well, Abello is not *Señor* Mendoza's plant, and he is an employee of Hampton Enterprises. Just as valuable as the person who had the courage to write that letter. Where I come from all employees are treated with respect, and I can assure you each of these employees in question will receive all the respect they deserve."

Ignoring Sam's comment, Enrico Blanco tendered a look of pity on yet another naïve American before he moved on with his next question. "You said you believed *Señor* Mendoza lied to you. May I ask why you believe this?"

Sam gave Blanco a brief account of his use of CRI and the information they supplied. How he used it to get Mendoza to lie. He did so without disclosing the exact nature of those facts. He was quick to respond and less deferential in his delivery. It was clear Sam was beginning to rub him the wrong way, a trait Sam seemed destined to display from time-to-time. Sam didn't care. He just wanted to get through this meeting, check it off his list, and get on with an investigation.

"*Señor* Blanco, you seem put-off by the use of deception in my interview with *Señor* Mendoza. Am I reading you correctly?"

He seemed a bit startled by Sam's directness but responded unapologetically. "We in my country are more courteous and respectful of others, but I understand how you Americans are at times."

"I see. So, courteous and respectful, you say. Well I have another impression of *Señor* Mendoza from my observations of how he treats his workers, especially the women; how he… " Sam caught himself and took a sip of his tea.

Blanco shifted in his chair. "Well, *Señor* Halloran, your observations of this one man should not reflect on all men of my country."

"Fair enough. Then I will ask the same of you."

Blanco was obviously taken off-guard but suddenly appeared more amenable. After a brief pause to allow the dust to settle, Sam returned to a more businesslike and courteous posture. "So, Veronica came down two days ago with a list of data requests that, due to unforeseen circumstances, they were not able to fulfill. Veronica, why don't you go through your list of what you found?"

"Sure, Sam." Turning to face Blanco, Veronica began giving him an account of what she found. She ended with, "I thought Miguel's explanation of events… odd."

"And why did you this think this odd?" Blanco asked in a dismissive tone.

"Because these people struggle to provide food on the table for their families," Veronica lashed out. "Makes no sense to commit a crime which would not produce anything of value for them. I haven't checked, but I doubt there is much of a market for used computer hard drives. Makes no sense."

Blanco stared at Veronica, not so quick to challenge her again.

Veronica gave him more details about how the *thieves* supposedly entered and what they took. Veronica then paused to take a sip of water, but what Blanco didn't realize was that this staging was all planned ahead by the two of them. Sam wanted her to deliver just the facts and allow the lawyer to give them his interpretation.

"So, what do you make of all this?" Sam asked.

Blanco began, "Well, I need to learn more, but it does strike me as odd there would be a break-in at the distillery and the thieves would spend such obvious amounts of time in the computer room, unless, of course, they were looking for data, or trying to cover-up something. Did they report anything of value taken from other parts of the plant?"

"You mean like a few hundred cases of rum? No, nothing. Nothing else was reported stolen. Only the theft of computer hard drives."

As Veronica continued, Blanco wrote something down and signaled to his clerk who dutifully hurried off with it. Veronica paused for a moment when he apologized for the interruption and asked her to continue.

Blanco looked to the ceiling as if pondering the scene and the report of computer hard drives being stolen. He continued to look bewildered, obviously playing out the scene in his mind's eye. "And what would they do with the hard drives? I just find that entire explanation completely preposterous," he finally said.

Unless this was just an incredible act to throw them off track, Blanco was doing a good job of convincing Sam he just might be on their side. Maybe Sam was too hasty in his profiling.

He motioned Veronica to continue.

"That's about it, except Miguel said due to what happened, they would not be able to comply with our data request." And with that, Veronica stopped and laid down her notes on the coffee table in front of her. Grabbing her tea, she crossed her legs and relaxed back into her chair while she and Sam sat silently waiting for Blanco to say something.

Blanco's clerk returned with a document and handed it to him stepping back, hands clasped in front of her waiting for his next command. He studied the document for a moment. "I asked my clerk to check and see if a report had been filed with the PNC, our national police. In my hands is a copy of a report filed with them all in the proper order. It was filed by Miguel Herrera who, if I remember correctly, you told me was the IT director. From my quick review, it appears to follow the chain of events and discoveries you have told me. So, if this was, as I am sure you suspect, a cover for them failing to honor your data request, they are at least taking it down the correct path."

"So, *Señor* Blanco, what do you recommend?"

He held his reading glasses by the stem with the other stem in his mouth and looking off. He laid his glasses on the coffee table, folded his hands across his ample belly, and repositioned himself in his queen Anne chair. "That depends on what you want to accomplish and how much time, effort, and money our client is willing to invest."

"*Señor* Blanco, *invest* is a strange word to use in this context."

"Because money expended for such purposes is money *invested* in relationships."

Sam cocked his head to indicate he did not understand. He actually did, but he wanted Blanco to say it.

"Shall I put it this way. This is a country where things are facilitated much the same way they are done in your country. Things, shall we say, one would not want the general public knowing about. In America, or so I understand it this way, such things are handled in remunerations made *under the table*; however, in my country, such things are handled *over the table* in plain sight. You see, my government does not pay their public servants well, such as police officers and judges, knowing they will supplement their incomes in resourceful ways. Am I making my point clear?"

"Very clear, I'm afraid. The problem is I am working for a US public company. As such, they are barred from making payments to influence actions and decisions on the part of those who participate in government, particularly with members of the judiciary and its enforcement officials. And Javier Mendoza, as an agent of Hampton Enterprises, enjoins the company in all his actions. So, if he's doing something illegal, Hampton Enterprises is doing something illegal." Blanco squinted and smirked at Sam.

"Hear me out, *Señor* Blanco," Sam said, holding up his hand as if to cement his point. "There is no way my client, our client, would consider paying bribes and kickbacks, and if they did occur, they would not have been sanctioned by corporate. Those would have been handled by local management, for sure."

Blanco shrugged his shoulders as if conceding the point but believing Sam was being naïve.

"With this option off the table, what legal means can you suggest for our client to pursue removing *Señor* Mendoza from his position as the general manager of Abello?"

"Absent engaging in the activities I mentioned, there are no legal options which could accomplish this for our client. None."

"I can't accept that."

"Let me explain further. The PNC will not investigate private actions, such as this break-in at the plant, unless you pay them out of corporate funds, an action I would not suggest as it would be a complete waste of time and money. Even if they did investigate and even if they did find evidence of a cover-up, which would be completely out of the realm of possibilities in my estimation, but let's suppose it happened that way, the only way to bring a penal action is through a local magistrate who reviews evidence and determines which matters may be actionable.

"*Señor* Mendoza will pay whatever is necessary to deny any action against him or his people. And the magistrate will gladly accept such payment. I expect he has done it many times before and will not hesitate to do it again. And let's suppose in the best of circumstances the magistrate agrees to bring charges and this matter finds its way into the courts, again, you will find *Señor* Mendoza bribing the sitting judge to obtain the ruling he desires. It is at this point our client will deeply regret pursuing an action against their GM. Because if we bring penal charges against a powerful and influential man such as *Señor* Mendoza and we lose, the defendant can then sue Hampton for damages.

"I can virtually guarantee such a lawsuit will most surely result in a large civil judgment in favor of *Señor* Mendoza. Hampton would appeal the decision, and it would take years to make it through the process. In the meantime, our client could, at any time, see the local authorities expropriate their plant to satisfy such judgment. Under the right circumstances and for the right money, the authorities might even sell it to *Señor* Mendoza at a nominal cost, all of which would be absorbed by the local courts to cover their *fees*."

Enrico Blanco paused to take a sip of his tea, patting his mouth with a cloth napkin, thus providing Sam time to consider his comments... warnings.

Sam got his meaning without further commentary or time to consider the implications. He didn't doubt Blanco's prophecy. It almost made his investigation a complete waste of time, but Sam wasn't willing to accept it. Still, there would be no point in challenging him. Better he believes Sam bought it all.

"I see," Sam said, trying hard to hold back his contempt for a lawyer who could work, day after day, in such a corrupt system. "It sounds like there are no viable options for Hampton to pursue a legal remedy to their predicament. What, then, would you suggest we do?"

"Your choices are quite limited at this point, and without being too critical of our client's past actions, I would say they should have set the ground rules and implemented proper monitoring safeguards long before breaking ground on the plant itself. So, many years down the road, we find ourselves in an awfully bad place and, in my view, Hampton is left with only one choice.

"The company must see they have learned a costly lesson, guard themselves with reliable security, get good insurance, don't place their trust in only one person, reestablish better controls and monitoring of activities, lick their wounds, learn from this, and move forward."

"Are you insane?" Sam was out of line, but he didn't care. "That's the best advice you can come up with? Just pick up our marbles, go home, and call it a day? This guy Mendoza is the devil incarnate!"

Enrico Blanco was unmoved by Sam's outburst.

"With the network of politicians, police, and other government officials he's been paying off," Sam continued, "he's likely putting the company in danger of violating US law, which is just a matter of time before it's discovered. And that's not to mention the deplorable conditions and acts of servitude he foists upon his employees daily that are morally repugnant.

"It sounds like you are suggesting we meet with Mendoza, concede this one, and negotiate a way to move forward with him still running the plant? You must be out of your mind if you honestly believe that's a suggestion I would countenance with any action on my part. That is a maniacal course of action."

Sam stood and grabbed his briefcase, signaling he was done. Veronica stood as well. Blanco rose and stepped in their path, both arms extended in a calm manner. He had one additional parting comment.

"Please, *Señor* and *Señorita*, I implore you both if you pursue what I believe you are planning and attempt in any way to try and dismantle the organization Javier Mendoza has spent the last nearly two decades investing in and building, it will most certainly end very badly for you and your client. Javier Mendoza retains all the power with his hold on Abello by virtue of the support of the company's stakeholders; and I am not speaking of the stakeholders of Hampton Enterprises worldwide, but of the facilitators and partners Mendoza has put in place.

"You must know also that your plant is sitting on sovereign soil, and he will do anything to protect his investment. Javier Mendoza is *the* legal representative of Hampton Enterprises in this country, and he could have you legally arrested, tried, convicted, and thrown in jail where I can assure you will never leave alive. This is the way things are in my country. I have given you good advice, and I beg that you sincerely consider it for your own safety."

Blanco had finished his speech, and for the moment Sam was pondering what Blanco had said. Sam's opinion of Blanco's loyalties had vacillated throughout the meeting, and at this point Sam still wasn't certain which side he was supporting. After a brief and silent analysis, he decided Blanco supported any client and any position where he could make a reasonable amount of money staying within not necessarily the rule of law but the expectations of those in power in this hellhole of a country.

Sam remained standing in the same place, a moment or two longer than he really wanted. He considered his options, not with rational thought but rather from instinct.

He did not want to do business with Enrico Blanco, but he didn't want to piss him off either. He knew Sam would be delivering a report directly to Hampton, a company Blanco knew had very deep pockets. Sam wanted to leave him with the impression that many US dollars could line his pockets.

There was, of course, the distinct possibility Blanco could be playing both sides. Actually, Sam suspected that the more likely scenario. It left Sam with very few options, none actually. Enrico Blanco was now part of the team, but Sam didn't like it one bit.

Sam extended his hand. "Enrico, I want to thank you for your time, your view of the way things are, and your most excellent advice. As you said, I'm sure it's good advice, and I will recommend our mutual client consider it."

He grasped Sam's hand, nodding and smiling and feeling confident he would soon be rolling in the dough of a big US consumer products giant.

"I do have one last question," Sam said. Blanco perked up like a puppy anticipating a treat. "What was the brand of tea you served us?" Looking at Veronica he said, "Veronica, wasn't that an amazing blend?"

"Marvelous, indeed," she said while smiling delightfully.

They both looked at him waiting for an answer.

His reaction was somewhere between befuddlement and avarice. Then, suddenly realizing he should say something, he managed, "I… I honestly do not know… but I will find out and deliver that information to your hotel." He looked at Sam first, then to Veronica for their reaction, as well as their approval.

"That would be delightful. Thank you so much," Sam finally said.

On that note, Veronica and Sam walked toward the door of the conference room, which Blanco opened with a smile. As they walked away from him, Sam could feel his stare burning a hole in his back, most likely thinking Sam daft. But Sam believed he had left Enrico Blanco with the right impression to take him out of the game; a game Sam was determined to win, however long the odds. Javier Mendoza was a pig wallowing in a country that was a stain on everything decent. Sam didn't know exactly how he would defeat him, but he knew he simply must.

ACT III

THIS MAY BE ONE WE CAN'T SOLVE

CHAPTER 29

NEARLY A MONTH had passed since their meeting with Enrico Blanco.

The day after their meeting with Blanco, Sam charged Veronica with securing two additional managers and a dozen staff from Chicago as well as various Hamilton Pierce offices in the States. All SOP in launching a full-scale investigation. The time for negotiation was over.

Alicia had virtually no experience in running a forensic accounting investigation but was proving to be a decent manager. She was the translator-in-chief. All day long she would work with the staff to resolve their translation issues in working with the many documents now flooding in from other sources.

All of them worked at the hotel in the *Pit*, affectionally dubbed by one of the staff for the large hotel conference room. Most days they had little respite from the Pit, even eating their lunch at the conference table where they worked.

Each day was the same routine: several of them would first make a trip to the bank, along with their security detail, to copy documents, mostly deposits and debits, and then back at the hotel they'd methodically log in that document production, distributing them to the various sub-teams working on payments, vendor payables, other cash transactions, and loan activity. All this was in an effort to reconstruct Abello's balance sheet and income statement in the absence of any real financial data. Sam had little contact with the staff but had to admit he didn't fully appreciate the effort they were going through each and every day and the stress building by not finding any evidence of crimes—at least nothing that could stand up to cross-examination.

Aside from that effort, Sam and Veronica had been working twelve-hour days interviewing Abello employees ferried out to the hotel by security managed by Manuel and Fernando. Sam placed a lot of hope on the interview process. His past experiences had proven in most major financial crimes there was at least one person—*one honest soul*—who would surface at some point and lead him and his team to the motherlode of evidence that always seemed to bust the case wide open. That Aha moment! Then, Sam would solve it and explain to his client all the details: who were the fraudsters, how long did it go on, how much did they steal, how they pulled it off, and where the remaining loot was stashed. He'd be the hero, but he knew he could never have accomplished this without a whistleblower coming forward. All he needed to do was provide the environment for that to occur.

During each interview Sam would communicate a sense that he cared and wanted to catch the bad guys before they'd do more harm to the company and its employees. It had worked so often in the past…. Sam was frustrated it didn't seem to be working this time, and he couldn't figure out why that was.

Sam and Veronica had worked together often over the past eight years but never had they been more committed to the same goal as on Project Vista.

But things were not going well. Sam feared Hampton might be growing weary of his investigation. March was closing in on them fast. Hampton had spent nearly two million dollars in fees to HP, plus another half-million in expenses, not counting the bundle their lawyers had to be billing them.

Steve emailed Sam saying the management committee would now be requiring daily conference call updates beginning tomorrow morning, and through it all they hadn't heard anything from Mendoza. He had to be laughing his ass off. He was winning.

He and Veronica had just completed their ninth interview of the day. Sam determined it was time for the two of them to take a break... poolside. It was only five o'clock, but maybe they'd knock off early today.

They sat in chairs on either side of a small glass-top table a few feet from the outdoor pool. Some of the other guests stared at them, probably because they were the only ones dressed in business casual dress and hard-soled shoes, not sandals or flip-flops like everyone else.

"Sam, you do realize everything our staff is doing is a total waste of time?"

He stared blankly at the table.

"Sam... Sam!"

"What?" he responded calmly.

"You going to answer my question?"

"You didn't ask a question."

"Dammit, Sam. You know what I mean. It's all bullshit. We haven't found shit, and we're never going to find the kind of evidence we need to nail this bastard by going through bank records."

"I know that."

"Then why the hell are we doing it?" Veronica said in complete frustration. She was glaring at Sam, expecting an answer.

Sam looked over at Veronica. "Look, kid. I'm as frustrated as you. Anxious, too. I have to believe Hampton's patience is wearing thin. Right now, they could be discussing pulling us out." He looked down at the table shaking his head. "So damn frustrating. I really thought something would turn up in all these interviews."

Five minutes of silence passed. Sam ordered each of them a Modelo Negra beer. Veronica had taken to liking them, a lot actually. Neither of them was eating healthy or sleeping well. Not exercising either. Each day turned into night, a few intermittent hours of sleep, then morning, and the same tired routine would begin again.

"Well, we're done for the week but have another twenty or so interviews scheduled for next week. Tomorrow is Friday, and you told me to keep Fridays open so you could catch up on the week. That still the case?"

Sam was only half-listening. "One honest soul… " he whispered.

"What?"

"We just need one honest soul to come forward. We know some-one knows everything. Someone close to him. It just takes *one* to come forward. For the life of me I don't know why we can't flush one of them out…. Dammit!"

Veronica didn't respond. Both of them now stared at the glass table as if that would help solve their dilemma. She reached into her purse.

"I didn't know you smoked," Sam said.

"I quit when I graduated from Mizzou," Veronica said with little feeling.

"How's that working out for you?"

"Apparently, not so well these days."

"Pass those over here."

Veronica slid a pack of Winston Reds and a Bic lighter over to Sam. He lit up.

"I didn't know you smoked."

"I quit when I went back to school."

"Which time?"

"When I got my MBA. Just before coming to HP. I used to work for the RJ Reynolds Tobacco Company and sold these things out of the trunk of my car."

"I didn't know that. I knew you had a sales job before HP but never imagined you selling cancer sticks."

"They weren't harmful back then. At least, that's what the company told us."

"And you believed them?"

"We tend to believe things that maintain the status quo, fit our own narrative, ignoring contradictory evidence."

"You mean like we're experiencing now?"

Sam looked at Veronica. "So you think we're wasting our time with these interviews, too?"

"I don't know what to think anymore. We've done more interviews on this engagement than any other. This may simply be one investigation that is not solvable."

"I'm starting to believe that may be the case," Sam said as he took a long drag. "But what else can I do? We have no digital data... no original documents. We've done over a couple hundred interviews here at the hotel, under our complete control, and we got crickets. *Nada!* Even offered money to his supervisors and managers and nothing. At least a dozen of them. Hell, they seemed scared to death sitting in our conference room an hour's drive from Mendoza. I thought that last one would piss his pants!"

"Yeah, pathetic," she said laughing.

"Am I supposed to give up?" Sam said while lighting up another Red.

Veronica didn't immediately respond. "No, Sam. But then, I don't know what to tell you."

"We're missing something."

Sam thought for a few moments. "We've done surprise inventory counts where we were absolutely certain we'd find a short count only to find it coming out perfect or in some cases over. We've even showed up at their homes in the evening, offering them money and protection if they would just point us in the right direction. That interview we did of Miguel, after we met with Blanco... he kept looking out the window. Said Mendoza was watching him. That it was impossible for anyone to escape his reach. Kept telling us to leave."

"This is crazy. I have never before run into a situation where no one, not one person, would tip us. Dammit!"

"Sam, let me ask you something."

"Anything."

"Don't make fun of me for reaching here."

"Veronica, nothing is off the table. What have you got?"

"What if our conference rooms are bugged?"

"You mean here at the hotel?"

"Yes."

"There's no way, Veronica. We've had these rooms under constant monitoring, day and night, by our own security from day one."

"But that was to protect our people and documents. What's to say one of Mendoza's louts compromised a hotel employee… or our own security? They all live here—all in need of money. We know bribes occur routinely in every facet of business and government life in this piss-ant country. Why not, Sam? Is that so unreasonable to believe?"

Sam stared off.

"So, what do you think?" Veronica asked, staring at Sam.

"I know just the person to run this by."

CHAPTER 30

VERONICA PUT OUT her cigarette and said she wanted to shower before dinner. Sam made his phone call and then went from the pool directly into the buffet line knowing he was a little early. He tried hard to wear a more positive attitude and wanted to greet his team and try to get them motivated. Maybe his presence would liven up his staff. He could only hope. He certainly needed a break. His first of the newly mandated daily management committee conference calls would begin tomorrow morning at eleven o'clock.

He was standing in the seating area waiting for his staff to file in when Alicia walked in. He jumped up like a teenager at a rock concert. "Alicia! Over here," Sam said waving her away from the buffet line. She immediately walked over to him right past the food. Sam realized how ridiculous he was acting. Alicia didn't seem to mind. "Please, get your food first, and we can sit together and catch up."

"No, I'm fine, Sam. Let's do talk."

They found a booth and slid in across from each other. "I'm really sorry we have not had a chance to talk much since Chicago. I'm hearing exceptionally good things from Veronica about you."

"She is kind. I am so thankful you assigned her as my mentor."

"So, how are you doing on your first real fraud investigation?"

"It is good. I am fine," she said, forcing a pleasant smile.

She wasn't fine. Alicia could never hide her feelings. Sam realized how absurd his question was. No one was having a good experience. Why would Alicia? "Hey, I get it. This isn't going so well for us. But I want you to know this is not the typical fraud investigation."

"You don't need to apologize, Sam. I am so incredibly happy to be a part of your team. Really, I am."

While Alicia acted sincere, Sam knew differently.

"I do have something I need to talk with you about. Something you should know," Alicia said haltingly, staring down at her lap. "Something you have a right to know."

Sam had no clue what was coming.

"Yesterday, I learned that I… I am with child." She immediately stared into Sam's face looking for a reaction.

Sam didn't flinch. He had been trained well over the years of handling shock and disappointment. No judgment. That logic seemed to apply at this very moment.

"And how do you feel about that?"

"I am so ashamed."

"I have a feeling it is not your fault."

"But of course it is. I could have quit, walked out, the first time he touched me. Staying and working for him just encouraged him. It *is* my fault. I wish I had met you and Veronica years ago."

Sam had to tread softly here. He had never been confronted with such an issue. "Have you considered an abortion?" Unfortunately, he thought of the practical solution and regretted suggesting it the moment he said it.

"Never could I even consider such a sin!" Alicia said in the sternest terms. Before Sam could backtrack, Alicia turned her right wrist over revealing a cross tattoo. "Sam, I do not know your faith, but my faith is strong. I want always to be reminded of my duty to God at all times. To live as Christ did. This reminds me," she said pointing to the cross.

"I am sorry, Alicia. I spoke too soon. I only want—"

Then she turned her left wrist around to reveal another tattoo, *PaPa*. "And if Christ seemed too distant to make me do the right thing, I would be reminded of what I would be doing to the memory of my PaPa, God rest his soul. What he would say?"

"Alicia, I deeply—"

"For Chrissake, Eric!" Marge screamed. "You have to be the first one in the buffet line for every meal."

Sam looked immediately up over Alicia's shoulder to the melee developing at the buffet line. They were at it again.

"Relax, Marge. Maybe you should have passed on your caffeine intake all day. Might help your attitude," Eric yelled back at Marge.

"Fuck you, asshole," Marge howled like she was at a professional wrestling event.

Sam's booth was about fifty feet away but facing them. Alicia had her back to them. "It's like that every day," Alicia said.

"Ignore them," Sam said, wanting to stay with Alicia at this extremely sensitive moment.

"We can talk later, Sam. You really should break them up. They make the staff extremely uncomfortable when they get this way. Really... go to them."

"Wait here. I'll be right back."

Eric's ear-to-ear smile displayed for Marge's consumption collapsed when he noticed Sam walking over to him. He left the line and walked up to meet him halfway.

"I know what you're going to say, Sam, but I'm telling you, that woman—"

"Not here," Sam said without emotion. He placed his arm on Eric's shoulder. "Follow me."

Eric Myers was an IT manager in Hamilton Pierce's Los Angeles office. Sam didn't know him well but had worked with him on one significant prior engagement. He was impressed with his knowledge, skills, and execution in IT and data mining. When looking for staff, Sam was a little concerned when Veronica jumped up with glee saying Eric was the perfect choice. She'd be happy to call him to check on his availability for Project Vista. Eric was also a hunk.

Eric had actually been performing well even though they had no data to mine. The staff liked him, and he was a particularly good manager. Organized. Methodical. Fun to be around, especially to cheer up the staff after a depressing day... which was almost every day.

Then, there was Marge Simon, a totally boring, aloof, and impish manager from the firm's New York City office. She was a stereotypical, green eyeshade accountant to the bone. Veronica suggested Marge for the project having worked with her in the past. She told Sam she was one of the smartest people she knew. An added plus, Veronica's description of Marge likened her to an unmarried schoolmarm. Sam thought she would be the perfect taskmaster they would need on Project Vista.

Marge and Eric were of equal rank, both managers. Oil and water from the start.

Safely inside the conference room with Eric, Sam closed the door and spoke first. "It all seems to be getting worse."

"What?"

Sam gave Eric a disgusted look.

"Oh, you mean that. I'm sorry, Sam, but—"

"Zip it."

Eric started to speak again, and Sam held up his finger to stop him. Eric hung his head, realizing a lecture was coming. But Sam deferred.

"Eric, what's with you and Marge?"

"She's a bitch. No one likes her because she treats everyone like shit, and it's wearing on everyone including me."

"Look, Eric. I need you both, but I need you both working together. I will be the first to admit Marge has her idiosyncrasies, but we need her, and we need you. Aside from Veronica, you two are my most experienced forensics managers."

Eric didn't respond immediately. Staring at the floor, hands on his hips, he began slowly, "Sam, what Marge and I are exhibiting is how everyone feels. They're as frustrated as we are but better about suppressing it. They're all stressed out. I'm not being critical of how you are running things; it's just the way it is. Plus, everyone knows how stressed you and Veronica are with the constant dour looks you wear all day. I don't have any suggestions for improving the situation. I just wanted you to be aware."

Sam considered his comments for a moment. "What do you want me to do?"

"Send Marge back to New York. I could cover what she does by saving all that time we spend arguing during the day! Plus, I guarantee the staff's attitude will improve immediately."

"Eric, I can't do that. I need you to find a way—any way—to get along with Marge. It would be nice if you could *mellow her out* a little. Quite frankly, I think it's an unreasonable expectation and I won't fault you if you fail, but it would be awesome if you could somehow manage it. I would be forever in your debt."

"So, you're asking me to suck up to Marge and yield to her demands the way every other staff person has been doing since day one?"

"No, not at all. I'm asking you to use your charm to woo her in any manner that accomplishes our purposes. You are the only one on the team that has any chance of that."

Sam wasn't saying what he really meant, but Eric seemed to get it. "Sooo, mellow her out? That's what you said, right?"

Sam nodded.

"That's a big ask, Sam."

"Yes, I am aware of that." He patted Eric on the shoulder and with a smile and a handshake they walked back to join their colleagues, all of them now eating and talking. Marge was, not surprisingly, off in a booth eating by herself and reading a book. Sam shook his head and then looked at Eric, who was looking at the same spectacle.

"I'll do my best, Sam."

"That's all I can ask, and I guarantee if you can pull this off, the staff will worship the ground you walk on." Eric was shaking his head as he walked over to Marge's booth.

When Sam returned to Alicia she was already talking and eating with other staff. Sam did not interrupt her. He was happy to see she had acclimated well with his team. She had come so far. He had big plans for her future... *and now this.* He'd circle back with her to finish their conversation later.

CHAPTER 31

SAM HAD BREAKFAST with his staff again but then returned to his room. His Fridays were reserved for assessing the previous week and planning the next. This morning he'd also need to review his notes in preparation for his eleven o'clock call with the management committee. Eric and Marge were noticeably absent from the buffet line. He wondered… maybe Eric moved that fast. At least the staff seemed more chipper and collegial this morning, not fearing another blowup between them. Sam hoped it was a good sign.

His BlackBerry buzzed: no name but a 212-area code. New York City. His son Will was in NYC. Still, he almost didn't answer it… and then he wished he hadn't.

"Hello."

"Is this Sam Halloran?"

"Who's this?"

"Martha Crunchner from Hamilton Pierce. I am trying to reach Sam Halloran on a matter of some urgency."

Dammit. It's her.

"This is Sam. How can I help you?" Sam balled his free hand into a fist.

"Sam. I'm calling on behalf of Firm Council," she began very un-partner-like, all business. "I know you have your hands full down there. Guatemala, right?"

"Yes. Terribly busy. Is this something that could wait?"

"Unfortunately, it cannot. Sam, I have been in contact with Louis Bittle. I understand you two have talked about the termination of a certain director in your practice. Am I correct?"

"Yes, but I can't carry out that instruction at the moment. Things here—"

"I'm sorry to interrupt, Sam, but this matter needs to be concluded today."

Sam clenched his jaw and tightened his grip on his BlackBerry. He wanted to tell her just where she could go, but he held back. He didn't care that she was on Firm Council. No one was going to tell him how to run his practice... no one.

"And what matter is that?" Sam said obnoxiously; he was never one for political games.

"The matter of one of your directors who has been terminated pending notification to the individual. Louis Bittle told me you indicated you should be the one who would be communicating that to the director. If that task has not been done it needs to be done today.

He was trying hard to remain calm.

"Sam... Sam... are you still there? Can you hear me?"

"I can hear you just fine. Now, you listen to me. In case you forgot her name, Veronica Martinez is now running one of the most difficult and sensitive investigations for one of this firm's largest clients. I have not informed Veronica of your decision to terminate her employment, and I have no intention of doing so while she is leading this matter. And—"

"Sam, it was not my decision alone but by unanimous vote of the entire Firm Council. Your director must be terminated today. Is that clear?"

It was the wrong thing to say, at the wrong time, to the wrong guy....

"If you interrupt me again I am hanging up," Sam said with bitter resentment. "I am going to say this just one more time, so listen closely.

"That *director* you keep mentioning has a name, Veronica Martinez. I hired her eight years ago; I trained her; I convinced her to follow me to Chicago; and I have made commitments to her I intend to honor. Neither you nor the entire Firm Council has any right to fire her without hearing me, Sam Halloran, the partner-in-charge of the Chicago Forensics practice, the largest such practice in the US Firm... yes, larger than your New York City practice.

"I had requested an audience with those who believe Veronica Martinez should be terminated, and until that happens, Veronica Martinez is not going anywhere. I am now hanging up because I have a scheduled conference call with my client, Hampton Enterprises, in just a few minutes. I will inform you when I have concluded this engagement in Guatemala and would be available for a face-to-face meeting in New York City to discuss this matter. Now, do I need to repeat anything?"

"Sam, maybe we can start over," Martha Crunchner said, conciliating. "We clearly have gotten off on the wrong foot. The longer your director continues working, the more risk you place on Hamilton Pierce's brand. It is our job—"

"Our job is to respond to our client's needs with the smartest, most capable staff we can place before them. One of whom you can't even say her name. So, I will say it once again for you to remember. Veronica Martinez is not going anywhere until I have my meeting. I will inform you when you can schedule that meeting after I conclude our services to our client and return to Chicago. Now, good day!"

Sam hit the red button. He sat down to assess just what he had done. Fortunately, there was a knock on his door.

"Veronica! How long were you standing there?"

"Long enough to hear you say my name several times interspersed with a lot of other action verbs that have me a little worried."

Sam stepped away from the door and walked into his living room as Veronica slowly followed him.

"Have a seat. I suppose now is as good a time as any," Sam said as he stood and then walked over to close the door to his suite.

Veronica looked worried... the first time Sam had ever seen her look worried.

"Sam... what is going on?"

Sam walked back and sat in the chair across from her.

"The name Brian Metcalf ring a bell?"

A moment passed. "This have anything to do with Disney World?"

"You might say that, and not in the sense of a fun vacation."

Veronica stared blankly to the side, away from Sam.

"OK, so I had a little too much to drink." She looked up at Sam and knew he was the best interviewer on the planet. She would not play games with him. It would just stretch out a process she knew would end badly for her. "I fucked up, Sam. How much trouble am I in?"

"Firm Council is terminating your employment."

She stood immediately, covered her mouth with both hands, and began to pace in all directions. Sam didn't say anything or move. She ended up at the patio doors, her back to Sam, but he could hear her sobbing.

Minutes passed without either saying anything. "So, do I need to pack and make arrangements to fly back to Chicago?"

"Come back over here and sit down."

She did, directly in front of Sam, elbows on her thighs, wiping away tears and annoyed her long hair wouldn't cooperate.

"Moral and ethical reasons aside, I am going to do everything in my power to save your job—"

"Thank you, Sam.... Oh, thank you so much—"

"I said nothing about being successful."

She sat back into the chair, staring directly into Sam's face.

"What can I do? I'll do anything. Please, Sam. Help me."

"Is that an admission you did something wrong?"

She thought for a moment. "Sam, I knew this day would come. Papa warned me years ago my ways would catch up to me. Momma, too. Looks like the party is over, huh?" She looked up at Sam.

"What is it going to take, Veronica?"

"This was it. I swear to you, Sam Halloran. If I dodge this bullet, I will become a nun. Sam, I can't go out like this. I screwed up. I know that. I always know it, but I swear to you this is the worst scare of my life. I will never forget what I did and never come close to disappointing you again. I suppose I needed this to happen to me. You have been my greatest supporter and mentor. Beyond embarrassing the firm, I am so, so angry at myself for disappointing you. Of all people… you, the one person who has done so much for me." She started to cry again.

Sam stood looking weary, like he didn't know what else to say, and he felt sorry for her. She stood directly in front of him, twisting her hands over and over nervously, then she leaned into him and placed her arms around his waist with her head on his chest and held him tight while she continued to sob. Sam wrapped his arms around her as well. After a minute, Sam patted her on her back several times. He leaned back a little, placing his hands on her shoulders, and then he looked into her face and said, "I'm hoping this leaves a mark on you. One you will remember for the rest of your career."

He looked over her shoulder at the clock on the wall. "My call with Hampton is in fifteen. Go to your room and clean yourself up, then take some time to regroup. I'll see you at lunch with the team."

She embraced him again. "Thank you, Sam. Thank you so much for your support. I will never disappoint you again."

"I know you won't. Now, please do as I ask." He smiled at her, she forced a smile, and then he walked her to the door.

Sam hadn't taken the time to assess the damage he had done to his own political capital. He was certain Martha Crunchner would carry his message back to the entire Firm Council… the same body that determined partner share allocations. He didn't care. If they decided to take out their angst on him, he had four other firms that would scoop him up in a heartbeat, along with his entire practice.

CHAPTER 32

THE APPOINTED HOUR came, and Sam dialed the prearranged number from his hotel room. He waited anxiously to be joined with the management committee conference call.

Steve would typically welcome everyone and then hand it over to Sam whereupon he would proceed with "news from the front," as Steve had humorously coined it. There was some laughter the first time he did. There would be no laughter on this call.

Sam began talking when the call connected, but after a couple of minutes he was interrupted.

"Sam, this is Garrett Barclay speaking."

"Good morning, Mr. Barclay. I'm pleased you could join us today. I was just updating the committee on our activities since our last call and—"

"Sam, please forgive me for interrupting again," Garrett said. "I don't mean to be rude, but I think it's time for us to make some decisions.

"I've calculated we have spent nearly two and a half million dollars in fees and expenses with your firm to support this effort you are leading in Guatemala. As it should be no surprise to a businessman like yourself, we cannot continue at this pace without some progress toward our goals.

"I want you to understand that while I cannot find criticism in the work you are doing, and while I do believe you are the best person for this job, it may just be that we are engaged in a folly where, at the end of the day, we will find ourselves spending millions of dollars and realizing little benefit.

"Here is what we are going to do, and I hope you understand in this instance I am not seeking your advice or comment. I am just asking you to carry out my instructions."

"I understand, Mr. Barclay," Sam said, now finding it difficult to swallow.

Sternly, Barclay continued, "I will agree to fund this operation for fourteen more days and not a day longer. If at the end of that period, we do not have something our lawyers tell us we can use, then we are done with the forensic accounting investigation phase of our efforts at Abello. Carry on with your daily updates and briefings, and I wish you all good fortune in your efforts."

After a minute of silence, Sam asked if he should continue with his update. He heard some papers rustling and the sound of chairs moving when someone, whose voice he did not recognize, asked, "Sam, do you have anything of substance to report to us?"

"I understand what you want to hear, and unfortunately, I cannot deliver that message at this time."

"That being the case, I want to thank you on behalf of the entire management committee for your efforts and your time today. We will reconvene at eleven a.m. on Monday for our next daily briefing. Good day."

Sam ended the call and sat for a moment to ponder what Barclay had dumped in his lap. He said they had just fourteen days rather than saying two weeks. It was obvious he wanted to emphasize that each and every day was critical. Sam was disappointed, but looking at it realistically, he had no reasonable grounds to push back and disagree.

He sat for a moment staring out his patio window trying to

remain calm, but that was not possible. Sam felt a rage building deep within him. The thought of Mendoza getting away with this caused him to feel like his head was going to explode. Maybe this shock to his system was just what he needed. Maybe it was time to think outside the box.

Sam was walking around his room almost bouncing off the walls and talking aloud even though he was the only person in the room. He was full of anger and could feel the adrenaline coursing through his entire body. He had to talk with his managers, then the staff, but he had to first cool off. *First Veronica, then this!* He fumed.

He regarded the treadmill across the room, all this time never using it. He quickly shed his clothes down to his boxer briefs, donned his running shoes and got on that machine. He cranked up the speed, and with the Guatemala City view in front of him he began pounding the treadmill like he was determined to run a marathon. He couldn't listen to music or watch TV. No, he had to think. The harder he pounded the treadmill the deeper his thought process.

He began to play in his head, over and over, the events transpiring all the way back to his first visit with Mendoza. He increased the incline, up and up, until sweat was pouring out of him.

After forty minutes, he slowed to a more comfortable and reasonable pace. He lowered the incline and locked into a methodical cadence, which seemed to compliment his thought process.

After an hour had passed, Sam slowed to a walk as he toweled himself off, feeling a cooling sense envelop his entire body. He felt relaxed, energized.

He emailed his managers inviting them to a meeting on his patio this afternoon at 4:00, after which they would dine poolside and be joined by a band.

Sam was upbeat.

He was still convinced Javier Mendoza was going down.

CHAPTER 33

IT WAS TWO o'clock when Sam hopped out of the shower and noticed a fax had been slipped under his door. Dave Rogers worked fast.

Still toweling off, Sam sat on his sofa reviewing the bio of a specialist Dave had faxed him. It was in response to Sam talking to him about the risk Mendoza might be bugging them.

Frank Wolf was a former FBI Special Agent with specific expertise in surveillance and subterfuge. Before that, he was a Navy SEAL deployed primarily in Southeast Asia and the Middle East. Before that, he served a tour in Vietnam immediately after graduating from West Point... plus, he was fluent in Spanish. Frank Wolf sounded more than qualified.

Sam called Frank and they talked. All the while it was just a formality to Sam. He couldn't wait to get Frank on board. He emailed Sam his fee schedule and an engagement letter. Sam agreed to engage him without bothering to clear it through Hampton. No time for red tape. This was one of those situations where it was better to apologize later than to ask for permission.

He might even find other uses for Frank Wolf beyond the possible bugging issues. Things were definitely looking up for Project Vista.

Moments later, Frank emailed him back. It sounded like the feeling was mutual. Frank's email read simply:

I booked a flight leaving at 7:20 a.m. out of O'Hare tomorrow (Saturday) morning. I'll arrive Guatemala City at 8:10 pm same day. Please confirm and inform me of the security personnel credentials meeting me at GUA.

Regards,
Frank Wolf

Sam felt less anxious about everything knowing Frank would soon arrive.

Sam received one additional email that reminded him he had others he was responsible to… or at least should occupy his thoughts from time to time. This one was from Sue.

As he clicked on it, he was feeling guilty about not staying in touch with his family. Fortunately, everything was fine. Sue mentioned Will was bringing a girl home to meet his family. She was checking to see if Sam might be available to join them. It was not surprising Will hadn't reached out to him personally.

In a previous email, Sue mentioned he had been serious about her for some time, but Sam never followed up with his son. Sam supposed this was Will's way of punishing him. Sam deserved it.

He typed a quick response thanking Sue for the message and especially for the invitation. As Sam typed his response, he couldn't remember if he had even told her, or the boys, of his investigation in Guatemala. Probably not. He was out of the country on an investigation with an indefinite timeline and could not attend… sorry. He didn't try and wordsmith, as they all knew the drill. Sam was rarely available for his family like any normal father or husband… now, ex-husband.

He didn't want to think about his past mistakes. He grabbed a seltzer and pulled the patio chairs into a circle where he could enjoy the afternoon sun. His managers would soon arrive. He stretched out on the chaise. It felt good, restorative almost, as if unplugging himself from a recharger. Sam must have dozed off when Eric was the first to arrive.

"Good afternoon, Eric." Eric walked with Sam out to his patio and took a seat.

"We missed you at lunch, Sam. How did the conference call go?"

"I'll be discussing that when the rest of the managers get here. "You and Marge were noticeably absent from breakfast. Where were you guys?" Sam had a suspicion.

"Wasn't feeling so good." *Both of them?*

Sam stared at Eric looking for any tells. "Humm… sorry to hear that. You OK now?"

"Sure, but Marge is still a little under the weather. She emailed me saying she was feeling nauseous and would be joining us later, maybe for dinner."

"How are you two getting along after yesterday?"

"I had a talk with her. She gets it. She'll be fine," Eric said, acting like he wanted to move on. "So, what's so important we need to meet?"

Veronica and Alicia joined them. Veronica wore dark, large sunglasses. After their talk that morning Sam felt certain she was stressed out. Who wouldn't be? Her great career was now at risk…. All she could do was wait. Alicia was her pleasant self, smiling and deferential. She was turning into the consummate professional. He suspected she knew this engagement was an extended interview. At this point, he felt confident that between his and Veronica's efforts she'd be joining their Chicago practice on a permanent basis.

"Thank you all for coming. I wanted to touch base with you following my call with the Hampton management committee update."

Sam was never one for beating around the bush and immediately laid out the fourteen-day notification, which was met with blank stares. In his mind he likened it to a boxer still holding on in the fifteenth round knowing he would be knocked out soon… just hanging on. Punch after punch and somehow he was still standing. The call today was just one more punch, not much different than those they had been sustaining each and every day.

"I gather you are likely disappointed with that decision," Sam said. "Any thoughts?"

"I'm not surprised," Eric said. "I get where they are coming from. Just a real downer we can't find the handle on this one."

Veronica said nothing, seemingly staring at Sam behind those enormous sunglasses. Maybe she was asleep. Alicia said she understood but would be disappointed if it came to an end without displacing Mendoza.

"Guys, I don't blame them in the least," Sam said. "They've spent a lot of money, and let's face it; we haven't produced any evidence of wrongdoing. I'm beginning to see what Dave Rogers has told Veronica and me about his days as a federal agent. They usually knew who was committing the crimes… just couldn't prove it. Frustrating as hell."

"I don't know what they expect us to do," Veronica finally spoke.

"Look, I feel their pain," Sam said. "They're businesspeople. They want to fire Mendoza and move on. The only reason they haven't was my recommendation not to. Heck, after listening to Blanco, firing Mendoza could send this investigation into overdrive. I'd rather have us back home when that happens. No telling how he'd react."

"Did you tell them that?" Alicia said.

"Not on that call, but I had briefed Steve on our meeting with Blanco. He just listened. I expect he informed the management committee."

"Two million to Hampton is a drop in the bucket," Veronica said in desultory fashion.

"OK, enough. All of you. Those are the cards we have been dealt. We play those cards."

After a few moments of quiet, Alicia asked, "What's the plan?"

Sam disclosed the good news of the day—bringing Frank Wolf down. They were all duly impressed with his credentials.

"So, you really believe they might be listening to us in the Pit?" Veronica asked.

"You put that thought into my head, and it makes sense to check it out. The Pit, our rooms—hell, everywhere. I'll defer to Frank when he gets here tomorrow night. This stuff is way out of my wheelhouse, and at this point I'm ready to consider anything."

Sam let a few moments pass without saying anything. "So, that's my agenda. You guys have anything to add? Questions? Criticisms?" Sam looked at each of them. No one spoke.

"OK then, I think we're done here. Weather looks really good tomorrow," Sam said in a jovial spirit. He was trying hard. "Maybe you should give everyone the day off. Some pool time might invigorate them. But I'll leave that up to you.

"And one last thing: Inform everyone to stay away from the conference rooms on Sunday. Frank will be doing his sweeps. Now, try and enjoy the weekend! We hit it hard again first thing Monday morning."

No one spoke. Eric nodded his head. Sam's team was suffering. He didn't have an answer for how to turn that around at the moment.

CHAPTER 34

MANUEL CALLED. FRANK Wolf's plane had landed. He would collect him in the baggage claim area and then leave for the hotel.

Sam said he'd meet Frank at the bar after which Manuel could knock-off for the evening.

Approaching eleven o'clock, Sam finally made his way down to the hotel lobby bar. He wasn't surprised to find Veronica already entertaining Frank. Veronica was sitting sideways on the barstool, legs crossed in front of her with one bouncing rhythmically to the sound of Madonna over the bar's speakers. With that admiring smile she threw Frank's way, Sam was quick to kill this action before it went too far. Hopefully, his earlier conversation with her had not worn off already… or maybe she had simply resigned herself to fate.

"Frank, it's nice to meet you in the flesh," Sam said, extending his hand. "Welcome to Guatemala City."

Frank Wolf stood to greet him. "Sam, it's good to meet you as well. I'm happy for the opportunity to work with you."

"Hey, what about me?" Veronica was never one to be cut out of a conversation.

"Oh, I didn't mean to ignore you. Goodnight, Veronica," Sam

said glibly as he moved Frank away from whatever Veronica was conjuring up, fully knowing it would lead to trouble.

"Party pooper. Just trying to enjoy my final days."

"Think positive, Veronica. I'm on it. Goodnight, dear."

Frank gave Sam a sideways glance. Sam ignored it and led him over to a distant table where they sat as Sam motioned the waiter. "What are you drinking, Frank?"

"Water's fine, thanks." Sam was surprised but ordered water as well, although he could really use a drink.

Frank was about as Sam had expected, except for the facial hair. Athletic frame, closely cropped hair, dark complexion, and a confident stare as he looked directly at his face when they talked. "So, how was your flight and getting your gear through customs?"

"No surprises. It was all good."

Sam and Frank talked about the usual stuff: Where they grew up, college, Frank's military and FBI experiences... how each chose their respective careers. Frank was also divorced, no kids. Both lamented choosing their work over family. Finally, they got down to business.

Sam talked non-stop bringing him up to speed on everything. Frank listened with few interruptions, intermittently taking notes. Lastly, he told Frank how he was concerned for the safety of his team. That got his attention. "I'm not surprised," Frank said.

"Why do you say that?"

Frank lowered his head seemingly reluctant to comment, but it was obvious to Sam he wanted to expand.

"Hey, Frank, you have complete license to tell me anything that's on your mind at any time. Please, don't hold back, especially when it comes to our safety."

Frank raised his head and looked directly into Sam's face. He hesitated for a moment, wondering if Sam was sincere. "Sam, you need to blend into your surroundings and not look like you're down here on a bird-watching trip. Your clean-shaven look, that Hawaiian shirt, the gold rings, necklace, and the Breitling Navitimer on your wrist signals to everyone who sees you: *Hey, I've got a ton of money and my employer has a bunch more. Please kidnap me. It sounds like fun!*"

"Really? I thought we'd be able to relax here at the hotel."

"I know you feel safe here, but think about it. If you're a bad guy, why not hang out at the local five-star hotel? This is where all the tourists with money are staying. I'm surprised you haven't had trouble before." Sam didn't know how to respond but felt a little embarrassed.

"Coming through the lobby," Frank continued, "I saw a couple of young guys laughing it up while walking from the cash cage, obviously on their way to the casino downstairs. They were each wearing ball caps, one wearing an Ohio State tee-shirt and both drawing attention to themselves. They were clueless but others were noticing. I'm guessing they're a couple of yours. Veronica is the only one dressed like she belongs here."

"What do you mean?" Sam said shocked.

"Sam, please take this the right way and I mean no disrespect to Veronica, but she was dressed like a rich-bitch tonight. Aloof, independent, spoken-for. A local would think twice about approaching her with the assumption she was in the harem of someone they would not care to tangle with. If I were passing out grades for appropriate costuming and demeanor, she'd get an A."

"And here I was about to say something to her tomorrow for the way she looked tonight thinking it inappropriate. Now you're telling me she was the only one of us who had it right all along."

"Regardless, for the remainder of your stay down here none of your female staff, including Veronica, should be alone in any public place at any time. It's not safe."

Sam sat silent for a few moments without responding, and Frank seemed to withdraw somewhat. Sam noticed. "Frank, I'm not discounting at all what you are saying. I'm trying to take it all in, and at the same time I'm pissed at myself for allowing it to happen because I think, no, I *know* you are making a good point. Let's talk more about this. You definitely have my attention. I will have that discussion with all the staff soon."

"Not telling you how to run your engagement, just saying."

"I really appreciate your advice, Frank. You have complete freedom to tell us what we need to hear to protect us from harm. In fact, what you have told me tonight makes me want to expand your role down here, and I hope you will consider staying on after you do your electronic sweeps. I hope that's something you'd consider."

"Let's see how tomorrow goes with the work you have already contracted me to do. Then we'll talk."

"Fair enough. As I think about our carefree attitudes down here, I was placing a lot of confidence in our contracted security guys to keep us safe. They're not here in the evening on my belief, rightly or wrongly, that we were safe inside the hotel, which appears to have an ample supply of their own security walking about."

Frank scanned the bar area. "I saw them when I entered, and I'm spotting a couple of them now, but what you have to realize, Sam, is these local guys who work for the hotel are loyal only to the one who pays the most. That means they could be working for the bad guys tomorrow. They'd be easily compromised to look the other way while you get snatched… or something worse. Keep in mind, they know your time here is temporary and when you leave this country, they and their families continue living and working here. Trust me when I say that fact of life is not falling silent on them."

Sam nodded his head and then shifted gears. "So, how do you want to play it tomorrow?"

"Well, I think you told me your team operates daily out of a large conference room."

"There are also two smaller conference rooms that can be accessed off of the larger one."

"And there will be no one working tomorrow in any of those rooms?"

"That's correct. We have been working six days a week with Sundays reserved for fun in the sun. I also have Manuel and Fernando join us poolside on Sundays. They were the first ones I retained through CRI, and they manage the other security guys furnished by CRI. Manuel picked you up at the airport."

"I know of CRI and have worked with them before. Good outfit."

"Lead guy is Derek Dorn. He's on another assignment now, but he's a friend. Called him immediately when I learned of this assignment back in January. He got everything in place before he left. Good guy. Good friend. I hope you get to meet him before you leave."

Frank nodded and switched the conversation back to the task at hand for Sunday. "Good that your staff has the day off. I will need complete quiet within the rooms I'll be sweeping tomorrow. I would like to meet your entire security team tomorrow as well. Right now, if it's OK with you, I'd like to turn-in."

"What time do you want to get started?"

"Would seven o'clock be too early?"

"Not at all," Sam said with a smile, "I'll be down here an hour earlier for breakfast if you'd like to join me."

"Thanks, but I like to work out at that time of day, so how about I just meet you in the restaurant a few minutes before seven. That work?"

"I'll see you then."

CHAPTER 35

FRANK SLID INTO Sam's booth in the restaurant. "Good morning, Sam."

Sam jumped a little.

"Sorry to sneak up on you like that."

"Guess I'm a little jumpy these days."

"Let's talk a bit before we enter the conference rooms. Now, when we do, you have to assume someone is listening or you're being recorded. Say nothing. Just find a seat away from the table and watch for my hand signals."

"Got it. But can you tell me what's about to happen?"

"Sure. It will take me about ten minutes to set everything up and another ten minutes to tune it in, but after that I'll need you perfectly still and seated so you will not make even the slightest sound which would distort my readings of the room. Need your mobile phone turned off as well."

"Won't talk, won't move. Mobile phone off. Got it."

"I'll warn you that this is not all that exciting to watch. I just keep an eye on the gauges as I slowly rotate the dial that changes the frequencies. As I do that, it will be searching for any emitting signals in the room. What I'm looking for are radio waves from any source. Since we are always impacted by radio waves, I'll be adjusting other dials and a directional finder such that I can isolate and identify all the individual waves. The harmless and expected ones are eliminated. I'm looking for ones I can't identify as harmless and follow those to the source of the frequency. If we pick up those waves, it will lead me to some sort of listening device. That's it. Are you ready?"

"Ready. Follow me," Sam said as he led Frank to the conference rooms.

When they walked into the main conference room, Frank pointed to a chair against the wall, and Sam took a seat. He sat in awe, completely focused on Frank setting up his equipment.

Thirty minutes passed when Frank began focusing on specific areas of the room. He was holding some sort of wand and walking toward the mantle over the faux fireplace. He held up his free hand to remind Sam not to move or make a sound. His wand was now passing in front of each of the objects on the fireplace mantle. They included a large clock and a couple of candle sticks on either side of it. Surrounding the clock centerpiece was a dotted selection of knickknacks.

Frank appeared to dismiss all but the clock, which he was laser focused on. He began feeling behind the clock. All at once he placed the wand on the table behind him, grabbed the clock carefully with both hands and turned it around to look at its back. Frank motioned Sam over to it with his head. Sam quietly and carefully inched close enough to see a small black device the size of a dime with a grill-like surface. Sam looked at Frank, who set the clock back on the mantel and pointed toward the door. They both exited the conference room.

"Was that—?" Sam started to ask.

Frank signaled Sam to be quiet and pointed in the direction of the pool deck.

Once outside, Frank turned to Sam. "That was clearly an eavesdropping device. There is always the chance it was meant for someone else, but I can tell you it is an active transmitting device most likely wirelessly connected to a nearby VOX recorder. I'd say within fifty feet or so. Let's leave the device where it is, continuing to transmit, while I look around to see if I can determine where it is transmitting to. Since we are on the ground floor, the most likely place is directly above which is where I am now headed.

"Why don't you go up to your room and I will meet you there after I sweep the other two conference rooms. We will need to sweep your room as well."

Sam acknowledged Frank and walked toward the elevators, still a bit struck that there was actually a bugging device in their conference room.

No wonder Mendoza had the drop on them for every surprise interview and inventory observation they had attempted to perform only to be met with silent witnesses and accurate counts. That also explained why all the employees they interviewed there were petrified likely knowing Mendoza's methods. What must they have thought? Sam began to think of other things he might have said in that room. He felt like a moron.

About forty-five minutes later, there was a knock at his door. It was Frank. He motioned Sam outside and down the hall a bit.

"I found similar transmitting devices in the other two conference rooms underneath the tables. There was a locked maintenance closet almost directly above. Once I jimmied the door open and moved a few cleaning supplies out of the way I was able to locate a VOX receiver and recorder. It was active and most definitely is the receiver that is recording everything coming out of your conference rooms."

"Can you pinpoint it to our target?"

"Not yet, but I did take down the serial number and will try to do that tomorrow. It's a long shot, but quite possibly someone close to our target registered the warranty and that would tell us a great deal. I'll let you know."

They then discussed similar procedures for sweeping Sam's suite and patio. Sam said he would sit quietly reading on the patio while Frank did the sweeps.

Thirty minutes later, Frank reported to Sam he found no bugs inside or out.

With that done and feeling somewhat relieved, Sam began to relax with his new friend, Frank Wolf. "I'm getting a refill on my coffee. How do you take yours?"

"Just water, thanks."

A few minutes later, they were both sitting on Sam's patio. "Now we know they are bugging us. So… what does it all mean?"

"Well, it could mean your target is a bad guy and doing bad things, or it could be he's in a powerful position and is a control freak and bugged your conference rooms just because he could. From what you've told me about the guy, he controls lots of government officials and hundreds of employees that work for him."

"You mean that work for *Hampton*. That simple point seems to escape everyone down here. They are not *his* employees. They are Hampton's employees."

"No, Sam. It is you that is missing the point. They *do* work for Mendoza. He is the only authority they know. Hampton is a distant name that occupies none of their waking thoughts. Mendoza holds a grip on at least his plant and much of his surroundings. He clearly can operate with impunity, and by what we have learned today, coupled with the things you told me last night, he sees you as a threat. That simple fact places you and your entire team in danger."

"Yeah, and as of yesterday we've got only fourteen days to nail the SOB.… Otherwise, he wins."

"Sam, he's already won. Sounds like he's been running things down here for an awfully long time, and you are just an annoying interruption in his normal routine. You have posed enough of a threat to where he needs to keep an eye on you, but I'm guessing he doesn't see you as capable of dislodging his grip on every authority around here. He likely views this entire project as something he shouldn't underestimate, but he does not see it as an imminent threat."

"I'm sure you're right, but I can't accept it just yet. I refuse to accept it."

"Well, you need to rethink a few things. Now, having said that, I want to make sure you are clear about one thing, Sam." Frank leaned in. "Given what I've observed, what you've told me, and what I know about this country, he might dispose of you just because he can. Just for fun."

Sam stared blankly at Frank, mulling over what he had just said. He knew the game had definitely changed upon discovering bugging devices. He needed no more convincing of the extreme threat Frank was portending. The only problem was he did not yet know how to move forward. But one thing was for sure: he had found a trusted adviser in Frank Wolf.

"Frank, if your intention was to scare me—"

"Good, stay scared."

"Your buddy Rogers told me the same thing."

"Great minds think alike."

They walked into Sam's living room, each picking a corner on the sofas outlining the large coffee table. Sam sat in quiet thought. Frank did not move or say another thing, probably believing he had communicated all he needed to say.

"Just tell me one more thing, Frank. Am I crazy to stay here… to keep pursuing Mendoza?"

"You're not crazy. You and I are a lot alike—mission-focused. And you care."

CHAPTER 36

Monday, February 23 (Midnight)—Hotel Barcelo

"*SEÑOR* HALLORAN, I am sorry to disturb you but there is a man on the phone for you. He says it is an emergency."

"No problem. Put him through," Sam said groggily after being awakened from a sound sleep.

Five minutes later, Sam was at the front desk pounding on the bell for service.

A lone desk clerk ambled around the corner from the office.

"Saint Peter's church. Where is it? How can I get there?" Sam demanded.

The clerk looked at Sam, his eyes assessing why a guy like him would want to go to a church at that late hour. Before he could speak in judgment, Sam shouted, "Saint Peter's, I need you to tell me how to get there! Nothing else!"

"*Señor*, if you could wait only five minutes, I can have one of our drivers take you there."

This was Guatemala. Five minutes meant at least some multiple longer. Sam wasn't about to wait a moment longer, and his temper was showing its ugly self. "Dammit! I swear if you don't direct me there immediately, the first thing I will do in the morning is walk into your manager's office and tell him of your lack of service tonight, and I'm guessing that might not be a good thing for your career."

The clerk moved so fast from behind the counter Sam almost felt guilty, but it was a fleeting thought as the hotel clerk motioned Sam to the front of the lobby and pointed to the path that would take him on the shortest route to the church. Sam could see the lighted steeple as he bolted through the front doors. This could be their big break!

There it was. Just a block away. Sam puzzled why he hadn't noticed it before. Still jogging, he looked at his wrist where his Breitling used to be… until Frank told him to ditch it. While still jogging, he groped his back pocket for his BlackBerry. Nearly 12:20. *I will be here until 12:30…. Hurry*, was what Miguel Herrera said on the phone. On the way, Sam questioned his sanity for doing this alone, but that didn't stop him. It was Miguel for sure on the phone. Sam was sure of it. If anyone else showed, Sam would abort.

He entered the church. A few steps into the sanctuary, the eerie quiet and darkness created the tension Sam was now feeling. Suddenly, moonlight streamed through the stained-glass windows painting the way toward the confessionals. That's where Miguel said to meet him. As Sam approached, he thought about the last time he had confessed his sins to a priest. It had been years… no, decades.

Three confessionals. He opened the first. No Miguel. He reached for the second—

Sam had never been hit on the head from behind, but moments later he found himself on the floor, dazed, disoriented, a ringing in his ears as pain enveloped his head. Other worldly. *Did I trip? Did something fall on me?*

A moment later, he felt as if a tree had fallen on him… instantly, a shooting pain on his side the likes of which he had never felt before. Then… nothing. No more pain. He had passed out.

"STAT" was the doctor's command that briefly awakened Sam.

Then, distant Spanish words being shouted about. Sam was able to open an eye but quickly closed it due to the blinding overhead light.

"*Eles Americano*" was the next thing Sam heard and then, "*Señor* Halloran, *Señor* Halloran. You are at Hospital Esperanza. Can you hear me? Squeeze my hand if you can hear me."

Sam could definitely hear someone and could somewhat understand what she was saying, but the noise, the pain.... He just wanted to sleep. No more pain. He felt himself fading in and out of consciousness and wanted to answer her but couldn't. Then, everything was quiet again as Sam fell into a deep sleep. He was falling, maybe drifting, rather floating. *Why am I floating? Where am I?* "Where am I?"

"You are back with us," said his attending doctor. It was the last thing Sam heard, in English or Spanish. Then, he slept again, only this time, he was out. He no longer fought whatever forces were pulling at him. He was secure in the belief that he had escaped something unexpected. He felt comfortable and warm but so very tired. Sam gave in peacefully and completely to sleep.

CHAPTER 37

Tuesday, February 24

SAM AWOKE TRYING desperately to focus on a figure standing a few feet away. He tried to speak. Again, he drifted away.

An hour later, hearing noises, he again opened his eyes. This time, he thought he had recognized the voice.

"Welcome back, pal."

"What?"

"It's Frank. You know. The guy who gave you some good advice meant to keep you alive down here. From the looks of you and piecing together what I could glean over the past twenty-four hours, it seems that advice went in one ear and right out the other."

"Frank. Yeah. Dave's friend," Sam slurred. He slowly began to piece it all together. Remembering seemed painful. *I was in Guatemala and running an investigation.* Sam couldn't recall details but at least remembered Frank.

Frank pulled up a chair next to Sam's hospital bed and sat.

"So, Sam, do you remember when we met at your hotel Saturday night? Do you remember what we did together the next day?"

"What is today?" Sam said, ignoring Frank's question.

"Today is Tuesday, February 24, 1998," Frank said, taking it slow, giving Sam time to get his bearings.

Sam was struggling to focus.

"Help me sit up."

Frank stood, taking Sam's arm, his other hand cradling his back to help him sit up.

"NOOO…! No, Frank. That won't work. Stabbing pain in my back." Frank deferred describing his wound but thought it a perceptive choice of words.

"Maybe just another pillow under my head."

"How's that?" Frank asked.

"Better. Why does my head hurt? The worst headache I've ever had. Pillow feels like a rock. Is that really a pillow?"

From his new perspective, Sam looked around. "Frank, am I in a hospital? What's going on?"

Frank sat again and began telling Sam everything that had transpired since those early morning hours yesterday—at least what he could piece together from the evidence. There was a lot he didn't know, which was one of the reasons he hung around Sam's room waiting for him to regain consciousness.

"I know from talking with the desk clerk," Frank said, "that you got a phone call around midnight yesterday morning. Then, you appeared downstairs demanding to know where St. Peter's church was."

"The last thing I remember is you did some sweeping of our conference rooms and my suite searching for bugs."

"Sam, it's good you remember that. What else do you remember about Sunday?"

Sam shifted in his hospital bed and let out a muffled groan again. "What the hell! Why so much pain?"

"You sustained a mild concussion. Also… you were stabbed."

"Stabbed! No! Seriously? Where? I don't remember anything."

"Right side, just nicking your kidney."

Sam was working hard to remember. Nothing. He reached around to his back and let out another groan as he felt the bandage.

"Sam, you need to stop moving around. Trust me when I tell you that you were stabbed."

"How the hell…?"

"I don't know. Doc said the concussion might cause short-term memory loss. That's why we're talking. I'm trying to help you recall."

"Don't *you* know what happened?"

"Well, I might," Frank said glibly, "had you taken my advice and called me before you ventured out of the hotel by yourself in the middle of the night. I've talked with all the staff and your security. No one has a clue what you were doing last—"

"He called me!" Sam said, remembering.

"Who called you?"

"Miguel… Miguel Herrera. Said to meet him at the church. St. Peter's. He's the IT director. The one Veronica met with on her first day in-country. He walked her through all the damage to the computer room. Since then, we've interviewed him twice. From their first meeting, she felt he was holding back." Sam rattled on like he was reading off of a list.

"He called me through the hotel. Told me he had a small window, but he wanted to meet me at St. Peter's church. Gave me the address. It was just a couple blocks from the hotel. He'd wait there just until 12:30. Bring no one. I had to hurry. No time to notify anyone. He said he was scared. Thought they were following him. Had just a little time. It was now or never. I felt I had no choice. He was the one who knew everything. Hotel clerk directed me. So… I left the hotel and ran over there… and now I'm here. That's all I remember." Sam let out a deep sigh.

"That's good, Sam. You're doing great, actually."

"What's the doctor say about my condition?"

"Beyond the hit on the head and the resulting concussion, he said the knife wound wouldn't pose a serious threat. Just painful for a time. With the proper rest you should be OK."

"I don't remember seeing Miguel. Maybe they got to him. Frank, you need to see if you can reach him!"

"Settle down, Sam. I'll put Veronica on that as soon as I leave here."

"Got to find Miguel. He's the key to everything," Sam said excitedly, fighting his shortness of breath.

Frank gave Sam a couple of minutes to regroup. "Anything else?" he asked, not wanting to push the envelope.

"Yeah, how did I get to this hospital?"

"I don't know, but that's a good question. Still investigating."

"When do I get out of here?"

"They expect you'll be released by week's end."

"I'm so tired. I need to rest just a little. Can you help me slide back down?"

Sam was asleep almost instantly.

On Wednesday morning, Sam awoke to a large flower bouquet sitting on the table next to him. He later learned they were from Hampton Enterprises. *All of us at Hampton Enterprises hope you have a speedy recovery. Best wishes, Steve.*

As if they had been waiting for him to awake, Eric, Marge, Veronica, and Alicia walked in.

"Well, I guess the rumors are true. You are alive!" Veronica said as she gave Sam a gentle hug. The others gathered at the foot of his bed.

"We heard what happened," Eric said. "Glad you're OK, but you still should have gotten one of us out of bed. I can't believe you didn't do that."

Marge looked uncomfortable but now saw an opening to say something. "I agree, you should have knocked on our door. Well, at least one of the guy's doors, Eric or Frank. You need to be more careful." Then, she gave Sam's foot a backhanded slap saying, "Now, you get well while we carry on doing all the work, as usual." She forced a thinly concocted smile and exited the room. Sam thanked her for coming and then smiled back.

After the door closed behind Marge, Eric said, "Compassionate Marge," as he shrugged his shoulders.

"OK, kiddies, recess is over, and now you have to scoot," said Nurse Ratched as she moved between them and Sam's bed. She began smoothing out his bed sheets at the foot and then picked up his chart. "Scoot, scoot! Mr. Halloran needs his rest. Go on now; you all need to leave," she said as she turned her attention entirely to the business at hand. On an earlier visit, it was Frank who dubbed Sam's nurse with that less than favorable name from the movie *One Flew over the Cuckoo's Nest.*

No one challenged her as they walked, single file, by Sam, tapping him on his arm. Veronica leaned in for a last hug. Sam waved them off but couldn't speak due to a thermometer the nurse had stuck in his mouth. He wanted to talk with his managers about the closing timeline, but as the nurse pumped up his blood pressure cuff he drifted off to sleep once again.

When Sam awoke later in the day, he lay there thinking he needed to get back to work. First, he had to get out of that hospital. He called Frank on his BlackBerry. Twenty minutes later, Frank was by his side.

Frank had called Steve Lemly at Hampton on Monday and told him about the attack on Sam. Steve was genuinely concerned and pushed hard for the investigation to be closed down—everyone should return home immediately. He eventually settled for Frank's suggestion to hold off on such a decision until Sam was back on his feet again. Let the emotion of this event pass.

"Did you tell him about finding the bugs?" Sam asked.

"I started with that. Got a weird response. I purposely paused and waited for his reaction before telling him about the attack on you. Seemed way too calm. Asked me to repeat what I had said about the attack. After he asked about your condition, he was silent for so long I asked if he was still on the line. Responded with a simple *yes*." Frank looked at his notepad. "Here's what he said: 'I suppose with what transpired last week none of this should surprise me. I guess I was not fully aware of the lengths Mendoza would go, but it seems now I should have. This is all my fault.'" Frank closed his notebook and looked at Sam.

"By his voice intonations and hesitations, he appeared embarrassed, saying he should have called you to discuss it. He was apologetic, saying he would call you immediately. I asked him to hold off calling you for now, that you'd call him when you could."

"What did he mean about *what happened last week*?" Sam said frowning.

"Don't know, Sam."

"Let's keep going. You said Steve wants to shut the whole thing down, reacting to the attack on me and not so much the bugging?"

"I think so, Sam. Anyway, we should call him soon."

"Why would he say it was his fault? How could he assume any blame for that?"

"Mystery. Just saying he seemed to blame himself and felt bad about the attack on you."

"Well, I should make that call now. Do you think we could get a speaker phone in here?"

"Are you crazy, pal?" Frank said, laughing. "You really think Nurse Ratched is going to let you turn this hospital room into an office. You must still be delusional."

"We probably should stop referring to her as Nurse Ratched. Do you know her real name?"

"I don't, but I'm fine calling her that."

"*Señor* Halloran, you and your *friend* need to heed my advice, or you will be in hospital very much longer than you expect. Am I making myself clear?" the nurse said, walking into the room.

She hesitated in shoving a thermometer into Sam's mouth until she received an answer.

"Yes, ma'am," Sam said, dutifully. He didn't know how old she was, but with her grey hair in a bun and those black horned-rimmed glasses, *ma'am* seemed appropriate.

She finished with Sam and walked out of the room, giving Frank a pernicious sneer.

Frank walked back to Sam's bedside.

"Aren't you a bit surprised the police didn't want to talk with me as soon as I regained consciousness? I get coldcocked and stabbed, and the cops are nowhere to be found."

"Actually, I talked with Manuel about that. He said there are so many bar fights, muggings, and stabbings all over town that unless someone died the cops don't care. So, I suppose, considering again where we are, it isn't much of a stretch to understand that."

"Fine. I can buy that. But I would like to know how I got to the hospital."

"Top of my list, pal."

Sam looked at the clock on the wall. "Frank, it's getting near dinnertime. I'm exhausted. I can't tell you how much I appreciate you being here," Sam placed his hand on Frank's forearm.

"This is a hell of a lot more fun than sweeping rooms. Happy I can help, pal."

CHAPTER 38

BY THURSDAY MORNING, Sam was feeling better. He was still sore but otherwise in good spirits. Frank came by for their planned call to Steve.

On the phone, Steve was gracious in every way. He kept apologizing. Sam had only one question: "What happened in Chicago last week?"

"Sam, I have to tell you something that causes me great pain and embarrassment," Steve began. "After the last conference call we had with you… last Friday… when Garrett told you he planned to shut it down in fourteen days."

"Yeah, I remember. What of it?"

"Well… there was a meeting held in Chicago that afternoon, between the management committee and… Javier Mendoza and his lawyer."

Sam was at first stunned and then furious. Javier Mendoza flew to Chicago for a meeting with the management committee, a meeting that certainly had to have been scheduled ahead of time, and *he* was just hearing about it now? Sam managed successfully to hold his tongue, simply repeating what he thought he had just heard, "Mendoza met with all of you in Chicago?"

"Sam, I know you are upset I didn't call earlier to inform you of that meeting, and you have every right to be."

Sam was beyond "upset" but held his temper.

"Mendoza's lawyer, his uncle actually, had called the previous Monday to arrange it. Said they had an offer for us to consider. That there would be no need for you at this meeting. The committee honored that request over my objections. That meeting was held a couple hours after our call with you last Friday.

"OK, Steve, you need to tell me what happened at that meeting."

"Right, so here is everything. It all began for me last week, Wednesday. I was called into a meeting of the management committee that had been arranged without my knowledge."

～

"Steve, thank you for joining us on short notice," Garrett Barclay stood to greet him, "Please, take a seat."

Steve looked around the table, seeing all the decision makers were there. His instincts told him this was not a meeting to discuss anything. This was a meeting to deliver a message.

Garrett continued, "Two days ago, Aaron Schmidt received a call from New York City attorney Jorge Mendoza, who relayed he was now representing his nephew in this matter. He called to propose a meeting between representatives of Hampton, him, and his nephew. The subject, we were told, would be the severance from his position as general manager of the Abello plant in Guatemala and the relinquishment of all claims past, present, and future. During the call, Aaron attempted to elicit more about their proposal, but he was unsuccessful. Jorge Mendoza simply continued to repeat the request for a meeting, telling Aaron he expected he would need to confer with others, but a return call would be expected within the next twenty-four hours.

"After Aaron had informed me of that call, I conferenced with most of the people you see gathered around this table now, and we agreed to the terms of that proposed meeting. I am now informing you that meeting will take place in two days' time, at one o'clock, this coming Friday afternoon in the board room. Your attendance is expected."

It was the first pause in Garrett's delivery, and Steve took the opportunity to probe for more information. When that attempt was abruptly denied, Steve addressed the committee for time to discuss the wisdom of meeting with the Mendozas. Garrett abruptly interrupted Steve, telling him the decision was final. Steve looked directly into Garrett's face and asked, "What do you want me to tell Sam with regard to this meeting?"

"Nothing," Garrett Barclay said tersely. "You are not to inform Sam Halloran of this meeting. Any resulting decisions that come out of the meeting are solely in the purview of this committee. If we need Sam's input, we know how to reach him."

"But Sam is the guy on the ground. He's running this investigation. It makes no sense to exclude him from these discussions and especially from this upcoming meeting. Sam needs to be in the room for such a discussion. Without Sam, we will be blind."

"Sam is *not* running this investigation," Garrett spoke tersely. "This committee is running this investigation, and Sam is working for *us* at *our* direction. We, and we alone, will make all decisions affecting the conduct, scope, and outcome of this investigation.

"I will tell you this," Garrett continued, "if their proposal is reasonable, it is more than likely we will accept it so we can be done with all of this and get back to running a very profitable business." Garrett looked away in disgust. "I wish you had never alerted us to that damn letter in the first place. This has all been a terrible waste of resources."

Garrett looked at Steve with a gaze challenging him to object. Hearing none, he continued. "I understand we have a scheduled call with Sam on Friday morning at eleven—two hours prior to our meeting with the Mendozas. I expect anything of importance to this committee will be communicated at that time." Garrett paused for effect, looked directly at Steve, then followed assertively, "Do you have any additional objections to present to me or this committee?"

Steve simply shook his head and slumped in his seat. At this point, his responsibilities regarding this investigation had been reduced to note-taking, messenger, and liar, all of which were roles Steve felt uncomfortable playing. He and Sam had become friends, taking their relationship far beyond simply client and *vendor*, which was how Garrett had referred to Sam more than once. Expeditious corporate politics—Steve had seen it before, and he knew what he would do. He'd do exactly as Garrett Barclay had instructed him. He didn't have to agree, but he would do it.

On Friday, at precisely one o'clock, the arrival of the Mendozas was announced to the waiting management committee already assembled in the board room. Garrett signaled for them to be led in.

As they entered, everyone was already seated, and the usual meet and greet was not on display. Only Garrett stood to simply point to two open seats at the opposite end of a fourteen-foot-long table. When the Mendozas were seated, Garrett took his seat, giving them a minute to lay out their papers and pour their own water. It was clear this was a meeting of adversaries, and there would be no extension of courtesy to these thieves.

"In the interest of clarity," Garrett said, "and as advised by counsel, a court reporter has been retained to make a record of these discussions and such record will be electronically supplied to the Mendozas within twenty-four hours. Today is Friday the 20th of February 1998, at one-ten p.m.," Barclay said, as though he were directing a courtroom drama. He then read into the record the names of the management committee members present and both Mendoza and his counsel.

With these preliminary matters concluded, Garrett opened the meeting, looking down the table at the Mendozas. "Gentlemen, as it was you who asked for this meeting, I would ask you to begin by stating your purpose."

Jorge Mendoza thanked the committee for their time to consider how to both fairly and adequately resolve the matter at hand, which he characterized as a misunderstanding of transactions and events. He never referred to the ongoing *investigation* of the Abello operations in Guatemala.

He began with a historical litany of his nephew's years of "faithful and loyal service" to Hampton Enterprises, emphasizing the sacrifices Javier Mendoza had made in building what was now the most profitable plant in the global Hampton family of distilleries. He concluded with how saddened his nephew was to now discuss a "parting of ways" with a fleeting and insincere reference to a rush to judgment on the part of the Hampton management team.

Through it all, Garrett Barclay patiently listened with a roll of his eyes here and there, realizing all this was complete posturing for the transcription but nonetheless would be made part of the permanent record. While he worked with lawyers on a routine basis, listening to Jorge Mendoza exemplified all he despised about them.

After breaking momentarily to take a sip of water, Jorge Mendoza continued to read from his prepared notes. Javier sat with his arms crossed, moving his stare from the table to the walls and to the ceiling and then the court reporter, but never toward any representative of the Hampton management committee.

Jorge Mendoza continued, "...and in respect of his nearly twenty years of loyal, honorable, and obedient service to Hampton Enterprises, whose management team has directed his every action in the building of the Guatemalan facility and the business, Javier Mendoza asks only for a reasonable severance package."

At the mention of who *directed* Javier Mendoza's actions, Barclay winced, believing that was a deliberate and veiled reference to Hampton's complicity in any alleged wrongdoing. He didn't get to where he was today by missing such things.

Javier slid a document forward as his uncle continued. "As described more fully in this document I have titled as Exhibit A, this severance package will include a release of all claims upon Javier Mendoza, his management team, and many of the loyal vendors of Abello. Additionally, this severance package will include a one-time payment of US $2 million for Mr. Mendoza and one-time payments totaling US $1 million to be distributed to the individuals listed on Exhibit A."

Barclay's jaw tightened, but he remained silent. Steve Lemly, showing no visible reaction, picked up the document and, scanning it, recognized many of the names on the list who likely participated in bribes and kickbacks in the millions of dollars over the years, including Mendoza's brother-in-law who owned the security company that provided Mendoza's army.

That said, and now removing his half-glasses, Jorge Mendoza calmly took another sip of water and then folded his hands over his rather large and protruding stomach, awaiting a reaction from the committee who all turned in unison toward their leader, Garrett Barclay.

For what seemed like the longest period of silence, Barclay cleared his voice and then began. "Without seeming to give your request a hint of credibility by referring to it as I am about to, over my dead body will Hampton Enterprises agree to give Mr. Mendoza one additional dollar to terminate our employment relationship with him.

"Now that you have had your moment to propose your ridiculous and raucously absurd proposal, it is now my turn to tell you exactly what we are prepared to do.

"In exchange for Mr. Mendoza's immediate agreement, as evidenced by his willing signature on this document, I am presenting you marked as Hampton Enterprises Exhibit A, this company forthwith agrees to release all civil claims past, present, and future against Javier Mendoza, but we will *not* do so against any other employee of Abello nor any vendor providing goods or services to Abello. Further, I am informing you that if Mr. Mendoza refuses to sign our Exhibit A, he will be served on a lawsuit to be filed by this company. He will receive such notice by a process server now standing just outside the door to this room. Additionally, there will be an immediate phone call made to the FBI informing them of federal statute violations perpetrated by Mr. Mendoza while falsely representing a US domiciled corporation in the country of Guatemala.

"Once notified and duly served, I expect Mr. Mendoza will be on his way to O'Hare International Airport. I expect that the FBI will proceed to prevent him from leaving this country, taking him into custody immediately so he can be arraigned and have a bail hearing, which I expect will be denied." Briefly pausing, Barclay leaned forward in his chair and with a most serious demeanor said directly to the person sitting at the end of the table from him, "Your move, Mr. Mendoza. This is a one-time offer. What's it going to be? Walk away now a man free of all claims against you, or walk into a federal prison? I need your answer within the next thirty minutes."

Both the Mendozas looked surprisingly calm, and they huddled, speaking in Spanish too low for anyone to hear. After several minutes had passed, Jorge Mendoza spoke calmly but affirmatively. "It is indeed unfortunate that you, the representatives of Hampton Enterprises, have chosen this path. I would again encourage you to take note of our Exhibit A. Should you refuse our very generous offer, my client will be forced to do his duty as a proud citizen of these United States of America and meet with a representative of the US Attorney's office seeking protection under the Uniform Whistleblower provisions afforded him by federal statute."

Barclay, no doubt from years of training to become a steely negotiator, did not tip his hand and offered no visible reaction; however, the other members of the management committee looked first at Barclay, then at the Mendozas, then back to Barclay, as if they had lost their resolve in the face of a threat they did not anticipate. Steve

Lemly appeared to come to grips immediately with the threat, seeing it as very credible. He was indeed familiar with the whistleblower statute Jorge Mendoza was referring to.

Physical reactions aside, no one in the room made a sound as Jorge Mendoza received tacit support for continuing. First, he walked to the stenographer and turned off her recorder and then looked at Barclay. He understood and instructed her to halt the transcription momentarily, and then Jorge pulled a document from his portfolio and began to read from it.

"Among the violations Mr. Mendoza has witnessed being executed in the country of Guatemala, and for the benefit of Hampton Enterprises, are bribes and kickbacks offered and paid to government officials and other persons and businesses operating in the US, Guatemala, as well as other countries, money-laundering and other crimes past and present." Jorge Mendoza, removing his glasses looked around the table into the faces of absolutely stunned and silent executives.

"Gentlemen, if you would like to see how quickly and efficiently your US Department of Justice can move against criminals of this great nation, I challenge you to make that call to have my nephew arrested as he attempts to travel back to his home. Pick up that phone now to make your call or go and prepare his wire transfer for $2 million. You will find those wire transfer instructions in our Exhibit A."

The smugness and confidence Jorge Mendoza exhibited toward Garrett Barclay and the committee was more than Barclay could stand. Veins now protruding from Barclay's neck and temples on a reddening face, he exploded from his seat, losing all form of business decorum. He had been insulted and humiliated, and if it was his last act on this earth he was going to tell these two hoodlums that he was a man of his word and immediately ordered his administrative assistant to get him the number of the Chicago FBI office.

Still calm and seated, the Mendozas quietly listened to Barclay's uncharacteristic tirade playout. Briefly pausing for effect, they both took a glance toward each other. It was now painfully obvious the Mendozas were about to conclude the execution of a very well-planned attack. Beginning this final salvo, Javier slowly stood and held up his hand like a crossing guard. "Mr. Barclay, you may wish to hear me out before making that call, as I can give you more relevant information to help you with such an important decision."

As Javier Mendoza stood looking down the table toward Garrett Barclay still standing at the other end, it looked like a standoff between the two remaining gunslingers at the *O.K. Corral*. Finally, Barclay looked over at his administrative assistant, who had dutifully obtained and was now handing Barclay the phone number he had just requested. Almost as if he knew where this was headed, he lowered his head and simply said, "Speak." Then, he returned to his seat, staring unflinchingly down the table toward his nemesis, Javier Mendoza. Sitting again himself, Javier Mendoza proceeded to speak without the aid of notes, being sure to make direct eye contact with each and every member of the management committee as if he were a master lion tamer performing in front of a rapt audience.

"Do any of you recall that when I was hired by Hampton my first task was to supervise the construction of the Abello plant?" He paused for a moment, appearing to make mental note of his certainty that at least some at the table remembered exactly what he was describing, although none acknowledged it. Mendoza, now realizing he likely was speaking rhetorically, continued staring into the faces of frightened executives anticipating what was coming and feeling powerless to stop it.

"We had many problems obtaining the proper government approvals and permitting. On a daily basis I was receiving calls to get it done. Whatever it took. We had to clear the way for construction. Crews and equipment were standing by at a cost of tens of thousands of dollars a day to the company. *You have to find a way*, I was told. Do you all remember what happened next?" Again, there was no response, but they all knew. "I got it done. I got the proper government approvals and permits, and we were able to proceed with construction."

Moving along, he gave a memorized list of law violations everyone now knew Mendoza would be pinning on the company as though he had been directed by some invisible hand of greed and corruption. "Shortly after we began production, we had labor trouble and again the calls from corporate came imploring me to fix it. *Get them back to work*, I was told. *Make it happen.* Then, what did happen? Pretty soon, as many of you had instructed me, I made it happen and we were back to full production."

The management committee looked sickened by the discovery of what they had suspected all along but never asked—that in order to do business in a corrupt country such as Guatemala, there were times when the company, in the interest of performing their mission and duty to the shareholders. Would need to bend a few laws. But then everyone was doing it because there was no other way to operate. If Hampton refused to play ball, they would be out of business in a heartbeat, and those left to suffer would be Guatemala's poor. In their minds, at least, it was all justified as if this were a humanitarian mission.

Hampton Enterprises would part the seas in this principled effort to reach out and help those poorest of the poor. After all, these pathetic people could not get that new job, as meager as the wages were, unless Hampton made the necessary *sacrifices* in an effort to help those poor citizens of a corrupt and dishonorable government. Hampton could not change the way things were, but they were the only thing that could keep these poor deserving Guatemalans alive. Surely, it would seem that accepting these law violations was perfectly justified. Any reasonable person could see that. Right? Or so the rationalizations likely unfolded at the time.

One by one around the table, each executive was now trying to justify, in their own minds, their criminal violations, but just as obvious were the dejected looks their faces displayed knowing full-well no US Justice Department official would see it their way. They violated federal law, and there were no excuses for what they did. It was greed, plain and simple, albeit rationalized to make it palatable enough for them to go home and sleep like a baby.

Beaten, yet refusing to cede any ground, the committee remained silent as Mendoza continued next with the payment of a *fine* for water pollution... the typical way to disguise a bribe paid to city officials. Then, there was the sabotaging of supplies at their competitors' plants when approached by those vendors making offers to do so, and if refused, such offers would be made to competitors to sabotage Abello's supplies instead. What could they do? They paid up, of course.

Over and over, Mendoza continued for more than thirty minutes, and still he had even more to disclose when finally, Garrett Barclay held his hand up as if it were a final act on the battlefield to stop the bloody onslaught. He had to mount a last-ditch effort to try and regain some lost ground where the only thing that remained were a few diehard Hampton soldiers left to carry the flag, bravely waving it to signal their refusal to surrender.

Barclay, more than any other, knew the battle had been lost, yet he would thrust his saber one last time. "We will make a strong case that you and you alone made the decisions resulting in breaking those laws you have now alleged, and we are hearing about for the first time. We have the resources and the courage to defeat you, and we will never rest until we do."

That was the last of Barclay's arsenal, and he hoped it had hit its mark but quickly realized the battle was utterly lost.

"Yes, you will. I am certain you will stand strong and proud to fight the good fight, first telling the US Attorney that you were duped, but they will not be dissuaded from opening up an investigation into Foreign Corrupt Practices Act violations because they are greedy, too. Yes, an onslaught of US Department of Justice lawyers

will race to show the world yet another selfish and greedy corporation which has used their vast financial empire to hold these poor
Guatemalans in blind and helpless servitude for their own benefit.
In the end, Hampton Enterprises was caught with their muddy
boot at the throat of a pathetic union of people who wanted nothing more than just a small sliver of the American dream... until a
dutiful whistleblower came to their rescue."

Finally, Javier Mendoza ended his cavalcade of horror stories and
premonitions, knowing he not only stopped his enemy's onslaught
of useless defenses but was now joyously believing he had severed the
head off the beast. Without another word being said, the Mendozas
calmly sat and awaited a response from Garrett Barclay, the now
defeated general leading this rabble of formerly distinguished executives of one of the world's largest and most profitable corporations.
They did not have to wait long for the terms of surrender to come.

"You will have our decision within twenty-four hours," he said,
and with that Garrett Barclay turned and walked out of the board-
room without any further acknowledgment of the scum gathered
at the other end of the table. The Mendozas calmly but deliberately
gathered their things and walked defiantly out of the conference
room by the same door they had entered an hour ago. They would
be headed to O'Hare airport without any fear of being detained.
One would head back to his New York City luxury office on Wall
Street in the same building as JP Morgan. The other, back to the
hellhole they call Guatemala to bask in the glory he knew was his
to enjoy. Both men assured that Hampton Enterprises would meet
their demands. What choice did they have? Child's play.

CHAPTER 39

STEVE FINISHED TELLING Sam all that had transpired at the meeting, but he hadn't yet delivered the news that caused the attack on Sam.

"Shortly after the committee arrived at a decision," Steve continued, "Garrett informed me to communicate to Mendoza's lawyer a complete rejection of their offer with no counter proposal—the investigation would continue. I did that via fax and email late Saturday morning. I suspect when Mendoza received that he hatched the plan to harm you. It was out of my control, Sam, and I feel like I really let you down. I am deeply sorry."

For the next few seconds there was silence.

"Sam, I should have informed you. Rejecting Mendoza's offer was obviously more significant than we anticipated. None of us ever imagined what happened to you was remotely possible. How could we know this madman would attempt to bring the investigation to a halt by attacking and possibly killing you? This is new territory for all of us. I hope you can understand, and I hope you can forgive me."

Frank and Sam looked at each other without saying a word. No one spoke. This time, Sam knew it was he who needed to break the silence. He was angry, sure, but what would expressing that anger accomplish? He moved on with just a slight edge to his usual levity.

"So, I'm guessing I no longer need to worry about Garrett's previously imposed fourteen-day timeframe, correct?"

"Sam, after telling Garrett of the attack on you, I've never seen him that upset. All he told me was 'Tell Mr. Halloran to do whatever is necessary to complete his objective. Tell him also that I apologize for not trusting his judgment.'

"I would venture to say he will make available any and all resources you request to ensure the removal of Javier Mendoza and his criminal enterprise at the earliest possible moment.

"I don't think I've ever said this before, but, Sam, it appears you have a blank check. Just tell me what it is you wish us to do."

Sam looked at Frank and smiled. "I appreciate your honesty and trust, Steve. I will reassess things down here and get back to you tomorrow." The call ended.

Sam and Frank sat thinking for a few moments. Frank spoke first, "So, what's the plan?"

"We starve the beast."

"You want to expand on that just a bit?"

"Sure. We can't get rid of him legally as local counsel Enrico Blanco told me earlier. Mendoza's network of paid protection can be summoned to do his bidding at any time; however, they do so only because they know he will pay them."

"So, you instruct Hampton to shut down the cash flow." Frank said. I get it, but will Hampton do it knowing it will cost them dearly?"

"After that call with Steve, this will be a good test of their will," Sam said. "Actually, it will be a test of wills for all parties, including the plant workers. If we shut off the cash, we effectively put Abello out of business. That plant runs six days a week, and for over nine-hundred people it is their only source of income. We'll be starving them.

"As for Mendoza," Sam continued, "I'm sure he's got sufficient reserves to hang on, but he may just get the message the end is near and decide to bolt with his remaining cash knowing it may be the last of it.

"But maybe not. He's used to getting his way. Wish there was a way we could speed things up."

"Actually, I think I have an idea," said Frank. "We take the plant away from him."

"Seriously? How do we accomplish that?"

"With a little help from our friends—the US Military!"

"Right. So, we just call them like we're ordering a taxi?"

"Sam, just hear me out. The US State Department has significant interests in Guatemala with relief efforts going on all over the country. And where those efforts are going on, you will find the US Military. I'm guessing Hampton has made some sizable political contributions. Maybe it's time to call in a favor?"

"Yeah, but Mendoza has his own small army, remember?"

Frank was really getting into it now. It was like he was back in Vietnam commanding his troops to take an objective. Sam was glad to see he still had that sense of mission accomplishment. Now on his feet and pacing as he talked, Sam had a sense he did.

"Here is the chain of events I see happening," Frank said. "First, Steve will make a call to Mendoza's brother-in-law, the guy who provides the security guards Mendoza considers his personal army. He'll set up our visit, stating you'll be acting on behalf of Hampton.

"Then, you walk into his office and fire him. Terminate his contract. The payments stop now. He'll be pissed, but I don't believe he will continue funding all those security guards knowing the cash train just ended. We've got to do it in person so we can gage his reaction. Just prior to that action, we contract to expand our own private security detail. I think an additional sixty men should do it. CRI can arrange it, and Manuel and Fernando can manage them."

"I'm beginning to see it, Frank. Steve can send down a new operational team to run the plant once we take it back. We get access to all the records and the employees. With the threat of Mendoza gone, I feel pretty certain someone at the plant will come forward and point us in the right direction. We get the right evidence on Mendoza on top of everything else, and he's got to bolt—or he gets arrested and extradited."

"He could decide to fight it out," Frank said warily.

"I suppose he could. What if he reaches out to the Guatemalan military? I'm sure he's paying the right people to make that happen."

"That's when we'll need the US base commander to make a courtesy call to the Guatemalan commander and remind him of the expected protocols."

"What *protocols*?"

"Those that never make it on the six o'clock news."

Sam nodded his approval. "Got it. As long as you realize that's your department."

"Can do, as long as Steve makes the introductory first call and gives them my name and number as the in-country authority."

"I'll get confirmation when I call Steve. Now, what are we forgetting?" Sam looked to Frank as the military strategist he was.

"Well, I'm thinking we can't run this operation with you lying in a hospital bed. You need to get released so we can execute this plan of attack."

"Who said anything about being *released*. Help me up. I'm walking out of here before Nurse Ratched has me tied to the bed."

"I wouldn't put it past her."

"Not gonna give her the opportunity, Frank. Not sure who I fear most, her or Mendoza!"

CHAPTER 40

"**W**HAT DO YOU want me to tell the team?" Frank asked as he helped Sam to his feet.

"I need to call Steve before we'll have authority to do anything, so hold tight for now. Email the managers to meet on my patio tonight at nine o'clock. Tell them I will let them know our plan for bringing this investigation to a successful conclusion very soon. That should pique their interest.

"I will not be spending another night here. On your way out, tell your girlfriend I need to see her."

Moments after Frank exited, Nurse Ratched walked into Sam's room. "Mr. Halloran, I am happy to see you and your friend are now respecting our visitation policy. He also said you asked to see me. What can I do for you?"

Sam made a direct beeline to his closet. Frank had brought over a new set of clothes for him given his old clothes were cut off him in the ER.

"I'm so sorry to say, nurse, I won't need to worry about visitation hours any longer, as I will be checking out of this fine establishment. Your care and service for my speedy recovery are very much appreciated, but I have important matters to attend to and must now take my leave."

The nurse stiffened like an oak tree, grabbing hold of her clipboard with both hands, her eyes wide as they could be. "*Señor* Halloran, you must return to your bed immediately! You will not be discharged until one of our doctors releases you, and that will not happen until he confers with me. Now, get back into your bed!"

He ignored her outburst and began buttoning his shirt and then heard her exit his room. No matter that she was pissed. He wouldn't need her for anything more. Sam finished dressing, grimacing from the pain on his right side. It was the first time he had been on his feet in four days.

Sam took a final scan of the room when Nurse Ratched walked in, this time with a doctor in tow. Sam ignored both of them.

"*Señor* Halloran, I understand you are not happy with our accommodations and wish to check out," said Sam's doctor, jovially.

"Doc, please don't take offense, but I've got a lot going on."

He then turned to his nurse. "Thank you, nurse, I can take it from here."

She looked at him with a subdued rage that didn't show other than her face was still a deep pink, approaching purple. "But doctor, hospital regulations stipulate—"

"Nurse, you do not need to quote hospital regulations to me. Now, please leave us."

"As you wish!"

With a slight smile, he balanced his stethoscope securely around his neck. Turning to ensure she was gone, he said, "Nurse Cruz is the best nurse on staff, and she is rarely wrong about such things as we are about to discuss, but for argument's sake, will you permit me to at least examine you before you walk out of here?"

Pausing and thinking it might not be a bad idea to let the good doctor examine him one last time, Sam acquiesced.

"OK, doc, but I am leaving."

Sam unbuttoned his shirt and sat on the bed.

"*Señor* Halloran, just so you are aware, if I do not officially release you there is not an airline in this country that will allow you to board a plane."

"Sure, and you really expect me to believe that?"

"I am not jesting with you, *Señor*. Please feel free to check with them yourself. It is for your own personal safety, as well as the safety of those who might be unfortunate to be on the same flight as you when you relapse, and the pilot is forced to turn around or engage in other more risky maneuvers in an attempt to save a dying passenger."

The word *dying* caught Sam's attention. He tucked in his shirt while the doctor made some notes on his chart. "You are serious. They won't let me board?"

"I'm afraid this is true, *Señor*. We will add your name to a database which each airline has access to. They will not allow you to board, ever, until you have an official doctor's release."

"Well, I'd call that having a powerful amount of control over us mere mortals. Who instituted that commie regulation?"

Sam thought for a moment. "Doc, I was not aware of that regulation, but I do believe you."

"You are a wise man, *Señor* Halloran," he said as he continued to write on Sam's chart, never looking up at him.

Sam considered his options quickly. He didn't have any if he ever wanted to fly out of this country. "Doc, it sounds like a good safety precaution, I will grant you that, but I have some special circumstances I am not at liberty to disclose. I'm asking for your trust. I simply must be discharged immediately."

"*Señor* Halloran, I know why you need to leave my hospital."

Sam looked into his face without responding.

"I overheard your friend talking on the phone Monday mentioning who it was who may have caused these injuries you have sustained. I heard him say the name Javier Mendoza."

Sam had no clue where this was going, but his doctor was clearly on a mission to tell him something, and Sam was suddenly eager for him to continue.

"*Señor*, my brother, four years ago, was running for mayor of Guatemala City on an anti-corruption platform. We, his family and friends, tried to convince him there was no use trying to defeat the incumbent mayor we all knew was corrupt. Things were moving in the direction where it was looking like my brother had a decent chance to win, until one night I see him lying on a gurney in my own emergency room, bloodied, beaten, and near death. He recovered. Lost an eye, but worse, he lost his passion to help change things for the better. So, my brother dropped his candidacy and returned to teaching."

Laying Sam's chart down on the bed, he turned to look directly into Sam's face. "Those who did this to my brother were never found, probably because the police suspected who did it and knew they could not do anything about it—not that they would want to anyway because many of them were on his payroll." Lowering his head, his lips trembling and his voice wavering, he said, "I hope you are successful in dislodging him from the death grip he has on us. I will pray for you and your team, but please be careful. Mendoza is an extremely dangerous man. God be with you."

To Sam's amazement, the good doctor was about to officially release him. Sam shook his hand and patted his shoulder at the same time, knowing nothing more needed to be said. As Sam turned to leave, the doctor held up a small paper and said, "*Señor*, your official release."

"Thank you for understanding, doctor."

"That will get you out of the country, but first, you need to successfully exit this hospital, which means getting past Nurse Cruz."

Sam laughed, even though it hurt like hell. He creeped out of his room ever vigilant for *her*, walking down the hall following the exit signs. That much Spanish he did know.

CHAPTER 41

SAM BROUGHT HIS managers up to speed regarding his call with Steve. They were relieved to hear Hampton had turned down Mendoza's offer. Sam needed his team on the same page and focused on executing a plan to bring this investigation to a successful conclusion, albeit not in the usual way for a forensic accounting investigation.

Sam laid out his preliminary plan but when pushed for specific details, Sam confessed it was all a work-in-progress at this stage. They seemed to understand the fluid nature of any plan from here forward and were pleased Frank and Sam were including them in its development. Frank had quickly become a respected member of the team, most likely resulting from his stepping in for Sam over the past few days.

"Sam, how do you expect to take control of the plant with all their security? What are you planning to do about them?" Veronica asked.

"Frank and I will be taking care of that tomorrow morning. Let's just say they will not pose a problem. Which reminds me, Marge, did you get the bank draft and copy of the contract?"

"Right here," Marge said, reaching into her portfolio.

"I'll get you the address and phone number in case you can't reach us by our mobiles if something comes up here. I'm told it's just a few miles away."

"How do you expect that will go?" Marge asked, surprising Sam. She usually sat mum at meetings unless she had something snarky to say.

"About the same way as any firing. They won't be happy, but what can they do?"

"They could shoot you both," Marge followed, expressing concern. Again, not the Marge that Sam knew.

"Don't be ridiculous," Sam replied and dismissed it with a smile.

"Sam, what do you expect will be the immediate result of this *siege*, as Eric put it?" Alicia asked.

"Good question, Alicia. I do not have a complete answer for you. What I'm hoping is Mendoza's existing security team will vacate the plant, given they're no longer on the payroll. Then, when we enter the plant, I'll have our lawyer explain to the employees what has transpired and assure them this marked a new day of freedom from the tyrannical leadership of Javier Mendoza."

What Sam expected to happen, what he prayed would happen, was someone in that crowd of employees would come forward with the information—the evidence—they needed to go after this scumbag legally and in a US federal district courtroom.

"But Mendoza lives here in Guatemala where Hampton won't be able to reach him," Eric said.

"True, not directly and immediately, but Javier Mendoza is a US Citizen. The documentary and testimonial evidence we expect to gather will ultimately be delivered to the US Justice Department. I doubt they will have much resistance in extraditing him and probably his wife as well. We learned they have a son at Princeton University, and his wife talks openly about her frequent shopping trips to New York and LA."

"And don't forget the ski lodge he owns in Aspen," Marge chimed in.

"Exactly! I doubt any of the Mendozas will be visiting the ski lodge ever again. I don't know how much cash he has stashed, but I've got to believe the execution of our plan will ensure he will run out of it soon enough."

Veronica asked, "But won't he simply hop on a plane and fly off to some country that doesn't have an extradition treaty with the US?"

"He may try, but keep in mind he'd have to keep an extremely low profile and continue paying-off government authorities to ensure his safety wherever he tries to hide. Plus, those countries without extradition are not the most hospitable environments—like Angola. How many less than honorable thieves would not hesitate to kidnap him for money? He'd have to include them on the payroll. Even he won't have enough to protect his entire family for a lifetime. And where does he hide all that cash? Sooner or later he'll be caught… or murdered by his own men hungry for his cash."

"Well, right now this is all a pipe-dream," said Eric. "We're sitting in a hotel in a country he's still running. This may make for a good movie script, but that's about it right now."

"True, absolutely true, indeed. But for the first time, I see a ray of hope that we can accomplish what we had set out to do." Sam paused to survey the room. "So, any more questions?" Sam asked, looking at each person individually.

"Good. I'll update the staff tomorrow morning at breakfast. Frank will be there in case they want to learn more about why we are taking the US Army with us." He chuckled as he said it, still in disbelief.

As they filed out of his room, Frank stood next to Sam, helping him assemble the notes and documents that were sprawled out on the coffee table as exhibits used in Sam's presentation. "What now, boss?"

Sam regarded him for a moment. "So, let me ask you, Frank, before I had the crap kicked out of me it was *pal* this and *pal* that. Now it's *boss*. Which is it, and why the flip?"

"Not sure, but it probably has something to do with respect."

Before Sam could say anything, Frank said, "You have had one exceptionally long day... and week. You look tired. I'm going to take off. I'll see you at breakfast tomorrow morning. Get a good night's rest. Things are about to move very quickly."

"Thanks, Frank."

Frank was right. Sam was not only exhausted but very anxious about what might lay ahead over the next few days. In spite of Frank's show of respect, Sam's mind began to wander. He knew all too well how things could go tragically wrong... so fast.

As Sam struggled to fall asleep, the possibilities for failure invaded his thoughts:

What if the State Department refuses Steve's request for assistance with the siege... and they are caught staring down the Guatemalan military?

What if Mendoza's brother-in-law keeps his security team in place despite not getting paid?

What if there is another attack on me—or worse, one of my team?

What if people start dying?

Sam rolled out of bed, grabbed a scotch and his pack of Reds, and headed for the patio. It was eleven o'clock. Dark. The cold stone bricks sent chills up his spine as he sat on the chaise lounge. His remedy was to drink more—smoke more too—as memories, bad ones, came flooding back.

I just wanted to expose them. I didn't mean for her to die.

CHAPTER 42

SAM AWOKE, STILL on his patio, to the sound of birds singing and felt the cool dew of the morning ritual playing out before him. The sun had not fully risen, but Sam could see it dawning just over the surrounding ivy-covered wall.

He'd be meeting Frank for breakfast shortly. He was ready. First step in his plan: fire the security company. He couldn't allow anything to cloud his judgment. He would not allow it. Today, they would light the fuse that would inform Javier Mendoza his days were numbered.

Standing for a moment at the entrance to the restaurant, Sam was relieved to see Frank already seated, a cup of coffee up to his lips, with his other hand waving Sam over.

"Don't tell me that's real coffee," Sam said.

"Go time, boss!" Frank said with flair to reveal his own anxiety for what this day held.

"Sounds like you're looking for a rumble today."

"Sam, I feel like I'm back in Nam, only this time the odds are in our favor."

"So, you really feel good about our chances at playing this out as we intend?"

"I do, I really do. I think the State Department is going to come through for us. I think Mendoza's brother-in-law is going to find the limits of family love and pull his team. I mean, why should he risk his entire business to face-off what he knows will be just a temporary stand. To ignore the threat you now represent and make a stand is a losing proposition. He'll see that immediately, and despite pleas from Mendoza, he will no longer support him. Trust me on this."

"I do trust your instincts, Frank, and I am glad to have you by my side."

"Heard back from Steve yet on the State Department call?" Frank asked.

"Just hung up with him. He seems to think it's a go for Monday."

"So, how and when will someone contact us?"

"Steve said he passed on your name and mobile. Someone should be calling you."

"When?"

"I don't know. I assumed it would be soon."

"Sam, we don't assume in this business."

"Sorry, running this type of engagement is not my forte."

"Steve does know the urgency of it all, right?" Frank asked.

"He does and I'm sure that, after last week's meeting with the Mendozas, Barclay has pulled out all the stops assuring the cooperation I requested. It's funny; a week ago, I was fighting to save this investigation from being scrapped, and today, I have a blank check."

"Yeah, and to think, all you had to do was engage in a near death experience to have it your way. You need to keep that tactic in mind next time you're not getting your way."

"Ha! No, thanks. I'm happy to leave the commando ops to guys like you. I'm poorly trained and not well equipped to work in that environment. Which reminds me, did you ever learn the identity of the guy who saved my life at the church?"

"Oh, damn, sorry, I did." Frank reached in his rear pants pocket pulling out his now famous flip notepad. "Pablo Escapa. Works as an independent limo driver. I've got his number, too. What do you want to do?"

Sam looked off… remembering.

"Where did you go, Sam?"

Sam smiled. "Make the call, Frank. I think we just found our newest team member."

He looked skinnier than Sam remembered him that day he drove Alicia and Sam to the airport, when they were fleeing the country. Considering all that had transpired since that day, *fleeing* seemed appropriate.

Approaching Pablo Escapa as he stood by the floor-to-ceiling windows in the hotel lobby, Sam had trouble realizing that, had Pablo not been there last Sunday night, he would have been murdered. What Sam needed to find out above all else was *why* Pablo was there. Sam didn't believe in coincidence. Pablo didn't look like the kind of guy to be hanging around churches in the middle of the night.

Pablo began to walk toward him, extending his hand. They connected, and Sam pulled Pablo close and embraced him with his other arm. "Pablo, you saved my life! How can I ever thank you?"

Pablo embraced Sam. Nothing more needed to be said. When they released, Sam said, "Let's sit." They picked an out-of-the-way corner of the lobby with windows to their backs and the expansive lobby in front of them. Sam was slowly learning from Frank… *always face the area with the greatest threat.*

"I'm guessing you remember driving us to the airport in early January?"

"*Sí, Señor*. I believe you were concerned a couple of men were following you. *Sí*, I remember."

"You were a huge help to us, and it now appears you have continued to be my guardian angel."

"*Sí*," Pablo said, humbly.

Sam waited, but Pablo was a man of few words. "No trouble with the police? About last Sunday?"

"No, *Señor*. The man who attack you, he run off. He not go to police. So, they don't know. The police, they know me anyway. They know what I do. They know I ask for no trouble from anyone, but they also know I will not run from trouble if it comes to me. No problem either way."

"Pablo, how did you happen to be at St. Peter's the same time I was there? Are you a religious man?"

Pablo did not speak immediately. He was remembering... painfully.

Breaking eye contact with Sam, he began with his head down. "My Molina... she was waitress at this hotel many years ago. She made good money. Not as much as I did, but good enough. My mother would watch our eleven-year-old son, Dario, while my wife worked. The work kept her busy with me being deployed... away.

"One Sunday night...."

Sam sat silently, waiting for Pablo to continue at his own pace.

"One Sunday night, about ten year ago, she get off at midnight but was not home at the usual time. My mother, she was very worried when it was an hour past the time, and she called the police. They would do nothing. They tell her wait twenty-four hours. My mother, she would not do this. So, with Dario asleep, my mother, she walked the same path my wife would take coming home from work. And then she saw the police lights at the church. She got close. In the back of the church... there... lying in the middle of trash, she found my Molina. Mother tell me later... my Molina... she had no clothes. When my mother screamed, the police see her standing behind them and took her around to their cruiser... put her in back seat. They later brought her home."

As Pablo spoke in deliberate monotones, Sam noticed him clenching his hands and twisting his wrists causing his forearm muscles to ripple. It was as if he was imagining twisting and then breaking an attacker's neck.

"My commander, when I tell him what happened, he got me out and back home in two days' time. When my mother first saw me, she fell to the ground and wept as she told all these terrible things she had seen. I left to see the police. I was out all night and then for two days more looking for the scum who do this to my Molina. My father, he told me when I come home that my mother cries herself to sleep each night. Even two, three day after when I see my mother again, she was upset to talk to me. My mother, she has never since talked of that night.

"Later, after Molina's funeral, the police come to me and talk. They said that reports were she taken by two men as she leave the church, taken to the back where they beat her, raped her, killed her, left her there like a piece of garbage. Police would not give me source."

Tensing again, the muscles in his forearm and neck rippling, Pablo spoke, "Every Sunday night since that day, I walk to the church and wait... hidden. At that same time. I do not know why. It is painful to do this, but I think whoever do these things to my Molina on that night... maybe they would return, and then I would kill them. But this does not happen... yet. But still, I feel closer to my Molina being there, and... maybe someday I find them."

Pablo sat in silence. "Pablo, your son Dario, he's what, about twenty-one? Is he still with you?"

"I have not seen my son since he finish secondary school. He left our home that summer. My son... he holds me at fault... for not having a mother. His memories of his mother are painful. My son I have not heard from for some years."

Pablo was done talking about the past, and Sam let him bury it, again. He quickly straightened as if a time machine had dropped him from above and the shock of hitting the ground awakened him once again.

"So, that is my story," he said. "Now, I drive car and I have enough. My father died last year, and my mother still lives with me. We have all we need." Pablo stood, extending his hand to shake Sam's. "I am glad to see you, *Señor* Halloran, and happy you have recovered."

With that, he turned to leave, and Sam reached out and touched his shoulder, stopping Pablo. "Pablo, what would you say about driving and providing personal protection for me for as much time as you can allow?" He seemed hesitant to react but did not say no.

"I'll pay you twice what you make a week now, and if you can figure out a way in light of your other obligations, taking care of your mother and such, I will double that figure and get you a room on our floor. You would be driving and providing security for me for most of the day, every day that I remain in this country."

Sam waited.

When Pablo agreed to the arrangement, Sam wrapped both his arms around him. Sam was relieved knowing there was no way anyone would get to him with Pablo as his constant companion. It was a good sign things might finally be going Sam's way. This would also free up Manuel and Fernando to look after Sam's team fulltime.

Sam introduced Pablo to Frank immediately. They shook hands. "Pablo," Sam said, "could you begin immediately? We have an important meeting at two o'clock today where we could really use your expertise."

Pablo thought for a minute. "I can begin for you this minute."

"Perfect! How about you do whatever you need to do, then come back here, and we'll discuss today's plan at lunch."

"This will work. Let me call my mother, and then I will meet you here."

When Pablo walked out of the hotel, Frank said, "Sam, I thought you were going to wait until I completed my background check of him?"

"Sorry, Frank. No time."

"Your call, but I have learned some from what CRI knows about him. Turns out your instincts were right. Pablo is well-trained.

284

Impressive credentials. Mid-eighties, he was a mercenary in the Angola and Mozambique insurgency and before that a little closer to home with the Sandinistas and Contras in Nicaragua."

"Which side did he work for?"

"Doesn't matter, Sam. He logged the right kind of experience either way—protect, cover, kill, if necessary. That's all I care about."

"If you're happy, I'm happy. When he gets back, the three of us will grab a bite to eat, and we'll lay it out for Pablo. We'll drive over with Pablo in his car."

The question of how Pablo happened to be at that church was now solved, but two questions remained: Why would Miguel set Sam up like that? And where is he?

CHAPTER 43

AT LUNCH, FRANK laid out their plan to Pablo. It was immediately clear they would bond quickly with their unique military experiences. Sam enjoyed listening to the two of them swapping old war stories when Sam's phone alarm signaled it was time to leave for their meeting with Philippe Cordova.

Sam checked his pocket, ensuring he had the envelope containing the $60,000 bank draft in payment of the contractual severance obligation. He wondered if that cancellation would be immediate on their part. Contractually, it was immediate, but there would be extenuating circumstances. Javier had to know a battle for the plant was coming and needed his army to defend his position. Sam wanted those guys out of the plant and out of their way, but there was no way to ensure that would happen on his timetable. Soon though, they would know for sure.

As the three of them drove over to *Protección* in Pablo's SUV, Sam was still rehearsing in his mind his planned script.

Having arrived at the *Protección* office, they were greeted by several military-looking men brandishing automatic rifles. They jumped up from their seated position and signaled Pablo to halt. Pablo rolled down his window, and the two exchanged curt passages, directing them further up the alley where they were to park. Pablo refused and insisted on parking in a different way. They finally came to an agreement, and Pablo worked to turn the SUV around, giving them a clear and straight-away exit to the street.

Pablo exited the SUV first and walked inside. Moments later, he signaled to Sam and Frank it was safe to exit the vehicle. One of the armed guards shouldered his rifle and walked up, motioning to follow him. Frank led the way. Pablo returned to the SUV. He'd leave it running.

Sam and Frank were led up a narrow staircase to Cordova's office. Along the way they passed a room with a door cracked open just enough to witness a guy being fondled by two women. He was lying shirtless and sitting up against the headrest of a king bed under a slowly oscillating ceiling fan. Sam paused to steal a longer look until a guard yelled at him. He ignored him. Nevertheless, the guard worked his way back to him and swiftly closed the door. "Follow me," was all he said.

Climbing yet another flight of stairs, Sam thought the women seemed quite young. He was reminded of an earlier conversation with Derek Dorn talking about the trafficking of underage women through this country and particularly Guatemala City. Sam thought of his side mission—his humanitarian mission undisclosed to the Hampton executives. He justified it, knowing how Mrs. Mumfry would admire him. The destruction of Mendoza's empire would be a nice side benefit to liberate a number of innocents such as the girls he just passed, but then he knew the whole sex trafficking issue was much bigger than just those girls. It saddened Sam to think about it.

At the top of the stairs, they finally entered the office of Philippe Cordova.

Cordova immediately stood up behind his massive, richly carved, black walnut desk, reaching over it to limply shake Sam's hand. Sam didn't want to provoke any trouble by making some statement about what he had just witnessed. That would be stupid, and Sam wanted to work hard at not being stupid anymore on this project.

Cordova motioned for them to sit in two overstuffed chairs in front of his desk. Frank had a different plan. He didn't shake Cordova's hand and positioned himself by a window looking down onto the street below. He and Pablo exchanged nods.

While Sam felt somewhat secure in the company of Frank and Pablo, there was one item noticeably missing from their attire—weapons. Caught with a firearm, they would be arrested for a capital offense. They didn't want to push that envelope, especially here where Mendoza controlled the law enforcement in the area. No, the plan was to conclude their business as quickly as possible and get the hell out.

"Mr. Cordova, I know you are a busy man, so I'll get right to the point of our visit." Sam handed him the envelope. "Enclosed you will find a faxed letter from Steve Lemly, the CFO of Abello Distilleries. It confirms that I am representing their interests in your contract to provide security personnel to the Abello plant." Sam felt the effects of adrenaline now coursing through his entire body, causing his voice to crack a little. It was embarrassing, but he could not control it. He was scared, and unfortunately, it was showing.

"This letter also states that Hampton is terminating the contract with your company effective immediately. At the end of this month, you will receive your final check for all services rendered to date.

"Additionally, you will find in the envelope a bank draft in the amount of $60,000 representing the contractual requirement for immediate termination. Hampton believes they have complied with all provisions of the contract."

In spite of how his body was reacting, Sam at least was able to deliver the message exactly as rehearsed. To make it clear there was no point in discussing any additional terms, Sam rose from his seat, still scared and glad he was wearing dark pants. "When do you expect to be removing your security from the plant?"

Cordova did not reply. He inspected the letter and then the check without speaking. He had to suspect this was coming. Nevertheless, he said, "But, *Señor*, I am surprised and disappointed with this action.

We have worked extremely hard to please Abello, and we want to continue providing our exceptional service to them and would beg to understand their reasons for this highly unexpected termination. Many employees I will have to let go. This is not a good event," Cordova said bitterly.

Cordova was showing the contents of the envelope to a suited man standing to his left and a little behind his chair, who acted like he was reading the letter with great interest and intensity. They seemed to be conferring, as the suited gentleman would speak for a bit and then point to something in the letter. Cordova would nod. They could have been discussing the weather for all Sam knew.

Sam feared this might be turning into a confrontation he had tried hard to avoid. Frank, sensing things were moving in the wrong direction, stood more erect. He looked down at Pablo and removed his cap with his right hand and smoothed back his hair with his left before replacing it. Frank then turned his back to the window to face Sam and Cordova. He stood rigid with arms at his side, as if preparing to fend off an attack. Never being in the military but having seen enough Harrison Ford movies, Sam sensed impending danger and a chill overcame him.

Two additional security guards entered the office and stood in front of the door. Sam felt something bad was about to happen. They were on the third floor. They could never make it down to Pablo in time. Even if they could, what good would that do? They were unarmed and surrounded by armed militia. More adrenaline pumped.

Then, Sam heard the faint sound of diesel motors. Frank heard them, too, as he turned toward the window and looked down onto the street. Two of Cordova's guards quickly stepped over to another open window and peered into the street where the noise, conversation, and commotion prompted even Cordova to rise from his throne.

Everyone in the room except Sam was positioned in front of an open window. A moment later, Sam heard the diesels idling and someone speaking in English from below.

"I am looking for Sam Halloran," he said, looking up at Frank.

"I am not, but I have accompanied him. He is in this room with me. I know he would appreciate an escort down."

"Copy that." Combined with the ear-to-ear grin on Frank's face, it could only mean one thing. The US Cavalry had arrived!

Frank moved to Sam's side. Both could hear what sounded like a legion of boots bounding up the stairway, constant thunder until they were standing in front of him, helmeted with glasses and AR rifles in hand pointed upward. "Are you Sam Halloran?"

"I am."

"How can we assist you, Mr. Halloran?"

"You can escort us out of this building," Sam said without cracking a single syllable, his confidence restored.

In seconds, Sam and Frank were surrounded by soldiers and escorted down the stairs and out of the building. Sam beamed with pride passing Cordova's men, who stood on the sidelines clearly afraid to engage.

Pablo was sitting behind the wheel of his vehicle, motor running. Behind and in front of him were two Humvees commanded by our very own US Military. There were not a lot of them, but then, they didn't need a lot. These were US Army Rangers heavily armed and prepared for anything. Sam felt the patriotism swell within him, almost beckoning him to shout out to Mendoza and his cronies to *bring it on*, but then he checked himself.

Frank escorted Sam past one Humvee and shoved him into the back seat of Pablo's SUV and then climbed in the front passenger seat. Atop both Humvees was a soldier with their hands on a Browning .50 caliber machine gun. As those diesel engines revved up, they raced away to safety knowing they would not be returning. Message delivered.

"Where the hell did they come from?" Frank said relieved. "Did you call them, Pablo?"

"No, *Señor*. Someone must have dispatched them to our aid. Thank you, Jesus!"

"Amen to that, Pablo!" Sam said.

"When dickhead began pushing back over your *take a hike* speech, I knew we were in trouble," said Frank. "I signaled Pablo to alert him to imminent danger."

"*Sí*, I was concerned when I hear the diesels, then I see the US flag on fender and smiled."

Pablo was working hard to keep up with the vehicle in the lead and struggled to drive and talk, clearly still excited. "While you guys coming downstairs, the colonel tell me they first stopped by the hotel and asked for you. A lady told him where you were. He told me the name, Mary something."

"Marge Simon?"

"Yeah, that's it, Marge Simon. Anyway, he say this Marge was standing at front desk and telling him you weren't there, but she knew of your location. And then they are here."

"I'll be damned," Sam said. "Marge sent them!" Slapping his thigh and still laughing at the thought of strait-laced Marge Simon taking charge on something that had nothing to do with her own workpapers.

Finally, on a paved road, Sam pulled out his BlackBerry. "Steve, it might have been nice if you had let me know you had coordinated with the military before going over to *Protección*." Sam wasn't angry, just excited from the stress of it all.

"Sam, no one from State let us know they had agreed. I'm sorry, but please believe me when I tell you we didn't get the call. I didn't screw it up this time."

"I believe you, Steve. I suppose they didn't want a record showing a link between a private corporation *renting* an army battalion. No matter. The timing could not have been better. Bad things were brewing, but the cavalry arrived just in time."

"Thank God for that."

Their vehicle stopped in front of the hotel lobby doors as Sam continued talking with Steve. Frank and Pablo jumped out and walked up to a distinguished older army officer standing between a couple of other uniformed men. Frank confirmed they came to the hotel just to review arrangements for the plant takeover on Monday.

"Steve, I've got to run. I need to coordinate with our new friends. Thank them, too."

"OK, but call me later to brief me. I wish I were there with you guys."

"Me too, but then you'd never again want to look at another debit or credit!" Both men laughed.

"Oh… one more thing, Steve. Please thank whoever it was that sent the cavalry."

"Actually, I know who that was, and I will pass along your appreciation to *her*."

"Don't tell me this went all the way to the top. Kate Hampton made the call?"

"She did, indeed. I wasn't in the room when she did, but I was told directly by Garrett, *Kate will need to make that call*."

"Wow. The heiress herself. I feel honored."

"You should. Katherine Hampton is now receiving daily updates on this engagement. Garrett told me he had never seen her so upset upon hearing about the attack on you. I was also told she wants to meet with you when this is all over and you are safely back in the US."

"I'm impressed. The iron lady herself wants to meet me."

"So please don't die, or it may turn out bad for me."

"Roger that, Steve. You can bet that's the only thing keeping me alive. I don't want you to look bad."

Both of them laughed again.

"Just stay safe, Sam."

"It's at the top of my list, Steve. Now, I really must get over there and find out what these guys are plotting. I'll be in touch. And thanks again, Steve. I feel safer knowing you are there for us."

CHAPTER 44

"I DON'T KNOW ABOUT you guys, but I could use a drink," Sam said after finalizing plans with the colonel regarding their assistance in the plant siege on Monday.

Sam, Frank, and Pablo turned and walked toward the pool bar. "I think after that experience, Hampton wouldn't mind us enjoying a bottle of Macallan 18," Sam said laughing.

At the pool bar, they discussed the siege just two days away. There was still much planning and coordinating to be done. Frank had taken care of the major details regarding their new security. Sam was hopeful Mendoza's guards, all 160 of them, were informed by Philippe Cordova that their services would no longer be needed and not to show up for work at Abello tomorrow, or the next day, or ever again.

The three of them sipped their scotch by the pool and talked about their planned tactics for Monday's siege. Sam delegated himself responsibility for directing the staff on the forensic accounting aspects once inside the plant. It would be a nice change of pace from the paramilitary life he had recently been experiencing.

That night, Sam wanted to have dinner in his room, alone. Frank understood and Sam thought Frank would be relieved he didn't have to look after him for a change. Besides, he and Pablo seemed to have bonded and were becoming fast friends. Sam was confident they'd find a quiet place to continue discussing their special ops experiences.

After finalizing things and retiring to his room, Sam was happy to have some alone time.

Stretching out on his patio chaise with the finest scotch whisky money could buy, he was reflective. Even though Frank and Pablo were still working out details, Sam was satisfied with their plans for taking over the plant. There was nothing more for him to do but try and relax.

Then, there was a knock at the door.

Sam opened it and was surprised to find Veronica standing there. "Sam, we need to talk." Veronica said as she walked into Sam's suite and sat on the sofa. She appeared pensive.

Sam sat near her. "What's up?"

"Got a call about an hour ago from Gabriela Castillo."

His face looked puzzled.

"Gabriela Castillo. Mendoza's secretary," Veronica said.

"Sorry… I do remember her from my first trip down here. What did she say?"

"Sam, she's scared. She's petrified of him!"

"What did he do to her?"

"What hasn't he done to her? But no sense going into all that now. She admitted to authoring the anonymous letter."

"Damn, nice work, Veronica!" Sam said as he sat up straight.

"She knows everything, and he trusts her with every detail of his entire criminal enterprise. She hates him, Sam. He treats her like his slave. Takes her on his business trips, mostly to Columbia, where he is deeply involved in the drug trade with the cartels. Trafficking in women, too." She started to cry.

"Take a breath, kid."

"Sam, he's a monster. That's where he gets most of his victims."

"What do you mean?"

"Gabriela told me. Favors the young ones. Right around sixteen, she said. Something about when he was that age everyone made fun of him about his looks, especially the girls. Said it's payback. Most come from the poorest cities in South and Central America. Girls are abandoned by the thousands as young as infants. He stores the younger ones in orphanages until they come of age. He gets them ready to ship off to better markets in the US, Middle East, Russia, but he brings some to work in the plant... until he decides he wants to rape them. Then, they disappear. No families. No one to search for them. No one cares."

"I care," Sam said, and he did, even though such an effort was not part of the Scope of Services in his engagement letter.

"It seems so hopeless, Sam."

"Veronica, what aren't you telling me? You didn't get all this in a phone call."

She ignored the inference. "And he is stealing from the company. Way more than expense reporting fraud. He's stealing a lot from the company according to her, but she didn't have details. She said we'd need Miguel for that. She and Miguel are extremely close."

"You mean the same Miguel that tried to get me killed?"

"She knew about that. Miguel called her after. To say goodbye. Sam, they held his family hostage in their own home forcing Miguel to call you. After they left, he grabbed them and fled. He wouldn't tell her where but said he'd contact her. He wants to come forward. He wants to help you in any way he can, but she hasn't heard from him since that call. She's worried something terrible has happened to him and his family."

Sam leaned forward and almost spilled his drink attempting to set it down. "You're telling me Miguel is willing to meet with us. Does he have evidence?"

"He has it all. Besides running the IT and data center for the company, Mendoza uses Miguel to keep the accounting for all the off-books stuff. Bribes and payoffs. The drugs. The sex trafficking and so much more.

"Gabriela said she and Miguel have been friends for a long time.

They'd see each other often. Well, before he skipped. Mendoza required Miguel to come to his office weekly to do all the off-book recordkeeping on Mendoza's desktop computer. He made it a habit to do it when Mendoza was gone. There, he and Gabriela had time to talk. They had both wanted to do something for a long time, only they never were sufficiently motivated, but now with us here, they are feeling emboldened."

Sam lay back into the sofa trying to take it all in. "Drugs? That'll get Hampton's attention! How long has that been going on?"

"According to Gabriela, the Colombians figured out a while ago it's a lot safer and more profitable to run their drugs from the Columbian labs through Central America and Mexico rather than try and outrun the US Coast Guard into Florida. They enlisted *El Gordo* from the *Cali Cartel* to do the running, and he got his cousin, Mendoza, involved. They use a network of Mexican gangs. Plus, Mendoza skims some of the cocaine for himself. Smuggles the coke in shipments of rum to the US."

"Veronica, I need to tell Steve about this. We've just moved to a whole new level. We need to get DEA involved."

"Not so fast. If we eventually go that route, fine, but right now obtaining the forensic evidence that would nail the son-of-a-bitch is within our grasp. Moving to get DEA involved now would slow it all down and we'd lose control. They'd run the operation. We're so close," she said, talking a mile a minute.

"That makes sense, but we've been working that angle with no luck."

"But now we have Gabriela and Miguel committing to help us."

"Except that Miguel has disappeared," Sam said as he placed his hands behind his head, trying to take it all in. "Veronica, this all sounds so farfetched."

"There's more. A lot more. We'd thought Saturdays were just another production day. It is, but *not* for the company. Saturday is when they manufacture Mendoza's own brand of rum. He uses

Hampton's resources in labor, equipment, and materials and then sells it under the brand name *Sophie's Pleasure* through the same distribution channels as all of Abello Distilleries' products throughout Latin and South America." Veronica paused to take a sip of her drink. Sam leaned forward, picking up his drink again.

"I've never heard of such a scheme." Sam contemplated how one could pull that off. He found himself almost admiring Mendoza's ingenuity.

"Me either. I've never encountered a fraudster so bold he would produce his own brand of the company's product and then sell it right under their noses through their own distribution network."

As Sam thought about all the accounting controls, the internal auditors, the external auditors, all the vendors, all the employees, how could it be possible to do something like that without detection? He sat there in amazement.

"Boss, you can close your mouth now. I know it sounds preposterous, but Gabriela has convinced me with these emails and bank records." She reached into her briefcase and pulled out the documents and began to lay them out in front of Sam.

"Hold on here, V. You could not have gotten all this on a phone call. You said Gabriela *called* you. Where did you get this stuff?"

"OK, I have a confession to make. Gabriela and I have been talking on the phone and meeting here and there for the past two weeks." Seeing Sam about to explode, Veronica held up both hands. "Hold on, Sam. I couldn't tell you before. I'd be betraying a source, and through it all I have followed the *Sam Halloran* book on cultivating a source, and it worked. The only reason we are having this discussion now is because she has finally given me permission to bring you in. So, relax. I did it your way, and your way worked."

Sam relented and calmed down. She was right to do it the way she did. He began leafing through the documents she laid before him. "I'm guessing you attached these translations to each document for my benefit. Nice going, kid."

Sam read through several pages. "This is unreal. These emails with distributors clearly show he's selling goods for his own purposes and not the company's." Sam held one up that Veronica had translated. "Look at this one." He began to read it.

Ender,

I look forward to the start of our new enterprise. We both seek to make much money, but only if you follow instructions to the letter. Gabriela Castillo, will be our intermediary. She will call you soon and you will trust her as you do me. She will send you the bank routing number, delivery schedules, and distribution information next week.

We both have much to gain, but also much to lose if her instructions are not carried out precisely as dictated.

I look forward to working with you on our new venture.

Your partner,

El Jefe

Sam read a few more aloud and then kept grabbing for another like a kid at a buffet line filled with desserts. "Just the fact Mendoza committed these schemes to writing shows how he acts with impunity."

"What else have you got? I mean, this is good, but we need more, a lot more. Like, we need his entire email archive."

"Way ahead of you, boss. After our meeting last night, I met with Gabriela at her house, and we had a long talk. This doesn't get us home but shows there is a pathway. Remember when we were notified that all the records were stolen, the hard drives gone?"

"How could I forget that absurd excuse?"

"Well, Gabriela said those hard drives are intact and under the watchful eye of Miguel Herrera."

"And she thinks he'll give them to us?"

"She's certain of it. It's always upset Miguel what Mendoza does, but threatening his family has taken this to a new level with him."

"But you said she hasn't heard from him?"

"Not since the attack on you last Sunday."

"Where does that leave us?"

"Screwed, at least for now," Veronica said with a downtrodden attitude.

Both sat contemplative for a few moments.

"OK, I guess we're through here," Sam said.

"I do have one question, boss."

"What?"

"If Miguel has possession of all the hard drives and access to the secret records on Mendoza's other criminal activities… tell me why we are raiding the plant on Monday?"

Sam breathed out a long sigh. "Good question. With this new information I guess the only answer I have is that someone has to take back the plant, and I, for one, am not going near that place without an army, which I now apparently have at my disposal. And who knows, maybe we get access to all the employees and Gabriela helps us convince some of them to help us. Hell, I don't know! Dammit!" Sam said, slamming his fist down on the coffee table. He placed his head in his hands and closed his eyes in frustration. A moment later, he felt Veronica's soothing hand on his shoulder.

"Sam, I wish I had answers for you. I think, at least for the moment, I've run out of them. I'll continue to hang with Gabriela and notify you the moment I learn anything new."

Without looking up, Sam touched Veronica's hand. "Thanks, kid. I know you will. Things have got to turn around for the better. They must. The good guys need a break here. We're so close."

Sam heard the door to his room softly close. He let out a sigh, pleased he still had a fully stocked bar in his room. It would be a long evening alone.

CHAPTER 45

Monday, March 2 (Early Morning)—Hotel Barcelo

SAM SPENT SATURDAY and Sunday finalizing plans for the siege. He was surprised how much preparation and coordination with the military was involved. They were thorough.

For his part, he had three primary objectives: pack up Mendoza's office, including, hopefully, his computer and Gabriela's; insert the new management team to operate the plant going forward; and interview the employees right after Enrico Blanco's speech—that Mendoza has been replaced and will never return to the plant. Mendoza's reign of terror was over. But even Sam doubted the workers would buy it. He could only hope.

Sam glanced over at his alarm clock—1:14 a.m. He let out a disgusted sigh. *Maybe I had too much scotch*, he thought. *I need to get some sleep.*

Then the phone rang.

"*Señor* Halloran. This is the front desk. My apologies at this late hour, but there is a person standing in front of me insisting you would want to meet with him. That you have been waiting for his call to you."

"No need to apologize. Thank you. I will be right down! Please make my guest comfortable. I'm coming down now!" Sam flew out of bed with his BlackBerry in his hand.

Pick up, pick up. Dammit!

"Do you know what time it is?"

"Time for the good guys to score a grand slam! I think it's him."

"Who?"

"Miguel. Or someone like him. I don't know who but… just get Pablo now and meet me at the elevator. I'm not going down to the lobby without you guys. I've learned my lesson."

Frank was in the hall pulling up his gym shorts and pounding on Pablo's door yelling for him to get up. Sam pushed the down arrow anticipating Pablo would be out quickly. He was right, but with how these guys were dressing in the hall, Sam was glad there were no women or children around.

On the way down, Sam recapped the call from the front desk. He was so excited he could hardly speak.

Sam was first out of the elevator. He had seen Miguel only a couple times, but he was sure it was him standing by the front desk. Standing next to him had to be his wife and two daughters. His whole family… here!

Sam calmed himself as he walked up to shake Miguel's hand, anticipating the reason he had come. "Miguel, I can't believe it is you in the flesh. It is so good to see you."

Miguel became emotional. "*Señor*, I had no choice. He had my family," he said, referring to the night he lured Sam to the church.

"Miguel, hold on. Stand here with Frank and Pablo. They work with me. I'll be right back. Don't move. We'll talk in a moment."

Sam walked up to the desk clerk. "I want a suite with at least three bedrooms for this family. Register him under the name Jose Velcro and put it on my master billing. Tell no one of this incident."

As the desk clerk handed Sam several room keys for Miguel's new suite, Sam handed him a C-note. "Tell no one… you hear me?"

"*Sí, Señor* Halloran. *Sí*, no one will know."

Moments later, Miguel's wife was tucking their daughters into bed, and Sam and Frank were huddled with Miguel in the living room. Pablo waited by the door, just in case. They were taking no chances.

"*Señor, Señor*, please forgive me. I had no choice," Miguel said as he began to get emotional again.

"Miguel, it makes no difference now. We'll talk about that later. Right now, please tell me why you are here. Where have you been? We thought—"

"I was away, but I am here now."

"Yes, you are. Thank God you are unharmed and your family too. Now, how can I help you?"

"I have it all. The hard drives. I have them to give you. They contain everything."

Sam could feel the adrenaline begin to course through his body, but this time it was a reaction to extreme stress relief. "The accounting records are contained on those hard drives?"

"*Sí*, all transactional data."

"The email archive for everyone, Mendoza too?"

"*Sí*. Everything. Everything is there."

Sam tasted blood in his mouth. He was so excited he bit through his lip without even feeling it.

"Where are the drives?"

Miguel was overly excited and having trouble getting it all out, still intermittently apologizing for that Sunday night.

"Miguel, calm down. Relax. You are safe here. Your family is safe here. You will never need fear for yourself or your family ever again. Do you understand me?"

"*Sí, Señor. Sí, Sí*. I understand, but I had no choice. He had my family."

"Miguel, we will talk about that in a minute. Let's talk about the hard drives. Where are they? Where are the hard drives at this minute?"

"They are with me. In the trunk of my car. Below. In the parking lot."

Sam turned to Pablo. "Go with Miguel and secure the hard drives now."

"Of course. Miguel, come with me," Pablo said. They took the stairs, Pablo not wanting to risk being caught in the elevator.

Sam sat on the floor, back against the sofa, elbows on his knees, head down. A huge sense of relief flooded over him. Frank joined him on the floor.

"Sam, you did it! This is the motherlode. You are the hero of the day! Congratulations!" They high fived each other, both grinning ear to ear.

Javier Mendoza couldn't sleep and paced on his back patio. Constanza had brought him his usual evening drink. He hadn't touched it. He could not remember having ever been so enraged… which was saying a lot. He was so incensed he could not enjoy his guest in the bedroom next to his. She would have to wait. He was mad with anger. Mad at his men, mad at his adversaries, mad at himself. Most of all, he hated Sam Halloran and wanted him dead.

Everything was falling apart. Everything he had built was disintegrating right in front of him. He was running out of options. Then, when he thought all was lost, he got a phone call.

"*Jefe*. We are at the Hotel Barcelo keeping an eye on Halloran and his people. Miguel showed up. He is here with his entire family."

Javier thought for a moment. "I want you to kill him," he said, calmly. Inside, he was ecstatic.

"What about his family?"

"I don't care about his family. If they get in the way, kill them too."

"His wife and daughters?"

"Listen, you idiot! Listen very closely. If the sun rises on this day and Miguel Herrera is still alive, I will kill you and *your* family in the most horrible of ways. Now, get it done."

"*Sí, Jefe*. He will die tonight."

"What about his car? Is it there? At the hotel?" Mendoza asked, calculating. Making sure he was being thorough.

"Yes. I can see it now."

"Blow it up."

"But it is parked next to other cars. In the hotel parking lot."

"How deaf are you? BLOW UP HIS FUCKING CAR!!! Now, did you hear that?"

"*Sí, Jefe*. We will blow it up."

"And call me the moment it is done. And Miguel is dead."

Javier hung up the phone. Suddenly, he experienced a pain in his left arm, his fingers tingling. He sat and took a sip of water. *Not now. I can't deal with this now.*

Javier's men huddled and waited. They waited for any sign of Miguel. But first they would lay a charge.

Bam! Bam! Bam!

"Sam, those are rifle shots," Frank yelled as he spread out on the floor, listening, trying to determine their direction.

Bam! Bam! Bam!

"They're NATO rounds. Stay down and cover."

There were screams all over.

Miguel's wife ran into her daughter's room.

There was more screaming, and then the gunshots continued.

Bam! Bam! Bam! Bam!

"Miguel and Pablo!" Sam yelled.

"On it! I'm headed downstairs," Frank said in surprisingly calm, measured speech.

"I'm right behind you."

They took the stairs and then crawled their way to the front desk, staying down and away from the hotel lobby's floor-to-ceiling windows, which remained intact. There were no more shots, but they were taking no chances.

Sam yelled to the desk clerks even though he could not see any. He assumed they, too, were hugging the floor.

Garbled Spanish was all he heard in response, but then a horrific explosion let off, totally obliterating the panes of the lobby windows as they blew inward, scattering shards of glass everywhere.

Alarms were sounding.

The lobby sprinkler system turned on.

There was screaming everywhere.

Frank jumped up and ran to the front entrance. He crouched down, surveying the parking lot and wishing he had a gun in his hand. Sam soon joined him. Off to the left, they saw several cars ablaze.

"Miguel… Pablo… are you OK?" Sam yelled into the night.

Nothing was heard in response.

Then, Frank noticed a body lying face down in the parking lot about seventy feet out, a straw hat several feet away from the body. It was just like the one he saw Miguel wearing before he left with Pablo. Frank ran to Miguel, but then quickly determined he was dead, lying in a pool of blood. Head shot… among others. Sam raced over.

"Sam, you shouldn't be here. The area is not secure."

Just then, there was another loud and horrific explosion… then another right after the first one. Gas tank explosions. There were now three cars engulfed in flames shooting twenty feet high. It was all happening over fifty feet away, yet Sam could feel the intense heat. There was pandemonium everywhere. Firetrucks were now arriving, police cars behind them, lights flashing, sirens blaring.

The hotel lobby was now filling with awakened guests responding to the automatic warning system that ordered everyone to the lobby. Sam stood while Frank was still attending to Miguel, searching for any sign of life.

"Pablo! Pablo!" Sam yelled, searching for his driver, protector, and friend.

He saw another body lying in an evergreen bush just outside a side entrance to the hotel. *Please God, let him be alive…. Please God!* He begged mentally.

When Sam reached the body, he lifted Pablo's head noting blood over one side of his face. He refused to believe he had been killed too. He cried out, "Pablo… NOOO! Damn you, Mendoza! Damn you!"

But then, Sam heard something. A groan. Pablo was alive!

"Frank, over here, Pablo… he's alive."

Frank soon joined him. He ripped off his own shirt to use as a cloth to wipe blood from the side of Pablo's head. Just above the ear was a two-inch gash. "It's a bullet wound, but just a grazing," Frank said. "He'll need stiches, but he will live. Pablo will be OK," he assured Sam.

Pablo was awakening.

"Pablo. It's Sam. You were grazed by a bullet, but you're going to be fine. Can you hear me? What happened?"

Pablo let out a few grunts and coughs and then maneuvered himself so that, with Sam's help, he was now sitting. Sam positioned him so his back was against the building.

"Miguel. Where's Miguel?" asked Pablo in slurred speech.

"He didn't make it, Pablo."

Frank had moved back to Miguel's body, which was now being attended by two paramedics administering CPR. Frank knew it was hopeless. He had seen more than his share of battlefield injuries and deaths. In a moment, they abandoned their efforts to save Miguel.

Police officers were now approaching. Frank moved toward Sam and Pablo. Another paramedic was now attending to the laceration on the side of Pablo's head, applying butterfly bandages. Frank stood next to Sam as they both surveyed the area.

The fire department had extinguished the fires that had engulfed the three cars. Both men suspected the worst; one of those cars was likely Miguel's. Sam glanced over toward Pablo. He was sitting up, his back against the building, talking with the paramedics. He'd be OK.

Sam and Frank walked toward the carnage for a closer look. The center vehicle's trunk had blown off. Inside lay the remains of small metal boxes, their plastic fronts melted away. Neither of them were forensics experts in the art of crime scene analysis, but it seemed clear they were staring at a bunch of hard drives that had seen better days. They would demand those drives be set aside for later examination, but they knew they would never see them again.

Police began pushing them back from the burned vehicles and lined the area with yellow tape. No, they would never see the charred remains of what Sam suspected was his golden ticket to solving this case.

"Sam, I heard gunshots!" said a frantic Veronica, who was on the floor next to her bed talking with Sam on their mobiles.

"Yeah, kid. Not good news to report. The trouble is over. Get word to the rest of the staff to remain in their rooms. As for you, I'd like you to go to room 2512. Take Alicia with you. Miguel's family is there. Stay with them. Try and keep them calm. I'll be up as soon as I can.

"Miguel's family? What are they doing here? Where's Miguel? What is going on?"

"I'll explain in a few. Right now, I'd like you to be with Miguel's wife and daughters. Try and keep them calm. I'll be up directly. I have some bad news to deliver to them."

CHAPTER 46

"**S**O, HOW DID I do?" Sam asked Veronica after talking with Miguel's wife… Veronica interpreting.

"Sam, you did the best you could. There's no way to prepare for something like that."

"I feel responsible," Sam said, disheartened that yet another person had died in an effort to help him.

"You shouldn't. Miguel came to you. I've talked with him more than you have. I guess he had seen enough."

"You're right there. I learned tonight why he called me that Sunday night. On that evening, when I went to the church, Mendoza visited Miguel's house while Miguel and his family were cleaning up after dinner. He asked Miguel to step out with one of his men. They took him to the plant where, for the next three hours, they tortured him trying to get him to make that call to me… to set me up. Miguel wouldn't do it. Then later, sitting at his office chair, bloodied and beaten, he was handed a mobile. At the other end was Mendoza. He was sitting in the bedroom of his daughter, Valeria, reading her a bedtime story. Miguel's wife was *entertaining Juan*, whatever the hell that meant. He agreed to do as Mendoza instructed. But throughout the beating, knowing he'd likely need to make that call to me, he had concocted a plan... *where* he would tell me to meet him and exactly *when*."

"He told you all this tonight?"

"No, we never had a chance to talk about it. He told Pablo on their way down to the parking lot... just before he was murdered. Miguel didn't know Pablo well, but he knew the story of how he lost his wife and his Sunday night routine since that day. Sam filled her in on the tragic details.

"Holy shit! So, if Pablo decided not to go to the church last Sunday, or was a little off on his timing...?"

"You got it. I'd be in a box being shipped back home right about now.

"So, let's talk about our whistleblower... Mendoza's secretary. When was the last time you talked to her?" Sam asked.

"Saturday morning, but I'm worried, Sam. I've been trying to call her all day. Left her messages but she hasn't returned my calls."

"So, what do you think?"

"I'm thinking it's not good. I'm worried she went ahead with that stupid plan of hers, which is probably why she didn't call me today... rather, yesterday. Afraid I'd talk her out of it."

"OK, back up. Come over here and sit."

Veronica walked to the sofa where Sam was seated.

She looked down at him, hesitant to speak. Sam stared into her face and waited. She sat next to him.

"On Saturday, Gabriela mentioned this wild-ass plan when she hadn't heard from Miguel. That the hard drives might be gone, along with him. That we would never find the evidence we needed."

"OK, but what *plan* are you talking about?"

Veronica took a moment. She folded her hands in her lap and lowered her head.

"Remember Friday when I told you about where Mendoza kept his records of all his extracurricular activities?"

"On his computer, in his office. Miguel would stop by weekly and log them."

"Yes. Well, on Saturday, she told me Miguel called her last Sunday…" she said haltingly, "about what he had done to lure you into a trap…."

"Take your time, V, this is good."

"…Miguel reminded her of a promise she had made to him some time ago. That if anything happened to him she'd need to download those files from Mendoza's computer and expose him. At that time, he told her the exact file name and its location on Mendoza's computer and gave her a microchip drive and showed her how to use it. Said it was small enough to easily hide in her office.

"On Saturday, she told me that all week long, not hearing from Miguel, she might have to follow through on that promise."

"You didn't tell her to go ahead with that, did you?"

"Of course not. I told her *not* to do that. That we were taking the plant back on Monday morning. We'd take his computer then."

"What did she say?"

"Well… she agreed with me. That there were eyes on his office all the time… that she could never work up the courage to do something like that. But now I fear she may have gone ahead with it… seeing it as her last chance, with Sunday being the only day the plant was closed."

"Let's slow down. Any chance Gabriela could be with a friend or relative?"

"She has a mother and younger sister, Evita, and a daughter. Her mother takes care of her daughter when she's away. Evita is about eighteen and still lives with her mother," Veronica said as she covered her face with her hands, pulling back her hair, her eyes tearing up around a reddening nose. She looked into Sam's face as reality hit her. "I've got no way to contact them!"

Sam gently grabbed her shoulders. "Calm down, V. Think. Do you know where Gabriela lives?

At that moment, Veronica brightened up. "I do! I have her address in my phone," she said quickly, standing up. Sam followed. She looked into Sam's face and grabbed his shoulders. "We need to go over there. She may be hurt." Veronica quickly morphed into a red-faced mess of tears and snot. "Sam, we need to go over there right now!"

"No, we're not doing that. You and I are staying here. I'll send Pablo and Frank over. Give me her address."

Sam relayed a brief update to Frank on his mobile, furnishing him with Gabriela's address. He and Pablo would go there now and report back.

Sam watched Veronica pacing back and forth.

"I need a damn cigarette. Where's my purse?"

Any other time, Sam would jump all over that request and their famous bantering would commence, but now was not the time. He handed over her purse.

"Let's wait on the patio," Sam said, trying to deflect her thoughts.

The trip over to Gabriela's house was about fifteen miles, which under normal circumstances would take about thirty minutes. Veronica was now on her fourth or fifth cigarette by the looks of the ashtray. She continued to pace on Sam's patio.

"It's been forty-five minutes! Why haven't they called? Maybe you gave them the wrong address or Frank wrote it down wrong?"

"I read it to him exactly as you gave it to me. He read it back to me. Pablo lives here. I've got to believe he can find it. Try and relax, Veronica. Let's give it a few more minutes before I call them."

That seemed to quiet her for another couple minutes, but then she exploded. "Sam, I can't wait any longer. Call them. Call them now!"

Sam picked up his phone. "Frank, what did you find?"

"Sam, put it on speaker! I need to hear." Sam complied.

"We're at Gabriela's home. I've been walking around the

perimeter while Pablo went inside, and he's coming out now. Give me a minute" ...She's not here, Sam. The place is empty, but there's no sign of a struggle."

Veronica shouted, "Frank, she has to be there! Are you sure you're in the right house?"

"It's the right house," said Pablo. "There was picture on the mantle of a little girl standing between her mother... and Mendoza."

Silence.

"What do you want us to do?"

Veronica was about to come unhinged, continuing to pace, her arms flailing. She talked incessantly, barking orders. "Sam, we should call the police. We need to call the police. Now!"

"Frank, what do you think? Should we get the police involved?"

"Problem is, Sam, if we do, we'll have to tell them why we're concerned for Gabriela's safety, and since they essentially work for Mendoza... we have to believe they'll contact him. Then, he'll no doubt begin searching for her as well. That is, unless...."

"Unless what, Frank?" Veronica said. "Unless he's already gotten to her? Is that what you were going to say?"

"Yes."

In low tones, Sam said, "That piece of shit!" He paced across the patio and into his suite, closing the doors behind him. He could hear Veronica screaming through the patio glass, and then she collapsed in tears on the chaise.

"Frank, what about neighbors, or...?" Sam stopped talking when he noticed Veronica had followed him into the kitchen.

"I had no backup plan. I really screwed this up! DAMMIT!" Veronica screamed in frustration.

Before Sam could react, Veronica grabbed her purse and stormed out.

"Frank, Veronica just took off. I need to stop her," he said, moving toward to door.

"Don't, Sam, let her go. She's just frustrated and worried. We have security in the lobby. I'll have Pablo alert them that Veronica should not be permitted to exit the hotel."

"Good, and make sure they understand completely. Tell them under no circumstances! She did grab her purse on the way out, which means she's got her mobile and we can track her down if we need to. She won't get far."

"What do you want us to do?"

"Here's a thought. We don't have an address for her mother, but maybe you guys could find an address in the house. Then check it out. Maybe she's there... I don't know."

"Will do. I'll call you as soon as we find anything helpful."

"Thanks, Frank."

Sam thought the best thing would be to stay in his room and wait. With security on alert for her, it was more likely than not Veronica would return to Sam's room.

Fifteen minutes later, Veronica walked through the door he had left open.

"Heard anything?" She was a lot calmer now, probably resigning herself to the reality there was nothing they could do but wait. Sam told her what he had assigned Frank and Pablo to do, which seemed to satisfy her. She fell into a chair, rummaging through her purse and cussing up a storm.

"Let me do that," he said, knowing what she was hunting for. He lit her up. She took a long drag and fell back into the chair, her hand over her eyes.

He reached for his own pack, lit one up, and began making each of them a drink.

It was already approaching four-thirty a.m. Expecting it to be a long day, he called room service and ordered two packs of Reds.

Any discovery occurring between now and dawn could not be good. He felt comfortable allowing Veronica to lose herself in liquor and tobacco if that's what it took to relax her. There was nothing else they could do having ruled out calling the police.

By five o'clock, he still heard nothing from Frank and Pablo, and Sam was beyond tired. Veronica had dozed off in the chair, clearly under the influence, but she still managed to slur out that she needed another cigarette. Sam lit another one for her.

By five-thirty, Veronica had fallen asleep.

They were all to gather downstairs in two hours and then head to the plant to take control of it. He couldn't stop thinking about Gabriela.

Veronica began to stir and then sat up straight. "I'm going to tell you what Gabriela told me in one of our meetings even though she swore me to confidence. You must understand, Sam, that Gabriela is deeply religious. She is convinced she will burn in hell for her sins."

CHAPTER 47

"**G**ABRIELA TOLD ME Mendoza was like a jailer in the worst prison on earth," Veronica began. "At work when she would be sitting at her desk and typing on her keyboard, she'd notice him walking out of his office and into hers. She tried ignoring him, fearing what was coming and hoped to become invisible.

∽

"His usual routine was to pull me from my chair, throw me on the sofa, and rape me… another session in hell with the devil. Door wide open. Sometimes, I would catch the guards in the hallway steal a glimpse, but mostly they would walk away. But then, there was this one time I will never forget….

"Mendoza walked into my office and stood silently behind my chair. I ignored him, continuing with my typing. He then walked to the outside door, closed it, and flipped the lock. He had never done that before. He approached me from behind. Whatever he had planned, I was powerless to change the coming course of events.

"I continued to ignore him, typing furiously, but all to no avail. He positioned himself behind my chair and began to massage my shoulders. Slowly around my neck, he would apply pressure. Then, with both palms flattened, slightly rippling over my collarbone, he eventually worked down to my breasts. I knew then, it was time.

"He began to tie my wrists. When I resisted, he slammed my head down into my desk, breaking my nose. I blacked out. When I awoke, I found myself hanging from a hook, facing the wall, naked. I screamed out, and he punched me in my side, breaking several ribs. The worst pain I had ever experienced, but he was just getting started.

"I struggled to keep my toes on the floor as the twine was cutting into my wrists, waiting for him to finish. *Soon this would be over*, I thought, but then I felt his hands around my neck. He began choking me. I increased my movements, struggling hopelessly to free myself. He squeezed his fingers into my throat. I couldn't breathe. I prayed Jesus to let me die. I passed out.

"Still hanging there and fading in and out of consciousness, I saw him open the door and grunt some instructions to his guards. Mercifully, I passed out again and awoke in hospital.

"I don't know how many days I was in their care, but they treated me in the strangest way. The only thing the nurses or doctors talked to me about was my medical condition. They exhibited feelings of subdued anger, as if it was my fault.

"On the day of my discharge, the doctor came to tell me my mother was in the waiting room to take me home. He then came uncomfortably close to my face, leaned toward my ear and whispered, "You are pregnant, whore."

"A nurse wheeled me down the hall toward my waiting mother. All the while, I tried to contemplate what I had been told.

"I was with child. I was going to be a mother. Even though I felt blessed to have survived such a brutal rape, even though I could see my mother ahead walking briskly toward me, I could only think that my child would also be the child of the man who owned me. The pig that had raped me in the past and would rape me repeatedly in the future. Now, he had fathered me a child, his child. What would the future hold for us?

"While at home and recuperating, my mother would not ask me anything. Even when I tried to tell her, she would caution me to stop. It was like she knew and condemned me for allowing it to happen—as if I could have stopped it—but that was the culture of my people. We did not own our own bodies, and if we were cursed with beauty, we were doomed to a life of servitude to any man having the resources to keep us alive, clothed, and close by. Close enough to serve him at his whim.

"After Sophie was born, he would still take me in various ways, but he seemed to treat me more gently. Later, I learned he still craved finding ways of satisfying his sadistic tendencies. Only now, with other women. Younger women. He liked to hurt them as he had done to me. On occasion, he would permit his closest managers to enjoy such *pleasures* as well. With others. Never with me. I belonged to him. Passing off other women to his men was his *pleasure gift*, and they would do anything he asked to be in his favor, waiting patiently for their next opportunity."

⁓

"Sophie is now fifteen," Veronica said, pausing, fighting back tears, but she continued.

"After Sophie was born, holding her in her arms the first time made Gabriela believe that things had to change... but she just couldn't commit. The rapes, the beatings, the inhumane treatments seemed the worst cross to experience; bearing his child, her Sophie, created a conflict within Gabriela too complex to reason through. But then, something happened that would force Gabriela's hand." Veronica paused to wipe away her tears.

As if this horrible story couldn't have gotten worse for Sam to stomach, it did. Veronica tossed a crumpled tissue and grabbed another. Facing Sam, now sitting up straight, she said, "I met Sophie a week ago when I was invited to dinner at Gabriela's house. She is the picture of her mother, beautiful and bright, but innocent... for now."

Seeming to dig deep for a reserve of strength she now needed, Veronica forced herself to continue. "Later that evening, we were sitting across from each other in the living room. After a time, Gabriela got up to check on Sophie asleep in her room. When she returned, she curled up next to me on the sofa, laid her head on my lap, and began to cry. I tried to comfort her, gently stroking her hair and shoulders, waiting, hoping she could relax and unwind, but Gabriela wasn't finished. Through stops and starts and sniffles she told me Mendoza was beginning to take an interest in Sophie… not in the way a father would admire his daughter. Unless that father was sick. Extremely sick.

"Just before last Christmas, the day after Sophie's fifteenth birthday party, which was thrown lavishly by Mendoza at a local restaurant, he instructed Gabriela to bring Sophie to work. He wanted to spend some *quality time* with his daughter. With tension infusing her body, Gabriela knew what he meant. Fear would now consume her. A fear all too familiar.

"Gabriela had come to the realization that same curse would soon befall her own daughter. There was no way of avoiding that plight for her Sophie, so she decided to do something—something drastic, but entirely necessary. That's when she sent the letter to corporate which, of course, is what brought us to this place."

Veronica moved over to Sam and sat next to him on the sofa. She took his hands into hers and looked into his face. "I've been watching you these past few days. I know you are thinking about past mistakes, doubting yourself… maybe believing it was a mistake to bring us all to this place…. Don't.

"Sam, Gabriela sees you as her savior. She sees this engagement as a rescue mission for her and her friends at Abello, but especially for her daughter, Sophie. Don't ever think for one minute that you have done the wrong thing in coming here. In the short time Gabriela and I have known each other, I have come to respect and admire that woman more than any woman I have ever met. She has begun a change in me, and I know I will become a better person for having known Gabriela Castillo.

"If that precious, brave woman has been harmed while doing what I have foolishly allowed her to do, it is I, and not you, that bears the guilt. One I shall never be able to erase."

Veronica buried her head into Sam's chest and sobbed.

After a few minutes passed, she stood stoically, glaring into Sam's face as she tossed yet another crumpled tissue into the trash, "Let's get that sick bastard."

Veronica was back.

ACT IV

COMMITTED BEYOND THEIR FEARS

CHAPTER 48

Monday morning, March 2, 1998

STANDING IN FRONT of the hotel with the rising sun, Sam had a renewed sense of confidence. He walked over to his now gathering team of managers by the front doors and thought what a beautiful day it was… just as the clouds rolled in and a few raindrops began forming on the lobby windows.

Sam surveyed his team being instructed by Frank; Pablo was standing by his side. Eric, Marge, and Alicia seemed like wide-eyed college freshmen at their campus orientation meeting. Veronica looked as if she could chew nails. Steely-eyed, determined. Sam worried about her a great deal. Still no word about Gabriela Castillo.

"Sam, I'm about done on the tactical issues, but Alicia has a question I can't answer."

"What happens after the military and our security team secures the plant?"

"Good question, Alicia," Sam said as he traded places with Frank.

"Hampton has sent a team to manage the plant with the expectation that, after today, Javier Mendoza will no longer be the general manager of Abello. That group of folks is actually standing over there," Sam said pointing off to the right. "I'll be meeting with them after I finish here. They are operational folks who couldn't care less what we accountants are doing, so they shouldn't get in our way. They know we'll be interviewing the employees today."

"On that point," Alicia continued, "You are all very experienced at this interrogation stuff. I'm not sure what to say to get the employees to talk, especially with all this disruption. I'd guess they'll have many questions."

"It's important to understand we will not be engaged in our typical interrogation tactics," Sam said, addressing his entire team. "I have given our local attorney a script he will read over the plant's loudspeakers. He will announce that every employee will receive a bonus today. That should get their attention. To receive their bonus, they will be instructed to form two lines at the administration building and be directed to one of you who will speak with them privately. You'll double-up on the interviews: Eric and Alicia, Marge and Veronica.

"In your packets, you will find your script. It's short and sweet. The most important question is, *Have you heard or seen anything that has made you feel uncomfortable?* If they do not answer after a short period, simply repeat the question. No one gets their check until you are satisfied they have told you all they know. If you need help with anyone, if you think they are holding back, call me on my mobile and one of us will come to your aid. It's important to stress we are here to help them from this day forward. Most importantly, they need to understand that Javier Mendoza's reign of terror is over. He is gone, never to return. If they believe he's listening or will return tomorrow, you are dead in the water. They must believe they will never have to deal with him again.

"You need to make it clear you represent the new reign of goodness, beginning with handing them a check equivalent to a month's wages. Be sure and have those checks plainly visible while you are talking to them. We want their eyes focused on the check. That should be a good start.

"And lastly, don't forget to hand them the business cards with Alicia and Veronica's mobile numbers. Any other questions?"

Sam surveyed his team one by one and then turned to Frank. "Frank, I think we are through here. Do you have anything more to say?"

"Nothing other than it's important to stick to the plan and not go off and do anything stupid like working alone. You need to think tactically today. I know none of you have any military training, but Mendoza is a smart guy. He's a bad guy, for sure, but he's cunning. I would expect he knows we are coming and has placed obstacles in our path to ensure our failure in today's effort. That may be in the form of loyalists on the inside, known to the workers and not to us. Maybe even with a message of their own to the workers reminding them of Mendoza's power, influence, and long reach. So, stick to the plan, work in your assigned pairs, communicate anything of concern to Sam or me, and we'll all arrive back here tonight celebrating our accomplishments today. Godspeed to all of you."

Sam surveyed his team one last time. "OK, I think we're good to go. The two military Humvees will pull out first, followed by the buses with our new security and the new management team, then us. Good luck today, team."

The storm had stopped, but the creek to Sam's right was swollen, and the rapidly moving waters caused debris to wash ashore or spin in whirlpools in certain spots. Discarded clothing, paper, plastic milk cartons, and other trash dotted the shoreline along the way. Just above, sparse vegetation covered the embankment up to the tree line. Surprisingly, those trees bore lush greenery laced together into a network of vines that reached across the creek, linking together the branches on both sides.

Pablo was driving the managers. Behind followed Frank and Sam driving together. The staff was in the rented box vans being driven by Manuel and Fernando. Sam hoped those vans would be packed with evidence later in the day… the primary purpose for the plant siege, as far as Sam was concerned.

Frank had instructed Pablo to lay back by a couple hundred feet until the military had signaled the "All Clear."

Soon, they had arrived. Fifteen minutes later, they could see the military and security personnel walking around with shouldered weapons, communicating they did not sense imminent danger. That was an instant relief.

The All Clear given, Pablo drove through the gate followed by Frank and Sam. They all stopped in the center of the yard. Frank instructed Sam to wait in the car. Pablo had done the same with the managers. Sam felt immensely secure having the two of them working together. He again wished he had had military training and then chuckled at the timing. He graduated high school in 1968. Had he joined the military, it would have been at the height of the Vietnam War. While immensely thankful to those who served, Sam was glad he was not drafted, knowing he'd have been KIA for sure. He didn't have the instincts.

"The colonel is deploying more troops to secure the perimeter," Frank reported back to Sam.

Sam hopped out of the car, eager to get to the motherlode. "Sounds good. I'm going to checkout Mendoza's office. How about you see if you can find any workers in the plant? Honestly, I expected to see more activity over there and hear production. I have a bad feeling about this."

"I'll check it out and meet you upstairs."

Sam needed to keep moving forward. Everything hinged on what he expected to find.

As he entered the administration building, he bolted up the stairs. Sam felt the adrenaline coursing through his body as he moved quickly through Gabriela's office and into Mendoza's.

No desktop computer. It was gone!

"Dammit!"

He fell into Mendoza's desk chair, elbows on the desk, hands grabbing the sides of his head. Mendoza had been one step ahead of them again.

Pablo entered the office. Sam looked at him and then immediately looked away. Pablo's elation deflated as he walked out without saying a word.

A few minutes later, Pablo returned. "The IT guys and some staff associates are here. What should I tell them?"

Sam hesitated, remembering his instructions to his team, his plan for when they took charge of the plant.... What a glorious day it should have been. Now, it seemed like a pipe dream.

"Stick to the plan. Gather it all up," Sam said as he stood and walked out to Gabriela's office. Not that he expected her desktop would be there, but still, he was disheartened when it was missing as well. Nothing to sit on either. He remembered a sofa and at least a couple of chairs. Nothing. Not even a desk chair. Why? It was odd. He began to recall that first day. He visualized how everything was when he first met Javier Mendoza.

...a huge, strapping, mustached man came out from a doorway to the left and greeted them. Javier Mendoza in the flesh. Sam had never seen a human being built in that way, reminding him of the cartoon character Shrek. Massive, thick. No neck.

Then, Sam remembered Gabriela... *who stood from behind her desk, extending her hand, announcing in surprisingly good English, "Welcome, I am Gabriela Castillo, Señor Mendoza's secretary. Please let me know if I can attend to you in any way."*

Even then, Mendoza treated her like a dog, cutting her off, dismissing her like a peasant. And all along, she was the whistleblower. *Where was she?*

There was a swirl of activity in Mendoza's office involved with placing Mendoza's books, possessions, and other items into banker's boxes. All would be flown up to Chicago shortly. Chain of custody protocols were in place. Sam watched his staff being instructed by

Eric, now directing someone with a hand truck lifting Mendoza's filing cabinets. Sam somehow knew this effort would be fruitless. The evidence he needed had already been burned, removed, or in some other way destroyed. Throughout it all, as Sam's depression grew, he heard a voice out in the hall that immediately brought hope back to him.

"Sam, you still in here?"

"Frank, I'm in here," Sam shouted out to him.

When Frank walked in, Sam looked up and said, "Please, no more bad news."

"Are you finding what you expected to find here?" Frank asked as his head swiftly darted around Gabriela's office and into Mendoza's.

"There's nothing of use to us in either office. It's all gone," Sam said completely haggard. "I feel beaten, Frank. The only hope we now have is if Blanco's appeal to the workers yields some evidence. Assuming, of course, some workers show up today... or ever."

"We're good on that. They're here," Frank said directing Sam to the windows overlooking the yard. Sam could see the workers slowly filling up the courtyard by the hundreds, all looking quite curious. Still, it seemed a lot less than the nine hundred employees they expected. Soon, Blanco would read the script into the plant's speakers. Then, Sam's team would commence the interview process with each of the workers individually, but still, he worried it would be a waste of time and felt like an idiot.

When Sam checked how the interviews were going a couple hours later, Veronica pulled him aside. She suspected yet another fraud they hadn't anticipated. Nearly all the *actual* employees were, in fact, here. The reported roster of employees apparently contained several hundred *ghost* employees. More money corporate believed was used for payroll when, in fact, Mendoza just pocketed it.

It was approaching one o'clock. "So, boss," Veronica said, "we're through at least a third of them. Sorry to say we've heard nothing of value yet." He looked away. "They were extremely pleased with the check, but I gotta tell you, Sam, they don't know anything. I mean, we didn't get the feeling anyone was holding back. You know… the way we felt Miguel was. Sorry, but don't count on this interview effort to produce anything. I'm just saying.…"

Sam nodded his head as if this were par for the course. "OK, thanks, V."

Going on six o'clock, Veronica and Alicia were interviewing the last of the workers. Sam had gathered in Mendoza's office with Frank, Pablo, Eric, and Marge. They sat in stone silence, staring at their inanimate object of choice having talked themselves out during the day. There were no words left to say.

A little while later, they looked up at the sound of footsteps on the stairway. Soon, Veronica and Alicia entered the office. All looked at them with no expectation, only vanquished hope at this point. There were no other seats in the office. "Well, tell me some good news," Sam said.

"There isn't any, boss," Veronica said, calmly. "Nothing at all to report."

Sam let out a long, deep sigh as if it were his last breath. "Steve's expecting a call from me. Guess all I can say is my arrogance got the better of me thinking we could solve this case."

"Well, I have about had it with this pity-party," Frank said. "I say we head back to the hotel, eat a lavish meal, and get stupid drunk."

"That's the most brilliant thing I've heard all day," Eric said.

"OK, all right," Sam said. "I think we all could use a little booze to wash away this disappointing day. You guys go ahead, and I'll catch up in a bit. Pablo will take me back, but right now I need to call Steve."

Before they filed out, Sam looked at Veronica walking away. He was tempted to ask if she'd heard any news of Gabriela but then checked himself. She'd have mentioned it.

Sam pulled out his BlackBerry and hit the speed-dial number for Steve.

Steve reacted a lot more understanding than Sam had thought he would. It was like he had already reconciled that, while Sam's team had to play out this day the way they did, there was really no expectation of success. He didn't say that, but Sam could discern his mood and thoughts from his voice. Steve would pass on the news to the management committee. Sam felt bad for Steve. He was Sam's most enthusiastic supporter, and he had let him down. Steve would disagree in his typically supportive manner, but it didn't change the facts.

CHAPTER 49

AFTER THE CALL, Sam and Pablo walked to the car. Everyone else had cleared out. "Pablo, I'm in no real hurry to get back to the hotel. Is there a back road you can take? I need time to think."

"There is another road, but it is dirt and slow-going, just so you know."

"Sounds perfect."

The cooler air passing through the open window was an elixir to a body completely drained from the constant shots of adrenaline Sam endured at different times throughout the day. Right about now, if everything had gone as planned, he would be ready to declare victory. Instead, he was wallowing in self-pity at such disappointing results.

The road Pablo had chosen was horrible, indeed. It was pothole infested and winding; they were weaving and braking like it was an amusement park ride through some Disney jungle gym adventure, but Sam didn't care and maintained his silence. Pablo was silent, as well, sensing rightly that Sam was in no mood to talk about anything.

After thirty minutes of quiet reflection, Sam could see up ahead what looked to be flashing red lights—emergency vehicles. As they got closer, a couple police cruisers and a boxy style ambulance came into view. They approached slowly, drawing scant attention from the officials working the scene. When they slowed even more to see what had happened, at first Sam could not determine the source of the commotion, but then he saw something disturbing... a body... a woman; he could tell from her long brown hair and petite size, and she was naked. He instantly yelled for Pablo to stop the car. He did not, continuing to move along at a slow pace. "*Señor*, Sam, the police, they will not allow us to stop."

Sam opened his door and jumped out of the moving vehicle as Pablo slammed on the brakes. Sam ran toward the lifeless body. An officer attempted to halt his advance, but Sam quickly sidestepped him, falling to the ground on his knees. The officer grabbed Sam's shoulders to pull him back, but he was close enough. He had found Gabriela Castillo.

Two other officers grabbed Sam's arms to lift and drag him back, but he fought them off and again fell to his knees. Pablo was out of his vehicle and yelling at them. Whatever he said made them stop tugging at Sam, but with firm hands on his shoulders they ensured he could no longer move forward.

Sam looked at her in horror. He could plainly see this poor woman dumped on the side of the road had been beaten. Her bloodied face. Her matted hair. Next to her were her clothes, shoes, purse... in a pile. Her light blue, pinstriped dress was bloodied, torn. He screamed with an emotion that consumed every inch of his body... struck with guilt that was overwhelming and debilitating. He sat up on his knees, hands behind his head, rocking back and forth mumbling indiscernible words. The officers no longer held him but stood ready by his side where Pablo had now kneeled.

Her arms, neck, and face were battered and bruised, signifying she had suffered terrible trauma before her death. Worse yet, her eyes were open. She was looking at Sam. Her mouth was slightly open, revealing blood-stained teeth. Sam let loose a stream of vomit. Even though he was gagging, he still tried to talk if only to say her name. "Gabriela. I am so, so sorry."

A moment later, Pablo helped Sam to his feet and leaned him against the fender of his car. He put his arm around Sam's shoulders to steady him, comfort him, and ensure he would not interfere with the officers again.

Volcanic rage consumed Sam so powerfully at the thought of Mendoza and what he did to this beautiful and vulnerable young woman, this mother to Sophie, who she predicted would be Mendoza's next plaything. *What would become of her?* Sam's thoughts were darting uncontrollably.

He felt totally alone now watching them administer to yet another dead body, their efficiency confirming this was a routine event.

Zipping up Gabriela Castillo in a black vinyl body bag signaled finality difficult to bear. With Gabriela out of the way, Mendoza would take his daughter without interference. Again, Sam let out the rage within him hopelessly and passionately, begging for there to be some other ending to this tragedy.

How can I tell Veronica?

Suddenly, Sam conjured a similar memory from fifteen years earlier, when another young mother had tragically been murdered attempting to aid in his investigation. He felt cursed. Sam turned toward Pablo and looked into his face. "I will kill that bastard if it is the last thing I do." Pablo didn't respond.

"*Señor*, do you know the victim?" asked one of the officers now standing in front of Sam.

Sam ignored him. He didn't care to help these Mendoza puppets. Pablo began speaking in Spanish to the officer, who was now taking notes. While Pablo continued to talk, Sam looked on as the paramedics closed the doors of the ambulance, Gabriela's body inside. One of her blood-stained sandals remained where she once lay, confirming their incompetence. They would never even investigate her murder.

Minutes later, the ambulance pulled away. Sam imagined her lifeless body soon lying on a slab in the morgue. Her mother, sister, and little girl would hear the awful news their loved one was gone.

As Sam watched the ambulance's lights slowly fade into the distance, Pablo turned to face him. "*Señor.* The officer... he has a few more questions for you."

"Tell him he can go to hell."

"Please, Sam. You must cooperate. If you do not, he may arrest you," Pablo said pleadingly.

Reality returned as Sam thought that was the last thing he needed. He nodded his head and turned to face the officer.

He asked a few more questions about whatever Sam could tell him of *the victim* and what his business was in Guatemala. Sam answered but felt distant... removed. Here and there, Sam would say something the officer would write in his notebook. Fifteen minutes later, with the officer seemingly satisfied, Pablo eased Sam into the passenger seat of his vehicle. He was making hurried movements, seemingly anxious to get back on the road and away from the police.

Sam now had a pounding headache. His knees and lower back were hurting as well, probably as a result of grappling with the officers earlier. He heard and felt the vibration of his BlackBerry and made no movement to answer it. He didn't care about anything at that point, only someone had to stop Mendoza. He had lost all belief he would be that person.

Shortly after Sam's phone stopped vibrating, Pablo's began. It must have been Frank trying to call him. He was now talking with Pablo. Pablo explained what they had discovered.

Things were spinning all around him. Sam continued to feel like he was asleep. Maybe he was. Maybe this was a bad dream. He lost track of time and didn't know how long he sat in the front seat of Pablo's SUV. It must have been some time, as he noticed Enrico Blanco now on the scene and talking to the officer who had interviewed him. It was obvious cooler heads, namely Pablo's, were now calling the shots.

Sam stared at Blanco, his hand on the officer's shoulder and moving him away, talking and waving his other arm as he always did when making an argument. Sam didn't try to figure out what they were discussing. He didn't care.

Then, he heard a familiar voice. "Sam, I'm so sorry," Frank said as he bent down in front of him, hand on his knee. Sam looked at Frank with no emotion, as if Frank had been there all along. "He killed her, Frank. She's dead. He murdered her."

"I know, Sam. Pablo filled me in while I was driving here with Blanco."

"He hurt her too, Frank. Her dress… her face…."

"It's not your fault, Sam. It's not anyone's fault. Gabriela reached out first. She did what she thought was the right thing to do. And it *was* the right thing to do. You too… with your attempts to help her. There is no fault here."

Sam looked at Frank sternly. "*He* is the fault, and he will pay dearly for what he has done to her. If it is the last thing I accomplish in my life, he will pay for what he has done to this woman… to these people."

Frank dropped his head like he had something to say.

"She doesn't know yet, does she?" Sam asked.

"No."

"Take me back to the hotel. Pablo can drive Blanco back. I need to do this tonight, and I need to do it in person."

"Whatever you say, Sam."

Frank stood and touched Sam's shoulder. "Wait here, and I'll tell them what we're doing."

Frank joined Pablo and Blanco in a small circle by the last remaining police cruiser.

A moment later, Sam joined them. They stopped talking and looked at him.

Sam stood in front of Enrico Blanco, so close that Blanco had to take a step backwards. Sam peered into his face, pointed his finger inches from his nose, and with all the conviction he could muster he said, "I want that police report. I don't care what you have to do to get it. I don't care what it costs, but I want it, and I want it tonight."

Nodding his head in agreement, he said, "You will have it as soon as I do, *Señor*."

Sam knew Blanco would have to bribe the officer. He didn't care. "Enrico… did you hear me? I don't care what you have to do to get it… just do it." Sam gave him one last look, pointing again at his face. "Tonight. I don't care how late."

Nodding his head in agreement, Blanco said, "And you will indeed, *Señor*. I promise you will have it tonight."

CHAPTER 50

AS SOON AS he entered his room, Sam made himself a scotch and moved to the patio. Frank and Pablo fixed themselves something at the bar and then joined him. He'd have to tell Veronica... but wanted to wait until he had received the police report. At nine-fifteen, it had been an hour since they returned. No one spoke. There was nothing to say or do... just to wait for the report. Sam continued drinking—a lot. Then, he fell asleep... but not for long.

He was awakened by a scream he realized had to be from Veronica. She had come to Sam's room upon learning they had returned. Sam jumped up and was now standing at the patio doors, looking in, watching her frenzied in Frank's arms, trying to push herself away from him. But he held her tight, comforting her.

"That bastard... that bastard... " she sobbed. "Promise me you'll make him pay. He must pay. Please, Frank... make him pay."

Frank realized Sam was in no condition to relay that news to Veronica... that Gabriela Castillo was dead.

Sam returned to his seat on the patio. He picked up what remained of his scotch and downed it. Pablo stood there with the bottle and refilled Sam's glass, probably hoping to use it as an inducement for him to sleep.

Frank had taken Veronica into Sam's guest bedroom. Hopefully, he was using liberal amounts of booze to assist him in consoling her.

Before they had left the scene where they found her body, Pablo offered to pay a visit to Gabriela's family and deliver the worst news. He did so after dropping off Blanco. He stood now, leaning against the patio wall, staring into the pool below. When Frank rejoined them on the patio and pulled a chair up close to Sam, Pablo did the same. Sam caught Pablo's face. "It is done. It did not go well. A neighbor and her daughter, Sophie's friend, are with them." Frank and Sam simply nodded.

Then, Pablo warned there might be even more tragic news ahead... Evita Castillo, Gabriela's sister, was not home. Her mother understood she would be with her sister. All three looked at each other, none of them offering a thought.

The phone rang. The front desk. A package had arrived for Sam.

Of course the police report was in Spanish. He handed it to Pablo and sat down.

It laid out the routine facts about their discovery and ended with, "There are no suspects at this time and our investigation is ongoing." But it was the accompanying coroner's report Sam wasn't prepared for.

It was horrifying. Pablo summarized, pausing frequently as the words carried with them their own reluctance to be spoken.

Sam had no words remaining.

Three days later, they attended Gabriela's funeral. Gabriela's sister Evita was still missing. Sam tried not to occupy his mind with that fact. Today's purpose was to honor the memory of Gabriela Castillo. He was pleased to see many others in attendance, so many they had to shut down the plant, which was the smart thing to do know-ing people would not have shown for their shifts anyway. Sam and his team stood in the back away from the crowd, not wanting to interfere with those who gathered to pay their respects to Gabriela's mother and daughter... and her closed coffin, which would soon be lowered beneath the earth. If this scene didn't define tragedy Sam didn't know what did. Unlike Gabriela, so many of these poor would survive, in spite of the hardships, for decades longer. It seemed such a miserable existence.

As he watched the proceeding, the outpouring of sorrow for her passing saddened him greatly. He wished he and his team had been able to make a difference in Gabriela's life. Sure, the company paid for the funeral and set up a trust fund that would ensure a safe and comfortable life for Gabriela's mother, sister, and daughter, but there were so many others that needed help; not only their own workers, but the overwhelming majority of this country's inhabitants. It seemed a problem too massive even for a company as rich and powerful as Hampton Enterprises. It seemed hopeless.

Then, there was still the matter of Javier Mendoza. His legacy was still working well in his disappearance, keeping everyone in line. At this point all Sam wanted to do was board a plane and leave this despicable country, never to return. All they had attempted to do seemed pointless. There were already indications it might be impossible to operate Abello legitimately in such a corrupt land.

Yesterday, the Ministry of Finance notified Enrico Blanco there had been an error in the calculation of the plant's property taxes. Not only would those taxes double on a go-forward basis, but they levied a one-hundred percent fine on over a decade of back taxes. They said they had informed Mendoza months ago and he had, purportedly, ignored their notices. Of course, it was all bogus, but it served as clear evidence Javier Mendoza was alive and well, still pulling all the strings in running his criminal enterprise and the country. Sam's investigation had been nothing more than an inconvenience. They would soon be gone, and Mendoza could resurface and resume his reign. Sam felt sick and nauseous and signaled to Pablo he was ready to leave, but the rest of his team, including a usually tough and unemotional Frank, said they wanted to stay a little longer.

By nine o'clock that evening, Sam had too much to drink. There was a knock at his door, and he would have ignored it if it hadn't been Frank.

"Hey, Frank," Sam said with little feeling, opening the door to his suite. "Come on in. Make yourself a drink. I'll be on the patio." Sam was working hard to stop the parallels from that prior investigation racing through his mind. One he would never be able to put behind him. It was impossible, especially with what he was encountering on Project Vista.

A few minutes later, Frank was sitting across from Sam. Neither spoke for a long time. Sam had not told him of the GEL investigation, but then it was all public. Maybe Frank had found out from news reports or maybe Dave Rogers had said something. Frank knew. He was too savvy an investigator to have taken this assignment without learning as much about his employer as he could. He never brought it up to Sam. Frank had his own tragedies—his own mistakes—when split-second decisions were made and regrets followed.

But now, two people had died, and one was still missing. Frank was very worried about Sam. Sam was staring into the night. Frank knew the routine. When you're not talking, you're thinking. He wanted to know what Sam was thinking about. At that moment, he began to explore.

"I'm curious, Sam. Why do this kind of work? I mean I know you don't do it for the money. I'm sure there are dozens of investigations you could run solely dealing with following-the-money. You could sit in your Chicago office on the phone all day telling others what to do and then spend your evenings politicking with household Chicago names mining for your next big fraud assignment. Yet, here you are in Guatemala dealing with all this crap. You have to know the odds are against you toppling a guy like Mendoza. You risk your life," he avoided saying the obvious about risking the lives of others. "I know that living this life has taken a toll on you. I know what it's done to your family. Bottom line, Sam, you don't look satisfied... you don't look happy. Why? I don't understand why you choose to do this?"

Sam lit up a Red and took a long draw. He thought of his childhood and growing up with the father he was cursed to have. He wondered what he'd do should he ever meet up with him again. He wanted to answer Frank's question, but then why go through it all again? He just cut to the chase.

"I know what it's like to live under a tyrant, to wake every morning fearful of what the day would bring. Petrified I'd say something to upset him, and if I did, what he might do to me and my mother. Every day I lived in fear. I prayed a lot back then... not so much since. Guess I lost faith, feeling God had abandoned me a long time ago. Seems he's abandoned a lot of people. Like the people we now see living under a tyrant, one who takes and takes until they have no more to give. Then, he finds other ways to take from them.

"Back then, I had neither the confidence nor the means to change my plight. I was his captive until the law took him away. These people don't have God or the law on their side. All they seem to have is me at the moment. I cannot... I will not desert them. This is very personal to me, Frank.

"The GEL investigation fifteen years ago was the first time in my life I really tried to make a difference. That experience affected me in ways difficult to explain. Mistakes were made. Someone I cared for was murdered; someone I loved was lost. I've not been the same since. And now, I find myself in similar circumstances. Conflicted by the risks to personal safety, I am possessed by a duty to stop an evil being, a man who takes advantage of others, just because he can. For that kind of person... criminal... I cannot turn away. But then, maybe I want it that way. No matter, I must stop him... if not me, then who?"

Sam looked at Frank as if challenging him to argue, to tell him his was wrong, to tell him to get on the next flight to Chicago and leave harm's way, but Sam knew Frank would not say that—which is why he found himself growing closer to Frank with each passing day.

They stared at each other until Frank spoke. "Let's nail this son of a bitch!"

CHAPTER 51

SAM AWOKE A little after noon and sat on the edge of his bed getting his bearings. Already it was Friday. *Where had the week gone?* At least he slept well, except he awoke with a pounding headache. He stood and walked to the bathroom on a mission: find an Excedrin. Then, his BlackBerry buzzed. It was Maggie.

"Are you still my secretary?"

"Of course, I am," she said softly, warmly. "Sam, I know you are up to your eyeballs, but I really need to pass along some messages. Is now a good time?" She said it absent her usual wit and humor.

"Why so serious?"

"Some of the staff has been keeping me abreast of all you guys have been going through. I'm so sorry, Sam. Sounds like this project has been tough for a lot of reasons." A moment of silence passed. "So, can I tell you a few things?"

"Sure," Sam said without responding to her expression of concern. No point in going into it.

"Not surprisingly, you've had a ton of calls and messages. Dave has been great at dealing with all the admin, including reviewing your messages. He told me to give you these three."

"Shoot."

"So, first the good news. Catherine Jennings has called several times. You never told me about her. Sounds sweet. She said she was just calling to tell you she missed you and looked forward to talking whenever you had a few moments. The times before when she called, she insisted that I not bother you, but this time she seemed really concerned. I tried to still her fears, that your absence was all in the normal course of running investigations abroad, but maybe you should call her. Just saying...."

"OK, next."

"Your favorite HR manager called to say the meeting you wanted was agreed to. Said to let him know when you had an idea of your return, and he'd set it up. Do you know what that's about?"

"You said three things."

"Well, the other one, Dave said not to bother you with given all you had going on down there."

"More bad news?"

"Not really sure. Dave apparently has been ruffling a lot of feathers on the Chicago Public Schools investigation. As you know, this was all on the q.t., but this morning's *Trib* ran a front-page headline: *Governor's Office Investigating CPS*. Anyway, Dave said if you ask about it, everything is under control... oh yeah... and he said Laura is working out great! Said she's really into it, and he's been using her for some interviews. Catches on fast and is wicked smart. Of course, she stops by frequently asking about you."

Hearing Maggie talk about some of the goings-on in his practice made him long to be there, at the helm of running it. "All sounds great, Maggie. Listen, I need to get back to it here."

"I understand, Sam. I do, but what should I tell Mr. Bittle?"

"I think you know the answer to that, Maggie. Gotta run. Thanks for holding down the fort."

Sam heard her come back, but he had already hit his favorite button on the BlackBerry—the red one.

At least the Excedrin was kicking in. He was pleased Laura

seemed to be doing well on the CPS investigation, but Dave was a great teacher, more patient than Sam and in many ways more knowledgeable about politics than Sam. Sam hated politics, and he knew the CPS job would bleed politics. It was better Dave was running that one. He had a lot more tact than Sam.

And then there was Cat. *Man, could I use an evening with her right now*, he thought. He did miss her and fought hard not to think about her. He had to fight the urge to fly up immediately and take her into his arms. He longed to be home, to be with her.

CHAPTER 52

MAGGIE'S CALL GAVE Sam a lot to think about. But he was exhausted and decided to lay down. He slept for nearly four hours. Missed having lunch with his team.

After a long shower, he decided to head poolside to see if he could reunite with everyone. Frank was the first to welcome him.

"Hey, Sam," Frank said, greeting him with a bear hug. "Really good to see you up and about."

"Good to be up," Sam said, joining Frank and Pablo. He pulled up a chair. It felt good to be with them.

"Where's Veronica? She still hurting?"

"She's doing much better, Sam. She and Alicia have been sitting off by themselves poolside. Left a few minutes ago… coping like the rest of us. Those two have really gotten close. Good they have each other to lean on, especially now."

"That's good to hear. Pablo, I interrupted you as I walked up, sorry."

"No, Sam, I was just talking about one of my missions. Not important."

"No, Pablo. That's a great story," Frank said. "You left off being in a firefight. Was it Angola?" Pablo continued with his story.

When he finished, Frank had a related story. The two went on for a couple of hours. Sam enjoyed listening and not being the center of attention for a change. Smoking Reds, sipping a beer, he felt himself relaxing… trying to forget… trying not to plan or think about anything related to Project Vista.

Suddenly, there was the sound of shattered glass followed immediately by blood curdling screams coming from the far end of the pool area. People close by were running in all directions.

None of them dared to move, relying first on their sight and hearing to determine the threat level. They heard whistles and then someone on a PA yelled something in Spanish, which Pablo quickly translated as "Everyone stand away. Clear this area." Frank was the first to leap out of his chair and immediately run toward the commotion. Sam and Pablo followed his lead.

The hotel security guards were lining up chairs cordoning off an area about twenty feet from the hotel tower of rooms. Sam approached, reluctantly, staying behind Frank and Pablo.

There was a body, or what was left of one, smashed through one of the oblong shaped, glass patio tables. Glass was everywhere. It was clear someone had fallen from one of the hotel balconies. A woman, face down. Her long brown hair atop an ever-expanding sea of red. The three of them studied the scene from about twenty feet away, but it was Frank who first reacted by standing in front of Sam, blocking his view and grabbing both shoulders.

"Frank, move away," Sam said attempting to look around him. He knew what Frank was doing. Shielding him. *But why?* He had to see for himself. He continued pushing Frank, but he was too strong for Sam and held him firm.

"Dammit, Frank. What are you doing? Get the hell out of my way."

But Frank would not yield. Finally, in a whisper with his head next to Sam, "I think it might be Veronica," Frank said, reluctantly. "I saw her in that blue satin jacket earlier today," Frank said.

Instantly, all of Sam's strength sapped and he fell to his knees, "No... No, Frank. God, No!" Sam said in low tones. Unbelieving.

He helped Sam rise but still held him by his shirt at his shoulders. Sam fought even harder to go around him, and then finally in a burst of strength he was around Frank and kneeling next to the bloody corpse. He suddenly believed.

Now both Frank and Pablo were kneeling with him, one on each side. Sam was sobbing uncontrollably. Inconsolable. Hands covering his face, rocking back and forth. "No, not Veronica. God, no. NOT HER TOO!"

Sam's knees completely gave out, slumping to the side, but Pablo steadied him.

Sam told himself *It couldn't be her* only to maintain his sanity. Then, he looked up, searching for some explanation. He saw drapes flowing in the wind from the patio doors on her balcony. That was definitely her suite... right next to his on the top floor.

There was only one way to be sure. Lucidity suddenly returned as Sam buried his grief. In seconds he was on his feet and bolted in the direction of the hotel doors charging through the makeshift of patio chairs lined up to keep the crowds back.

The hotel guards and then Frank and Pablo ran close behind in pursuit. The guards caught up to Sam first, restraining him. Local police were now arriving through the hotel doors fifteen feet in front of Sam. That distracted the guards and Sam broke their restraint, running against the stream of police and into the hotel.

Frank and Pablo caught up to Sam at the elevator bank hitting the up arrow and screaming, "Her room. We need to go there now!" Two police officers were now standing there, too, arms restraining Sam, yelling at him.

Frank and Pablo were frantically trying to explain to them who they were and their relationship to the victim. When convinced of their legitimacy, the police entered the elevator with them as Sam hit the button to Veronica's floor... his floor.

It did not fall silent on any of them that whoever had done this might still be there. Maybe they were involved in a struggle with Alicia.

One of the officers got on the radio to dispatch more officers to the lobby in the event the perpetrators were running off.

When they arrived at Veronica's room, the door was propped open. Inside were two hotel security guards, one of whom blocked them from coming into the room. The police officers took over and ordered the guards out of the room. "Crime scene. You need to leave."

The scene was chaotic. The guards left immediately as the officers ran to the balcony. Frank grabbed Sam's arm, pulling him into the bedroom and closing the door. Pablo did not follow opting instead to run into the hallway and yelling to the police. Whatever he said caused them to bolt from the room and run down the hallway toward where Pablo was pointing. He then joined Sam and Frank in the bedroom hoping to find some explanation for what they had witnessed below. All three standing still, they heard crying coming from the closet.

Frank opened the closet door to discover a woman crouched in the back. It wasn't Alicia, although she, too, was Latina.

Pablo remained by the bedroom door, holding it open only a crack... listening. As Frank gently lowered himself to her level, he began talking with her in calming tones, in Spanish, extending his hand toward her.

Pablo warned them the police would return soon. They had to move fast.

Frank looked back toward Sam, "Sam, this is Evita Castillo. Gabriela's sister."

Frank coaxed her out of the closet, tossing a blanket over her shivering body. He cradled her in his arms. Flanked by Sam and Pablo, they were now standing in the hallway considering their next move.

As if sent from God, Eric and Marge appeared.

"What the hell is going on?" Eric said.

Sam realized Marge's room was just down the hall. He yelled at her to give him her room key making no comment about the bathrobe she was wearing standing next to Eric, who was wearing only a pair of gym shorts.

Marge started to speak, but Sam cut her off in stark and demanding tones. "Marge, give me your room key now!" She rifled her pocket so fast her robe flipped open revealing her nakedness, which momentarily caused her to halt her search until Sam screamed at her one last time, "Give me the key or I'll rip it from you!"

With Sam now in possession of her key, they raced down toward Marge's room, Evita still cradled in Frank's arms. Sam yelled back to the love birds, "Get lost. Say nothing to the police." They both bolted down the hall in the opposite direction.

Sam held open the door to Marge's room as Frank carried Evita, who was now shivering uncontrollably. He eased her into the bed and laid a couple layers of blankets over her. "I think she's going into shock. We need to get her medical attention immediately," Frank said.

"I'm not letting this girl out of my sight until I find out what happened," Sam said. "Do whatever you need to do, but she's not leaving this room, and we're not calling anyone." Frank stared at Sam.

"Frank, Veronica is dead, and Evita shows up after disappearing for five days. We need her right now to explain what the hell was going on. Do you really want to trust the police to question her?"

Without saying another word, Frank began speaking to Evita again, in Spanish, and comforting her, trying to get her to take a sip of water, keeping her legs elevated. Pablo and Sam stepped back to let Frank work on her. Sam felt sorry for her as he looked on. None of this was her fault, but she was now their only hope of determining what had happened in Veronica's hotel room… and maybe where Alicia might be.

Pablo and Sam stood next to the door, listening.

"I think they are doing search, room by room," Pablo said.

"Damn," Sam said as he looked over at Frank still nursing Evita. He motioned Frank over to them.

"Frank, we don't have a lot of time here. We need to question her."

"You gotta buy me more time. She is not ready to talk. Still shaking. She's just a kid, Sam, and she's petrified."

Sam thought for a moment. He reached into his pocket and pulled out a wad of bills, peeling off several C-notes. He handed them to Pablo who understood instantly, nodded his head, and stepped into the hallway. Sam closed the door and prayed.

Moments later, Pablo reentered the room and winked at Sam. "There will be no problem."

"Good, now I have another mission for you. We are still missing Alicia. Go down to the lobby and ask around."

"*Sí*, Sam. I know the hotel guards. Maybe Manuel or Fernando are there. I will see and then call you."

"Perfect," Sam said, handing him several more C-notes. "This should help with your conversations."

Sam returned to focusing on Evita Castillo lying on the bed covered in blankets. *Where had she been over the last five days?*

Frank continued to stroke Evita's hair, whispering assurances in the hope of calming her. She was conscious and not shivering as much. Frank's approach was working, but she still had not said a word.

After a few more moments, Frank helped her to sit up in bed against the headboard. She was now drinking water and pointing over to the minibar. Sam touched various packages until reaching the cookies and candies. She lit up. He grabbed them and handed to her as she furiously tore into them, devouring one package after the other. It was then Sam really pitied her. *Does she know her sister's fate?*

Sam studied her. Her hair was matted, and her face and shoulders were dirty with some small cuts and abrasions. The sun dress she was wearing was filthy, with one of the shoulder straps broken and lying across her chest, revealing lighter skin as if she had been in the sun for some time, not burned but deeply tanned even beyond her naturally brown skin. She was eating so fast she choked, and Frank helped her again. Sam shot Frank a glance. He worried they had little time to get out of Evita where she had been and more importantly what she had seen. If the police found her she'd be gone from them.

After fifteen minutes, all cookies and candies fully devoured, Evita Castillo curled into a ball, burying her head into the pillow, sobbing.

CHAPTER 53

Earlier that same day

VERONICA AND ALICIA spent the better part of the day at the pool. They had become friends from the moment they met in Chicago but grown much closer through this tortuous investigation. The brutal murder of Gabriela Castillo left so much uncertainty… many questions unanswered. Still, they tried to put it out of their minds while spending time together, beginning with a room service lunch on Veronica's balcony and then the afternoon poolside. Everyone left them alone, knowing how hard Veronica had taken Gabriela's death.

Then, there was the concern Evita was still missing, and they were no further along on accomplishing their mission. The end of Project Vista seemed near, and they wanted to spend as much time together before Hampton pulled the plug and sent them home… in different directions.

Alicia had become enamored with everything about Veronica. Question after question she lobbed at her. But then, the two began discussing shopping on Chicago's Magnificent Mile… clothes, shoes and purses. Veronica invited Alicia to her room in search for the perfect outfit for dinner with her new best friend. While Alicia was exploring her American friend's wardrobe, Veronica went down to the restaurant. She wanted the private dining room that was typically reserved for those with power and money, neither of which she possessed, but she did have a Latina charm which she would turn on for the restaurant manager, completely confident she'd persuade him.

Returning to her room, Veronica pushed the up arrow at the hotel lobby elevator bank. As if God were answering her prayers, Evita appeared out of nowhere.

"Veronica!" Evita said, jumping out of her blind in the lobby's assortment of tropical plants. "Do you remember me? I am Evita Castillo—"

"Where have you been!" Veronica shouted, grabbing her shoulders.

In an instant, they were on them, two men groping at Evita. No one else mattered. They pushed, shoved, and grabbed, but they hadn't counted on dealing with a pissed-off Veronica Martinez.

The one who was grasping Evita's arm received a well-placed fist to his thorax and went down immediately, clutching his throat gasping for air. The elevator doors opened, and Veronica shoved Evita in and then turned to measure the threat level. The other one attempted to enter as well, but a swift kick to the groin changed his options. He went down too. The doors closed with both of them inside, alone.

Evita was hysterical, her eyes shut, arms flailing as if fighting off an unseen enemy. "Evita, they are gone. You are safe," Veronica said, finally able to wrap her arms around Evita. She stopped moving and hugged Veronica as the elevator rose to Veronica's floor.

"I will take you to my room and call for help. We have security and they will protect you," Veronica said while clutching Evita close to her. "Thank God you are alive. I am so incredibly happy you chose to come to me."

Evita stopped crying, remembering her mission—what her sister had died trying to accomplish. "Veronica, here, take this," she said, handing her the microchip drive. Veronica knew instantly what it was and its importance from her earlier conversation with Gabriela. She was euphoric and hugged Evita again just as they reached the twenty-fifth floor.

With her free hand, she grabbed Evita's hand. "Quickly, Evita, we must get you to my room. My friend, Alicia, will be there. We will protect you until I can get help. Hurry!" She opened the door to her room and then slammed it shut, throwing on the security chain.

Veronica called out, "Alicia, quickly, I've found Evita."

Alicia ran into the foyer; the three of them hugged, but the threat was not over. Veronica was cursing herself for not dialing one of the guys while in the elevator. She pulled her phone out and dropped it. She picked it up but fumbled with it, still holding the one thing that would justify all their efforts and sacrifice.

"Alicia, take this!" Veronica said, freeing up both hands to call the one man who could help them.

"Open up! This is the police." They pounded at the door. "You must open this door immediately!"

"Come with me, Evita," Veronica pulled her into her bedroom and then shoved her into the closet. "Get on the floor, in the back. Stay hidden until I come back for you. Be quiet… not a peep!" She closed the closet door not waiting for an answer. Evita pushed back into the corner, hands covering her mouth to silence herself. She was shaking all over, petrified.

When Veronica exited her bedroom, she slammed the door closed.

"Veronica, the doorknob is turning. What should I do?" Alicia yelled. Soon, there was screaming. Evita covered her ears trying desperately to ignore whatever was happening outside her respite. Then, there was quiet.

CHAPTER 54

EVITA WAS CRYING and began once again shivering. Frank attended to her, coaxing her to sip more water. He had a tough exterior but was gifted with a kindness Evita warmed to.

A short time later, with Frank still comforting her, she began talking about the day her nightmare began, when she was last with her family at her mother's house; Sunday noon meal was a tradition.

Following their meal, the family would sit together on the porch and talk about the week that had passed and the week in front of them.

But this Sunday would be different. Gabriela had met a new friend at work, and they had made plans to spend the afternoon and evening together. At least, that had been what her sister told them. In fact, Gabriela would be spending the night with this friend and asked her mother if she'd look after Sophie. Of course, it was all a lie. Gabriela had other plans.

The plant was closed on Sunday, but she was Javier Mendoza's private secretary. There was no trouble entering the plant. The guard recognized Gabriela immediately and opened the gate. Soon after she entered her office with her keys, she stopped briefly at her desk to drop her purse and grab something out of her desk drawer. She reached way in the back of the drawer and pulled out a sealed yellow envelope, ripped it open, and pulled something from it. Moments later, she inserted a key to enter her boss's office door.

It didn't take her long. Miguel had given her written instructions, which she followed to the letter. Fifteen minutes later, she was done but then heard something in her office.

"Who's there?" she yelled out with some authority. There was no answer. She shut down Mendoza's computer, walked into her office, and screamed upon seeing her sister standing against the wall behind her desk, making no attempt to hide her presence. Upon her discovery and reacting to Gabriela's shriek, Evita ran into her sister's arms hugging and saying, "I'm sorry, sister. I should not have come. I should not be here. I'm so sorry. Please, forgive me."

Gabriela hugged and comforted her sister, "Evita, don't be upset. Don't cry. But why are you here? How did you get here?"

"I hid in the back seat of your car. I thought you were going to a fun place with Veronica, and I wanted to experience fun, and now I know it was wrong, and I am so sorry, sister. Please, forgive me."

"Evita, it's all right, but we must leave right now, and you must hide again in my back seat until we are safely outside the gates. Now, take my hand and do exactly as I say."

But it was too late. As they turned toward the door, they heard a car door close, followed by footsteps on the staircase rising to the hallway outside Gabriela's office. Gabriela gasped at the knowledge there was no other exit from her office, or Mendoza's, and whoever was coming toward them on this Sunday could not be good. Gabriela was almost paralyzed with fear and turned toward her sister. The fearful look on Gabriela's face now caused Evita to gasp and begin to cry softly, but Gabriela quickly cupped her hand over Evita's mouth and said in a low hushed voice, "Under my desk, hurry. There is no time."

Taking instructions from her older sister as if she knew their situation was precarious, Evita quickly slid into the well under

Gabriela's desk. Suddenly her sister flew out of her vision, and she could hear voices. Male voices. There were at least two of them, and Evita cupped her mouth to ensure she would not make a sound.

"*Señores*, what are you doing in my office?" Gabriela tried to sound authoritative in the hopes it would dissuade two unknown men from advancing any further into her office, but it fell on deaf ears.

As one of them drew closer toward her, she backed up against the front of her desk and continued to bark orders commanding them to leave immediately. The other man casually walked toward Mendoza's office and peeked inside.

"Why is *Señor* Mendoza's office door open? It is never open on Sunday. Were you messing with *El Jefe*'s things? Maybe he would like to know this."

Gabriela now pressed up against the front of her desk, her arms in front of her preparing to shove away the man who continued walking slowly toward her. She continued to speak with authority threatening to "pick up the phone and call *Señor* Mendoza." But the man now inches away from her was not dissuaded and said, "Good idea. Why don't you do that?"

Broad-shaped and strong, he was now pressing his body against hers. Gabriela had no chance shoving him off of her. Holding both her wrists, he displayed a lustful, grinning smile revealing a couple of missing teeth, the rest blackened from years of chewing cheap tobacco. Gabriela feared what was about to happen and was more fearful her sister might be discovered. *Please God, not my innocent sister!* She prayed.

Undeterred, the man now tightening his grip on Gabriela's wrists said, "Go ahead and call him. I just got off the phone with *El Jefe* to ask why you might be here on a Sunday. He said whatever reason was no good." The gate security guard had called Mendoza upon her arrival.

His face was now hovering over Gabriela's, and she could smell his pungent body odor.

Still gripping her wrists tightly, he forcefully moved her forearms behind her, gripped her in the small of her back and pulled her toward him. Scratching his scraggly beard across her lips slowly, he said, "I ask *Señor* Mendoza, what should we do with this woman? He say do whatever we like. He say he is replacing you. He say you are too loose, like a whore. He say you are too old. He say we can fuck the bitch until she bleeds. He say when we are finished to take you home for my brothers to fuck."

With a quickness that surprised her, he flipped her around then slammed her upper torso onto the desk, causing her head to crash into the desktop. She saw stars but managed to stay conscious. He pulled her dress up to her waist, ripped her panties off with one hard pull and then entered her. Immediately, he began thrusting. With each grunt she tried hard to stay conscious, to stay focused, to look for an opportunity. His constant thrusting forced her closer and closer to the back edge of her desk. Through all the pain and humiliation of what she endured, her only thoughts were of her sister, and the small object she was still clutching in the palm of her right hand.

Thrust after thrust, she now almost welcomed it as it preoccupied her attacker and moved her into a position where she was now peering over the edge of her desk. She could see her sister's foot on the floor beneath her. She reached forward with her closed fist and inched it downward ever so slowly until Evita touched her and then held her sister's fist. Gabriela opened her palm and released into Evita's hand the object that would make it all seem to have a purpose just as the pig on top of her climaxed.

As he lay there, her next attacker was egging him off saying, "Get off of her. You'll smother the bitch. It's my turn." At that moment, Gabriela lost consciousness, but in her heart she was prepared and prayed it would all soon end.

She awakened again to find herself face down on the sofa. Again, she was being raped, and she was in excruciating pain. She let out muffled cries. Powerless to stop her attacker, she prayed to her Lord to fade away from the humiliation of what was happening to her. She no longer wanted to live.

A few minutes later, she felt hands envelop her neck. Fingers closed on her throat, pressure so deep and so intense she knew her prayer would soon be answered.

Finally finished, her attacker stood, attempting to put on his pants, but all the exertion, coupled with an afternoon of drinking, caused him to lose his balance. He crashed into the front of Gabriela's desk, shoving it back hard with a jolt to the stowaway beneath… who let out a slight noise. Unfortunately, it was just enough.

CHAPTER 55

H E GRABBED A corner of Gabriela's desk and swung it out.
"Look what we have here. More fun!" he said, his face
lighting up with joy at his discovery.

Evita crammed herself back into the well, cringed from fear,
and shrieked as never before. The attacker grabbed her ankle and
dragged her forward into the center of the room. With every part
of her body in movement, she kicked and screamed and broke free.
Quickly standing, she darted for the outer door in the disquieted
hope she could somehow escape her sister's demise. He grabbed her
torso preventing her from reaching the door. Evita let out a scream,
silenced only by seeing the looming figure now standing in the
entrance to Gabriela's office—*El Jefe.*

Evita threw herself to the floor and slid on her butt to the sofa
where her sister lay. She turned to confront Gabriela's bloody mouth
and open eyes… but there was no life in them. Evita shrieked again
as she scooted back on the floor until she met the wall. There, she
curled up her knees and buried her head in them, wrapped by her
arms, and she began reciting Hail Marys aloud.

Mendoza shifted his eyes from Evita to Gabriela. "What the fuck
did you boys do?" bellowed Javier Mendoza as he loomed over them.
Like chickens in a caged pen, they both ran to opposite corners of

the office inviting distance between them and *El Jefe*. With Mendoza's stare fully upon them, shifting from one to the other, they acted like two small children fearing their father's discipline would soon be upon them and pleaded in incoherent terms, begging.

"But *Señor Jefe*, you say to me, you say do as we want to her. You tell me, it is OK. We just do as you order. As always, we are your servants."

But Mendoza wasn't listening as he focused on a new gem. "Ahhh... I know you," he said bending slightly at the waist and reaching out his hand. "You are Gabriela's sister... Evita, no?"

Evita stood and approached him, acting like she was reaching for his hand, then made a quick move to the left, but not quickly enough. Instantly, he grasped her. She bit his arm. He released her, throwing her off like a bug. She crashed into the wall, stood again, and moved to an unoccupied corner clutching the standing coat tree.

Mendoza moved to the center of the room, standing between her and the open doorway, staring at her in anticipation that she might try to make a break for the door again. When another of Mendoza's men came up to check on him, Evita collapsed onto the floor, curling into a ball, sobbing, pleading to go home.

Mendoza shifted his attention back to his two gorillas cowering on opposite walls, still pleading with their boss for mercy. They moved around indiscriminately like a teenager needing to pee. Then, Mendoza glanced back at Evita. Regarding her for what seemed minutes he began to approach her as if he had found a new bobble. Evita's sobbing became louder, more desperate, as she shuffled her feet back and forth in an effort to blend into the wall. Begging, pleading, crying, she closed her eyes, turned away, and covered up.

"You are a pretty one, even more so than your sister," he said leering at her. "How old are you?" Again, she ignored him.

Crouching down to her level, maintaining a comfortable distance, Mendoza said, "Child, are you all right? Did these men hurt you?" Evita wasn't having any of it. She did not speak and pulled her legs toward her, trying to disappear into the corner. Mendoza was instinctively aware he was staring at a young, innocent girl. A virgin. He liked virgins a great deal. He was running out of them. He could feel himself getting hard.

He did not grab at her. He just dropped to one knee and used logic attempting to coax her into his arms. "Sweetheart, these are awfully bad men, and I will not allow them to harm you. But I must go now, and should I leave you with them I fear they *will* harm you," He looked over to the lifeless corpse of Gabriela still lying on the sofa and then back to Evita. "Well, I don't want to say, but I do not think it a good idea for you to remain here with these men. Now, please, last chance. Won't you come with me? I will take you to your mother's. There you will be safe." He extended his hand and waited.

She did not trust Mendoza, but she knew she could not remain there and decided to take it a step at a time. Right now, Mendoza was offering to take her away from this place. She suspected he would do that, but then what? She was the only witness to the murder of her sister. She could implicate them all. There was no way he would let her live, but maybe she could buy time. That was it… buy time and do what Mendoza commanded. Maybe, just maybe, she could survive… at least long enough.

When they exited the building, Mendoza's driver and bodyguard were patiently waiting for him. He handed Evita to his driver and she pulled back, resisting, but his comforting words moved her in the direction he wanted. "Hugo, take this child and put her in the back seat. Give her a blanket and some water."

Mendoza looked into Evita's face and assured her he would be just a moment and then would take her to her mother's. He had to get some things from upstairs.

When he returned to Gabriela's office, he was infuriated with his two men now sitting on side chairs and bragging about their fun adventure. They both jumped immediately to their feet and quickly put distance between themselves and Mendoza, who looked like he was about to shoot both of them. Again, they pleaded with him, spewing sorrowful excuses about any misunderstanding until he commanded, "Shut up, you fools!"

Mendoza looked around the room at the disarray, finally settling on Gabriela's lifeless, naked, bruised, and bloodied corpse. "Clean up this place!" He commanded. "But before you do that, I want you to carry both her computer and my computer to my car." Looking back toward Gabriela's corpse, he seemed to ponder the times he himself had enjoyed her on the very sofa where she now lay dead. He remained angry at the two fools now moving with haste to follow his latest command. He slowly turned their way and in a disgusted tone said, "Then, get rid of that body… and all signs of what you have done here. If you don't do exactly as I am telling you, both of you will end up lying next to her before the sun rises. Now, move!"

Mendoza's attention then moved to look upon the open door to his office. He had a clear view of his desktop computer. He stared at it for a moment and then shifted his stare toward Gabriela's computer and then Gabriela's body. He knew she had not visited here on this Sunday to do some typing. He was no fool. And why was his office unlocked? He thought of Sam Halloran and grew enraged.

He watched one of his men preparing his computer and then told him to stop. Mendoza walked up to the back of his computer and placed his hand on a two-foot-long black cable plugged into it. The other side looked like it, too, should be plugged into something… something that was missing. He looked over at Gabriela and thought, *What were you up to, you bitch?*

He walked to her body and turned her over. He felt for a pulse, dropped her arm, and then grunted. He then searched around the office. Continuing to scan her office, he found her purse, picked it up, and dumped its contents on her desk and rifled through it, looking for something…. Walking into his office, Mendoza pushed his man aside and sat down at his computer. It was turned off. He stared at his desktop wishing he had been more computer savvy. He tried to think about what she could have done that would later cause him trouble and then slammed his fist on his keyboard in frustration. He wished now he hadn't scared Miguel into a disappearing act.

Then, it hit him. Evita! He raced down to the vehicle and flung open the back seat and then dragged her from her temporary respite. She screamed as he ripped her dress off, then her panties and bra, pulling and tearing at her as if skinning a rabbit he'd just shot. Both his driver and bodyguard stood back in shock. Even for Mendoza, this behavior was unusual.

"Boss, what can we do?"

"Stay the fuck back," Mendoza bellowed. "That's what you can do."

In frustration and with Evita crying hysterically and screaming, Mendoza groped and clutched her, turning her in different positions, forcing his hand into her mouth and then her vagina as she let out a blood curdling scream. "Shut up, bitch." He flipped her around and did the same to her anus and she screamed again. He was looking for something. Something Gabriela may have passed on to her sister, but it was too late. Evita had already swallowed it.

Fortunately for her, Mendoza did not think of that or even if he had, he was not ready to slice open her gizzards, not just yet anyway. As he grabbed Evita by her hair and looked into her face, he began to loosen his grip as calm was restored. Realizing how shaken and scared Evita now was, he proceeded to stroke her hair gently, pulling her closer to him. "We are all done, my child. I'm sorry for the rough treatment. You are safe once again. Daddy's going to take exceptionally good care of my Evita. Just calm yourself for now. Daddy is taking you home." She continued to whimper.

He blanketed her naked body, stroking her hair while supporting her weight. Slowly, he guided Evita back inside his car and gently laid her once again in his back seat. Evita was shaking uncontrollably. She now feared a horrible journey awaited her, and she quietly sobbed. "Soon, you will be home," Mendoza said in calming tones, as he gently closed the door. *Home* did not mean her home.

He stood by the car, turned to his driver, and commanded, "Pick up her clothes." As he turned to face the administration building, he saw Gabriela's attackers walking down the stairs, each carrying his and Gabriela's computers. His bodyguard opened the back hatch to the Suburban as Mendoza stood there looking off into the darkness.

"Boss, you look troubled," Hugo said. "What can I do?"

"Have a good look around you, Hugo. This will be the last time you see Abello for a long time, maybe forever." Somehow, Mendoza knew of the siege being implemented tomorrow morning. He was a man of impeccable planning and cunning, but tonight he felt uneasy knowing there were forces at play hoping to dismantle his empire. For the first time since building this plant, he was worried *they* might be gaining the upper hand. He was frustrated and angry, but all he could manage to do was curse and kick the side of his vehicle, yelling to his driver, "Pack it up! Take me home." As Mendoza jumped in the back seat, his thoughts were focused on making the right moves, fearing with one false move his dynasty may come to an abrupt end.

Pulling away, he saw Gabriela's corpse being thrown onto the bed of a pickup truck, soon to be laid to rest on the side of some desolate road. He shifted his attention to his new jewel sitting next to him. Evita was still whimpering, still shaking. Mendoza wrapped his arm around her shoulders and began to stroke her hair as he would do to his dogs after a hunt. "Relax my precious, be calm, Daddy's going to take very good care of you."

Evita knew any pleas for mercy would fall on deaf ears. She also knew any resistance now would be foolish. As she played the submission game, she instinctively knew what Mendoza expected of her, but that next chapter had not yet been written. Gritting her teeth, she vowed to herself she would not let this monster do to her what he had done to her sister. With her blanket clutched in both hands crossed on her chest, she pulled the wrap tighter around her body as she snuggled closer to her captor. She would do whatever was needed to stay alive for as long as it took.

CHAPTER 56

WHEN THEY ARRIVED at Mendoza's ranch, he was the first to exit the car.

"Give her to Constanza," he commanded his driver. "Tell her to clean her up and put her in the guest room next to my bedroom."

Another man then came out to greet him, and Mendoza barked orders to him. "My scotch and cigar box to the south balcony. I need a shower."

Constanza, Mendoza's female house servant, walked Evita upstairs. She knew the drill. Comforting Evita with gentle strokes and a soothing voice she said, "Now, child, you come with me, and we will clean you up. Do not worry, my child, you will be fine. I will bathe you and dress you. You will be fine, just fine." Evita walked alongside her not saying a word, staring blankly ahead like she was sleepwalking.

Even as she spoke those words, Constanza knew in her heart things would not be fine. She knew Mendoza had terrible habits when it came to women, especially young, beautiful women. Constanza suspected on this night Mendoza had brought Evita here for other purposes, but as he waited for those purposes to present themselves, she knew he would enjoy his new toy in ways that sickened her—like a cat would play with a cornered and helpless mouse.

But no longer would Constanza allow such horrors to occur. The sins she had committed over the years, looking the other way… those days were over. The Lord had seen to it she would no longer assist her *Jefe* in these disgusting encounters. This would be her final act of repentance. The cancer would see to that. Still, she thanked Him for the opportunity to redeem herself.

At least Evita would be safe tonight. Constanza knew Mendoza hadn't the strength to play now. He looked exhausted, and a cigar and scotch were the last ritual of every day. He would soon sleep, but he would awaken and again begin another day of terror. There was little time; she had to act fast.

Constanza awoke a little after one a.m. hearing Mendoza stomping about, cursing, and then throwing something that shattered against his bedroom wall. At first, she feared he had found Evita, and then she calmed herself when she saw him pacing the hallway while still on the phone. Still, she waited, all the time watching, protecting the child next door to him. A while later, Mendoza had returned to his bedroom. From under the door, she noticed his light was extinguished. Evita would be safe tonight.

Morning dawned with cloudy skies and the threat of rain. Whatever was going on this day had upset her boss. She was relieved when he stormed out of the house without saying a word to her or even mentioning his new house guest still upstairs in bed. Unbeknownst to her, the siege had begun.

After Mendoza left, Constanza entered Evita's room and panicked not finding her in bed. Constanza had locked her door for her own safety. Knowing she had to be in this room somewhere, she first looked under the bed, not finding her. There was only one other place she could be.

Upon opening the closet door, she noticed Evita's bare feet retreat slightly upon discovery. Being careful not to startle her,

Constanza said, "My child, you need not fear me. I am here to take you to safety. Please, give me your hand." Almost immediately, Evita extended her hand in a show of trust, most likely earned from the gentle and loving care Constanza offered her last night. For a brief moment, they hugged and then Constanza said, "We must hurry. I have arranged for your escape. I will help you get dressed and then we will go."

Evita said in a nervous manner, "But you must call the police. My sister was murdered by his men yesterday. You must call them now. They will take me home and punish him for what he has done to my sister."

"My dear, there is no time to explain, but you need to trust me. The police are the last people you want to call. No dear, your journey home will be a long and difficult one. You are far away and deep in the rainforest. There is not another soul for many miles. My brother Mario, you can trust him, he will take you to a place you can hide until he can determine the best way to return you to safety."

With Evita now fully clothed, Constanza led her downstairs and into the kitchen. "Here is enough food and water for the two of you to last for several days. Stay with my brother, he will keep you safe."

Evita looked into Constanza's face and was overcome with emotion at her charity. She began to cry as she hugged her, struggling to find words to thank Constanza. "I will pray for you," Evita said.

"I will be just fine," Constanza said, briefly but firmly hugging her. "Now, child, you must go."

Constanza took Evita's hand and walked to the back of the house and through a service door onto a deck. At the bottom of the stairs stood her brother, Mario, which momentarily startled Evita and she drew closer to Constanza.

"Do not be afraid, my child. This is my brother, Mario." Mario smiled and tipped his hat toward Evita.

Evita relaxed a little but still clung to Constanza.

"Mario, help me with this child."

Mario was the perfect caricature of a ranch hand, short and skinny with a grizzled face looking more like a detailed 3D road map showing all the contours and valleys of the rough terrain surrounding them. He was clothed in denim from his boots to his neck and wore a weathered, sweat-stained, tan cowboy hat. He stood slumped over, the result of a nasty fall some years ago while working the annual cattle drive. Now approaching fifty years old, damaged and limping, Mendoza kept him around and close to the house to do minor repairs.

Mario slowly and cautiously ascended the narrow stairway. He extended his hand and waited for Evita to take it. "Child, please come with me. I will keep you safe. Please, this way. I will protect you."

Evita said nothing but stared directly into his face, measuring him. After yesterday's events, she was slow and deliberate in everything she did. Gone forever was the playful and carefree young girl she would never be again. Her innocence lost, she could only hope and pray she would survive this ordeal and soon be reunited with her mother. She slowly reconciled in her mind that Mario appeared to be her only ticket to that reunion. Evita slowly but firmly took Mario's hand. He led her to descend from the deck and from the house, which would most certainly have turned into her prison had Constanza not saved her this day.

When Evita reached the bottom of the stairs, Mario put an arm around her shoulder and walked off into the murkiness of a brewing storm. Their long journey had begun. Evita looked over her shoulder to regard Constanza one last time.

CHAPTER 57

WHILE EVITA SLEPT inside, Sam and Frank sat together on the balcony of Marge's room, both contemplating what Evita had told them about her terrifying experience. No one should have to go through all she had, but beyond the unfairness of it all, only one thing remained on Sam's mind. "Frank, where do you think that drive is now?"

"Your guess is as good as mine."

"It's got to be back in the room."

"Or on Veronica."

"They'll never let you search her. You do know that?"

"I do," Sam said as he turned to steal a look at Evita getting some well-deserved sleep.

"Poor kid," Frank said. "I can't imagine all she endured to get the drive to us. I refuse to believe it's gone."

"Frank, I realize you should be the one to go back to Veronica's room and look for it, but if Evita wakes up and you're not here she'll freak out." Frank nodded. Sam had to be the one.

With Pablo gone in search of Alicia, and Veronica dead, Sam had no interpreter as he stood at the entrance to Veronica's room. Across the door was yellow tape with something stenciled on it that Sam assumed read *crime scene*. Inside he saw three officials moving about—two in uniform and one in a suit. Sam chose the suit to speak to. Fortunately, he spoke English.

"Officer, could I please speak with you?"

He ignored Sam.

"Excuse me, officer, sir, I need to speak with you. Veronica Martinez worked for me. Here is my ID. I need to speak with someone in charge."

He looked over at Sam and then walked toward him and took his ID to examine it. He handed it back and said, "Detective Lieutenant."

"Sorry, what?"

"You may refer to me as Detective Lieutenant Nogales," he said sternly as if demanding respect from this gringo—at least, that was how Sam felt.

"Sorry, Detective Lieutenant Nogales. Veronica worked for me and—"

"You said that. This is an active crime scene, and you are not to enter. Give me your card, and I will have someone notify you when you may come back. Right now, you are interfering with an investigation, and I will have you arrested if you do not leave immediately," he said without once looking at Sam.

Sam wanted to tell him to stick his crime scene up his ass but decided on a different approach.

"Sorry, again, Detective Lieutenant Nogales," he said solemnly, "but Veronica Martinez was not only an employee of mine but a dear friend. I need to call her parents and tell them their daughter is dead."

That got his attention. He walked over to Sam, who was still standing at the door on the other side of the yellow tape which was about chest-high to Sam.

Sam was holding out his business card. The Lieutenant took it and read from it. "My apologies, *Señor* Halloran. Please excuse my shortness." He stepped on Sam's side of the tape, placed a comforting hand on Sam's shoulder, and walked with him to a bench seat in the elevator lobby area.

"May we start at the beginning, please," said the detective, who then pulled out a notepad and jotted something down.

They talked for twenty minutes. Sam told him about the engagement for Hampton and gave him the name of Enrico Blanco as local counsel. He continued to take notes. When Sam felt he had given the detective enough information, he asked him for the courtesy of taking a quick run through Veronica's room.

Abruptly, Detective Nogales stood and said, "I am sorry, Mr. Halloran, but I cannot assist you any further." He started to walk away. Sam was pissed.

"Wait a minute. I thought you were going to help me?" Sam said as he leaped up.

Nogales stopped and turned. "I *am* helping you, *Señor* Halloran. Stop in your persistence, or you will join your precious Veronica Martinez in heaven… or hell. It matters not to me."

Sam saw red and started toward him. When the detective took a step forward, Sam stopped. He was no match for him. He likely wanted Sam to try something so he could shoot him and collect an even larger bonus from the man Sam now knew was still calling the shots.

"You are a total piece of shit. Along with your boss."

"I will pass on your sentiments to *Señor* Mendoza, who, by the way, sends his regards." He said it with a smirk and gleam in his eyes.

Sam knew when he needed to back off. He turned and pushed the down elevator button. He needed to walk it off. Besides, Pablo had been gone for some time. He should check on him. On the way down the elevator, Sam was beating himself up for letting Nogales play him like a deck of cards… a totally stacked deck.

But Sam could play that game, too. He knew exactly what needed to be done; he stepped off the elevator in the lobby and dialed his number.

"Steve, it's Sam."

"Of course it's you. Who else would call me in the middle of the night?"

In no mood for bantering, Sam got right to it and gave him an abbreviated version of the events that led to the death of Veronica Martinez. He told Steve about finding Evita and her story about the microchip drive. Steve was, of course, horrified. Before he could ask what he could do to help, Sam told him, like Steve was one of his staff.

Steve got it immediately, and they hung up so he could make the necessary phone calls that would move the State Department to act in the timeframe Sam needed. Now, there was nothing for Sam's team to do but wait. A scotch for him, maybe, but he knew this night might just be getting started and thought it best to stay alert. He looked around the lobby. Pablo was nowhere in sight. Sam went back to Marge's room.

When Sam opened the door to her room, he was surprised to see Eric sitting in the living room. He instantly panicked, but Eric, sensing his surprise, stood and moved toward him. The police were searching his room and told him to leave. Evita was in the bathtub and Marge was attending to her.

"Marge is giving Evita a bath?" Sam said, surprised.

Eric shrugged his shoulders. "Maybe Marge has some sensitive genes after all."

Sam asked about Frank's whereabouts. Eric said Frank wanted to see what activity was occurring down where Veronica's body lay, and he took off in the direction of the elevator banks, said he would meet Sam back here.

Sam nodded his head and then walked out onto Marge's balcony. Eric remained inside.

After being mocked by Detective Lieutenant Nogales, Sam wanted to stomp on his authority. He wanted to punch him in the face, but that would not get him what he really wanted—what he needed—to advance his plan. He needed to stay cool, collected, and calculating. This was a test of right over wrong. He had to trust that right would prevail... even in such a corrupt country. But then, why not use that fact? Corruption needed constant feeding.

The US government provided over a quarter-billion dollars annually in aid to the government of Guatemala. They actually calculated that about twenty percent was skimmed off the top by government officials and then a like amount was *lost* in traveling to its final destination: the poorest of the poor of this country. But without the US supplying some monetary help, these people would suffer even greater hardships, so they feed corruption to get some money to those who needed it most. Overhead costs. That was the way US officials viewed it. And now, it could actually help in his investigation. Money talks, and Sam was ready to hear it scream loudly.

He had made the call to Steve. He was certain Steve would make it happen. There was nothing to do but wait. It was killing Sam.

Down below, Sam could see a great deal of activity at the scene. Even though he couldn't make out anyone in particular, he knew Frank was down there. He still couldn't believe Veronica had been added to a growing list of people who were killed assisting Sam in his investigation. He fought back tears. He loved her like the daughter he never had, much like Laura Wittford. He was cursed, for sure.

Sam sat and replayed everything, trying to make sense of it. Maybe there was a clue he had been missing. *This couldn't be the way this ended,* he thought. *We were so damn close. Keep thinking through the problem,* he told himself. *There must be a solution, something we could do that we're not thinking of yet.*

But nothing came to mind. Everything that needed to be done was in the works. They needed access to the crime scene with trusted investigators, an autopsy of Veronica's body in the event that she, too, swallowed the drive, and access to everything the police were doing: collecting evidence or destroying it.

That was the hardest part because Mendoza still pulled those strings. Even if Sam were to get such access, the whole process would be corrupted by now.

Sam rewound the tape in his mind imagining what had transpired.

Whatever happened after Veronica left Evita in her bedroom is a mystery, but it seems from what Evita could recall, it happened very quickly. Evita said she gave Veronica the drive while coming up the elevator. In that case, Veronica did not have much time to do something with it. But Veronica is a smart gal (he cursed himself—*was*) *and sensing danger, she would have hidden it before answering the door. She either swallowed it, handed it off to Alicia, or hid it somewhere in her room.*

And now those corrupt cops were going through her room. And some corrupt coroner is going through her body... literally.

The thought made him sick to his stomach.

Then, there's the mystery about Alicia. Where is she? Evita said Veronica mentioned a friend in her room that would help them. She had to be talking about Alicia.

The emotion must have shown on his face when he went inside. After a time, Eric said, "Sam, I'm so sorry. Veronica was an amazing person. I didn't know her well, but I understand what a loss this must be for you. Please let me know if there is anything I can do for you."

It was a thoughtful gesture, but Sam was not in the mood for thoughtful gestures. If he had used better judgement, he would have put them on a plane and Veronica would still be alive. *Hell, if I could have replayed the entire engagement, we never would have left Chicago.*

He stood and walked toward the door upon hearing a knock followed quickly by, "It's Frank."

Sam opened the door and anxiously waited for a good report. Frank said the area was cordoned off, and Veronica's body was gone, no doubt sitting on some stainless-steel table at the morgue. If they hadn't found the drive yet, they'd be x-raying her to see if she had swallowed it. At any rate, Mendoza still held all the cards.

Sam motioned for Frank to follow him out and then turned and said to Eric, "Keep Evita here until we figure out what to do with her. We'll be back in a few. Do not leave this room."

The look on Eric's face revealed he didn't enjoy being kept on the sidelines, but Eric seemed to know instinctively now was not the time to bargain with his boss.

They stood outside the room as Sam updated Frank on his call with Steve. Frank agreed there was nothing else they could do but wait to hear from Steve. They walked down to the pool bar, but it had been closed off entirely. They walked inside and each grabbed a seat at the lobby bar but waived off the bartender. Sam thought it impressive how quickly they cleaned up the lobby and replaced all the windows after Miguel's murder.

As they sat watching all the commotion, Sam overheard some people talking about all that happened, one saying it was a suicide. He had a feeling who was spreading that rumor.

Sam recalled the first day he met Frank right at this very bar. It seemed a lifetime ago. He recalled Frank telling him to get rid of his Breitling Navitimer, which he had not seen since he placed it in the hotel safe... hoping it was still there. All that initial instructive advice was meant to keep them safe. For all the good that did.

"Frank, it's going on two a.m. I'm not sure Steve is going to get this done tonight, what do you think?"

"You civilians crack me up," Frank said with a sarcastic chuckle. "You think the State Department closes when nighttime falls? Like, we can't invade a country until everyone wakes up, takes a shower, and eats a good breakfast."

"OK, so I wasn't in the military. I get it!" Sam said, frustrated.

Sam's BlackBerry hummed. "Talk to me, Steve."

"Sam, your State contact is Don Mann. He will be meeting you shortly in the hotel lobby with the local police chief, Manalo

Bosque. Together, they should be able to get whatever you need. And, Sam, I am so sorry about Veronica. I don't know what to say."

Before Sam could respond, Steve continued. "One thing they require though, Sam, and I know this will be difficult for you, they need you to make a positive identification at the morgue. I said you would do that."

Silence.

Sam cleared his throat, "Thanks for everything, Steve. You're always there for me. And yes... I will take care of that. I'll also call her parents after."

Sam had repeated the names Steve relayed to him. Frank wrote them down.

Just then, Sam saw a police cruiser pull up and several officers rushing over to it. He guessed they recognized their chief's car. When Sam saw the American stepping from the passenger side, he knew they had their man.

"Frank, they're here. Let's go." Both hopped off their barstools.

Neither lost a second knowing how they risked losing an opportunity to recover the drive. Sam met them at the lobby doors, shaking hands and moving forward through the lobby. Frank redirected them toward the elevator bank. "Sam, how about you head up to her room," Frank said, "and get the chief to have someone take me to the morgue so I can get a glimpse of the autopsy. You can join us later."

"Makes sense."

After a brief discussion, the chief motioned to two of his men who stood attentive while he instructed them. A minute later, Sam and Frank went in different directions.

Before they entered Veronica's room, Sam pulled Don Mann aside and briefed him with just the salient details and their objective: to find the microchip drive. When they got to Veronica's room, one police officer remained but was seated and writing in his notepad. Someone in a white lab coat carrying a large case was walking out of the room. Sam was told he was the forensics guy. The balcony doors were still open and the drapes were blowing inward now. He stood in the doorway surveying the room. Upon seeing one of Veronica's shoes laying sideways near the wall he felt tormented knowing what had transpired in that room just a few hours earlier.

The chief was talking with another officer and then relayed to Sam they had cleared the room. Two men appeared at the doorway.

"A couple crime scene guys I phoned to meet us here," Don said. "I'll just be a moment."

Sam withdrew to the balcony to get some fresh air. What he saw did not help his current state.

With his back on the railing he viewed something he would not soon forget. There was a blood spatter on the building wall beginning about a foot off the balcony floor upwards about a foot and two inches wide. In the corner on the floor was a massive pool of blood. He had to work hard to keep from getting sick. Sam couldn't imagine what was going through her mind during those last seconds as she struggled with whoever broke into her room.

What did you do with that drive, Veronica?

He walked back inside and sat in a chair by a small hutch in the foyer, placed his head between his knees, and took deep breaths. A few minutes later, he felt his breathing settle and his vision return to normal.

Sam reminded himself why he wanted to visit Veronica's room and then set upon doing what he came to do. He had never examined a murder scene before but chose to do what he did on most of his investigations: simply observe and imagine what was going on between the characters involved. And so, he began.

First, he studied the door to the unit. He remembered Evita said a man was pounding on the door, saying he was police and demanding to be let in.

The safety chain had been ripped off, but there seemed to be no damage to the doorknob or frame. That told Sam that Veronica

opened the door with the safety latch on and he pushed his way in…
or she didn't open the door. He did with a key.

The bedroom where Veronica had stowed Evita was only five feet
away and behind a closed door, so she could have dispensed with
Evita quickly. Between the front door and the balcony lay about
thirty some feet straight back from the front door. If Veronica were
holding the drive, with him pounding on the door, she had very few
options to hide it. Sam began looking around the area.

He stood from his chair and walked toward the balcony. Don
walked in with one of his inspectors. He motioned Sam off to the
side and just above a whisper he said, "He's a blood spatter expert.
Sam… he said the intruder slit her throat while he had her pinned to
the balcony floor. That's why she couldn't scream. Also, based on the
large pool of blood, he likely examined the contents of her larynx.
Only after did he throw her over the side. She was dead before she
hit the ground."

Sam paused for a moment trying to maintain his composure.
"But then why toss her over the railing drawing all that attention below?"

"Easiest way to get the body out quickly," Don said. "To someplace they controlled—the morgue."

Don walked away leaving Sam to his thoughts. Sam managed to
make it back to the chair he had been sitting in. He imagined the
horror she must have suffered. *Maybe that's how it came down. So,
it's gone… the drive is gone.*

CHAPTER 58

AS DON'S GUYS were completing their pictures and write-up, Sam watched Chief Bosque standing outside the doorway with one of his men. The chief looked at his phone, put it to his ear, then moved down the hall. Sam thought of Mendoza. Of course, this police chief was on his payroll, playing both sides. Sam tried to remain calm and restrained. *The chief could play us tonight and keep Mendoza informed on events. It was so unfair.*

When he finished his call and stepped back into the room, he motioned for Don to come over. They spoke briefly. The chief had cleared the room. He and his men were leaving. Maybe that call informed Mendoza they did indeed have it… the drive.

Another thirty minutes passed when the hypnotic, steady rhythm of the damp air blowing through the open balcony window was broken by Sam's BlackBerry buzzing. It was Frank.

"Sam, they did take x-rays, and I was able to see them. Nothing resembling any foreign object anywhere in her digestive tract. Coroner said based on the timing of events I communicated to him, it would still be in her upper thorax area if she had swallowed it."

"Frank, how do you even know you were looking at Veronica's x-ray?"

"I don't for sure, but the wounds on the x-ray appear consistent with a fall like she sustained… as well as her throat being examined. The hyoid bone, the one that protects the throat, was broken. The coroner explained it to me. I'll confirm it later myself but seemed legit."

They were both silent, thinking the same thing: *If you're going to shove someone off a twenty-five-story balcony, why take the time to slit their throat?* "Frank, I know what you're thinking. Maybe her attacker saw her swallow it which is why he slit her throat."

"I'm sorry, Sam. I don't know what to say. I suppose we'll never know exactly what happened unless we catch the bastard who did this."

"Like that could ever happen in this God-forsaken place."

Neither spoke for a few moments.

"All right, Frank, anything else you can think of that we aren't doing at this point?"

"I guess just one more thing. I wasn't going to mention this, but when are you planning to come down here?"

"Not sure. I wanted to sit in Veronica's room for a while. This may sound crazy, but I knew her pretty well. I want to imagine what she might have been thinking just moments before that hoodlum broke into her room… where she might have hidden the drive. I know that's a long shot, but I'm out of options."

"Maybe you should come down here right now while we still have the chance."

"Why? I'm not exactly in a hurry to see her. Besides, you know what Veronica looked like. I know they want me, but you did see her, right?"

"That's just it, Sam. They refuse to show me her body. Said their instructions are to show the body only to the one who is to ID her. I wish I could save you the torment, but I can't ID her."

"OK, Frank. I'll talk to Don to ensure this place will be secure, and then I'll come down there and get it over with."

"Sounds good. I'll see you soon."

Sam walked over to where Don was watching his men work. "Don, can I talk to you a moment?"

He relayed his conversation with Frank. "Has to be me," they said. "I should get down to the morgue."

"I understand, Sam. I'll make sure this room is secure with one of my men standing outside for as long as you need it." He handed Sam a key.

Frank met Sam just outside the front door. He nodded, respectfully. Neither said anything. Neither wanted to be there but both understood what had to be done... and who had to be the one to do it.

A technician in a white coat told Frank he'd need to wait outside but after Frank said something in Spanish, tersely, the technician backed down. He directed them downstairs and took them into a room with several stainless-steel tables and what looked like refrigerator doors... cold slabs. *Veronica was in one of those.*

The attendant instructed Sam where to stand and then pulled on a handle resembling a large metal filing cabinet drawer. He pulled it out completely. Sam's eyes were closed.

"*Señor,*" The technician said to Sam.

Sam opened his eyes. He was looking at a white sheet covering someone he did not want to see like this. He wondered if he would ever forget what he was about to see. He fought hard to maintain some semblance of decorum. He had underestimated how difficult this would be.

When the sheet was pulled back from her face it was the most hideous thing Sam had ever witnessed. Even the warning he had received could not have prepared him for this. Her face... was gone. *How could I possibly make a positive ID?*

The attendant spoke in monotone. "This is the body of a female Caucasian. Height five feet and five inches, weight 118 pounds. She has tattoos on the underside of each wrist and one on her left buttock."

Sam held up his hand to stop the technician. "I need to see her wrists," he said balanced, steadied, self-controlled.

The attendant pulled each arm from under the sheet and laid them on top. Then, he turned over her right wrist exposing a cross; on the left was *PaPa*.

"This is not Veronica. It's Alicia… Alicia Lopez," Sam said with gut-wrenching relief mixed with utmost sadness.

Frank immediately grabbed Sam around his shoulders.

"I need to sit down," Sam said. Someone slid a metal chair under him.

"I would ask if you are sure, but I'm certain you are," Frank said. "I saw them both during the day… then when I saw… the victim, wearing the same jacket I saw Veronica in…." Frank was seemingly apologizing for his earlier error.

"Not your fault, Frank. They were like a couple of teens together," Sam said. "Alicia must have wanted to try on Veronica's outfits."

"That would explain it."

"Let's get out of here, Frank."

On the drive back to the hotel, Frank and Sam were in the back seat being driven by one of their security.

"You thinking what I'm thinking, Frank?"

"If Veronica is still alive, where the hell is she?"

"And where is the drive?"

CHAPTER 59

Earlier that same day

THE TWO THUGS from the lobby were now pouring into Veronica's room, ripping the security chain off the door frame like it wasn't even there. One grabbed Alicia, wrestling with her. The other did not see Veronica jump him from behind, gouging at his eyes and screaming for help, but he was a large man. He backed into the door, causing Veronica's head to hit it with a force rendering her unconscious.

Hugo was waiting in his car behind the hotel near the loading docks. He saw one of his men exit with a woman slung over his shoulder. He smiled as he got out and opened the liftgate of the Suburban, and she was flopped onto the floor.

"This is not her. Where is Evita?"

"Jose is dealing with her. He will be down soon."

Hugo leaned on the hood of his SUV, focused on the door to the loading dock. "Jose had better be bringing her soon, or he will have to answer to *El Jefe* himself."

Veronica was lying in the back—blindfolded, bound, and gagged. She had now regained consciousness but was powerless to make a sound. She was their prisoner.

Hugo slammed the hood in frustration when he saw Jose exit the hotel empty-handed. "Where is the girl?" he yelled.

"She is dead. I slit her throat and searched her. Nothing. Let's go. They are coming!"

"Shit... fuck!" Hugo knew he could not run back upstairs. That room would be swarming with police; he couldn't count on them being the ones they owned.

Jose slid into the backseat. "You said to get the girl. I did. She had nothing on her. She is dead. Now, GO!"

Hugo sped off, already crafting a believable story to tell *El Jefe*.

Mendoza paced the floor of the kitchen at Del Griego, his favorite steakhouse in Guatemala City, while Hugo told him what happened. He didn't have the *drive thing* Mendoza had told him to find. Said he must have been mistaken. There was no such thing to find.

Mendoza wasn't buying it, but that didn't matter right now. He would soon get to the bottom of it. He had a prize. He would see for himself if she might be carrying it someplace hidden very cleverly. Mendoza laughed to himself of the fun he'd have retrieving it.

He had her, that little shit who followed Sam Halloran everywhere. Enrico Blanco had told him about her. Smart ass Mexican. Thought she was some bigshot American. Soon, she would tell Javier all he wanted to know. Then, he would please himself with that Mexican-American slut.

Pablo had just hung up with Sam after learning of Alicia's fate and that Veronica was still alive... as far as they knew. He was now in search of her. He decided to pay a visit to the security camera room. After paying the requisite bribes, he sat down and began searching. Soon, he found what he was looking for.

He began to scan the tapes, beginning with the footage of Evita and Veronica reuniting in front of the lobby elevators. He thought it impressive how Veronica had subdued her two attackers. Then, he watched camera footage from the twenty-fifth floor as Veronica and Evita ran down the hallway and entered her room.

He watched and waited for the men who broke into her room. Two minutes and thirty-three seconds later, two men dressed as commandos were pounding on her door. Another half-minute later, they came through the door. Pablo waited and logged the time. Two minutes and sixteen seconds later, one man left with what appeared to be a woman slung over his shoulder, walking toward the stairs. The man moved fast, and Pablo couldn't make out much but assumed that was Veronica. By the way her arms were dangling, she was unconscious.

There was one man left in the room. He waited, logging the time. He felt sick to his stomach knowing what that man was doing to Alicia on the balcony. Five minutes and twenty-one seconds later, he also left headed for the stairway—empty-handed.

Another five minutes passed before two hotel security guards entered the room. Still, Pablo waited, confirming his understanding. Seven minutes and twenty-six seconds later, it was he, Sam, and Frank entering her room accompanied by two police officers. Next, he saw the two hotel security guards dispatched by the officers. Fifty-six seconds later, the two officers left the room running down the hallway toward the stairs, courtesy of his warning of two fictitious men.

Finally, nearly a minute later, he, then Sam, exited the room, looking both ways, and then Frank followed, carrying Evita.

Pablo continued searching other security footage, which took him an additional twenty minutes. He wanted to see where they had taken Veronica but could not confirm. The loading dock camera was nonfunctioning. Like Sam, he, too, did not believe in coincidence. He presumed she was removed from the hotel after her kidnappers had disabled that camera. Another room was a possibility, but he couldn't waste time searching other floor cams. Veronica was in *his* hands... the hands of a madman. He felt certain she was no longer in the hotel; he needed more clues as to where she might be.

He called Sam to let him know what he had found. "What do you want me to do now?"

"I don't know, Pablo, I'll defer to your judgment."

"Maybe I should go back down to the lobby and walk around. Maybe something more will surface."

Sam thought for a moment. "I think that makes sense, but call me back in an hour no matter what. I'm in Veronica's room trying to piece it all together."

Pablo made it back to the lobby. He chose to sit on a bench by the elevator bank where the first attempt to get the girls began.

Ten minutes later, he noticed a man just outside the pool door standing and smoking a cigarette. That wasn't why Pablo noticed him. It was the way he was dressed: blue jean pants and shirt, red bandana around his neck, leather gloves hanging out of his back pocket, and an oversized well-worn cowboy hat. By the look of his face and dress, he didn't belong anywhere near a five-star hotel. He looked more at home on a cattle drive.

Pablo stood, continuing to regard the man on the other side of the glass doors. He started to walk toward him. Before he pushed on the doors, the man turned and noticed Pablo. Suddenly, he flicked his cigarette and then started to run, or rather limp, away. Pablo gave chase, although it took only a few steps to catch up to him.

"*Señor*, please do not run. I will not harm you."

He turned to look at Pablo and then slowed his pace.

Pablo walked to within a couple feet of him and said, "Please, *Señor*. I just want to ask you something. Can we talk for a moment?"

The man stopped and waited for Pablo to join him by his side. A few words were exchanged and then the two men sat on a bench.

Like Sam and Frank, Pablo also had a knack for calming people and gaining their confidence. Very soon, Pablo realized what a treasure he had found. Moments later, Mario told him about their journey.

Pablo gave him some money and invited him to have a meal in

the restaurant, and they would talk later. He promised Mario he would see Evita, so he could report back to his sister that she was in good hands.

Fifteen minutes later, Pablo was sitting in his SUV outside of the restaurant. A trained military tactician, he would wait and observe before entering. He also thought he could use some help and knew who to call.

"You are where?" Frank said.

"I am sitting in my car with eyes on the Del Griego restaurant. I think Veronica may be inside."

"Veronica… are you sure?"

"Not certain, but the source is good". He told Frank about his conversation with Mario, that Mario had overheard Hugo on the phone with his boss and mentioned Del Griego.

"That was it? Just the name?"

"Mario said they talked on the phone for a minute or so and that was the only thing that stuck with him." That name meant something to Mario. It was the largest steakhouse in all of Guatemala City and a buyer of Mendoza cattle. Mario would not forget such a thing.

"I could use your help, but should we run this by Sam?"

"Sam is really in a bad way right now. He's up in Veronica's room with investigators."

"I agree. We talked a while ago."

"He definitely needs some space. So, what's your plan?"

"Frank, this may turn out to be a dead end, but my gut tells me she's here with Mendoza. I have not seen any sign of them, but I have identified four security personnel at various stations around the perimeter. Mendoza would have his guards do this. I think it's worth checking out. I have been here before. They have a large walkout basement for banquets, which I cannot see at this moment."

"I trust your instincts, Pablo. Give me the address." Frank wrote it in his notepad. "I'll see you there soon."

When Frank arrived, he slid into the passenger seat of Pablo's vehicle. "Have you seen any sign of Veronica?"

"Nothing yet."

"You know, the longer she's in there, the more danger she's in."

"Then we should go in and get her now," Pablo said as he pulled a concealed 9mm Glock 19 from his back. "I have a piece for you in my glove box."

Frank thought for a minute. "Pablo, much as I'd like to do this with you, I'm thinking Sam would advise otherwise. Plus, we don't know what to expect. He could have a dozen men with him in there. It's probably best we call Sam."

"But we do not know she is there. We should first make sure of this."

"I don't see where that gets us. This is time sensitive. I say we call Sam. He can call his State Department contact that can get the chief out here. You know... the cop working both ends."

Pablo thought a minute. He flicked the safety on his Glock and placed it on his lap. "It seems yours is the wiser move. Call him."

Frank made the call, and twenty minutes later the area lit up with red and blue lights. Patrons of the restaurant began slowly filing out.

Frank and Pablo identified themselves to the chief, who allowed them to follow his men into the basement.

Of course, no one remained in the basement thanks to the heads-up call the chief had made to Mendoza. No matter, the only person they cared about at the moment was there.

Veronica was doped up and bruised but otherwise unharmed. They had just begun to work on her.

Mission accomplished.

It was good to see Don Mann could still wield influence over the police chief, but then the US Army Rangers behind them probably had some influence, too.

Frank untied Veronica from a chair while speaking calming

words. She was slowly coming back. Pablo was already calling Sam to update him.

When she recognized Frank, she laid an arm on his shoulder. She was groggy, but her tears confirmed how happy she was to see him.

He steadied her, holding a glass of water while she took sips. Five minutes later, she was able to speak. "Oh my God… it is so good to see you!" she said, hugging him with both arms.

"Were you harmed in any way?"

"Just my pride and about the worst headache I've ever had. Where's Sam?"

"There's something I need to tell you."

"Oh my God!" Veronica said covering her mouth.

"No, no, I'm sorry… no, Sam is fine. I should have told you immediately."

Veronica breathed a huge sigh of relief.

As Frank held her hands, he told her all that happened after she was taken… but for the moment, he held back on the worst of it. She looked bewildered searching her memory…. She remembered the men crashing through the door to her room, but that was all. She didn't remember the microchip drive or finding Evita.

Then, he told her of Alicia's fate, and Veronica collapsed into him, sobbing, shaking, and cursing. He held her tight as she wept. A few minutes later, she sat up straight, still crying intermittently. She asked a few questions.

After Frank had satisfied her questions, Veronica's memory returned.

"The drive! I passed it to Alicia! Do you have it?"

"No, we don't. Sam has been sitting in your room for some time trying to retrace everything. He suspected you must have given it to Alicia."

"How could he know that?"

Frank did not want to say why. She'd learn the gruesome facts soon enough.

"Good instincts, I suppose."

Veronica nodded her head.

"I'll take you there now. Maybe both of you can figure it out together."

"And Evita?"

"Probably still asleep in Marge's room."

"Whaaat?"

"Long story."

CHAPTER 60

AFTER IDENTIFYING ALICIA'S body, Sam headed back to Veronica's room so he could continue where he left off. Pablo had updated him on Veronica's rescue. She would be with him soon. With all that had happened, he thanked God for sparing Veronica.

Before he left the morgue, Sam was given Alicia's personal belongings. Included among them was her BlackBerry. He momentarily marveled at the fact that falling twenty-five stories did not appear to have damaged it. It had to have been in her back pocket. Sam pushed the power button—dead.

He searched for and found a charger on the hutch and plugged it in. It wouldn't be long.

He lay on the sofa and closed his eyes. Ten minutes later, her phone sprang to life with several vibrations. She had a voicemail, but he needed a password to unlock it. He thought for a moment and then guessed it on the first try. The man she most respected in this world.

The call had come in only an hour ago. Of course, the voicemail was in Spanish. He redialed the caller. Fortunately, she spoke English.

The call was to confirm Alicia had received the Danta Chocolates

Deluxe Assortment. It should have been delivered to her room yesterday. *Why did it matter, anyway?* He didn't know if it had and told the caller. He was about to hang up and then looked up and saw a tall gold foil bag on the bookshelf above the hutch. He asked her to describe it. As she did, he walked up to it for a closer look and then confirmed delivery and said goodbye. Who knew why it now sat in Veronica's room? Who cared?

His thoughts turned back to the drive. *Where was it? Did he have it?*

His eyes set again on that box of Danta Chocolates. He stared at it and then focused on something hanging from the side handle—a small envelope. Nothing was written on it.

He pulled a card out of the envelope, feeling somewhat like he was prying… but then he was glad he had.

> *Sam,*
>
> *I cannot begin to express my gratitude for all you have taught me in so short a time. I hope to continue to learn from you and your entire team. And maybe I have taught you something too—Guatemalan chocolates were the first and the best!*
>
> *Respectfully,*
>
> *Alicia*

Standing there, he recalled their first meeting at Miami Airport; then, he reflected upon how much she had changed. He became overwhelmed with emotion and sat in the chair next to the hutch. She had become a completely different person in such a short period of time. He, too, wished he could have worked with her more. *With all she had going on down here, she thought of me.*

Sam recalled one night while several of them were gathered poolside shortly after arriving. The hotel staff brought them a boxed assortment of chocolates as a welcoming gift. As he sampled them, he was not saying nice things about Guatemala, reflecting, of course, on the target of his investigation.

Alicia took to defending the country. "Sam, those chocolates you are eating were likely made in Guatemala. You may not be aware the Mayan people first discovered chocolate over a thousand years ago."

Sam remembered breaking out in a hearty laugh. "You'll never convince me. That's absurd! These chocolates taste amazing! They have to be Swiss made. Something this good could never have come from this worthless country."

They bantered back and forth. Alicia wouldn't let it go. Finally, he said, "Whatever... it's just a box of chocolates."

He now recalled how she ended the debate. *"But it does matter, Sam. Life is like a box of chocolates. You never know what you're gonna get."*

How embarrassed and foolish he now felt.

This was the last memory he would have of Alicia, and this thoughtful gesture may have been one of her last acts before she left them in such a violent way. It caused him to reach up and take them into his hands... this gift of Danta Chocolates.

Sam held the box in his hands, admiring it.

He thought of Alicia's death and the deaths of Miguel, Gabriela, and of the perilous fate awaiting Evita, her mother and niece. He fought back tears for the sacrifices they had made to expose a monster and bring the hope of a better life for so many. They had come so close.

Finally, he set the box down and walked toward the door to leave Veronica's room. Then, he had another thought.

Alicia knew I would end up with this box of chocolates... even if she was no longer around to gift it to me... her very last thought.

Sam turned to look at it again. He picked it up and slowly examined it from top to bottom.

Along the sides at the top, it was easy to separate the foil. Easy enough to slip something slim inside, yet no one would suspect this from looking at the box. *It's just a box of chocolates....*

Sam explored a little... then smiled.

Thank you, Alicia!

CHAPTER 61

THREE DAYS HAD passed since Sam recovered the microchip drive from where Alicia had left it for him. He immediately charged one of his team with delivering it personally to Chicago's forensic IT group for analysis. Sam would not take any chances with something so valuable; something many suffered to obtain… some who had even given their lives to deliver to him.

Sam's BlackBerry vibrated. "Hey, Sam, it's Jack. This a good time to talk?"

Jack Coulter was one of Sam's Chicago partners. They had grown to become the best of friends, probably because they were of the same ilk—good at what they did and impatient with others who got in their way. Sam met Jack several years ago when Jack was hired into Chicago to support Sam's growing investigations practice. He had a law degree but soon tired of the law and began specializing in Information Technology (IT), his undergraduate major.

Data interrogation was a critical part of performing financial crime investigations, and Sam needed a competent IT practice close by. He had been relying on the Dallas IT group, but they couldn't keep up with the frenetic pace at which Sam's practice was growing.

Jack quickly established a group of professionals always ready and willing to respond to Sam's IT needs no matter the time of day or night. His IT practice grew along with Sam's practice. Jack got it.

"Only if you're calling me with good news," Sam said, his knee bouncing nervously, anxious to hear Jack's report. Everything hinged on what evidence of crimes Sam hoped was on that drive.

"I am. Some sectors were damaged, but the lawyer in me thinks you've got enough to interest the US Attorney's office into pursuing a criminal investigation against Mr. Mendoza, AKA rapist, extortioner, drug lord."

"I didn't say anything to you about him being a rapist."

"You didn't have to. What I saw confirms this guy is a sick dude."

"Saw?"

"Pictures, Sam. Disgusting ones."

"I don't need to see them, but can you send me a printout of the drive's contents?"

"I've got more than that for you. Dave Rogers and his staff have been working side-by-side with my guys on three shifts to analyze and research the data as we extracted it. I know they are still working on it, but they've prepared a preliminary report that should be ready for you at the end of today. Dave said you were landing Chicago early evening. That right?"

"Not exactly. I'll soon be boarding a flight to New York. Won't be back in Chicago until late tomorrow."

"New York. You going to go kiss the ring?"

"I'll do anything to save her."

"Who?"

"Never mind. Need to tell you all that over a scotch."

"Sounds like an interesting story."

"I could do with a lot less *interesting* in my life these days."

"Well, in that case, do you want me to fetch Dave to brief you now? I can see him in our forensics lab working with my team."

"That would be great. Put him on."

"Hey, Sam," Dave said solemnly. He'd heard of the tragedies but hadn't had a chance to talk with Sam about them. "Sounds like you had a rough week down there."

"You could say that. I know I owe you a call. You need to be aware of all that's happened down here. I'm sure the staff is hearing bits and pieces. I'll need to address it with them soon. I'm just not ready. But right now, I need to hear what you've found on that drive... of a financial nature."

"We've found plenty, Sam. Trust me when I say you and the US Attorney are going to become best friends."

"Talk to me, Dave."

"The most compelling evidence is Mendoza's spreadsheet log of payoffs to all sorts of people, most of whom are in Guatemala and Columbia... dates and amounts. Many FCPA violations. Some with what looks to be bank routing and account numbers, the others appearing to be cash payments. I had Laura track down the routing numbers. One you'll find of particular interest. It's to a US bank—LaSalle Bank."

Sam thought for a moment. "As in the Chicago variety? Presumably, payoffs to someone at corporate?"

"That's my thought as well. It seems a significant source of funding were cash transfers from corporate to the Abello plant. All made as debits to the intercompany account on the corporate side. Of course, the only auditing done on those accounts is simply to match the corresponding period-end balances. If the debit on corporate's side matched the credit on Abello's side that was proof enough."

"Doesn't surprise me, Dave. Auditors audit balances, not transactions—at least, of this variety."

"That's what Laura told me, too, but this time she took it a step further to look at the actual detailed transactions on the corporate side. She was able to confirm the corresponding cash transfers to the Abello plant's cash account."

"That would explain a lot. Mendoza must have someone at

corporate working for him. Which would explain the payoffs wired to LaSalle Bank. We'll have to sort that out. OK, what else?"

"Lots of instructional documents on how and when to process certain transactions," Dave said. "That's where Laura's audit experience seems to be coming into play. She said that, aside from the cash transfers to Abello, there were lots of debits in A/P (accounts payable). Said what Abello likely did was to charge A/P when they would withdraw cash for whatever reason. She found macro formulas that, once activated, blew out those balance sheet debits to over 1,500 expense accounts so no one account would draw attention."

"But that would ensure Abello would show losses," Sam said quizzically.

"And that's why they created bogus sale transactions. Laura also found evidence indicating large sale transactions were created with corresponding receivables. Included in the document on the drive were instructions on how and when to re-age the receivables on the balance sheet to escape detection from the auditors."

"So they covered up the influx of expenses with bogus sales—sales that would have corresponding receivables that would never be collected. That made Abello look profitable… as profitable as they wanted to be at any point in time," Sam said almost admiringly.

"I would expect auditors should catch stuff like that," Dave said.

"That's why they call it *the expectations gap*—the difference between what the public would *expect* the auditors to do and what they are trained to do.

"They rarely, if ever, audit the income statement, favoring instead to perform fluctuation analysis. As long as the ratios do not significantly differ from previous year's amounts, they wouldn't give it a second look. And assuming Mendoza has been perpetrating these frauds for some time, the fluctuations wouldn't be significant."

"Ha! So he had to continue stealing from the company so no one would notice. The only part he needed outside help with was a steady source of cash funding his criminal empire."

"Hate to say it, but aside from his perverse nature he seemed to be one slick fraudster. He fooled everyone and no telling if he ever would have been caught. Hampton Enterprises likely lost tens of millions to him, but that's a drop in the bucket compared to the billions in cash generated by their global operations. Steve's going to have his work cut out for him nailing down what exactly happened and how it escaped their internal auditors."

Dave moved to the next item on his list. "Next scam we've discovered: Laura found a list of charitable foundations. Gave it to me asking if it was important. I'm sure you know what that might be indicating."

"Sure do. I've seen it many times. It's a common cover for illegal bribes. The government official sets up a bogus foundation when in fact he or his wife owns that foundation. Sending the check to the foundation is less likely to draw attention."

"Any other scams detected?"

"One final one related to the financials… this one off-books. Inflated invoicing. Again, we're assuming these occurred, as we don't have the actual transactional details."

"I get that. All the accounting documents were *stolen* by the peasant workers, right?" Sam said sarcastically.

"How could I forget? Veronica's initial trip."

"There appears to be some communication showing commissions each Abello vendor paid to Mendoza ranging between five and ten percent. Laura is continuing to work on that scam, but it sure seemed that Mendoza had all bases covered."

"It does. And he had absolutely no fear of being caught by either the internal or external auditors. To corporate, he was a god due to his apparent success when in fact he was robbing them blind."

"That's what we've found so far on our side. You ready to talk about Mendoza's hobbies?"

"Not really, but through some interviews down here post

Mendoza fleeing, we've had a peek into what you're about to say. Tell me what you've found first."

"A lot of recordkeeping on cocaine shipments and on sex trafficking. They go back at least a decade. Laura and her staff are still working on it. A lot of data, Sam. Spreadsheet after spreadsheet."

"We're finding the same is true in our interviews," Sam said. "With Mendoza gone, we've actually been able to compromise a few of his inner circle into cooperating. Money talks. Mendoza wasted no time in cutting off payments to them. We're hearing that he had regular shipments of cocaine in dummy rum casks. Cash was funneled back to him in the returned casks from previous shipments to Abello's bottling plant in Texas."

"Sounds like another investigation into the manager of that plant."

"I think with all this fallout down here, that manager will cave without too much coaxing. Just get Steve's agreement and give this opportunity to one of our forensics managers. Some good admission-seeking interview experience," Sam said clearly exhausted.

"Sounds like a lot of loose ends to wrap up."

"Right now, I've got bigger fish to fry in New York. You know Fitzgerald, right?"

"Patrick and I go way back. I knew a long time ago he'd be the US Attorney in the seventh circuit one day. He'll take my call and be happy to look over the evidence. I'll set up a meeting for you and me. Should I notify that Bruce & Bishop partner?"

Sam had forgotten he was technically working at the direction of Rodney Phillips at Bruce & Bishop. The whole reason Hampton engaged Hamilton Pierce through outside counsel was to maintain the privilege. Sam realized that was an important aspect of his investigation. This one was so successful he wouldn't want to risk losing the privilege. "Inform Phillips *after* you have set things up with Fitzgerald. I suppose we'll have to invite him to that meeting," Sam said with disgust. There were some rules he did need to follow.

"Dave, thanks for all your work on this, but before I let you go, tell me how Laura performed."

"You've got a winner in that one, Sam. She's as smart as they come. She'll do very well here. And by the way, don't worry that she's still pissed at you for not assigning her to Guatemala. She thinks the world of you."

"Good to hear. Gotta run," Sam said. He was relieved he hadn't lost Laura's confidence. His promise to her mother still carried an immeasurable importance to him.

CHAPTER 62

FRANK HAD NOT left the country yet. He told Sam he wanted to spend some time with the new plant operational crew to ensure a smooth transition. Even though Javier Mendoza had fled, there remained many loyal to him—well, his money, anyway, but they were slowly coming to the realization that money had dried up.

Sam knew this to be his last eggs benedict with Frank in the hotel restaurant. "You know, Frank, this breakfast is the only memorable thing, in a pleasant sort of way, about this entire country," Sam said, trying to act light-hearted in spite of all the tragedies he'd witnessed—*caused*.... He'd be telling himself that for some time.

"You're selling yourself short, Sam. You ran one hell of an investigation here, and you've done a lot to get the ball rolling on cleaning up this country. At least with him gone, his political connections seem to be taking a different view of things. That tax lien on the plant was just lifted and the judgement vacated. The mayor has had several meetings with the new plant manager offering to help in anyway."

"Like he helped Mendoza?" Sam said jokingly.

"Nope. He was sincere. He knows the party is over," Frank said. "He's in survival mode now."

"That's good to hear, but I still feel a big hole with Mendoza on the run."

"Yeah, well, it shouldn't be long before he's apprehended. There's now an INTERPOL Wanted Notice, which means Javier Mendoza is an international fugitive. And with the reward for his capture set at a quarter-million, courtesy of Hampton Enterprises, I'm certain he won't know whom to trust any longer."

Sam wasn't so sure. "You're forgetting about who his cousin is."

"Ha! You mean The Fat Man, *El Gordo*. Yeah, I get it. I try not to think about that. I'd rather keep hoping he'll get nailed someday... soon."

"I won't believe it until I read about it in the papers someday."

Sam focused on someone walking up to their table. He hopped up and embraced him. "Derek, I'm so happy you could make it," Sam said as he pulled up a chair so his friend could sit.

"Frank, I want you to meet Derek Dorn from CRI. You weren't around for the start of this gig, but Derek was the guy who got me great intel on Mendoza for my first trip down here and initial interview of Mendoza."

The two shook hands, although Derek held on to Frank's hand longer. He looked at Sam. "You didn't tell me Frank was a brother!" Derek said, smiling at Sam still holding onto Frank's hand.

"Why would I? You know me better than that," Sam said and then shifted his focus to the front of the hotel. "You guys are competing special forces, Delta and SEALs. I see Pablo just pulled up. Swap some war stories. I'll be right back."

The two began talking and swapping stories like they had been longtime friends, and then Derek gave Frank a long look. "Frank, Sam and I had a number of calls, and he talked about all the help you've given him, even saving his life, but he never told me you were black," Derek said seemingly surprised.

"But does that surprise you about Sam? Never told me you were black either."

"He does break the mold, doesn't he?"

"He does indeed," Frank said admiringly. "The more I get to know him, the more I'm impressed with him."

Derek nodded.

"Right on time as usual," Sam said, glancing at the time on his phone. He laughed, realizing he was again wearing his Breitling Navitimer that Frank warned him not to wear for the rest of his stay. That seemed ages ago. He'd have to retrain himself to look at it again.

"Your flight on time?" Pablo said.

"Just confirmed a little while ago."

"Good, I am eager to see you off and then I am having the best day in a very long time," Pablo said smiling ear to ear. Sam had never seen him smile with such joy.

"I am happy, *Señor*. Maybe I am happy for the first time in many, many years. I learned this morning that my son, Dario, he is here."

"He's in Guatemala City?" Sam said surprised.

"*Sí*, he is here. I learned he has been *under my nose* I think you would say," Pablo said, still smiling.

Sam laughed. "Where?"

"He has been driving delivery truck at the Abello plant. My priest, he asked me how Dario was doing. I said I did not know. Then he backed away. We talked. He finally say he saw Dario last month. But in confidence. That he confessed to him. That Dario said he would see me soon. He say Dario was so happy."

Sam was excited father and son would be reunited. "Pablo and Dario Escapa are soon once again a family. I am happy for you, Pablo!"

"Well, I'm told he changed his name to Castro for some reason. Still, no matter, we will soon be together."

"I'm ready to leave. Just need to say goodbye to Frank. Why don't you join me?"

"No, *Señor*. I will see Frank later. I must make some calls now," Pablo said, still excited with the news about his son.

Sam didn't want to delay Pablo on his reunion with his son. He returned to the table to give his apologies to Derek and Frank for his quick exit. He gave them each a final man hug—a one arm embrace, two quick pats.

"Walk with me, Frank," Sam said as they walked toward the lobby door. "Do me a last favor."

"Name it."

"Pablo just told me some incredibly good news. I'll let him tell you, but I'd like you to go with us as he drops me off at the airport. Then stay with him."

"Got it. We've been hanging out together. Supposed to have dinner tonight."

"Those plans may change," Sam said.

"Pablo is a good man. I'll help him anyway I can."

"I know you will, and call me... soon," Sam said.

"Count on it."

CHAPTER 63

ON THE DRIVE to the airport, Pablo filled Frank in on his news. Frank acted happy for Pablo but seemed to have reservations, like Sam. Something didn't seem right.

Pablo pulled up behind the bus carrying Project Vista's staff, all of whom were excited to be going home. Sam had already said his goodbyes to them last night at a final gathering by the hotel pool. It was an emotional goodbye.

He got out of Pablo's vehicle the same time they were exiting the bus. The first one off was Marge and then behind her, Eric. He caught Sam's attention and said something to Marge. She waved, and Sam waved back. Eric ran toward Sam.

"Sam, I just want to thank you for all you taught me on this engagement," Eric said, extending his hand. "I hope you'll keep me in mind anytime you need additional staffing."

"I certainly will, Eric. Anyone who takes my instructions and executes as well as you did deserves remembering." Eric smiled. He knew exactly what Sam was referring to. They both looked at Marge as she waved again.

"I'm sure you'll be happy to be back in LA?"

"Not yet. Marge got me assigned to a NYC engagement. They're headed to an investigation in India in a few days. She invited me to go along. Thought it would be good experience." Marge called out to Eric... warmly this time. It appeared she had picked up a few new skills as well.

As more staff filed off the bus, Sam exchanged waves to them as Frank talked with Pablo while getting Sam's bags. Sam thought back to the day when he first met Pablo, how he had escorted and protected Alicia and him to the airport as Mendoza's thugs followed close behind. His was the first personal commentary on how evil Javier Mendoza was. Of course, he was right. *I should have listened to him.*

Sam thought back on the sadness that had occurred with the loss of lives. He still held out hope their sacrifices would have a permanent impact on changing things for the better for so many families. Hampton had pledged to do what they could to turn things around.

Pablo set Sam's bags down at his feet. Frank gave Sam a nod and then hopped in the car to give them some time alone. They embraced one last time. When they separated, Pablo wiped a tear away, turned quickly, slid into his car, and drove off. Sam was anxious about what Pablo would find as he searched for his son, Dario, but he was relieved Frank would be with him.

As Sam walked toward the terminal, he wondered how Veronica was doing. She left yesterday without saying goodbye to Sam. She knew where he was off to and she would see him in a couple of days... maybe for the last time.

CHAPTER 64

ON THE FLIGHT to NYC, Sam reviewed his notes. Louis Bittle had arranged for Sam's meeting before the Hamilton Pierce Firm Council just as Sam had demanded. In a couple of hours, Sam would have to face off with the most senior partners in the firm to try and save Veronica Martinez's job... her career. If she were fired from Hamilton Pierce, no one would touch her. She'd be through with the consulting business.

Sam had only one friend on the Council, Ann Williams. Ann was a good friend, and Sam knew she would do all she could to help him achieve his objective. Sure, Ann was disgusted with what Veronica had done, sleeping with an intern, her mentee. Ann told Sam it was inexcusable, and she agreed with the Council's unanimous decision to terminate Veronica's employment. Yes, Ann, too, voted to fire Veronica Martinez.

What Veronica did was wrong, no argument there, but Sam knew the reason, and in a way he could identify with it having suffered through his own childhood trauma. In a different way, Veronica had suffered unthinkable trauma—at the innocent age of thirteen, she was raped by her babysitter's boyfriend. Then, he threatened he'd murder her parents if she revealed it. She was a traumatized child, so of course she believed him and remained quiet. She had told Sam the story after Sam was berating her for her indiscretion with her mentee. There were a lot of starts and stops and quiet moments during that session between the two of them. She told Sam the only way she had reconciled herself to the event, the rape, was to reduce the act of having sex to something less invasive. *Like getting drunk and passing out,* she told him.

Sam was no counselor but knew enough to get Veronica to agree she needed one. "It was time," she admitted. Sam asked her for permission to disclose that trauma to the Council, but she refused. "You'll have to get it done another way, Sam. Sorry." Sam didn't push back.

This would be the toughest selling job Sam had ever done. The odds were against him, but he owed it to his star athlete to try. Sam valued loyalty and, in spite of Veronica's indiscretion, he would do his best to save her. Plus, he had a plan they would never expect.

"Mr. Halloran, the Council will see you now," said the receptionist. Sam followed her into a room that looked like a smaller version of the UN Security Council. He was instructed to make his presentation from a podium directly in front of him. As he stepped up to it, the Twin Towers came into view off to his left through the twenty-foot floor-to-ceiling windows. Off to the right through a matching massive window, the Empire State Building loomed just a block away. He'd be addressing all twelve members of Firm Council, who were seated on a semicircle platform elevated a couple of feet above the floor. Even for a guy like Sam, who had testified dozens of times and given hundreds of speeches, it was imposing… intimidating.

He heard a voice off to his left from someone seated apart from the Council with a machine in front of her. She'd be the transcriber. "Mr. Halloran, we are meeting in the matter of the termination of… " All he heard was Veronica Martinez. Everything else that followed was inaudible to Sam. He focused on his argument, waiting for someone to instruct him to speak.

"Mr. Halloran, I am Chairman Mattingly and will conduct this session. As you are aware, this council has previously determined Veronica Martinez, a director in your Chicago practice, has been terminated pursuant to policy violations warranting such treatment. That decision is binding. Your presence here is only out of respect for your wishes to be heard. You have fifteen minutes to state your case. Please, begin."

"Partners, thank you for seeing me on this important matter. Veronica Martinez has admitted to the charges and offers no defense. I have talked with her numerous times about this matter. She knows it was wrong and… " Sam hesitated, thinking about his conversation with Veronica. *No, get it done another way.* But what if he couldn't? He looked toward his partners, settling his eyes on Ann Williams. She met his stare. Sam wanted to offer the *why* but knew he could not. He'd be violating Veronica's trust, so he continued. "Veronica offers no excuse for her actions."

Sam knew the Council would be familiar with Veronica's outstanding achievements over her career, so he thought he'd give them a closer look at Veronica the person. Sam proceeded to share with the Council Veronica Martinez's history, beginning with her father's entry illegally to the US and then marrying a US Citizen and later raising three girls: a US Congresswoman, a CFO of a Fortune 500 company, and their youngest: Veronica.

Sam then read comments from others, staff and clients alike, ending with a citation issued by Illinois Governor Jim Edger in 1996 for her role in breaking up a Medicaid fraud scam resulting in over $60 million in recovery to the state of Illinois. After that, Sam scanned the faces of the Council and determined he was not getting through to any one of them. He'd have to play his hole card.

"Sam, thank you for your presentation—"

"I'm sorry, Chairman Mattingly, but I am not quite through."

"I'm afraid you have exceeded your time limit and we must bring this to a close."

"I beg the Council's indulgence to hear from someone who may be able to shed a different light on this matter. He is standing by waiting for a call. May I proceed?"

"You may not proceed! This is highly irregular—"

"Chairman, you will want to hear from this person. Trust me on this."

Mattingly had the gavel in his hand and was ready to slam it down to end Sam's appeal but was interrupted.

"Chairman Mattingly," spoke Ann Williams. "I have known Sam Halloran my entire career. If he insists this Council take the time to hear from someone with an interest in this matter, I believe we should allow it, but then it is your decision."

Mattingly, still holding the gavel, looked at Ann and around the room to his fellow partners. Some offered a nod, others a shoulder shrug. He then looked toward Sam and said, "I'll allow it."

Sam immediately passed on the phone number and stood back waiting for the connection to go through. When it did, Sam said, "I will allow the caller to introduce himself and to state his purpose."

"Good afternoon. My name is Henry Metcalf, Managing Partner of the Chicago law firm, Lawrence & Metcalf. Brian Metcalf, the victim in this matter, is my son."

Immediately, the Council members began rumbling to themselves. Mattingly gaveled to bring order. "Mr. Metcalf, this is highly irregular, and I cannot allow your testimony here to continue. It is totally inappropriate for you to present yourself before us in the representation of your son. I am disconnecting—"

"But I am not representing my son. I am representing Veronica Martinez... well, only if it comes to that."

Every person in the room looked toward the speaker phone as if it were a live person.

"Look," Henry Metcalf continued, "I realize this may be a bit irregular, but I hope you will hear me out. There is no pending litigation, and I am not making any threats, nor has Ms. Martinez.

In fact, I doubt she has any knowledge of my call here today. That's because I am making a plea to you on behalf of my role not as a litigator but as a father." He had their attention. Sam knew Henry quite well, as he was responsible for twenty percent of Sam's revenue and had recently engaged Sam's practice as the expert forensic accountants in the Chicago Public Schools matter that Dave Rogers was running.

"I agree with Sam that Ms. Martinez's actions were wrong, and I cannot disagree with the action the Council has taken to terminate her employment. But this is not the first time my son has done something like this." Henry hesitated, as if the lawyer in him was coming out. "Let's just say Ms. Martinez was influenced by forces outside of her control, those she was not aware of, and it would be unfair if she were to have her career destroyed." Henry was obviously struggling to find the right words.

"Look, I want to teach my son a lesson. I will only say he was complicit in what happened and shares in the responsibility of the events Ms. Martinez is charged with. My son has some matters of character he needs to work out."

"Mr. Metcalf, I can appreciate you feel an obligation to give this Council the other side of the story, and I can sympathize with your concerns as a father, but that has nothing to do with our obligations as the leaders of this firm. It's really quite simple: Veronica Martinez has violated our policy and standards, and we believe her termination was appropriate. This stands as our final decision. Now, I thank you for—"

"Well, there is just one more thing you need to be aware of," Henry continued. "If this Council persists in affecting this decision, then you give me no choice but to represent Ms. Martinez in a wrongful termination lawsuit against Hamilton Pierce."

"That is absolutely absurd!" yelled Mattingly as the rest of the Council talked among themselves. Well, everyone but Ann. She was staring at Sam with pursed lips but with a glint in her eyes, admiring him as she had so often in the past. More than any other on that Council, Ann Williams knew what Sam had experienced as a child and struggling young adult and all it taught him about compassion and persistence. She now knew exactly how this matter would turn out, and she couldn't be prouder of her partner and friend. Sam caught her stare and gave her a discrete nod.

Sam felt Henry had done an excellent job introducing additional facts for the Council to mull over. Sam wanted to give the Council something additional to ease the pain of reversing their decision. "Partners, I have one last piece of information for your consideration. As I said, I have had a few conversations with Ms. Martinez about her actions. Should she be reinstated at her former position, with no damage to her partner ambitions, she will submit to regular behavioral counseling for as long as necessary to help her act in a more responsible manner. She wants very much to be a partner in this firm and will do what it takes to achieve that goal. She will also agree to community service activities, say, 250 hours over the next two years. That should help keep her busy in addition to her job responsibilities. Again, she sincerely regrets her actions and is embarrassed the matter has reached the attention of this Council."

After a brief pause, Ann Williams stood. "Mr. Chairman, we have heard from relevant and credible witnesses. They have presented new facts. Facts I suggest this Council consider and deliberate upon to ensure we have rendered the appropriate disciplinary action in keeping with our policies, for sure, but also our values." The room quieted.

Mattingly cleared his throat. "Ms. Williams makes an excellent suggestion, and we will proceed accordingly.

"Mr. Metcalf, we thank you for your testimony today." He then looked at Sam, "Sam, we will consider what we have heard today, and I will inform you of our decision when we have one." He gave a nod to Sam as a show of respect. "Thank you for appearing today, Sam."

Before the doors closed on the plane, Sam received a call from Vince Mattingly. In a split decision, Veronica Martinez's position with Hamilton Pierce was reinstated… "this one time," he added. Sam breathed a sigh of relief. He'd let Veronica sweat this one out another couple of hours before he'd call her.

CHAPTER 65

"**S**AM HALLORAN SPEAKING."

"Not much of a greeting to someone you're supposedly fond of."

"Oh, Cat. Sorry. I didn't look at the display. It's really good to hear your voice."

"How is Guatemala?"

Immediately, Sam felt guilty for not keeping in touch with Cat. Just a few other things on his mind. He couldn't even remember the last time he'd talked with her. "I'm actually in a cab on my way to my condo," he said, half expecting her to demand he reroute himself to her townhouse. When she didn't, he knew there was a problem.

"I won't keep you. I'm in my car. I'm leaving for a few days and wanted to make sure I didn't miss you if you happened to plan a visit back home."

"Sounds like I'm going to miss you. Where are you headed?"

Sam heard crying. "Cat, are you OK?"

"Not really." More crying.

"Cat, what's wrong?"

"I'm fine. It's my father. He's in trouble, Sam."

"What's going on?"

"I don't understand any of it. He stopped by to see me yesterday.

Said he had some business in the city, but I found out he was really meeting with his lawyer. When he stopped by my home after his meeting, he took a call and walked off. I heard him on the phone. When he got off I asked him what it was about. Said he couldn't say much… only that he had a meeting with someone at the Federal Building on Dearborn. He wouldn't give me any details, but I know he's in trouble. I've never seen him like that. Left soon after that call. None of it makes sense to me. Something about the FBI calling him an *interesting person*. I don't know," Cat said sniffling, crying softly.

"Could it be a person-of-interest?"

"Yeah, that's it. A person-of-interest… in some investigation they are doing."

"Damn, Cat, I'm so sorry. Do you know anything more?"

"I don't, Sam. I went to bed after he left but couldn't sleep. I'm on my way to see him."

"Where?"

"Home. Where I grew up. Kenilworth. All I know is that it has something to do with his business."

"I should probably know this, but what does your dad do?" Sam said apologetically.

"Textbooks and school supplies. School consulting. Tutoring services. Lots of stuff related to schools. Not much more I can tell you, Sam. But one thing I can say is my father is the most honest person I know. Whatever they are investigating him for is bullshit!" She started crying again.

Sam thought a moment. *Could it be related?*

"Cat, where's your father's business located?"

"Chicago. Chicago Public Schools is his largest client. Why?"

"Just curious." He couldn't say, but he'd be making another call in a moment. He could ask Cat more questions to be sure, but he had enough and was already pretty certain he had a conflict.

"Sam, I really should pay attention to my driving," she said sadly but no longer crying.

"OK, but I'm worried about you. When can I see you?"

"I don't know, Sam. Daddy's pretty upset. Mom too. My first obligation is to them. I'll just have to let you know."

"I understand. Be careful, Cat. I'll be thinking about you."

"Thanks, Sam." She hung up.

"Hey, Dave. Sorry for the hour, but—"

"You sold it, right?"

"What?"

"Come on. Don't play with me. Veronica? They going to let her stay?"

Finally, Sam came around to what Dave was talking about. Sam couldn't even take a moment to savor the success of saving Veronica before he was hit with another problem.

"Sorry, Dave. Yeah, I did. But don't tell her. I'll call her in a few. But that's not why I'm calling you."

Dave confirmed they had uncovered suspicious documents from several vendors, the largest of which was Jennings Schools Services, Inc. "So what have you found so far?"

"The usual: inflated invoicing, bogus tutoring sign-in sheets, email communications with school principals strongly suggesting payments of some sort. Bribes. Like I said, the usual stuff. Why are you asking?"

"I've been dating a gal," Sam said, hesitant to say more. Not out of deception but rather embarrassment.

"Well, that's good to hear. About time you got back in the saddle."

"Yes and no. Her name is Catherine Jennings."

"As in Jennings School Services?"

"Looking that way. Not her, but her father."

"So you have a conflict."

"I do. I'll have to figure out a way to tell her. But right now, Dave, can you tell me how serious the Feds might be on him?"

"Sam, I didn't even know the Feds had opened a file, but I can tell you this. If they are pursuing an investigation against Jennings you can bet he's guilty as hell. They walk away from solid cases for lack of resources, so if they decide to take a case… it's rock solid. Your girlfriend's dad is in the crosshairs."

"I hear you, Dave. How about I stop by first thing in the morning and you can bring me up to speed on what you've found so far?"

"OK, but what are you—"

"No need to tell her now. I can buy another day before I make that call. Plus, I'll need to disclose all this to Henry Metcalf first. But honestly, Dave, it's approaching midnight, and I just don't have another ounce of energy. Walking into my condo now. I'll see you in the morning."

At one o'clock in the morning, Sam found himself in a familiar place with a familiar beverage in his hand—Macallan 18. He was also staring at a familiar sight: the lighthouse at the entrance to Monroe Harbor, imagining the foghorn warning summertime boaters to be wary. Then, his trance was interrupted by a call from Frank.

"Sam, sorry to call at this hour, but I was finally able to leave Pablo for just a minute," Frank said. "He's inconsolable. Dario, his son, is dead. Murdered by Mendoza in the most horrible of ways…. Sam, you still there?"

EPILOGE

Guatemala City, Guatemala

NEITHER OF THEM got much, if any, sleep. Sam had arranged for Frank to move into his vacated suite of rooms at the Hotel Barcelo. It was plenty of room for both of them, Pablo and Frank.

Frank was sitting on the patio nursing an orange juice and waiting for Pablo to rise. After learning his son was dead, murdered by Mendoza in front of some of the plant workers and in such a horrible manner, Pablo nearly went mad last night. If he had known where Mendoza was he'd have gone there, killed every one of his protection detail, and ripped Mendoza limb from limb… literally. Frank saw something in Pablo he hadn't seen before—the mercenary soldier he used to be. Then, there he was, standing in the kitchen staring at an empty coffee pot.

Frank slowly slid open the patio doors. "Pablo. What can I get you?"

"I am good, Frank. Thank you," Pablo said in a surprisingly calm manner.

Frank was now inside and standing a few feet from Pablo, observing him. "Do you want to order some breakfast? I can call room service and—"

"Breakfast sounds good. Cheese omelet, tortilla, and beans for me. Four eggs. No meat. Coffee. I will take a shower, eat with you, but then I must leave."

"But where—?"

"We will talk at breakfast," he said.

Thirty minutes later, Frank answered the door where the server wheeled in their breakfast order. While placing their servings on the dining table, Pablo walked out of his room, dressed in the same clothes he had worn the previous day, and took a seat at the table. Frank also took a seat and began to eat, waiting for Pablo to speak. He didn't look right.

"Frank, I must leave you, but I want to thank you for being with me yesterday and last night. It was… a bad time for me. I consider you a good friend and last night proves this."

A few minutes passed where they ate quietly. Finally, Frank broke the silence.

"Pablo, I know you are planning something in your head. Will you tell me what?"

"This is not your fight, Frank."

"That's where you're wrong, Pablo. This absolutely is my fight, too. I am with you in this." Frank watched Pablo lap up the last of his beans with his tortilla.

"You have duties to do here. For Sam. To watch over things. I will handle this on my own."

"You're going after him, aren't you?"

Pablo looked at him, still chewing. He wiped his mouth and, standing, took a large gulp of coffee, finishing it off. "This is my fight," he said placing his hat on his head and then turning toward the guest room.

Frank came around to his side of the table and gently placed his hand on Pablo's shoulder. He could feel Pablo's muscles ripple as if he were about to act in a hostile manner, but Frank knew otherwise. He held his shoulder firm. Pablo turned to face him.

"Pablo, I'm serious. You are going after Mendoza, and I can help. I think we both know where he went. I have in-country resources that can help. You are not doing this without me. We've been through a lot so far. Let me help you finish this…. Please."

A full minute passed. Pablo placed his hand on Frank's forearm. "Thank you, my friend. For helping me avenge the death of my son."

Six weeks later…

Chicago—Sam's office

Things were going great. Business was pouring in; the practice was hopping. Dave's Chicago Public Schools investigation was still proceeding with a parallel FBI investigation. Everything was good… except Sam missed Cat very much. He told her only that he had a conflict and could not get involved in her father's problems. She didn't understand and hung up on him.

Maggie walked into Sam's office, smiling.

"Get out of here. I'm busy," Sam said, playfully.

"Oh, hush up!" Maggie said with that look she wore when one of her ideas panned out. "Remember my idea about subscribing to that Lexus/Nexus service? Well, I think it just paid off in spades! Have a look at what just turned up," she said as she laid an AP Newswire release in front of Sam.

Prominent Guatemalan Businessman Found Brutally Murdered

AP Newswire: April 22, 1998 Cali, Columbia

(*for immediate release*)

The body of Javier Mendoza was found yesterday by farmers in what authorities are calling a *Blood Eagle* execution style slaying. The coroner reported it as an excruciating way to die. "Señor Mendoza hung spread eagle for at least two days before he died from exposure."

Those same sources say regardless of who's involvement, the victim, and the manner of slaying, all point to signs of another narcoterrorism murder that will likely never be solved.

Mendoza was recently terminated as the General Manager of the Abello Distillery located in Palencia, Guatemala. Abello is a division of Hampton Enterprises, a US domiciled global company. The company's press office would only confirm Mendoza is no longer an employee of the company and offered no additional information.

The Mayor of Palencia, Guatemala, Marcelo Rodriguez said, "Javier was a pillar of the community, caring deeply for the people of Palencia and unbounded in his generosity to everyone he touched. He was especially kind to abandoned girls for whom he made jobs available at the plant. He will be sorely missed."

ABOUT THE AUTHOR

Tom Golden is a retired PricewaterhouseCoopers (PwC) Partner and former leader of PwC's Chicago Forensic Accounting Investigation practice. When he began his accounting and auditing career with PwC little did his know that his first public company audit would result in changing his career. It was on that audit where he discovered a massive fraud eventually destroying the company and launching Tom's forensic accounting career—the inspiration for his first novel *Sunday Night Fears*.

His many investigations performed over the past three decades led to numerous engagements performing fraud investigation training seminars for both domestic and foreign organizations including the FBI and IRS.

Tom was the lead author of the award-winning Wiley book *A Guide to Forensic Accounting Investigation*, now in its second edition. He earned his MBA from Indiana University, is a CPA and Certified Fraud Examiner (CFE). He consulted on and appeared in the 2017 film *All the Queen's Horses* documenting the largest municipal fraud in our nation's history.

Tom was an adjunct professor at DePaul University, developing and teaching the school's first Forensic Accounting Investigation course in 2002 on the heels of the infamous Enron and then World-Com financial frauds.

Tom retired from PwC in 2008 but continued to conduct high-profile investigations that will inspire future novels. Together with his wife of fifty years, a retired schoolteacher, they now live in the middle of the woods about a hundred miles west of Chicago. Their sons' families live a short distance away—allowing precious time to spend with their four grandchildren. Life is good!

SUNDAY NIGHT FEARS

Book 1 in the Sam Halloran Thriller Series

A fraud uncovered... A past haunting him... He had something to prove in this gripping thriller reviewers are calling "fresh," "page-turning," "captivating," and "inspiring."

Sam Halloran is ambitious, a bit desperate, and running from an ugly past. He's got a family to support and everything hinges on his job as a newly minted auditor. But when he gets assigned to his first public company audit, he discovers something no one else did. Fraud... massive fraud!

That's when the walls start to close in.

As Sam struggles with what to do and confronts the pain of his past, the company's smart, seductive accounting manager becomes both ally and temptation. With each piece of evidence painting a bigger target on his back, Sam wonders if she would rather help him uncover the truth or lead him straight into a deadly trap....

Suddenly, average-joe-Sam becomes modern-day David, up against an unforeseen giant that could crush him in an instant. He'll remind you a lot of Mitch McDeere in **John Grisham**'s pioneering legal thriller, **THE FIRM**, a guy in so deep, so suddenly, he hasn't yet checked the exits. And now it's too late to run.

—Exclusively on Amazon—

ABOUT FORENSIC ACCOUNTING INVESTIGATION

Tom Golden stumbled into a career in forensic accounting investigation, but you don't have to if the field interests you. He has been affiliated with the Association of Certified Fraud Examiners (ACFE) since 1991 in various capacities and heartily recommends visiting their website below to see the enormous opportunities that are available to you.

Founded in 1988 by Dr. Joseph T. Wells, CFE, CPA, the ACFE is the world's largest anti-fraud organization and premier provider of anti-fraud training and education. Together with more than 85,000 members in more than 150 countries, the ACFE is reducing business fraud worldwide and providing the training and resources needed to fight fraud more effectively.

The positive effects of anti-fraud training are far-reaching. Clearly, the best way to combat fraud is to educate anyone engaged in fighting fraud on how to effectively prevent, detect and investigate it. By educating, uniting and supporting the global anti-fraud community with the tools to fight fraud more effectively, the ACFE is reducing business fraud worldwide and inspiring public confidence in the integrity and objectivity of the profession.

The ACFE offers its members the opportunity for professional certification. The Certified Fraud Examiner (CFE) credential is preferred by businesses and government entities around the world and indicates expertise in fraud prevention and detection.

Learn more about the ACFE at *www.acfe.com*

Tell them Tom Golden sent you!

ACKNOWLEDGMENTS

Whenever tackling a major project, like an investigation, I am reluctant to cede control. Same goes for publishing my novels. I know enough about the publishing industry to be able to choose those publishing consultants that will give me what I require. With their expert help, I can place in front of my readers nothing but the absolute best story writing and packaging collectively produced. If you ever get around to writing that novel which resides in most of us, this author recommends these professionals to you:

Publishing industry consulting: www.janefriedman.com
Editing: www.authormarkspencer.com
Proofreading: www.bronteelise.wixsite.com/brontepearson
Website design: www.stormhillmedia.com
Marketing: www.authormedia.com
Publishing: www.kdp.com
Audio Production: www.acx.com
Cover and Formatting: www.Damonza.com

To My Beta Readers

It would be impossible to properly thank this group of readers who have been committed from the start of this project. It takes courage, patience and stamina to slog through a first draft, then offering (sometimes demanding) edits. The thoughtful work they performed enabled me to create a work which is the best that I could produce. I am eternally indebted to these readers. Thank you!

To My Launch Team

Beyond the production and publication of a novel I am fortunate to have another dedicated group of readers who are committed to helping me achieve my goals. Their only compensation being my unending gratitude.

SPEECHES AND SEMINARS

Tom's presentation style is unique and can be tailored to each specific audience. Whether he speaks from a podium or freely moves around an open stage, he delivers common sense techniques which internal auditors and financial executives can use to spot and avoid fraud.

Tom's presentations highlight his real-life experiences conducting large-scale investigations bringing to life his investigative techniques to create an experience sure to enhance learning in a memorable, oftentimes humorous, fashion. He literally "wrote the book on fraud," and you are guaranteed to walk away a savvier businessperson having attended one of his sessions.

Tom enjoys speaking about fraud almost as much as performing investigations.

He especially enjoys teaching others how to prevent fraud or chase down perpetrators bringing them to justice. That is why he discounts, by half, his fee to schools.

Tom is also available as a Podcast Guest
He can be contacted at tom@tomgoldenbooks.com

Made in the USA
Monee, IL
27 July 2021